Praise for

Diary of a Mad Fat

"*Diary of a Mad Fat Girl* is bawdy, sexy Southern-fried fun. McAfee makes a powerhouse debut that readers will love."

—Valerie Frankel, author of *It's Hard Not to Hate You*

"Fresh and funny. Ace Jones is a hoot! This is what *Sex and the City* might have been if Carrie and friends were looking for love in Bugtussle, Mississippi, instead of Manhattan."

—Wendy Wax, author of *Ten Beach Road*

"Ace Jones is my kind of girl: Her outsize appetite for life, plus a dangerously low tolerance for losers, gets her into one impossible fix after another. In addition to involving a delightfully madcap crew of friends and acquaintances in her quest for justice, Ace is aided, abetted, and occasionally bedded by some delicious Southern gentlemen. Ace prevails with humor, heart, and a speed-dial relationship with the pizza guy."

—Sophie Littlefield, award-winning author of
A Bad Day for Scandal

"Stephanie McAfee, in creating Ace Jones, has written a character that will grab you by the shirtfront and take you with her on her ride, and oh, what a wild ride it is. *Diary of a Mad Fat Girl* is pure fun."

—Rachael Herron, author of *Wishes & Stitches*

DIARY OF A
MAD FAT GIRL

Stephanie McAfee

NEW AMERICAN LIBRARY

NEW AMERICAN LIBRARY
Published by New American Library, a division of
Penguin Group (USA) Inc., 375 Hudson Street,
New York, New York 10014, USA
Penguin Group (Canada), 90 Eglinton Avenue East, Suite 700, Toronto,
Ontario M4P 2Y3, Canada (a division of Pearson Penguin Canada Inc.)
Penguin Books Ltd., 80 Strand, London WC2R 0RL, England
Penguin Ireland, 25 St. Stephen's Green, Dublin 2,
Ireland (a division of Penguin Books Ltd.)
Penguin Group (Australia), 250 Camberwell Road, Camberwell, Victoria 3124,
Australia (a division of Pearson Australia Group Pty. Ltd.)
Penguin Books India Pvt. Ltd., 11 Community Centre, Panchsheel Park,
New Delhi - 110 017, India
Penguin Group (NZ), 67 Apollo Drive, Rosedale, Auckland 0632,
New Zealand (a division of Pearson New Zealand Ltd.)
Penguin Books (South Africa) (Pty.) Ltd., 24 Sturdee Avenue,
Rosebank, Johannesburg 2196, South Africa

Penguin Books Ltd., Registered Offices:
80 Strand, London WC2R 0RL, England

Published by New American Library, a division of Penguin Group (USA) Inc. Original edition published
by the author in digital form.

First New American Library Printing, February 2012
10 9 8 7 6 5 4 3 2 1

 REGISTERED TRADEMARK—MARCA REGISTRADA

LIBRARY OF CONGRESS CATALOGING-IN-PUBLICATION DATA:

McAfee, Stephanie.
   Diary of a mad fat girl/Stephanie McAfee.
      p. cm.
   ISBN 978-0-451-23649-4
   1. Overweight women—Fiction. 2. Female friendship—Fiction.
   3. Mississippi—Fiction. I. Title.
   PS3613.C2635D53 2012
   813'.6—dc23   2011043820

Set in Carre Noir STD
Designed by Alissa Amell

Printed in the United States of America

For Carson
It's all because of you.

DIARY OF A
MAD FAT GIRL

1

◇◇◇

All of my bags are packed and I'm ready to go. If I had some white shoe polish, I'd do like we did in the nineties and scribble "Panama City Beach or BUST" on my back windshield.

Spring break is finally here, and for the next week I'm a free woman. No students to teach, no projects to grade, no paintbrushes to wash, and, best of all, no bitchy Catherine Hilliard riding my ass like a fat lady on a Rascal.

I'm sick of her and I'm tired of my job and I need a vacation worse than Nancy Grace needs a chill pill. I wish we were leaving tonight. I squeeze a lime into my beer and head out the back door with Señor Buster Loo Bluefeather hot on my heels. While Buster Loo does speedy-dog crazy eights around my flower beds, I flip on the multicolored Christmas lights, settle into my overstuffed lounger, and start daydreaming about white sandy beaches, piña coladas, and hot men in their twenties.

My phone dings and in the two seconds it takes me to look at the caller ID, I wish a thousand times it was a text from Mason McKenzie.

I wouldn't give Mason McKenzie the time of day, and he knows I wouldn't give him the time of day, so it's ridiculous for me to wish that he would text me, but I still do. Every day.

Of course, it's not a text from him; it's one from my best bud, Lilly Lane.

Call me. I will never understand the logic of sending a text message that says *call me.* Lilly Lane is one of those cellular addicts who could carry on a full-fledged six-hour conversation via text message. Sometimes her messages are so encrypted with abbreviations that I just pick up the phone and call her, which pisses her off. She's like, "I'm texting you. Why are you calling me? If I wanted to talk to you I would've texted you and told you to call me."

Oh, so I'm the idiot? Right.

Then I'll say something like, "Hey, heifer, save it for someone who cares and tell me what the hell that last message was supposed to mean. I'm not Robert Langdon. I can't decode symbols, and if you don't want me to call you, then send me some crap I can read."

But I can read this particular text, so I prop my feet up on the lounger and give her a call.

"Ace," she says, and it sounds like she's been running, but she's not a runner. "I'm not gonna be able to go to Florida."

"What are you talking about?" I'm confused because spending spring break in Panama City Beach is one of our most sacred and beloved traditions.

"I can't go." She pauses. "I'm sorry."

"Sorry?" I yell into the phone. "Are you freakin' kidding me? We're supposed to leave in the morning, Lilly! Like nine hours from *right now*! What the hell do you mean you can't go?"

Silence. And then it dawns on me.

For the past five months, Lilly has been seeing someone on the sly whom she will only call the Gentleman, and she's more tightlipped about him than she was about the time she got a hot dog stuck in her cooter. I think he might be a gross old man with tons of money. I thought about making a list of all the gross old men with money in Bugtussle, Mississippi, and doing some investigating, but I'm not much of a list maker so I probably won't do that.

Lilly, however, is a habitual list maker, and I don't mean the kind of list you take to the grocery store. She can go on a date with some dude and by the time they get to wherever they're going, she's got a list a mile long of everything she thinks is wrong with him.

I know this because she keeps me updated with a continuous stream of text messages. Not because I ask for them. I don't.

After the date is over, she documents the potential suitor's faults on a piece or twelve of loose-leaf paper that she then files in an alphabet-ized four-inch binder. I mean, God forbid she should forget one small thing about a guy nice enough to take her goofy ass out to dinner and a movie.

Some poor fellows hang around long enough to have their list read to them, and the truly unfortunate get shown the actual notebook. Imagine a man looking at a hot pink polka-dot binder stuffed with more than ten years' worth of documentation on Mr. Wrong.

The Gentleman, however, does not have a list. As far as I can tell, he has only an itinerary. Since the commencement of her supersecret affair, Lilly has been to New York City, Los Angeles, and Chicago. In the past five months. *Five months.* And she returns from these esca-pades with truckloads of fancy shopping bags stuffed with extravagant gifts.

I guess she may have finally found her Mr. Right, although I have serious doubts about how right a man can be who requires such se-crecy concerning his identity.

Further adding to the mystery of this surreptitious affair is that new BMW convertible she started driving about two months ago. I mean, she has some serious cash stacked up from her days as a lingerie model, but I don't think she'd blow every last dime of it on an automobile. Maybe the Gentleman is a rich man in a midlife crisis. The car is red.

Whoever he is, I hate his guts because I'm relatively certain he's the reason my vacation plans are now in ruins.

"Oh," I say, "I get it. It's him. The Gentleman's got bigger plans for you, Lilly? A little trip down to the Redneck Riviera doesn't quite measure up to your new travel standards? I can't buy you six pairs of Manolos and three Gucci purses so I'm out now?"

"Ace, please don't do this to me. Just get someone else to go."

"Don't do this to *you*?" I yell and feel my face getting hot. "How about you don't do this to *me*? And who the hell am I gonna get who can pack up and be ready on such short notice? I'm the only person I know who is that spontaneous."

"You could ask Chloe," she peeps.

"Oh, yeah, that's a great idea. I mean, Chloe can't go to the mailbox without being watched, so I'm sure her *adoring* husband would just love it if she took off on a trip to the beach, where she might actually get to relax and enjoy herself. Why can't I come up with ideas that brilliant?"

Chloe is married to Richard Stacks the Fourth, a prominent pillar in the Bugtussle community who puts a ridiculous amount of effort into his let-me-get-that-door-for-you-my-sweet-beloved-wife-because-I'm-a-perfect-husband persona. In private, however, he talks to Chloe like she's a shit-eating dog. It's been almost six years since that midnight phone call when Chloe quietly confided the details of her first verbal beat-down. She'd only been married a few months and asked me what I thought she should do. I told her to pack her crap and come to my house. She wouldn't. I told her to go in the bedroom and super-glue his lips together. She wouldn't do that, either. I was about to ask her why she called me if she wasn't going to heed my stellar advice, when it dawned on me that what she needed was for me to clarify who the bad guy was and that it wasn't her. Soon afterward, Richard had an affair with a skanky-ass local woman who, upon discovering that she was not his only mistress, told everyone in town that he was a grue-some nymphomaniac with a weird, tiny penis. His other concubines obviously didn't mind sharing, and rumors of his sexual deviance be-came standard fodder for the rumor mill.

Chloe refuses to acknowledge his infidelity, shrouds herself in ig-norance, and stands by in silence as he flaunts his gentlemanly man-ners in public. She won't entertain even the slightest suggestion of divorce and ignores me when I say he should be killed. I've offered to do just that on several occasions and come up with some good places to hide the body, but she is determined to make her marriage work because she thinks he can change. I think the only thing that can change a man like that is a bullet to the skull. Just like that Dixie Chicks song about Earl.

Silence on the line.

"Well," I say.

"Well," she says, "I think you should go on down to Florida and try to patch things up with Mason. You could stop by Pelican Cove on your way to Panama City and y'all could have lunch or something, and maybe work things out. When I was at the bar the other day, Ethan Allen told me he isn't seeing anybody and, honestly, Ace, I think he's just waiting on you to come back."

"Is that what you think?" I ask, heavy on the sarcasm. "How could you even bring that up right now? What the hell is wrong with you?"

I pause. "But, hey. I do appreciate you sitting up at the bar and hashing out my personal business with Ethan Allen."

"Ace, I'm sorry but you're the only person who doesn't see what a big mistake you made when you packed up and left Mason in one of your famous fits of rage! No one else will say anything to you because they know you'll go ape-shit crazy—"

"Just stop right there," I interrupt. My face is on fire. "You have got to be out of your damn mind. I mean, first you text me and tell me to call you, which is stupid as shit by the way; then you tell me you're ditching our trip, a trip we take every year and you *know* how much it means to me; *then* you suggest I take along our poor little friend who can't go to the grocery store without being interrogated; and after *all of that*, you have the balls to start babbling about how I need to patch things up with Mason. Seriously, Lilly?" I take a deep breath. "Is that what you really think, or is this you worming your way out of our trip because your Gentleman came calling?"

She doesn't say anything.

"You have to admit it's a pretty convenient thing to bring up now."

Silence still.

"You're gonna ditch me the night before we leave?" I ask, making a legitimate effort to be calm. "Really?"

"I'm sorry. It's not what you think. I have to be somewhere."

"You have to be somewhere?" The sarcasm oozes like lava. "Where exactly do you have to be, Lilly?"

"Paris." She sounds like a baby frog trying to find its first croak.

"Really, I thought you quit modeling because you found the lifestyle too exhausting and unfulfilling, and that's why you came home and started teaching school. Am I right about that?"

"You know I'm not modeling."

"Just trying to be a better French teacher?"

"Ace, please—"

"Spring break in Paris," I say with the sarcasm full throttle. "Well, don't that just take the cake? I'm so happy for you and your Gentleman friend. Or should I say your Gentleman financier." I put a little French twist on the last syllable. For effect.

"You are so cruel," she whispers.

"Oh, yeah, I'm definitely the bitch in this relationship." I pause. "Tell me who it is, Lilly. Who is this Gentleman whose plans for you are so much more important than the plans you made with me?"

"You know I can't tell you who he is."

"Why not? I really wanna know."

"Ace, stop, please. I can't."

"Right. Of course you can't. I mean, why would you? It's not like you can trust me. It's not like we're best friends, good ol' BFFs forever, right, Lilly?"

"Ace," she says, and I can tell she's about to start her stupid squalling like she always does when she needs people to come around to her way of thinking.

"Okay, well. Hey! Thanks for waiting until Friday afternoon to let me know. Have a great trip and I'll talk to you later—" I pause. "Or maybe not."

She starts mumbling a string of apologies and I push the red button on my phone with enough pressure to drive a nail through wood. Sorry means as much to me as that dog turd Buster Loo just dropped in that dwarf yaupon holly.

2

<><><><><><><><><><><><><><><><><><><><><><><><><><><><><><><><><><><><>

All I see when I open my eyes is a wet black nose and dog whiskers. Buster Loo is standing on my pillow, resting his snout on my face. I pat him on the head and reach for my cell phone as the sun pours through the open blinds like a giant laser designed to obliterate my eyeballs.

Lilly and I should be well on our way to the Emerald Coast by now. I think for a second about throwing my bags in the car and setting out solo, but how pathetic would that be? What kind of idiot goes to Panama City Beach alone during spring break? I think for one miserable second about how nice it would be to hang out with Mason McKenzie, but I wouldn't try to get in touch with him if my life depended on it. He's probably got a lap full of college girls right now and it's only eleven thirty in the morning.

I get out of bed and make my way to the kitchen, where I take four ibuprofen and fix myself a Sprite on the rocks. With six cherries. I grab some saltines, wobble into the living room, and ease onto the sofa.

Buster Loo appears from what he thinks is his secret hiding place behind the love seat and curls up in the bend of my legs.

I flip on the television just in time to catch a commercial for the gym that docks my checking account $40 a month and seeing that makes me feel worse than I already do.

What the hell was I thinking when I gave a voided check to that Ken doll–looking man with no hair on his arms? Was I thinking that I'd go to the gym five times a week and love every minute of it? Was I thinking I'd lose that extra twenty pounds I've packed on since I broke up with Mason and strut around in those superexpensive jeans he bought me that have been hanging in my closet, haunting me since last summer?

I don't know what I was thinking and I'm not in the mood to try and remember. I don't want to think about anything.

I don't want to think about the damned gym. I don't want to think about Lilly sitting pretty in her first-class seat en route to Charles de Gaulle. I don't want to think about all the beer I drank last night. I don't want to think about the beach or the ocean or all the raw oysters I'd planned on eating this week. And I don't need to think about Mason McKenzie.

The only problem is that I like thinking about him. It's one of many bad habits that I have no desire to break.

I met Jonathan Mason McKenzie shortly after my family moved to Bugtussle when I was eleven years old. I remember Daddy was so happy when he got that job down here, and Gramma Jones was positively thrilled that her boy was moving back home. My mom, however, didn't share their enthusiasm. She had no affection for Bugtussle, and our visits here had always been brief. My mom was born and raised in Nashville, Tennessee. That's where she met and married my dad; that's where she had me; and that's where she'd planned to spend the rest of her life.

She did her best to be excited and supportive, but it was easy to see that she was heartbroken. And she didn't adjust well to small-town life. Isabella Jones drank beer and didn't care who saw her, and that just wasn't the way women did things in Bugtussle. Add to that the fact that she won at everything she did, and you've got a recipe for social disaster.

Whether she was on the golf course, the tennis court, or at the bunco table, my mother was merciless. I think it was her way of showing a few pesky ladies that she didn't just *think* she was better than them, she really *was*.

We joined the Methodist church the first Sunday we attended, and Brother Rankle slapped Daddy on the back and said, "Jake, it's so good to have you back!" After lunch at Gramma Jones's house that day, Daddy sat me down and told me I could meet some good friends if I went to the youth fellowship meeting that afternoon. I didn't want to go, but I did just to please him.

My mom dropped me off at the church twenty minutes early because she always got everywhere twenty minutes early and thought everyone else should do the same. I distinctly remember sitting in the far corner of that rectangular room in a cold metal folding chair, all alone and completely terrified. The youth leader wasn't even there yet.

After ten long minutes of pure agony, other kids started to show up, and I stared at the floor because I was embarrassed at being there so early. I could sense the room was filling up, but the chair beside mine remained unoccupied. I had considered bolting to the bathroom, where I could hide until the evening services, when Mason McKenzie made his noisy, dramatic entrance.

I looked up when I heard his voice, and the moment I saw him I fell madly and deeply in love. My young heart was beating like a jungle drum as I watched him survey the room, looking for a place to sit.

All the angels in heaven started to sing when he chose the seat next to mine.

I stared at the floor because I felt like I might die if I didn't. He tapped me on the arm and said, "Hey! I haven't seen you here before. Who are you?" He smiled at me and I felt like I'd been swept up into a beautiful, wonderful dream.

"Graciela," I whispered. "But everyone calls me Ace."

"Ace," he said, "I like that."

All I could do was grin like a buffoon.

"Well, Ace," he said, "I'm Mason"—he held out his hand—"Mason McKenzie. Nice to meet you." I took his hand and he gave mine a good, firm shake, then pointed to the boy behind him. "This here is Ethan Allen Harwood and he thinks he's a handsome fellow, but he's not."

I giggled and Ethan Allen punched him in the arm and they both got in trouble with the youth leader.

"I'm sorry, Brother Henry," Mason said somberly. "I am not acting like the Southern gentleman that my mamma has raised me to be."

"Brother McKenzie, don't make me have to speak with your mamma again," Brother Henry said as he flipped open his Bible.

"No, sir, Brother Henry, that will not be necessary, sir." Mason stole a quick glance at me, then leaned over and whispered, "Ethan Allen has a face that only a mamma could love."

I thought Ethan Allen was cute, really cute, as a matter of fact, but I decided it was in my best interest to go along with the joke. "Not even a grandma?" I whispered back.

"Not even," he said and grinned.

I stifled a giggle and Mason McKenzie bowed his head to pray.

From there on out, I couldn't get enough of going to church. My parents were so pleased with my newfound dedication to the Lord that they took me to the pool at the country club almost every time I asked. Daddy was happy because he thought I was trying to make friends, and Mom was happy just because I was happy, so I considered it a triple-win situation.

I didn't bother telling them that the only reason I wanted to go was because I was desperate to get a glimpse of Mason on the golf course. I did hang out with a few other girls my age at the pool, but their petty conversations could hardly distract me from the love of my eleven-year-old life.

I couldn't wait for school to start, and remember thinking that July had to be the longest month of the year. I spent a considerable amount of time hoping that "J for Jones" was close enough to "M for McKenzie" for us to be in the same homeroom.

August finally arrived, and the Saturday before school started Ethan Allen's parents threw him a birthday party at their farm. I couldn't have been more excited if I'd gotten an invitation to join the Mickey Mouse Club with Britney Spears and Justin Timberlake. Mom took me shopping and bought me a new outfit to wear to the party. I spent almost an hour curling my dark wavy hair with a big-barrel curling iron because I wanted to look just like Jessie on *Saved by the Bell*.

My parents dropped me off twenty minutes before the party started and that was fine with me. I volunteered to help Ethan Allen's mom set out the food because that afforded me the opportunity to discreetly check my reflection in the china cabinet mirror every time I walked past.

As other kids drifted in, I noticed a passel of girls congregating at the foot of the stairs. I didn't pay much attention to them because I didn't pay much attention to anyone other than Mason. I was somewhat aware that I was earning a reputation as a snob, but I didn't care. I was in love.

Six o'clock came and went and Mason had yet to arrive. I was standing in the foyer peeking out toward the driveway when I felt a tap on my shoulder. I turned to find a slender girl with long blond hair and long tan legs looking down at me with ice blue eyes. She appeared to be the self-appointed leader of the group I'd seen by the stairs.

"Hello," I said, trying to act like she wasn't getting on my nerves.

"Hello, yourself, shorty," she said, and the edge in her voice made my knees weak. "Are you looking for my boyfriend, *Mason*?"

I was overwhelmed with shock and disappointment, and when I opened my mouth to speak, nothing came out. She smiled at my reaction.

"When he gets here, tell him his *girl*friend is on the patio waiting for him," she said with a wicked smile.

"Who are you?" I finally managed to sputter.

"I'm Lilly Lane," she said proudly, "and don't you forget it." With that she turned and led her entourage through the living room, out the French doors, and onto the patio.

"She ain't Mason's girlfriend," Ethan Allen said, and I almost jumped out of my skin at the sound of his voice. "She's my girlfriend."

"What?" was all I could manage because I felt as if I might vomit at any given second.

"Yeah, she's my girlfriend," he said, like it was no big deal. "Has been off and on since kindergarten. She's just mad at me right now because she asked who you were and I told her we went to church together, and she asked if I thought you were pretty and I told her yeah and she got mad and ran over here to make a scene."

I just stared at him.

"I do think you're pretty. I wasn't gonna lie with my mamma standing right over there in the kitchen." He nodded toward his mother, who was wiping down the countertop and smiling at him. "I think Lilly's pretty, too, and I tried to tell her that but she wouldn't listen."

"Oh, okay," I said, sure I was about to pass out.

"Don't worry. Mason will be here in a minute. His mamma and daddy always run late to everything. You'll see when school starts. He'll be late almost every day." Ethan Allen smiled. "But just don't you worry, Ace. He'll be here tonight, okay?"

"Okay," I said and started fanning myself with my hand.

"Can I get you something to drink?" Ethan Allen asked. "You look kinda thirsty."

"Sure," I said, eyeballing the patio. "Did your mamma make some tea?"

"Of course!" he said. "I'll be right back."

Ethan Allen went to the kitchen and returned a second later with a mug of sweet iced tea.

"Look at that," he said, pointing. "Even got you a lemon."

"Ethan Allen, you're the best," I said, and I really meant it.

"Thanks," he said. "Just do me a favor and don't tell Lilly you think that. She'd be mad for sure then."

"Don't worry," I said. "I'm gonna try real hard not to talk to her unless I absolutely have to."

"Aw, she's all right," he said. "You just gotta get to know her."

I wanted to roll my eyes and say, "Yeah, right," but it *was* his girlfriend we were talking about, so I just smiled and nodded my head in agreement.

"Well, I guess I better get on out there and see if I can get my love life straightened out." He winked at me. "And don't worry. Mason's coming. I promise."

I'd almost given up on that promise by the time Mason arrived thirty minutes later. After greeting literally everyone at the party, including chaperones, Mason came into the living room and sat next to me on the sofa.

"I just saw your mamma and daddy at the store," he said.

"What were you doing at the store?"

"Well, buying Ethan Allen a birthday present, of course!"

"You bought him a present on the way to the party?"

"Yeah," he said, like that was perfectly normal. "When did you get him one?"

"My mom took me the day after we got the invitation."

"Two weeks ago?" he exclaimed.

"Yeah, two weeks ago," I said. "What's wrong with that?"

"Well, not a thing," he said, smiling. "Hey, why does your mamma always wear orange?"

"'Cause she's a Volunteer fan!"

"Oh, that's awful," he said and snarled. "Why is your mamma, of all things, a Tennessee Volunteer fan?"

"Same reason your daddy is an Ole Miss Rebel fan."

"She went to school there?"

"Yes, she did," I said proudly. "Good ol' Rocky Top."

"Well, I guess it's better than her bein' an Alabama fan."

"Or Auburn!" I said. "Ugh!"

He laughed for a second, then leaned over close to me. "Hey, Ace," he whispered, "you wanna see some chickens?"

"Chickens?"

"Yeah," he said with a devilish smile. "Mr. Harwood's got lots of 'em out behind the barn."

"Well, I'd love to see some chickens," I lied. I could not have cared less about seeing some feathery farm animals, but I wasn't about to turn down the opportunity to be alone with him.

We got up and I was relieved that he led me out the carport, thus avoiding the crowd on the patio. I didn't want to run into Lilly Lane and her little minions. When we got behind the barn, Mason took my hand and led me around some hay bales to a huge pen where there were indeed a lot of chickens.

I was a nervous wreck standing there holding his hand, and just when I thought my heart couldn't beat any faster, he looked at me and said, "Ace, do you have a boyfriend?" I shook my head no and he smiled and said, "Do you want one?" I nodded my head yes. He giggled a little and said, "Cat got your tongue?" I shook my head no, grinned, and felt my cheeks getting red. "Chicken?" he asked, looking at me sideways.

I laughed and he smiled and said, "You're even prettier when you laugh."

I stopped laughing and stood completely still. I was afraid my heart would pound a hole in my chest. He took a step closer to me, reached out, and took my face into his hands.

"What would happen if I kissed you?"

Finally finding the capacity to speak, I whispered, "Guess you'll have to do it and see."

As he leaned closer to my face, I closed my eyes like all those girls in the movies. When his lips touched mine, it was the softest, sweetest thing I'd ever experienced in my life. I felt like Alice in Wonderland falling through the rabbit hole.

On the walk back, he held my hand all the way to the house. Everyone was inside eating, so we fixed our plates and sat together on the stairs. I ended up wasting a few sausage balls and a whole pile of cocktail weenies, but I couldn't help it. I was too intoxicated from the magic of my first kiss to worry about some silly appetizers.

When school finally started, I was thrilled to find that *J* was indeed close enough to *M* to land us in the same homeroom. What I hadn't factored in was the *L* that would come between us in the form of one prissy, bossy drama queen named Lilly Lane.

Looking back now, it's funny to think about how badly she hated me that whole first year we knew each other. Little did I know that she would become the best friend I'd ever have that very next summer.

I feel whiskers on my arm and look down to see Buster Loo sniffing at the cracker in my hand. I give it to him and he crunches and munches it to pieces, sending crumbs flying everywhere, and I remind myself, yet again, to only give him snacks in the kitchen.

"C'mon, little buddy," I say, setting my empty glass on the coffee table. "Let's go for a walk."

3

<<<<<<<<<<<<<<<<<<<<<<<<<<<<<<<<<<<<<<<<<<<<<<<<<<<<<<<<<<

It's cloudy and a little cool, so I pull on a windbreaker and put a doggie shirt on Buster Loo before heading out the door. Not many people are at the park, most likely because of the dreary weather, and I get all pissed off thinking about Lilly strolling the streets of Paris while I'm stuck here walking the streets of Bugtussle.

"We should be on the beach right now," I tell Buster Loo, who gives me a little goose honk as a reply.

My mind wanders, and I find myself thinking about the day Lilly and I buried the hatchet and became friends. Looking back now, it had to be fate that threw us together like that. As if somebody somewhere knew I'd need a friend soon, so they sent that lunatic my way.

It was the summer after sixth grade when Lilly and I found ourselves stuck together as roommates at basketball camp.

I was there because I loved basketball and was, in most people's opinion, a lot better than pretty good. She was there because she was tall. The junior high basketball coach had talked her daddy into sending her to camp because his post player had moved on to the high school team and he was in need of a tall girl.

Lilly did not want to be there, and I heard her whining to her mother as they made their way down the hallway. I couldn't believe that she was at basketball camp. Her mom was very sympathetic, but also very clear on the fact that Lilly would be spending the week in the dorm. I was smoothing the sheets on my squeaky twin bed when she and her mom walked into my room. I almost died when her mom double-checked the room number and said, "This is it!" When Lilly looked around and saw me standing there, she came unglued for real.

A few of the camp counselors heard the commotion and came running down to see what all the fuss was about. I just stood there and stared at her because if I'd ever seen anyone pitch a bigger fit, I couldn't remember when. She stomped and cried and fussed and demanded another roommate.

When the camp director arrived on the scene, she got right to the point. It was impossible to change rooms, she said, because if they started switching rooms for a bunch of eleven- and twelve-year-old girls, it would never stop.

Lilly's mom understood, but Lilly did not.

She skipped the evening meal and got out of bed the next morning only because the camp counselor threatened to call her daddy. On the way to the gym, some girls from out of town started making fun of her for being a crybaby. Then when she got on the court, they made fun of her even worse because Lilly was about as coordinated as a newborn giraffe.

I thought it was all pretty funny until I listened to her cry herself to sleep that night. The next day when the same girls started in on her again, I decided to intervene.

I told them I was from Nashville, where they beat people to death in the streets, and that really got their attention. I'd never actually heard of anything like that happening when I lived there, but I thought it made me sound like a real badass to say something so shocking. The three of them studied me for a minute, like they didn't know what to make of that comment, so I went on to tell them that I was a black belt in karate and I'd whip every one of their asses if they said another word to Lilly. I got in trouble with the camp counselors and had to do push-ups at half court in front of everybody, but I didn't care.

Lilly sat with me at dinner that night and asked me how long it took to become a black belt in karate. I told her I had no idea because I'd never taken a karate lesson in my life so it was a good thing those girls didn't call my bluff. She thought that was pretty funny. That night, instead of crying herself to sleep, we stayed up all night talking and giggling.

Three weeks after that, I was at Lilly's house on a Sunday afternoon when Gramma Jones came to pick me up. I told her that my parents were supposed to pick me up when they got back from their weekend trip to Nashville. Gramma Jones told me that there had been a terrible accident.

Lilly sat with me at my mom's funeral, and then stayed with me for the better part of the next three days while I sat, hoping and praying that my dad would pull through. Her whole family was there with Gramma Jones and me when they told us that he didn't. I'd never met Lilly's grandfather before that awful day, but I loved him forevermore after watching him hold my grandmother's hand when they gave her the news about her only child.

My mom's parents had long since passed away, so I had no choice but to move in with Gramma Jones. I think it did us both good, having each other so close during that time.

Lilly helped me pack up all my stuff at my parents' house. Ethan

Allen's parents and grandparents made it their personal mission to help Gramma Jones get the place ready to sell. Mason and I had been broken up for several months, but he came with Ethan Allen every day for the entire two weeks and did anything and everything my grandmother asked him to do.

He was picking up sticks in the yard one day in what I considered to be unbearable heat, so I fixed him some sweet tea and invited him to sit with me in the swing under the big shade tree. He put his arm around me and said, "No matter what happens for the rest of our lives, whether you're my girlfriend or not, I will always be around when you need me."

"Thanks, Mason," I said, feeling those old familiar butterflies.

"So, you wanna be my girlfriend again?" I couldn't remember why we'd broken up.

"That would be great," I said and smiled for the first time since the day Gramma Jones had picked me up at Lilly's.

We were on again, off again all that next year and the next.

In high school, we were the couple who always ended up getting back together. We did a ridiculous amount of making up and breaking up. We fought with each other while we dated other people. If I was going out with someone he didn't approve of, we'd argue about that. If he was seeing someone I thought was a ditz, I'd call him on it. More times than not, those arguments ended up with us dumping whoever else was involved and getting back together. Again.

We squabbled all the time. In the tenth grade, we didn't speak for two months because we got into a fight about whether or not Pindarus had a right to stab Cassius in *Julius Caesar.*

We argued a lot about where to eat lunch after church on Sundays. I always wanted to eat with Gramma Jones and never wanted to eat with his family. I knew this wasn't fair to him, but I always felt like his parents would've preferred for him to have a girlfriend with a bit more social status. I can't say for sure that's what they thought, but I was never comfortable at his house.

His two older sisters were supermodel skinny and gorgeous, as was his mom, and I was always ten or fifteen pounds overweight and wondering how they all kept their hair so straight and shiny. They were serious tennis players and, even though I could've beaten them into submission on the court, I always allowed them to play a close set. Maybe the lovely ladies in Mason's family would've liked me better if I'd allowed them to win a match every now and then. But I just wasn't willing to do that. Mason loved the fact that they couldn't beat me, and that was all the justification I needed to keep winning.

The longest and most successful run we had as a couple started on New Year's Eve our junior year and ended just before graduation our senior year. A knee injury had just put an end to my basketball scholarship dreams, while Mason had just signed to play football at Ole Miss. I was angry and bitter and jealous and started a big fight over nothing just so I could break up with him. Thus began the great divide. We went our separate ways and barely spoke the few times we saw each other that summer after graduation.

After a year at the local community college, Lilly and I decided to pursue our higher education at Mississippi State University. I selected art history as my major because I loved to paint, and she went with French because she wanted to live in Paris. We were looking for a cool place to live when we ran into poor, nervous Chloe Barksdale tacking up posters outside the campus bookstore.

She'd graduated from one of those big fancy Catholic schools in Jackson, and, after she'd spent the requisite year in the dorm, her daddy had bought (not rented, actually purchased) her a four-bedroom house in the Cotton District. She had one roommate already, a cousin of hers who was a junior at Mississippi State. She told us her daddy wanted her to "branch out and meet new people," and that's why she was out there tacking up "Roommates Wanted" flyers.

When we found out her house was in the Cotton District, we made a decision on the spot to move in. Lilly and I both thought she was a little weird, but not in a bad way, and certainly not weird enough to cause us to pass up that prime location. We moved in a few days later and discovered that she wasn't weird, just really serious and incredibly gullible.

Her cousin turned out to be more concerned with smoking pot than earning credits, so she was gone by Thanksgiving because her parents pulled her out of school and put her in a rehab clinic. Chloe was glad to see her go. She told Lilly and me that her cousin made her nervous, always sitting on the porch smoking weird-smelling cigarettes.

Chloe begged her dad not to make her find another roommate, claiming that she'd just moved in two perfect strangers and simply couldn't tolerate another new personality. He acquiesced and it was just the three of us for the next two years.

I dated a few other guys but couldn't find anyone that took my mind off of Mason. When I went home to stay with Gramma Jones during the break between semesters my junior year, I ran into him at the Christmas program at church. We ended up riding around till after midnight, then going parking like a couple of horny teenagers. After school started back in January, we saw each other as often as we could, but that wasn't very much.

The weather had just gone from pleasantly warm to unpleasantly hot the spring semester of my junior year, when I got a phone call on a Tuesday afternoon from Mrs. Lowberg, a good friend of Gramma's. She was crying and told me that Gramma had had a heart attack while working in her garden. Mason came to the funeral and was very kind, but my emotions were so raw I couldn't muster up much interest or enthusiasm in anyone or anything. He was preparing to apply for law school, and I knew what little time he had for me would be gone soon after that.

In the months that followed, I endured an insufferable bout of depression and probably would've dropped out of school had it not been for Chloe and Lilly's constant care and attention. I decided that I needed a break and found the perfect escape in a twelve-month study-abroad program. I left for Europe three days before my twenty-first birthday and didn't step foot on American soil until the following year.

When I got home, Lilly told me that she'd been "discovered" on a recent trip to New York City and was leaving immediately after graduation to start her career as a model. I was floored by the news and couldn't believe her luck. I was happy for her because she was so excited, but sad at the same time because I'd missed her so much while I was gone. What could I do besides bid her a fond farewell?

Chloe begged me to move back in with her so she wouldn't have to look for a new roommate. She was tackling her master's degree, and I had decided it would be stupid not to finish my bachelor's when I was so close to being done, so I spent another year with Chloe in the Cotton District.

After graduation, I decided to move into Gramma Jones's house in Bugtussle. It had been empty for more than two years and was stuffy and stinky inside, but being there made me feel good. The ladies of the Bugtussle Garden Club had taken it upon themselves to maintain her ornate yard and garden as a way to honor her passing. They were positively thrilled when I told them I'd decided to keep the place. They'd been worried sick I'd sell it to someone who wouldn't take care of the yard.

I lucked up and landed a job at the high school from which I'd graduated five years earlier. My old art teacher, Mrs. Jennings, had just retired and stopped by the house one day and told me I should apply for the job. I'm pretty sure I got hired not because of her recommendation or because anyone on the school board liked me, but because I was the only qualified applicant.

I heard a rumor that, due to high enrollment numbers, the board was looking to hire one more counselor for the high school, so I called Chloe and she came up immediately. She'd been staying with her parents since graduation and was thankful for the chance to put some distance between her and her mother's expectations.

She submitted her application and, according to her, knocked the interview out of the park. I'm pretty sure she was hired not because of her fantastic qualifications or stellar interviewing skills, but rather because she came from old money and her last name was Barksdale.

Chloe moved in with me and I had the idea that she might date Ethan Allen, but she had a moral issue with that because Lilly had dated him in high school. Instead, she ended up with that asshole Richard Stacks, who was probably more impressed with her family heritage than her sweet personality and stunning good looks.

Richard Stacks the Fourth had just moved to Bugtussle from Tupelo to open a branch of his father's insurance company when he ran across Chloe Barksdale at the Fall Festival. She'd caught his eye when she wandered by his booth, and when he found out who she was, he was not to be deterred. We begged her not to marry him, but she had fallen for his wolf-in-sheep's-clothing act hook, line, and sinker.

Not long after their absurdly extravagant wedding atop the Peabody Hotel in Memphis, Richard's mother, Mrs. Bobbie Sue Stacks, decided to depart from the lower ranks of Tupelo society in favor of being a "bigger fish in a smaller pond" in Bugtussle. She bought a house at the country club and set about establishing herself as a "Queen Bee of Bugtussle Society." She was enthusiastically accepted by the very same women who had scorned the presence of my mother.

Chloe moved out of my house and into the elegant home that Richard bought for them with her daddy's money and life got pretty boring for me. I started having an affair with Logan Hatter, the new baseball coach, who was from the Delta and liked to party. I had a great time with him, but he was not, by any stretch of the imagination, "the marrying kind."

I found myself spending more and more time daydreaming about quitting my job and moving to the big city, any big city, and opening my own art studio. I was drawing floor plans for this imaginary studio the day Lilly called me and told me she was finished with modeling.

"Why?" I asked her. "You're making crazy money and getting to travel all over the world."

"It's just not worth it," she said and I could tell she'd been crying. "I'm sick of it, and the money isn't worth it. I'm lonely, I'm miserable, and I want to come home."

"Well, come on!" I told her and forgot about the art studio for a while.

It was easy for Lilly to get a job working with Chloe and me at the high school. She was fluent in French, and foreign language teachers are hard to come by in North Mississippi. As a matter of fact, she had three other job offers on the table when she accepted the position at Bugtussle.

It was great having her home again. Ethan Allen had just bought the old beer joint downtown and we spent most of our time off helping him fix up the place. She liked Logan Hatter, but didn't like that I was having a fling with him because she thought that he was too much of a ladies' man. She felt better when I told her that we were pretty much just friends with benefits. Logan was a regular at the bar as soon as it opened so the four of us got to where we spent a lot of time together.

Then came the day that I ran into Mason McKenzie at the Grove in Oxford during the Egg Bowl. The Egg Bowl, arguably the biggest event of the year for college football fans in Mississippi, is always the last scheduled game for the Ole Miss Rebels and the Mississippi State Bulldogs, and most people forget about the rest of the season and focus on the outcome of this one game because the winner gets bragging rights for the following twelve months. It was in this atmosphere of rivalry and tradition that Mason, a Rebel fan, begged me, a Bulldog fan, to move to Florida and marry him. I quickly agreed. We were both thoroughly intoxicated at the time.

I spent the week after Christmas at his place and couldn't wait to go back during spring break. When he came home for Easter, we had a sober conversation that didn't include a marriage proposal but did include a serious invitation for me to move in with him. I was bored with my life, hated my boss, and was very much in love with him. The day after school was out, I moved into his three-story house two blocks from the ocean in Pelican Cove, Florida.

I was so happy I couldn't stand myself. I laughed more in the six weeks I spent with him than I had my whole life up until then. We walked on the beach and drank beer out of plastic wineglasses. We told each other our wildest dreams and darkest fears. We shopped at the local farmers' markets and ate boiled shrimp and raw oysters whenever we liked. He bought me a sweet little chiweenie puppy and it took us two weeks to come up with the name Señor Buster Loo Bluefeather. I went to bed every night with the man of my dreams and woke up every morning to the smell of salt water and gourmet coffee.

Then a girl named Allison showed up at his door and, after watching them stand in the driveway and talk for almost an hour, I got mad and left. I had just turned thirty but had yet to master the demon of jealousy. I moved back to Bugtussle just before school started and justified my irrational decision by claiming Mason couldn't be trusted. Shortly after, Lilly told me that Mason had a ring in his pocket the night I left. Then Ethan Allen let it slip that Mason had purchased a building for me in Pelican Cove. Ethan Allen asked me what I would've done with a building, and I couldn't bring myself to tell him about my dream of owning an art studio.

I put on ten pounds in two months, and had I not had Buster Loo to take walking I probably would've gained a hundred. I couldn't bear to see Mason or talk to him, so I ignored all of his text messages and phone calls and locked the door and hid in the bedroom when he came to my house. I didn't go to church or Ethan Allen's when Lilly told me he was in town.

I feel a tug on the leash and turn around to see Buster Loo lying in the grass beside the walking trail.

"Oh, goodness, Buster Loo!" I say, looking at my watch. "We've been walking for over an hour. I'm so sorry! Here," I say, leaning down to pick him up, "let me carry you home, little buddy!"

4

<><><><><><><><><><><><><><><><><><><><><><><><><><><><><><><><><><>

I skip church Sunday because I don't feel like answering ten thousand questions about why I'm still in Bugtussle, Mississippi, when I'm supposed to be at the beach in Florida. Everyone will be asking where Lilly is and I don't feel like lying to church people on the Lord's Day.

Against my better judgment, I decide to spend the morning at the gym instead. I pull into the parking lot, hoping against hope that a good endorphin rush will lift my spirits, or, at the very least, make me feel better about those stupid monthly payments. As soon as I'm in the front door, however, I pick up on something very peculiar that somehow escaped my notice during my two previous visits.

I am, without a doubt, the fattest girl in this place.

I look around to see if anyone else notices that I'm the only person in the building who has to shop in the big and not so tall department, but no one seems to be paying attention. So I try to forget about it.

But I can't forget about it.

I am keenly aware of my fatness as I feign invisibility on a walk of shame past a never-ending line of big fancy treadmills with micro-LCD screens and more USB ports than my home computer.

"Who needs all that crap?" I mumble under my breath. "It's a freakin' treadmill, not a Boeing 747."

Even if I had sense enough to work one of those monsters, I wouldn't step foot on it if my life depended on it. I mean, I would literally die before I hopped up there with that Bratz pack of little jogger ladies with their shiny, straight ponytails and their little gym shorts stretched over their tight little rumps.

I make my way back to the old clunker treadmills, and it only takes a second for me to spot the one I'm looking for. It's parked between two dusty machines with "out of order" signs taped to the monitors. No Bratz dolls on either side of me. Those little fitness freaks wouldn't dream of abandoning their front-and-center Boeing 747 treadmills, and I don't give a rat's ass anyway because I happen to prefer the privacy.

Plus I don't need some hairy-ass bald man, sweating all over the place, trying to talk to me about the economy or the weather or some stupid crap like that. I mean, how does a man lose every sprig of hair on his head but look like a woolly mammoth from the ears down? I honestly feel sorry for those dudes, just not sorry enough to listen to their annoying opinions regarding the state of affairs in the world today.

I push the start button and tell myself not to look down at the timer, but all I can do is look down at the timer. I look at it every three or four seconds. I try to stop but I can't. It makes me dizzy staring at that stupid monitor, but the only other place to rest my eyes is on that floor-to-ceiling wall-to-wall mirror, and goodness knows, I don't want to see that. Mirrors that size are not natural or normal, and they insult my intelligence because they cannot reveal *to* me a single thing *about* me that I don't already know.

I know my pie-shaped face is red as a beet and my frizzy hair is soaking wet with sweat after ten minutes of warm-up. I know my black yoga pants are spotted with bleach specks from the knees down, but it's the only pair I have that aren't worn out in the thighs, and I know my socks don't match each other *or* this XL Fudpuckers T-shirt I've had since 2005. I don't need mirrors to know this. And I don't need mirrors reflecting every other female in this place, all of whom are dressed like Under Armour mannequins at Dick's Sporting Goods.

What the hell am I doing here?

And why doesn't this gym have a separate area for fat girls? Girls who need to lose a little more than that last five pounds.

That last five pounds. Is that supposed to be some kind of a joke? If I got that close to my ideal weight, I'd throw myself a three-keg pizza party. And that's why I'll never have to worry about that last five pounds, because I'll always be battling that first fifteen.

At any rate, these gym owners need to take a hint from department stores and designate a *plus size* or a *women's* area. We need a place of our own so we don't offend the Under Armour–wearing Bratz packs of the workout world with our fatassness.

I fantasize about having a place to stretch without someone thinking I look like the Michelin Man on a Twister mat. Or doing sit-ups without worrying about a roll of fat slipping out somewhere and being mistaken for a renegade boob.

I think I'll send an e-mail to the gym manager and suggest he designate a separate room for big girls, and while I'm at it, I'll tell him to take down those billboard-sized mirrors and put up some posters of Justin Timberlake and Marky Mark. Then all the chubby girls could have their very own private room in the gym and maybe I wouldn't be the only one here.

A Fat Girls Only Work-Out Room.

Throw in a big-screen TV and every season of the *Biggest Loser* and we're talking about fitness center perfection. Who knows, if I could exercise with other chubby ladies while watching Bob and Jillian work their sadistic magic, I might come to the gym more than once a month. I might turn my flabby body into a Bratz doll, go buy a flat iron, and take a class on how to work those big fancy treadmills.

Hell, no, I won't.

My left knee hurts and my hands are numb and I've only been on this bastard for thirty-one minutes and forty-two seconds.

I'm going home.

5

◇◇

It rains Monday, Tuesday, and Wednesday, then gets hot enough Thursday to kill a camel. The weekend passes without much ado and Monday morning arrives too soon.

Back to school. Another day, another dollar, another antidepressant.

I sign in fifteen minutes late and wish it was thirty. Coach Logan Hatter is standing in his usual spot between our classrooms with a smug look on his face.

"Still hungover?" he asks, smiling. "You didn't get much of a tan. Don't tell me you've started using sunscreen."

"Not hardly, Hatt," I mumble. "We didn't go."

"What? Didn't go? What are you talking about?"

"Lilly couldn't make it, so I stayed home and cleaned out my closets."

That got a laugh out of him. "Cleaned out your *closets*? Why didn't you call *me*?" And there is a shining example of why guy friends are easier to get along with than girlfriends. They don't want a bunch of details; they aren't interested in all the drama; they just want a little action if they can get it.

"You had baseball games, Coach Hatter, remember?"

"Yeah, but I like knowing I *could've* gone." He grins and his navy blue eyes sparkle. "You know you would've had a good time if I'd gone down there with ya."

"Are you about to slap me on the ass?" He looks guilty. "Please don't, because here comes Cruella de Vil."

I'd rather be shot in the face than listen to anything Principal Catherine Hilliard has to say to me this morning.

"Miss Jones, I'd like to see you in my office during your planning period this afternoon," she hisses through crusty chapped lips, "and try to be on time if it wouldn't put you out too much."

"I'll check my planner and see what I can do, Mrs. Hilliard," I retort with all the smart-assness I can muster.

"Your planner," she says, "now says to be in my office at one thirty-five sharp."

Coach Hatter fidgets with his keys and looks like he's squeezing back a surge of diarrhea.

"I'll see what I can do." I swear if I had a gun I would stop talking about it and shoot myself. Or her. "What's this concerning?"

"A private matter. I'm sure you don't want to discuss it here."

"I don't mind discussing it here."

Catherine Hilliard is the worst thing to happen to Bugtussle High School since they started having Meat Loaf Monday in the cafeteria. I liked my job until Mr. Landing retired two years ago. He was absolutely the best principal a teacher could ask for, so I guess we were due for an asshole, and boy, did we get one.

Usually the district hires someone already in the system or at least someone local, but for some odd reason that dipshit Ardie Griffith brought in Catherine Hilliard from some school in south Mississippi, and, in an unparalleled display of small-town political favoritism, pretty much forced the board to approve her.

Mr. Landing held teachers' meetings every Thursday that lasted about thirty or forty-five minutes. He said what needed to be said and we were on our way. Now we have ninety-minute meetings twice a week because Catherine Hilliard loves to command the attention of a captive audience. And I mean *captive* in the most literal way.

If she had any interest whatsoever in improving the school or the students' educational experience, the meetings might be tolerable, but she doesn't so they're not. She always spends the first fifteen or twenty minutes chewing on our collective asses for miscellaneous petty shit, then veers off on speeches and soapboxes that couldn't be more irrelevant to education.

We spent forty-five minutes one afternoon listening to her recap a detailed roster of Dr. Oz anecdotes. Lara Beth Harrison, a feisty science teacher, got sick of it and filed a grievance with the school board. At the meeting, Superintendent Griffith promptly dismissed her complaint and asked her to leave before she even had a chance to speak. She tried calling a few members of the board but got nowhere with it.

Lara Beth led the first wave of the mass exodus. About a dozen teachers transferred or retired after the first year Catherine Hilliard was in charge, and several more are leaving at the end of this year. I wouldn't mind joining them, but if I left there wouldn't be anybody to rub that bitch the wrong way, and I can't have that.

Principal Catherine Hilliard makes the students more miserable than she does the teachers. As soon as she took over, she cracked down on the dress code, shortened breaks, and threatened to cancel the weekly pep rallies if the halls didn't get quieter between classes. She ground student morale into the dirt, and it shows in their lack of gusto in the classroom.

She tried to punish the entire football team for showing too much spirit during school hours, but that caused a backlash even Ardie Griffith couldn't save her from. She found out the hard way that nobody messes with the Bugtussle Rockets. Amanda Tanner, president of the Booster Club and mom of beloved Rocket quarterback Zac Tanner, showed up at one of our ninety-minute meetings and, in front of every teacher in the library, told Mrs. Hilliard that she would whip her ass all over Bugtussle if she ever got on her kid again for being too rowdy at a pep rally. I watched with delight as Catherine Hilliard stuttered something unintelligible, and Amanda Tanner pointed her finger in her face and told her to shut her mouth and never say another word to her or about her.

Since then, it's been an all-out war between Catherine Hilliard and pretty much everyone who has anything to do with the school. Mrs. Hilliard has but one ally, the superintendent, which is a small but rather powerful alliance to have.

I just don't know what the hell she thinks she's accomplishing by acting like she does. Anybody with a grain of sense can see she's doing more harm than good and is obviously in the wrong profession. That's not to say I'm in the right one, but at least I have enough sense to understand the responsibility I have to my students.

I can't say that I love teaching, because I don't, but what I lack in professional interest I try to make up for with enthusiasm for my subject matter. I have good credibility with my students, many of whom have never left the state of Mississippi, because I spent that year studying art history in Europe.

I can start class with something like, "When I saw Michelangelo's *Last Judgment* in the Sistine Chapel in Rome . . . ," and bingo! I have their undivided attention. I'm proud to say that I've cultivated some serious talent and spurred some genuine interest in the minds of my students, who, for the most part, are great kids. And even the ones I don't like don't deserve to have their high school experience ruined by a self-serving hag like Catherine Hilliard. She goes out of her way to make this place a living hell, and that's why I don't miss an opportunity to piss her off.

"Be there, Miss Jones," she says and smirks. "On time."

She turns to Coach Hatter, who flashes her a big shaky smile.

"Good morning, Mrs. Hilliard, good to see you. How was your break?"

Catherine Hilliard glares at him like she's about to cram her fist down his throat, rip his heart out, and eat it with a side of fries.

She says nothing.

His smile falters and he looks at the floor.

She turns and clicks down the hallway, maroon pumps keeping time with the beating of her sadistic heart.

"What was that all about?" Coach Hatter asks, obviously stung by her rudeness.

"Hell if I know." I watch her tromp past my students' art displays without so much as turning her head. "Maybe she didn't get to drown any puppies on her way to work this morning."

"You are crazy," Logan says and starts that ridiculous, obnoxious snigger of his that always cracks me up, so we just stand there laughing like hyenas waiting for the first bell to ring.

6

<><><><><><><><><><><><><><><><><><><><><><><><><><><><><><><><><>

At lunch, Chloe Stacks is a nervous wreck.

Chloe takes her job, her life, and her self very seriously. Too seriously in my opinion, but that's just me. She's the best school counselor in the state of Mississippi and has the plaques in her office to prove it.

"What's wrong, sweet Chloe?" I ask. "Have you had to counsel some nutcases this morning?" She gracefully takes the seat across from me and places her lavender monogrammed lunch bag on the table.

"You don't know?" she asks, like I'm stupid.

"Know what?" I'm not stupid, so I look at her like she's crazy.

"You really do not know?" She's staring me down with those big brown saucer-shaped eyes.

"Well, obviously I don't, Chloe. What's up? We gonna have a state test in art this year and you just found out?" I snort at my own joke and open a ketchup packet with my teeth.

She stares at me like I'm an insolent child misbehaving in church. During prayer.

"What? Why are you looking at me like that?"

"How do you not know what just happened to your best friend?"

"Lilly?" My mind starts spinning the crazy *what-if* scenarios. What if she got kidnapped in Paris? What if her plane crashed? What if it got hijacked? What if she tried to screw one of the hijackers? What if she got carjacked in Memphis and she's sitting on the side of the road up there in the big city? What if she had a wreck on the way home from the airport? What if the Gentleman's wife found out about her and hacked her to death with a pickax? It's amazing how many ludicrous thoughts can dart through your mind in a millisecond.

"She was fired this morning," Chloe whispers.

"What?" I spray the table with tater tots and get the insolent child stare again. "What for? Are you serious?"

"I overheard it this morning while I was in the conference room," she whispers. "Cheap walls, very thin." She eyeballs the other teachers filing into the cafeteria. "If you don't know, then probably no one does. I guess they're not going to make it public."

"Make what public?"

She cups her hands around her mouth and whispers, "She was fired after Catherine Hilliard accused her of having an affair with one of her students."

I choke on my chocolate milk and it takes me a second to recover.

"Would you please stop eating for a second?" Chloe asks, wiping milk and tater tots off her side of the table.

"She's banging one of her kids. No shit? Which one?"

"Watch your *language*! Does it matter which one?"

"Hell, yeah, it matters."

"No, it does *not* matter because she would *not* do that." A thoughtful pause. "What are we going to do, Ace?"

"Nothing. Watch her on the news tonight, I guess." I'm not feeling the pity-party vibe for the promiscuous Lilly Lane. Not even a little bit.

"So you think she's guilty? You think she did this?" Chloe is giving me her saucer-eyed stare again. "Because I do *not* think that she would do such a thing, and I think we need to help her."

"Help her what? Clean out her desk and find a lawyer?"

"You think she would do something like that?" Now she's boring a hole through me with those eyes. Perfectly arched eyebrows drawn; perfectly lined lips quivering. "How could you *say* that? She is our *best* friend. What is *wrong* with you today?"

"I don't know, Chloe." I can see she's about to burst into tears so I paddle backward like I usually do when having a conversation with her. "No. You know what, Chloe? I do not think that Lilly did anything wrong. There is absolutely no way she would do something like that."

"So we're going to help her then?" Her brown eyes light up and she smiles like a little girl looking at lollipop balloons.

"Yes. Absolutely. We are going to help her." I look down at the tater tot shrapnel floating in a pool of chocolate milk on my plastic lunch tray. "Forget lunch. Let's go check out her classroom. See what we can find out."

"Yes, let's do that!" She jumps up and runs right into Logan Hatter.

Coach Hatter eats lunch with us every day, but Chloe can't tell her husband that.

"Hey, ladies, where y'all off to?" He looks at Chloe, then eyeballs me. "What's wrong? What's going on?"

"We gotta run, Hatt. I'll fill you in later, I promise."

"So I'm eatin' by myself? That's no fun. Where's Lilly?"

Awkward silence.

"Here comes Coach Wills. He'll keep you company." I give him a quick wink and he rolls his eyes. He can't stand Coach Wills.

The hallway is empty so I imagine for one disillusioned second that this might go off without a hitch. The door to Lilly's classroom is slightly ajar, so we scurry down there like field mice sneaking past a sleeping cat. I stop short and Chloe bumps into me from behind. I spin around and put a finger over my mouth.

Someone is in Lilly's classroom.

We freeze.

And wait.

Then, a voice.

It's Catherine Hilliard.

I can't tell if she's talking on a cell phone or just mumbling to herself, but either way, she's stupid and I want to knock her ass over with a tire tool. I can't make out what she's saying; I can only hear papers rattling and stuff hitting the floor.

Suddenly, she articulates a sentence that comes through loud and clear.

"Who? Oh, of course. Right now? Out in the hallway?"

"Shit!" I whisper and Chloe takes off running in a dead sprint to the girls' bathroom. "What are you doing? Get back here!" I scream-whisper, but she's gone.

I smell mothballs and old lady muff powder and turn around like a girl in a horror movie about to get axed in the skull. I'm eye level with a giant gold cross hanging on a thin rope chain. There is a tiny Jesus on the cross.

"Just what do you think you're doing, Miss Jones? And where did Mrs. Stacks run off to?"

"I don't know what you're talking about." Probably not the best response I've ever come up with.

She stares at me like I'm a dog turd in the lima beans on the Sunday dinner table. I look back down at Jesus.

"You should've taken Miss Lane to Florida like you always do."

That catches me off guard.

"Okay, seriously, Mrs. Hilliard, now I really don't know what you're talking about."

"You will. Now, why don't you be a nice girl and get in there and clean out Miss Lane's personal effects?"

"Why? Is she getting a new classroom?"

She points into the classroom and glares down at me as if her dreadful stare will force me into action.

"What's that you have in your hand there, Mrs. Hilliard?"

"School property."

"A picture frame and some postcards are school property?" I wonder when the picture was taken and where the postcards are from. I wonder why I can't keep my mouth shut and live a normal life. I think about grabbing that stuff out of her hand and throwing it down the hallway just for fun.

"Don't stand there and act like you don't know what's going on, Graciela Jones. I haven't decided yet what *your* role is in all of this," she hisses.

This bitch is driving me crazy. I think about drawing back and trying to slap the ugly off her face, but I don't think I could hit her hard enough.

"All of what, Mrs. Hilliard?" I'm not sure I want The-Whole-Truth-So-Help-Me-God when it comes to what's going on with Lilly, but I press on anyway. "I came down here to check on Lilly because she wasn't at lunch, and find you going through her personal stuff, so pardon me if I'm not connecting the dots."

"Don't play stupid with me, Miss Jones, even though we both know how good you are at that." She smirks, and I fight off the urge to gouge her eyes out with the dry-erase marker in my back pocket. She continues, "So tell me, why were you standing at the door eavesdropping? And where is your prim little sidekick?"

"Well, she ran to the bathroom, so common sense would dictate that she had to pee. I was standing outside the door here because you don't look or sound *any*thing like Lilly Lane."

"You are on thin ice, Miss Jones, and you better tread lightly."

"I think you mean skate. And is that a threat? Do I need to call the Mississippi Association of Educators and report that?" I can feel my face burning.

"Like that would make any difference," she says. "By the way, your presence is no longer required in my office this afternoon because, as it turns out, something far more important has come up."

"Oh, really? Like what?"

"I'll be at the district office," she says and smiles at me with her gigantic horse teeth, "filing a complaint to have Miss Lane's teaching license revoked."

I watch in stunned silence as she stomps off down the hallway. She stops at the girls' bathroom and calls, "Yoo-hoo, Mrs. Stacks, you can come out now. Coast is clear."

"What the hell is going on?" I whisper to myself. Could Lilly really be sleeping with one of her students? Wonder which one it is? Why is Catherine Hilliard such a hateful bitch? Could I kill her and make it look like an accident? What the hell does she think I've done? What did Chloe accomplish by running to the bathroom and leaving me here by myself looking like an idiot? What was Catherine Hilliard looking for in Lilly's classroom? Why didn't Lilly talk to Chloe before she left? Would she really do it with one of her kids and risk throwing her entire career away? Could Lilly possibly be that stupid?

I've always admired Lilly's genuine passion for teaching, but the question on my mind at the present moment is how her passion fits into her getting her ass fired. If she ditched our trip to Florida so she could screw around with some teenage boy, then this could be the end of our friendship.

It takes Chloe a full two minutes to creep out of the bathroom. I stare at the "Springtime in Paris" poster stuck to Lilly's door and try to wrap my mind around what's going on, but none of this crap makes any sense. Nothing lines up.

"Ace, how did she know we were out here?" Chloe asks. "That's creepy."

I nod my head toward the security camera mounted at the end of the hallway.

"Someone was *watching* us! Those monitors are in her office! Someone *was* watching us!"

"Chloe, someone was watching out for her and saw us." I walk in Lilly's room and motion for her to join me. "Let's get Lilly's stuff packed up before Cruella comes back and throws it all in the trash."

I turn to the security camera and throw up my middle finger, then mouth the phrase that goes along with the gesture. I'd like to moon whoever has the bird's-eye view up there, but I know I couldn't get my pants back up before Chloe saw what I was doing.

7

<><><><><><><><><><><><><><><><><><><><><><><><><><><><><><><><><><><><><><><>

My students are getting ready to start on their art fair projects so the rest of the day passes off quickly. Art fair is one of my favorite ventures, second only to annual field trips, because I never cease to be amazed by the creativity of my students when they are allowed to let their imaginations run wild. It also means the end of the school year is near.

When the last bell rings, I breathe an audible, "Thank you, Jesus," and get a few funny looks from my students. "Just ready to head home," I say, and they nod in understanding.

I grab the box with Lilly's stuff in it and make my way to the parking lot while the buses are still loading. I'm not in the mood to stand around doing nothing for fifteen minutes, then get behind thirteen buses that stop every ten yards for twenty-six miles. At least six other teachers see me leave, so that pretty much guarantees I'll get a good ass chewing for committing the dreadful sin of leaving school early. I head home and throw on a T-shirt, shorts, and flip-flops; I feed Buster Loo, take him for a walk, then get down in the grass for some speedychiweenie playtime. After a few minutes, Buster Loo looks up at the sky, barks two times, and takes off for his doggie door as fast as his two-inch legs will take him. I go in to check on him and he's in his secret hiding place behind the love seat with his eyes squeezed shut, which is Buster Loo speak for "I'm finished playing. Now bug off."

I grab my keys and head out the door. I'm going to get some answers from Lilly Lane.

I swing by China Kitchen and pick up some kung pao chicken and cream cheese wontons. She'll think I'm trying to be nice by bringing over a tasty peace offering, but the truth is that I need a snack to calm my nerves.

I pull up at the pink and white dollhouse that is the home of Lilly Lucille Lane. I park my dirty Maxima behind her badass BMW and wonder for the hundredth time what the hell is going on with her.

I grab the Chinese food and go around to the back door, which is unlocked as always. I go in and put the food on the table and hear a commotion going on in the living room. I turn around to see Zac Tanner—All-American, All-Star, All-State, Mr. Bugtussle High School himself—sitting on Lilly's sofa wearing only swimming trunks.

Lilly is perched on the love seat like the cat who swallowed the canary and all I can do is stare.

"Not what it looks like, Ace, I swear," she says, shaking her head and rocking back and forth like a crack addict.

"It never is, is it, Lilly?" I absolutely do not know what to do at this point, so I say, "This is too much. Gotta get outta here."

"Miss Jones, I promise—" Zac Tanner begins.

I cut him off quick. "You"—I point at him—"you shut your mouth, go put on a shirt, and get the hell out of here. Don't say another word to me. Got it?"

"Ace." Lilly stands up but doesn't take a step forward.

"You're on your own with this one, sister." I turn to leave. "I cannot believe this."

"Ace! Wait!" she calls as I'm walking out the door, but I don't look back.

I pop the trunk, grab the box of junk from her classroom, and sling that mess all over her front yard. I hear a heated exchange going on inside but could not care less what's being said. I get in my car and get out of there.

I tell myself I'm wrong. I tell myself that she's telling me the truth and it really isn't what it looks like but, damn it, the facts are staring me right in the face. She dropped our annual trip to the beach to screw around with Zac Tanner.

The Gentleman is an eighteen-year-old kid.

That pisses me off so much I think I might pass out.

I bet she went to Paris over spring break.

Paris, Tennessee, maybe.

I stop by the Hill Top Country Store and buy two packs of cigarettes and a 40-ounce Corona, then hit the back roads. I haven't smoked since I was a teenager, but today is turning out to be a good day to fall back on some bad habits. My phone is buzzing like a pack of bees at a garden festival, but I don't give a rat's ass. I need some time to think.

When it gets dark, I take a paved road back to town and head to Ethan Allen's. The bar, not the furniture store. People in Bugtussle don't get the two confused because the only Ethan Allen they've ever heard of besides the one who owns the bar is the Revolutionary War hero who founded the state of Vermont.

8

◇◇

I walk in at 8:55 and Ethan Allen smiles and switches off the neon signs. Everything in Bugtussle closes at 9:00 p.m. He fills a frosty mug with Killian's Red and puts it down on a beverage napkin.

"Hey, babe!" he says affectionately. "You look like you could use a drink."

Ethan Allen Harwood spends his days on a tractor, his nights at the bar, and his Sunday mornings at the Methodist church sitting next to his grandparents. He drives a spotless Chevrolet pickup with gigantic mud tires and listens only to country music. He's got on his usual getup, which consists of Wrangler jeans, a plaid shirt with metal buttons, worn-out cowboy boots, and one of his four state championship rings. His dusty Stetson hangs on a hook next to the liquor shelf.

"What's goin' on, gal?" He fixes himself a frosty mug of Mountain Dew and sniffs the air. "You been smokin'?"

"You might as well sit down, Ethan Allen," I say, "'cause this is gonna take a while."

He walks around the bar and parks his long lean body on the stool next to mine and listens with great interest as I tell him everything that's transpired. He asks a bunch of questions like he always does, and when his antique cuckoo clock strikes ten, I get up to go to the bathroom and realize I'm too drunk to walk.

"I'm hammered, Ethan Allen," I slur.

"Really, Ace? I hadn't noticed." He laughs and pats me on the butt as I teeter past him. Ethan Allen is the most eligible bachelor in Bugtussle, Mississippi, but not because he wants to be. He just can't find a woman that wants to live on a farm with a man who owns a bar. Since we've both been single for most of the past year, Ethan Allen and I have spent a lot of time together drinking and solving each other's problems. I've told him that he might want to think about selling the bar or maybe hiring someone to run it so he'd have more time for the ladies. He's told me that I need to calm down and think about being nicer to people who care about me. He never said he was talking about Mason, but I always knew he was.

I feel my way back to the restroom, and when I get back out to the bar he has his cowboy hat on and my keys in his hand.

"C'mon. I'm taking you home," he says with a warm smile. "I know you gotta go to work in the morning. You know the drill."

He holds my hand while we walk across the parking lot, then helps me up into his huge truck.

"Is this a monster truck, Ethan Allen? Is that what you're going for here?"

He laughs, pops in a Toby Keith CD, and starts singing to me about the red, white, and blue. After helping me out of his huge truck, he walks me around to the back door like he's done a million times before, and I know that my car will be parked in my driveway before the sun comes up in the morning.

"Ace, your backyard out here is unbelievable. Your Gramma Jones would be so proud of you for taking care of this place like you do," he says as he squints into the dark. "Is that okra stalks comin' up over there?"

"Sure is, buddy. You like it pickled or fried? I do it both ways." I start sniggering. "Okra that is, you pervert." I almost lose my balance laughing at my own idiotic joke and Ethan Allen puts a hand on my hip to steady me.

"You are plum retarded, Ace, plum flippin' retarded."

"Thank you very much." I hear a small commotion and turn to see Buster Loo running speedy-dog circles around the patio table. "What the hell is my dog doin' out here, Ethan Allen? He is not a night crawler. Buster Loo does not like to be outside in the dark."

"Maybe he wants up in that chair." Ethan Allen walks over to the table, leans down, and says, "Why is there bacon on your out-a-doors table, Ace? That's mighty unsightly."

"I'm puttin' it in the black-eyed peas I'm cookin' tomorrow. Okay, not really. I'm havin' it for breakfast in an omelet. Oh, no, wait, that's not it. I'm savin' it for a midnight BLT. You got any lettuce I can borrow?" I turn around and look at him, snorting and laughing. "Seriously, Ethan Allen, what are you talking about?"

"There's bacon on your table and that's what your little dog here wants. You want me to give it to him?"

I walk over to get a closer look at the alleged bacon. I see two strips of precooked bacon laid in an "X" on the center of my patio table.

"What the hell is that doing on my table? I don't eat that weird-ass bacon from a box." Buster Loo is bouncing like a ball and whining like a derelict feline.

"Me neither, sister, that's some nasty stuff right there," he says as he snarls. "It ain't right. Bacon is meant to be fried in a pan, not processed and sold at room temperature."

I pick up the bacon and toss it to Buster Loo and he gulps it down in three hasty bites. I see a pink piece of paper on the table, and when I reach for it, it flitters off in the direction of my potted herb garden.

"What the hell?" Ethan Allen hollers, watching the note fly through the air. "Somebody stuck bacon on top of a note on your out-a-doors table? Now that beats all I ever saw."

I make a move to catch the note, trip over Buster Loo, and go down face-first onto the porch. I land close to my Christmas lights, so I reach over and plug those in like that was my plan all along. Buster Loo is clucking like a chicken and looking like his feelings are hurt, so I pull him over and apologize for booting him in his little chiweenie ribs. He shows his forgiveness by speed-licking my right eyeball and pawing me on the head.

Ethan Allen is laughing his ass off, and when he gets his breath back he says, "Oh, so I guess that's how you always get them lights on? I'm gonna go get you a football helmet to wear around here, girl." Still chuckling, he asks, "That little Mexican wiener dog okay?"

"He's fine. Did you see where that note went?"

"Landed in your marijuana grove over here." He waves the rectangular-shaped paper back and forth. "Pink polka-dot paper. Wonder who that's from?"

"That's an herb garden, you geek." I squint at the note. "And I know who it's from and so do you. You gonna read it?"

"Ain't my note. Ain't my business."

"Oh, good word, Ethan Allen Harwood! I just spent over an hour giving you the juiciest news in town and now you're gonna stand there and act like you're a mind-your-own-business kind of guy? Puh-leese. I don't even care what it says! Throw it away then."

"Okay, jus' calm down and I'll see what it says." He unfolds the paper, reads the note, then gives me an odd look.

"What?" I ask, feeling a killer headache coming on.

He looks down at the paper, out toward the yard, then back at me.

"You look like you saw a ghost, Ethan Allen. What is it?"

"You better look at it. I don't think I was meant to read this."

"Lilly Lane and her stupid pink-polka-dot-stationery-using ass ditched me the night before we were supposed to go to the beach so she could screw around with a stupid kid, and I spent my spring break cleaning out my stupid closets. Then she gets her stupid self fired and Catherine Hilliard's stupid ass wants to see me go down with her and now she's stuck a stupid note out here and used stupid fake bacon as a stupid paperweight so my dog would be going crazy, and you think I give a stupid flyin' shit what it says?"

"No, really, you better read it."

"I don't give a shit what she has to say, Ethan Allen!"

"Ace, get up and read it yourself. It's about Chloe." He walks over and holds out both hands. "Here. C'mon, now."

He pulls me up and I'm thankful he's a big strong country boy because I don't think a little fellow could get the job done.

I squint down at the note and sobriety comes fast and hard.

"I've gotta get to the hospital, Ethan Allen. Can you take me?" He looks at me, obviously concerned about my level of intoxication. "Will you take me? Please?"

"I don't know if you should—"

"I have to go. You know I have to go."

"All righty then. Whatever you need."

I run inside with Buster Loo hot on my heels, splash water all over my face, and grab a Diet Mountain Dew out of the fridge.

"You want a drink?"

"I don't think now's the time—"

"Not a *drink* drink! Some water or a Coke or something."

"Naw, I got a dip, but grab me an empty bottle if you got one handy."

I grab a water bottle, blow Buster Loo a kiss, and run out the door. Ethan Allen helps me climb back into his massive truck and he leaves rubber on the road at the end of my driveway.

9

◇◇◇

Lilly is sitting alone in the lobby of Bugtussle Memorial Hospital. She doesn't see us come in and we startle her out of a daze.

"Did you know he had started hitting her?" she asks quietly, looking at the floor.

"I had no idea." I focus on trying not to hurl. When my nerves are shot, my stomach gets really upset, and that's without nine beers and a pack of Virginia Slims. I look around for a vending machine. I need a 7-Up and some crackers.

"I didn't either," she says, still looking at the floor.

"Have you seen her, Lilly?" Ethan Allen asks.

"No," she mumbles. "Richard had security escort me down here and said he'd call if anything changed."

"Security? Are you kidding me?" I yell, and then a little quieter say, "You know, Lilly, maybe they just don't allow pedophiles in the ICU."

"Ace!" Ethan Allen barks.

"What? Sorry." I'm really not sorry at all, so I continue. "But I

mean, you never know when Chris Hansen and his Pedophile Preven-
tion Van might roll up, and I'm just sayin' that maybe the doctors and
nurses don't wanna be featured on an episode of *To Catch a Predator.*"

"Ace," Ethan Allen says and shakes his head back and forth.

I walk to the elevator and punch the button and stand there for
what seems like twelve hours. I look back and see that Ethan Allen has
his arm around Lilly and her head is on his shoulder. I put my finger
on the little silver button and punch it and punch it till the doors finally open. There is nary a soul in sight, yet the elevator takes seventy
hours to get to the lobby. And then it's empty. Go figure.

When I arrive on the ICU floor, I see Richard Stacks the Fourth
standing with his pastor and a bunch of random Bugtussle assholes.
He comes over and makes a move to hug me and I shove him away like
he just climbed out of a manure pile.

"Don't make a scene, Graciela," he whispers sharply.

"I'm going to see her, so back up out of my face, Richard."

The waiting room gets a little quieter and people are trying to act
like they aren't looking. My stomach is churning, my head is pounding,
and I feel like I might pass out.

"You look sick, Ace," he snarls. "You been drinking?"

I try to push past him, but he grabs my arm and I turn on him like
a pit bull.

"You get your hands off of me!" I say a little too loud and people
stop pretending not to look. I see Brother Berkin distracting people
with head nods and hand gestures.

"I'm going to see Chloe," I say, not quite as loud.

"No, I don't think you will, Graciela." He takes a step closer to me
and, in a low voice, says, "You don't run over me like you do everybody
else in this town, Ace Jones. I'm a man and you need to learn your
place."

"I need to learn my place, Richard?" I practically shout. "Why don't you tell me what my place is, Richard? Because I have *so* much respect for *your* opinion."

He grabs my elbow and tries to force me to move, but I don't budge.

"Let go of my arm!" I yell. "Get your hands off of me right now!"

Now everyone is staring. Even Brother Berkin.

"Don't make a scene, you worthless, fat-ass whore," he whispers, smiling at everyone who is staring, "and get out of here before I do something that you will regret."

I look him right in the eye and say, "Do it." He doesn't move.

"Do something, Richard Stacks. Do it right here, right now, in front of your *audience*." I wave my arm at the onlookers. "I dare you, you big pussy."

He looks at our audience, smiles, and says, "Sorry, folks, she's just really upset about all this."

I get up in his face and say, "Do. It. Do something, Richard."

He turns to me and whispers, "You can bet your fat ass I'm going to. Just not here."

The air is thick with tension as Richard Stacks steps away from me and flips open his cell phone. Brother Berkin comes over and pats me on the shoulder.

"Have you seen her, Brother Berkin?" I'm antsy and ready to make a move because I'm feeling sicker by the second and I'm mad as hell on top of that.

"No, Ace," he says quietly, "Mr. Stacks thinks it's best if we don't disturb her, so I think we should honor his wishes."

"There's a lot you don't know about him." I nod toward Richard and cross and uncross and recross my arms. "I mean, I'm sure you know about the affairs because everyone in town knows about those, but not many people know how he treats his wife behind closed doors."

Brother Berkin looks at me like I'm speaking ancient Hebrew. "Yeah, he's an emotional terrorist and has been for years, and now look where we are." I wave a hand around. "The hospital."

"Chloe fell down the stairs, Graciela, and Mr. Stacks is very upset about it and your acting like this is not helping."

"Fell down the stairs my—" I stop myself. "Brother Berkin, Richard Stacks is not the man you think he is." I'm wringing my hands and staring a hole in Richard, trying to decide if I want to grab his cell phone and beat his eyes shut or make a run to see Chloe before security gets here. "Fell down the stairs, please. Brother Berkin, Chloe is not that clumsy of a woman." I can't stop fidgeting. "She does *yoga* for Christ's sake."

"Graciela," Brother Berkin begins, "now is not the time for such talk and—"

"Yeah, I know," I say and pat him on the shoulder, "never is, is it?"

I take off like a prison escapee and bolt through the double doors and into the hallway. Nurses are calling out for me to stop but I keep moving, scanning the nameplates until I find Chloe's. I duck inside her room and stop short. "Oh, my God, Chloe," I whisper, and I can't move my feet. I bend over and throw up on the floor. I raise my head and look at her swollen, scuffed-up face and start feeling like I might pass out for real. I struggle to catch my breath, but I can't, so I put my hands on my knees and throw up again. I raise up, wipe my face on my shirt, then put my arms around her legs and start to cry. She moves and mumbles something I don't understand.

"Chloe, can you hear me?" I whisper. "I'm here now and I'm going to take care of you. I will never let this happen to you again. I promise."

She turns her head from side to side but doesn't open her eyes.

"Chloe," I whisper, "please say something."

She mumbles a string of incoherent sounds, then stops moving and starts to snore very quietly.

A herd of Bugtussle's heaviest nurses bustle into the room; then the doctor bursts through the door followed by a passel of security guards. I put my hand on her arm and tell her one last time that it's going to be all right, but she doesn't move.

"Miss Jones, you have to leave," Dr. Rain says in his usual condescending tone. "We have a strict privacy policy and I expect you to honor that!"

"Are you blind, Dr. Rain? Or just stupid?" I point to Chloe. "Does this look like something that happened from falling down the fucking stairs?"

"Her injuries are consistent with a fall down a flight of stairs," Dr. Rain says drily.

"Yeah, maybe if she slid down face-first!"

"Get out!" He points toward the door.

"Well, could you tell me before I go, good doctor, why she's comatose?" I say sarcastically. "Is that consistent with a fall down some stairs? Being doped up out of your damned mind?"

"Get out of this room immediately or I will have you arrested!"

"I wish you would," I say and turn to go. One of the guards reaches for my arm and I jerk it out of his grasp. "Do not touch me!" I say and he pauses. "I'm going. Just don't!"

As I push past the pack of nurses, I hear Dr. Rain demanding to know how the word spread so fast about Chloe being hospitalized and I wonder for a second how Lilly found out.

I walk back into the waiting room, where Richard Stacks is soothing the crowd in his best used-car salesman tone. Brother Berkin is sitting across the room, away from the crowd, and I make my way toward him. "Go look at her, Brother Berkin. That's all I ask. Just go look at her face."

"Graciela, I won't go against Mr. Stacks's wishes."

"Brother Berkin, I'm telling you that the only way Chloe Stacks fell down any stairs is if she was pushed. I'm telling you that Richard Stacks is an emotional abuser who has crossed the line and become a physical abuser. And I'm telling you—" He looks up nervously and I turn to see Richard Stacks coming our way, taking long strides with both fists clenched. It dawns on me that no woman has ever stood up to the great coward Richard Stacks. Not his beautiful, delicate wife and certainly not his despicable mother.

"The police are waiting on you downstairs, Miss Jones. Scurry along now."

"The police need to be waiting on you, dick face, because I'm not the criminal here. You are." I turn to the pastor. "Sorry for the language, Brother Berkin."

Richard Stacks takes a deep breath and I can tell that he is teetering between upholding his fine Bugtussle image and choking me to death. He goes with his image.

"Miss Jones, would you please leave now?" His face is bloodred.

"I'm still waiting on you to do something." I lift my chin and say, "Be a man. Do something I'll regret."

"Oh, you can bet I will," he whispers through clenched teeth.

"Bet you will what, Mr. Stacks, if you don't mind my asking?" Brother Berkin asks, giving Richard a curious look.

"I do mind you asking," Richard Stacks the Fourth tells his spiritual leader. "Now, have a seat somewhere else please, Brother Berkin."

"Well, listen to Mr. Holy Roller talking to his preacher like a yard dog," I say loud enough for everyone in the waiting room to hear, and since I have an attentive audience, I decide to take full advantage. "Hey, everybody," I yell to the increasingly nervous crowd, "would you like to know what really happened to Chloe?" I look at Richard and he looks like he's about to blow a gasket. "Richard Stacks the Fourth here has always verbally abused his sweet little wife and now here we all are, in the hospital. Would anyone like to guess why?" I ask. "No? Well, let me break it down for you. He finally crossed the line from a talker to a doer and I think you know what I mean, so if you would all kindly keep that in mind while you're standing around praying here for him, that would be great, okay?"

Gasps and covered mouths all around.

"Shut your stupid mouth!" He comes at me with his right fist in the air and I jump on him like a bitch dog that's lost a pup. He tries to get his hands around my throat but I'm hitting him so hard in the face that all he can do is flail around and cuss.

The security guards grab me and pull me back and Richard Stacks opens his mouth to say something and I kick him in the stomach and scream, "I am going to kill you! I am going to fucking kill you if it's the last thing I do."

Brother Berkin steps forward and holds out his arms. "Please, please, in the name of God, please stop!"

I jerk and wiggle away from the security guards and grab Brother Berkin by the hand.

"Just go look at her!" I whisper and take off running toward the stairs. I get to the lobby and see two police cars parked outside and Lilly and Ethan Allen talking to Sheriff J. J. Jackson, who is looking down at the pavement and shaking his head. I stop running, try to catch my breath, and walk slowly through the sliding doors.

Sheriff Jackson looks at me, makes an awful face, and says, "Ace, what in the hell are you doing? Look at you."

I turn to check my reflection in the glass doors that just slid shut behind me and I am truly shocked by what I see. My hair is frizzy and wild and wet with sweat. My face is beet red and my cheeks are streaked with mascara. My Pineapple Willy's T-shirt has vomit all over it and somewhere along the way I lost a flip-flop. I turn to look at my friends and they are staring at me like I'm a wild animal. With rabies.

"You know you gotta come with me now, right?" Sheriff Jackson says in a quiet voice.

I nod my head and another cop, new to the area and apparently anxious for action, comes up and tries to cuff me, but Sheriff Jackson orders him back to his patrol car. The sheriff opens the back door of his squad car and motions for me to get inside.

In a calm voice I say, "J.J., if you want to arrest someone who is really guilty of something, why don't you go arrest Richard Stacks?"

"Ace, lay off it, okay?" the sheriff says. "You've caused quite a scene and we just need to get you out of here."

"How was she, Ace?" Ethan Allen asks.

"Awful," I say and feel tears welling up. "She was awful! Her face is all banged up, and for some odd reason she's totally incoherent."

"She took some pills," Lilly mumbles.

"What?" Ethan Allen and J.J. say at the same time.

"She took a bunch of Xanax. I don't know how much."

"Oh, God," Ethan Allen says. "Please tell me she didn't try to—"

"How do you know this, Lilly?" I yell. "And how did you know she was in the hospital? I know Richard Stacks's sorry ass didn't call you!"

"Calm down, Ace," J.J. says.

"I can't say how I know," Lilly mumbles.

"What the fuck do you mean you can't say, Lilly?" I yell. "You damn well better tell us what you know!"

"All right, Ace, knock it off and get in the car!" J. J. Jackson says sternly. "That's enough for tonight!"

"Nobody is going to do anything about this, are they?" I ask as he escorts me around the back of his patrol car.

"Chloe is the one who will have to press charges, and I give you my word that I'll talk to her about that as soon as she's able, okay? Now get in the car."

The hospital doors slide open again and Richard Stacks comes running toward us screaming obscenities. I notice with great satisfaction that his nose is bleeding and his left eye is slightly swollen. I start to go after him but Sheriff Jackson grabs me and wrestles me into the back of his patrol car.

Richard keeps yelling and cussing, and just before the sheriff slams the door I hear Ethan Allen say, "Hey, buddy, why don't you shut your mouth before I bust your other eye?"

Deputy Dumbass jumps out of his car and runs up to the fray with his hand on his pistol, and all of a sudden the big bad Richard Stacks isn't saying a word. Sheriff Jackson walks over to him and says something I can't hear. Richard gets in the sheriff's face, and they have what looks like a heated exchange. Then, in the blink of an eye, the sheriff spins him around, slaps cuffs on him, and barks something at his deputy, who runs to his patrol car and opens the back door.

I say a silent prayer that we'll be in the same cell. Gramma Jones used to warn me about praying for things that weren't what she called "issues of the Lord," but I think she would let this one slide.

As luck would have it, however, neither of us goes any farther than the holding area. Ethan Allen is waiting for me, and Richard's dreadful mother is waiting for him, and before that crazy bitch leaves, she makes all kinds of threats that everyone within ten miles hears because she's running around yelling like an idiot. According to her, nobody in the Bugtussle County Jail will have a job when she finishes the phone calls she's about to go home and make.

Ethan Allen walks me out, helps me into his truck, and we ride in silence back to my house. His cell phone rings, and when he hangs up he tells me that Adrianna Lane, Lilly's cousin and head nurse of the night shift, was just quietly escorted out the back door of Bugtussle Memorial with all of her personal effects because when Dr. Rain asked her if she'd told anyone about Chloe's being there, she didn't lie and say she didn't.

Dr. Sebastian Rain and Mr. Richard Stacks are big-time golfing buddies and they had every intention of chalking this up as an accident and sweeping it all under the rug.

I hope Adrianna Lane sues the hell out of Bugtussle Memorial Hospital and gets filthy rich and never has to work again. Unless she just wants to.

◇◇◇

10

Tuesday morning I call in sick to work for ten thousand different reasons, not the least of which is my pounding head and aching body. I sleep most of the day away with Buster Loo snuggled up beside me. I get up after lunch, fill his doggie bowl, and sit on the floor with him while he eats.

"Buster Loo," I whine, "we're gonna skip the park today and just hang out in the backyard, okay?"

Buster Loo snorts and keeps eating. When he finishes, we head out to the back porch. I flip on the fans and curl up on the lounger while he runs speedy-dog circles around the yard. After about thirty minutes, he looks up at the sky, barks twice, and hauls ass for the doggie door. Instead of rocket launching himself back into the house, he pauses and looks my way. As if sensing my sadness, he jumps up into my lap, lays his little chiweenie head on my shoulder, and plants a few quick love licks on my cheek. I scoop him up, go inside, and get back in the bed.

"Buster Loo, I'd be lost without you, little fella," I tell him as he burrows into the covers.

When the alarm goes off for the fifth time on Wednesday morning, I roll over and tell Buster Loo that I'd rather take a bath in boiling water than go to work today. He snuggles down further into the covers as if to rub it in that he can spend all day in bed if he so desires. A dog's life, indeed.

I get to school ten minutes late. Coach Hatter is in his usual spot between our classrooms, and I can tell by the look on his face that he's heard all about it.

"You all right?" he asks.

"Fine," I mumble. I walk into my classroom and plop down in my chair. Coach Hatter leans against the door frame and raises his eyebrows at me.

"So what'd you hear?" I ask, not really wanting to know.

"Well," he says, smiling a big mischievous smile, "I heard you had a tell-all session with Brother Berkin at the hospital, then beat one of Rich Stacks's eyes shut." He starts that ridiculous sniggering and I smile despite myself.

"Well, Hatt, I guess that'd be one way to put it," I say and suddenly realize how lucky I am that Logan Hatter's classroom is right next door to mine.

"Been a long time comin'," he says, shaking his head. "Just didn't think you'd be the one dolin' it out to him."

"Fuck him," I whisper and Coach Hatter cracks up again.

"How's Chloe?" he asks, looking down at his shoes.

"Oh, God, Logan," I say and squeeze my eyes shut. "Oh, you don't even want to know."

"She should leave him and go out with the sheriff," he says.

"Yeah, she should. Right after she ties Richard *and* his ridiculous mother to a stump somewhere way out in the woods."

He continues to look at the floor.

"Let's go to Ethan Allen's tonight, Ace. I wanna be the man on your elbow when you walk in that place." He pauses and looks at me sideways. "You know Ethan Allen is just dyin' for you to come down there and tell everybody your side of the story. Says he can only say so much until you come in to verify the details. I swear he's worse than a woman about that gossiping."

"What's that supposed to mean, Hatt?" I ask just as the bell rings.

"Saved by the bell," he chirps. "Pick you up at eight?"

"Maybe."

Just before lunch, I check my e-mail and, lo and behold, there's a message from Catherine Hilliard summoning me to her nasty little office. During lunch. Great. Hatter will just have to tough it out again today with Coach Wills.

When the time comes, I reluctantly make my way up the hallway and through the commons area to the office. When I walk into the lobby, I notice a handwritten note on Chloe's door and go over to inspect it. *Mrs. Stacks will be out of the office until further notice. Please see Mrs. Marshall.*

"Miss Jones," Catherine Hilliard booms from behind me, and I jump like somebody stuck a hot poker to my ass.

"Yes, ma'am?" My stomach knots up as I turn around.

"In here, please, *ma'am.*" She piles on the sarcasm when she says *ma'am* and motions me into her office.

I sit down in a dusty navy blue chair that looks like it had its heyday back when J. Lo was dating Puff Daddy. Mrs. Hilliard comes in and starts digging through a junky filing cabinet behind her desk and pulls out a yellow slip of paper. I realize with no small amount of apprehension that I have put my job in serious jeopardy.

"For you, Miss Jones," she says in her most vindictive tone, "to reward you for your most inappropriate conduct which resulted in your arrest Monday night." She looks at me with pure disgust. "Such unbecoming behavior for an educational professional, and I'm using that term loosely in reference to you. You should be ashamed of yourself."

"Are you aware of what he did to his wife, Mrs. Hilliard, who works two doors down from you every day?" She doesn't say a word. She just stares at me like I have an arm growing out of my forehead.

"It would be in your best interest to start keeping your mouth shut and minding your own business, Miss Jones," she says curtly and slides the ominous yellow slip across the desk. "One more write-up and you *will* be suspended." She flips open a folder on her desk and appears to be counting. "Looks like just one more tardy is all you'll need and you will be out of here." She looks at me and flashes a wide yellow-toothed smile.

"What?" I practically shout. "You've already written me up for that, remember?"

"I wrote you up *once*," she says with no small amount of delight. "When I could and *should* have written you up *twice*."

"Well, maybe if you didn't force us all to get here forty-five minutes before the first bell, it wouldn't be so hard to be on time." I give her my best evil eye. "There is no reason for teachers to be at this school that early and you know it. Mr. Landing—"

"Mr. Landing is retired, Miss Jones," she says curtly, "and if you don't like how I run things around here, then maybe you should take it up with the board."

"Yeah, like Lara Beth Harrison did?" I say. "Get 'dismissed' from the meeting by Superintendent Griffith before I utter one word. No, thanks." She leans back in her chair and smiles and that pisses me off, so I add, "What is it with you two anyway? A little personal favoritism there maybe?"

"Say one more word and I will fire you on the spot," she hisses.

"Fine, Mrs. Hilliard," I say.

I feel the fury welling up in my gut and I am overcome with the urge to jump across her junky-ass desk and hit her in the head with that 1979 model calculator.

But I don't because I can't. She's got me by the ol' metaphorical balls.

I get up, snatch the paper off her filthy desk, and turn to leave.

"Toodle-loo, Miss Jones," she calls as I walk out the door. "Have a great day!"

I resist the urge to give her the finger.

I speed walk back to my classroom and stew over my yellow slips until the bell rings to start fifth period, which, thankfully, is my good class.

"What's wrong, Miss Jones?" Olivia West, one of my all-time favorite students, asks as she drops her backpack on the floor beside her easel. "Are you still upset about what happened at the hospital?"

"Olivia, come here." I wave her up to my desk and whisper, "What did you hear about that?"

"I heard that Mrs. Stacks fell down the stairs and you went to the hospital and accused her husband of beating her and everyone there got all mad at you until Mr. Stacks tried to hit you and then they all started wondering what really happened."

"Really?" That makes me feel a little better.

"Yep, and get this." Olivia leans in closer and lowers her voice. "My mom's best friend, Sandy Taggert, was doing hospital visitation with some ladies from church when Brother Berkin called and asked if they were still there, which, of course, they were. She said Brother Berkin told her that he'd received a strange phone call from a lady who told him that a member of the congregation had just been admitted to the hospital. When he asked who it was, she didn't say anything. When he asked who was calling, she hung up."

"Oh, really," I whisper, thinking of Adrianna Lane.

"Yes, really," Olivia whispers back. "So Brother Berkin asks Sandy to check around and see if she sees anyone from church, and when she got to the second floor she saw Richard Stacks standing in the corner of the waiting room on his cell phone. She said he looked like a deer caught in headlights when he saw her and that he got off his phone really fast and claimed to be calling Brother Berkin." Olivia pauses, looks around to make sure the coast is still clear, then continues, "So Sandy calls Brother Berkin, who says he hasn't heard from Richard Stacks."

"Very interesting, Olivia, thank you for sharing."

"Well, Miss Jones, I'm worried about you." Olivia sighs and looks at the floor.

"Why?"

"Because you're my favorite teacher and Sandy told my mom that Richard Stacks said he was gonna get you fired."

"You don't worry about that, Olivia, okay?" I say with a sense of confidence I don't feel. "You just worry about what I'm going to do without you next year when you're off at college painting priceless masterpieces and I'm here with no one to keep me posted on the gossip!"

The tardy bell rings and Olivia returns to her easel, giggling.

"Okay, class," I say, "before we get started on those art fair projects, let's talk for a minute about Francisco Goya. This guy lived during a time of upheaval in Spain that included war with France, the Inquisition, and the rule of Napoleon's brother—bet he was really popular with the Spaniards, huh? And later the reign of a king known as Ferdinand the Desired. How's that for an interesting time to be an artist?"

When the final bell rings, I sit and stare out my window at the buses because I dare not leave before they do. I decide to sit around an extra fifteen minutes to let the traffic die down. Then I get in my dirty Maxima and go home. I feed Buster Loo, who, after scarfing his food, runs to the front door and starts jumping at his leash.

"Buster Loo wanna go for a walk?" I say, antagonizing him. "Buster Loo wanna go outside?"

I hook him up and we head down to the park, where I ignore everyone on the walking trail for fear someone might try and start a conversation with me about, hell, anything.

11

◇◇

I am a celebrity. At least at Ethan Allen's anyway.

I walk in to a standing ovation, and Logan Hatter puts his arm around me and smiles like he's Clint Eastwood and I'm Hillary Swank with a much wider ass.

Ethan Allen pours a Killian's Red and puts it down on the bar with great theatrical flair, and people form a line on either side of me like I'm the winning quarterback at the state championship football game. I get hugs and pats on the back and high fives and smiles and winks from the working people of Bugtussle, who love nothing more than a good story about a white-collar asshole getting punched in the eyeball.

I polish off a few beers and, after much pomp and circumstance, I beguile them with the details of everything that happened from the moment I stepped off the elevator until Sheriff Jackson stuffed me into the back of his patrol car. I'm quite the storyteller, if I do say so myself.

The place erupts with laughter and cheers, and a few guys from the feed store break out in an Irish jig. I don't mention that I puked my brains out when I saw Chloe. Instead, while I have the floor, I decide to tell them about Catherine Hilliard calling me into her dirty stinking office and telling me to mind my own business, and that I was about to get fired because I wouldn't get to work on time. Then I do what I believe is a fantastic impersonation of her and, judging from the laughs I get, the crowd seems to agree.

It didn't occur to me that everyone dining on the patio over at Pier Six Pizza could hear every word I said. Obviously it didn't occur to anyone else at Ethan Allen's, either, because no one brought it to my attention.

I feel a tap on my shoulder and turn around to see Pete the Tire Man. He's a cool little dude who has more money than the bank, but you can't tell it by looking at his overalls and dusty mesh hat.

"Hey, Ace," he asks, "where's ol' Lilly Lane at tonight?"

"Aw, I don't know, Pete," I say with a shrug. "I guess she's at home."

"Well, call her and tell her she's missing the party!" I assume by this exchange that word isn't out about the allegations against Lilly and, for some reason, I'm relieved. I look to Ethan Allen for help.

"Hey, Petey," he hollers, "I talked to her earlier and she's watchin' *The Bachelorette* tonight." Ethan Allen winks at me and pours four shots of Jack Daniel's.

"The what?" Pete asks and makes a funny face.

"C'mon, Petey." I grab him by the arm. "Let's dance."

Everyone drinks and laughs and has a good time, and Ethan Allen drives Logan and me home. On the way, we rehash the moment again and again when Ethan Allen threatened to bust Rich Stacks's other eye.

"Well, Ace, I'm sure glad there ain't no precooked bacon on your table out here tonight," Ethan Allen says, keeping his hand on my hip. He holds my screen door open while I poke around in my purse for my keys.

"Tell me about it, Ethan Allen," I say, unlocking the door. "Tell Logan I'll pick him up in the morning and take him to school and we'll do our best to get there on time so he won't get fired for riding with me."

"Will do, Ace." He kisses me on the head and turns to go. "Good night, sweetheart."

I hear his cowboy boots clomping off the porch, and a second later he peels out of my driveway like the true-blue country boy that he is. I imagine him and Logan laughing their hillbilly asses off all the way down the road.

12

<><><><><><><><><><><><><><><><><><><><><><><><><><><><><><><><><>

I pick up Coach Hatter Thursday morning and we arrive at school ten minutes early. He goes to the athletic office to partake in that sacred, time-honored Bugtussle Rocket tradition called Coach Coffee, which means if you ain't a coach, you ain't getting any of their precious coffee.

Lilly and I snuck in there one morning during a pep rally and sampled a little bit of their Coach Coffee, and I think I would've better enjoyed a cup of cough syrup flavored with monkey piss. I take off to the teachers' lounge, where I purchase my breakfast from the vending machine, check my mailbox, and sign in early for the first time in a long time. I walk down to my classroom and, much to my dismay, find Catherine Hilliard perched outside my door.

"In," she hisses through those thin crusty lips.

"Good morning, Mrs. Hilliard," I say and offer her a powdered doughnut as I walk past her and into my classroom. She declines. "You sure? They're real good." I pop a whole one in my mouth.

"Sit," she says, like I'm a dog.

"I'd rather stand. Or I could roll over, if you like."

She glares at me and I decide to sit on top of my desk.

"You," she says and points to me, "think you are so funny and so *cool*."

I nod my head in agreement and she continues, speaking slowly. "As long as I have had the displeasure of knowing you, you have conducted yourself like no one in your entire life has ever taught you *anything*."

"Are you talking about my mamma?" I ask, getting offended, "because she was a good woman and it would be awful tacky of you to speak ill of the dead."

"I am most certainly *not* talking about your mother. I am talking about you," she says. "You run around and think you are so"—she pauses—"so entertaining with your mindless stupidity telling everybody everything you know all the time. You think—"

"Whoa, now, Mrs. Hilliard," I cut her off. "I don't like the direction this is going."

"You humiliate yourself, yet you think you're so comical. Well, let me tell you something—"

"When did I humiliate myself?" I ask with a mouthful of doughnut. "Because I don't recollect."

"You had the nerve, the audacity, to go out in public, a *bar* of all places, and *shamelessly* run your loud mouth about an incident that landed you in *jail*. Then you decide to really get funny and start making fun of *me* and the fact that you are about to lose your *job*. Do you think you can make fun of *me* and get away with it? Who do you think you are?" It never fails. News travels at the speed of light in Bugtussle, Mississippi.

"Pretty sure I'm Ace Jones. Art teacher. Chiweenie lover. Pizza addict." She just stares at me so I add, "Consumer of alcoholic beverages." She keeps glaring at me, so I continue.

"What are you gonna do, Mrs. Hilliard?" I ask and give up trying to play it cool. "Write me up for drinking a beer and hanging out with my friends? I mean, I do realize that drinking beer is considered a mortal sin by you fine upstanding hypocrites over at the First Self-Righteous Church, where it's okay to beat your wife and say she fell down the stairs, but the simple fact of the matter is, and I hate to disappoint you with this, but nobody's going to hell for drinking a beer, regardless of what your personal opinion is, so why don't you just drop that, okay?" She opens her mouth, but I keep going. "And as far as what I said inside my friend Ethan Allen's place of business, well, I pledge allegiance to the flag of the United States of America and to the Republic for which it stands, because in this one nation under God, I enjoy a little perk called freedom of speech."

"Let me tell you something, Ace Jones, I will get rid of you," she hisses. "That is a promise. I will get rid of you *and* that slutty little friend of yours."

"What?" I yell, and I'm seriously about to go nuts on this hag. "Well, let me tell you something. From here on out, I will be recording all of our conversations, *and* I'll contact the Mississippi Association of Educators and let them know about your big plans to fire me *and my slutty little friend!*"

"You call whoever you want. It's not going to make any difference," she says and leans toward me, and I can smell coffee on her breath. "You are an embarrassment to the teaching profession, Miss Jones."

"And you are a scab on the ass of humanity, Mrs. Hilliard." I smile at her.

"Be in my office at lunchtime," she says and stomps toward the door.

"I'll probably be on the phone with my attorney during lunch."

"Really," she says, spinning around to face me. "I thought things didn't work out very well for you and your *attorney*. Terrible mess from what I heard. You moving to Florida and thinking he was going to marry you when he had another woman all along. Tragic." She turns around and walks toward the door.

"That's not exactly right," I stammer, "but what do you care about what's right or wrong? Self-service is your only concern."

"Miss Jones," she says as she reaches for the doorknob, "have you ever heard the phrase *quit while you're behind*? You might want to consider that."

She jerks the door open and nearly bulldozes Logan Hatter.

"Excuse me, Mrs. Hilliard," he says politely and holds out his hand. "Come on out."

"Out of my way, Hatter!" she shouts and stomps past him.

Coach Hatter comes into my classroom with wide eyes and a questioning look.

"I'm really startin' not to like her," he says with boyish innocence. "I have never been anything but nice and respectful to that woman and she treats me like I stole something out of her yard."

"You're guilty by association, Hatter," I tell him. "Find some friends that she likes and she will certainly shower you with approval. Heck, you might even get to knock off a piece."

He makes a gagging sound and the bell rings; I decide right then and there to take Friday off. I've had all the fun I can stand for one week. And if Catherine Hilliard and Richard Stacks both want me fired, then it's only a matter of time before I get canned, so I might as well start using up those personal days I've been saving for the past seven years.

13

◇◇◇

Thursday night, I hang out with Buster Loo, eat leftover pizza and potato chips for supper, and watch everything I have recorded on the DVR.

It's times like this, when I feel my life starting to crumble, that I miss my parents the most. I would give anything if I had somebody, hell, anybody, to sit here beside me and tell me it's going to be okay, that I'm okay, and that everything is going to be just fine.

I have no brothers or sisters, no aunts or uncles or cousins. I'm the only child of only children and that makes for an awful lonely existence sometimes.

My only family is my friends, and thanks to Lilly, I'm down one of those now. I'd like to think that Lilly wouldn't ditch a trip with me so she could sneak around and have sex with Zac Tanner, but seeing him sitting half naked on her couch is fairly hard evidence that she has. And I know Lilly Lane well enough to know that she is, in reality, an incredibly spoiled and self-centered soul.

I am so sick of living in Bugtussle, Mississippi. There are many folks here I can't stand the sight of, and every time I leave the house, I see at least ten people I want to punch in the face. Lilly is always telling me that people are basically the same no matter where you go, but I don't buy into that way of thinking.

I'm quite certain that Bugtussle has a surplus of idiots and assholes, most of whom are pious fanatics who love to bash you over the head with their religion. They have their socially acceptable sins, like gluttony, fornication, and adultery, to which they easily turn a blind eye, but if you drink beer or happen to be gay, then the wrath of the fat fornicators and judgmental adulterers will descend upon you like fire from the pits of a twisted hell. And almost all of them go to church with Catherine Hilliard over at the First Self-Righteous Church of Bugtussle.

I'd like to pick up and move away from here, but the problem is that I don't have anywhere to go. I mean, there's a lot of different places I could go that would be more fun and exciting, but that would mean leaving Chloe, Logan, Ethan Allen, and that damn Lilly, and I just can't bring myself to do that. I've thought about going back to Nashville and looking up the friends I had there, but who knows if they're still around, and if they are, how much they might have changed since the fifth grade.

The bottom line is that I'm scared. I'm scared to leave the comfortable little existence that I've carved out for myself here in Bugtussle. I've had this hole in my heart since I lost my mom and dad, and I just don't think I could stand to leave the only people who have ever come close to filling it. Well, not counting Mason, whose presence has the power to completely and totally wax over my pain.

I wish I felt better about my decision to pack up and leave him. I wish I could have just a *little* peace of mind about it, but I can't because the questions never go away. Why did that stupid Allison have to show up that night? Why didn't he just ask her to leave? Why did he walk out there and talk to her for so long? What did he expect me to do? Then the questions get tougher. What if I was wrong? Would he have asked me to move in with him if he wasn't committed to our relationship? What if that girl meant nothing to him and he was just trying to be nice? What if I would've stayed? Why do I always get so mad?

I look over at my phone. No one has called or texted me all day long.

I pull Buster Loo up a little closer to me, snuggle down into the sofa, and pray for sleep to come quickly.

14

◇◇◇

Early Friday morning, Chloe calls, and I gladly accept her invitation to come over for a visit. After picking up a nice bouquet and two cups of Starbucks coffee, I head over to her place, nervous as a cat.

I get a dreadful feeling when I think about seeing her face-to-face and end up driving past her house twice before parking on the street and getting out. I have knots in my stomach as I walk up the driveway, and by the time I ring the doorbell, I feel like I'm going to hurl.

When she opens the door, she's wearing a scarf around her head and a pair of gigantic sunshades. Even with bruises showing through her makeup, she still somehow manages to look glamorous.

"Well, hello, Ace," she says sweetly, but I can tell she's nervous, too. "Come on in."

"For you, my love," I say dramatically and present the flowers to her with such flourish that she starts to giggle.

I take a seat in her lavish living room and she arranges the flowers in an expensive-looking crystal vase. She sits down across from me and takes the lid off her coffee. "Thank you so much, Ace." I try to think of something to say, but nothing comes to mind, so I just sit there looking like I've lapsed into some kind of idiotic stupor. The doorbell rings just as I'm starting to feel super-awkward, and I notice that Chloe doesn't look particularly surprised. She hops up and scurries into the foyer and I hear her whispering with whoever is at the door. She returns to the living room, followed by Lilly Lane, and at that very moment I realize I've been ambushed.

"I wanted to speak with both of you so I hope it's all right that I invited Lilly over," Chloe says sweetly and looks at me with those big round puppy-dog eyes.

"That's fine, Chloe," I say and give Lilly the evil eye. "Sorry, but I didn't know you were going to be here so I didn't get you any coffee." Lilly just scowls at me so I turn to Chloe. "What's on your mind?"

"I'm pretty sure Richard is cheating on me," she begins slowly, and I want to roll my eyes and snort, but I don't, "and I think it's with more than one person. I think it's been going on for a while." She holds up both hands like she's surrendering to something. "I know y'all have suspected such for a long time, but I'm asking you to be patient with me as I try to work my way through this." She looks down at the floor. "I'm ready to do something, and I can't do it without y'all, but it has to be done on my terms."

"Okay," we say in unison.

"First of all, I want you guys to hug and make up."

"What?!" I yell. "Chloe, seriously?"

"Yes, Ace," she says. "I need you both to help me and I won't tell you what I found until you hug Lilly and tell her y'all are friends again."

"Oh, good word," I say, and this time I do roll my eyes.

"I've been trying to call you, Ace," Lilly says smartly.

"Oh, really? Well, after I deleted your name from my contacts, I must not have recognized your number."

"Am I that bad, Ace?" Lilly snorts like a real smart-ass.

"Don't start with me," I fire back.

"Please, don't do this," Chloe says, "or I promise I won't give you the passwords to Richard's e-mail accounts."

That got my attention. "Where did you get those?" I ask.

"Hug Lilly and I'll tell you."

Lilly gets up, smiling like the kid who deserved a spanking but didn't get it. I stand up and give her a quick hug. At least Chloe didn't ask me to help Lilly out of the bind she's screwed herself into. I guess Lilly warned her that I would only go so far.

"Lilly," I say, drilling her with the evil eye, "we are officially friends again, but only because I am committed to helping Chloe do whatever she needs done." I look at Chloe. "Is that good enough? I hope so because it's really all I can manage right now."

"That will do for now," Chloe says, smiling. "Now let's go to Richard's office."

I spend the next thirty minutes downloading all kinds of names, addresses, phone numbers, and e-mails from Richard Stacks's personal computer. The creep has six different e-mail accounts and Chloe found the user names and passwords written on the bottom of his mouse pad. There is so much random information that it's impossible to link one woman to one phone number or physical address, but knowing their names and having their e-mail addresses is a good starting point.

"I'm going to take this list and cross-reference it with the little black book he keeps in his briefcase and try to put some names together with a phone number or an address or, if I'm lucky, both."

"He doesn't keep his briefcase locked?" Lilly asks.

"No," she says. "I guess he thinks I'm too dumb or scared to root through his things, but I'm here to tell you, girls," she says with a sigh, "I'm a changed woman after what he did to me."

"Do you want to talk about that?" Lilly asks quietly.

"No, I don't," she says. "Not now, not ever. I think you both know that I didn't fall down the damn stairs." I want to ask her about the pills, but can't bring myself to mention it. It's apparent she's doing all she can do to hold herself together. She closes her eyes, takes a deep breath, and continues. "Richard crossed a line from which there is no coming back. There will be no reconciliation."

"Hell, yeah!" I say and give her a very gentle hug.

"But"—Chloe gives me a hard look—"I plan on ending my marriage in a decent and civilized manner. No shenanigans. That's why everything has to be done my way."

"Chloe," Lilly says, "we will do anything and everything just like you want it done. That's a promise."

"Thank you," Chloe says, "and I know y'all love me enough to do this together." She goes to the closet and brings out a box. "Here, use this. It's a fourteen-hundred-dollar camera that I got for Christmas last year and I've never used it, so y'all will have to figure it out on your own." She hands it to me. "Get me some proof. I know you both are skilled and proficient stalkers, so I trust you can do this without getting yourselves in trouble."

"Absolutely," I say, inspecting the camera. "Nothing to worry about."

"Okay, so do what you can now and I'll e-mail you in a few days."

Before either of us has time to respond, the doorbell rings, and this time Chloe not only looks surprised but becomes visibly nervous. So nervous, in fact, that she starts to shake.

"What is it, Chloe?" I ask. "Do you want me to get the door?"

"No," she says, "I'll get it. Just go through there and wait in the sunroom if you don't mind."

Lilly and I hustle into the sunroom, and after what seems like an eternity Chloe comes back, smiling.

"It's Brother Berkin," she says, looking a little embarrassed. "Sorry about that."

"Not a problem," I say.

"No problem at all," Lilly chimes in.

"Okay," she whispers, "do we have a plan?"

"Yes, we most certainly do," I whisper back. "We'll check out the local addresses tonight."

"Tonight?" Chloe asks with palpable enthusiasm.

"Of course tonight!" Lilly replies.

Brother Berkin greets us in the foyer and we exchange polite pleasantries before Lilly and I head out the door.

Once we're outside, Lilly turns to me with a pleading look on her face.

"Ace, I need some help," she says. "I'm asking you as a friend to help me. I can't do it alone."

"Lilly, I'll do whatever I can to help Chloe, but your problem," I say and shake my head, "I'm not going near that."

"Look, I know how bad it all looks, Ace, but you're putting the pieces together wrong, I swear. You have got to trust me—"

"Lilly, please, I'm not in the mood to listen to this right now. Just tell me what you want."

"Catherine Hilliard has something of mine that I desperately need to get back. It has nothing whatsoever to do with Zac Tanner, I swear to God."

"Fine, Lilly," I say, "but if you dupe me on this, I will whip your ass. Got it?"

"Got it."

"When do you want to do this?"

"Just before dark tonight."

"Okay, I'm going home to spend the day with Buster Loo. I'll pick you up at your place around seven."

"Thanks, Ace."

When I get home, I find Buster Loo napping in the backyard with all four paws in the air.

"Hey, little buddy, wanna go for a walk?" I ask, closing the gate door behind me. In one quick motion, Buster Loo flips off of his back onto his feet and runs full speed toward the doggie door. When I get inside, he's standing by the front door, barking at his leash. I hook him up and we head to the park.

I love getting out and about on days I'm supposed to be at work, and today is the perfect day to do just that. Not too hot. Not too cold. A bit of a breeze. It's an ideal spring morning and the park is all but deserted, which I love because I can let Buster Loo off his leash when we get around to the wooded section of the trail. I think he really appreciates some time to poke around at his own pace.

When we round the bend and turn into the woods, I don't see anyone anywhere so I let Buster Loo go, and he gets busy with the sniffing. I'm walking along, savoring the peaceful quiet, when Buster Loo stops, bristles up, and starts to growl.

"What is it, Buster Loo?" I whisper. He starts sniffing the air, and I try to get him to keep walking, but he won't move.

"C'mon, Buster Loo, I'm putting you back on the leash if you're gonna act like this." When I reach down to hook him back up, he lurches forward and starts running speedy-dog circles around my feet.

"What are you doing?" I ask, like I actually expect an answer. "Have you lost your little doggie mind?" Buster Loo stops and stands at attention and that's when I hear the voice.

It's a man's voice.

I can hear him, but I can't see him.

Buster Loo starts to growl again and I shush him, and that does as much good as it always does, which is not a bit. I take a few steps with Buster Loo right behind me and look around to see if I can see where this voice is coming from.

"Yes, I just found out that I'll be going to Phoenix next month," I hear the man say. "Oh, yes, you'll definitely need your golf clubs for this trip. We'll play at Scottsdale." A pause. "Great, talk to you soon." I hear the crunching of leaves and branches and turn around to see Reece Hilliard coming up a narrow pathway that links the walking trail to his affluent subdivision.

He has a cell phone in one hand and Daisy's leash in the other. Daisy is a golden retriever whose hair is more lush and beautiful than the models in shampoo commercials. I don't mean dog shampoo commercials. I mean commercials like those freaky women who have fake orgasms while shampooing their hair on an airplane.

Buster Loo starts to bark and go nuts, and I make a quick move to grab him, but it's too late. He takes off, barking his brains out and I take off after him.

Reece Hilliard hears the commotion and his cell phone disappears as he steps out onto the walking trail behind Daisy. I'm running to catch up with Buster Loo, who is hauling chiweenie ass toward his target. Daisy finds the perfect place to hunch over and relieve herself just about the time Buster Loo leaps off the trail, heading straight for her. I'm running behind him shouting, "No! Bad dog! Buster Loo! Stop!" but that doesn't even slow him down. He mounts Daisy's rump and starts humping like they're the last two dogs on the planet and he's solely responsible for the survival of his species.

Daisy springs up and whirls to face her violator but doesn't get a chance because Buster Loo runs around and buries his snout in the fuzziness under her tail. I reach down, snatch him up, and turn to face Reece Hilliard, my face burning with embarrassment.

"Enthusiastic little guy," Mr. Hilliard says, laughing.

"Yeah, I'm so sorry about that, Mr. Hilliard," I say. "I just let him off his leash back here sometimes because it's the only place he gets to run around except for the backyard and—"

He pats me on the shoulder and says, "No worries, Miss Jones, no worries at all." Daisy snarls at Buster Loo, then takes off behind Mr. Hilliard, who starts whistling as he walks away.

"Buster Loo, I cannot believe you just did that," I say, hooking him to his leash and putting him down. "I will never let you ramble around here again!"

15

◇◇◇

Wicked is as wicked does. Or was that stupid?

"Lilly," I say as she settles into the passenger seat, "do me a favor and tell me how I'm supposed to be putting the puzzle together. And keep in mind I'm working with some really dubious pieces."

"Ace," she says with a heavy sigh, "you have been my best friend since we were twelve and you know I love you like a sister, right?"

"Lilly, I'm *not* detecting an answer in that gibberish. If you want me to put this car in reverse, then you better cease and desist with the sentimental bullshit and give me a legitimate explanation."

"You said you weren't in the mood—"

"I wasn't in the mood when we were walking through Richard Stacks's finely manicured lawn. I just wanted to get out of there."

"Why can't you just trust me?" she whines. "Just believe me when I tell you it's not what it looks like—"

"This car isn't moving from this driveway until you tell me what's going on."

She takes a deep breath and looks out the passenger-side window.

"I am accompanying a married man on business trips who is having an affair with another man, and I'm just there to make them look not"—she pauses—"gay."

"That's the craziest shit I've ever heard, Lilly."

"Well, I told you. Are you happy now?"

"I'm not understanding this. I mean, how would your presence make anyone look any less gay, and why would you be a part of a cover-up like that?"

"The married man has a job that requires a lot of travel, working for a company who frowns on same-sex relationships. He's two months away from retirement and doesn't want to lose his benefits. The other man's job allows plenty of time for him to travel and those trips are the only opportunity they have to spend quality time together. Obviously a married man everyone assumes is heterosexual can't go gallivanting around Bugtussle with his homosexual partner."

"Holy shit," I say. "And you help how?"

"I go to the hotel on the businessman's arm and appear to be his mistress. A little later, the other man checks into the same hotel, and he and I switch keys. After that, I meet the businessman in the hallway and go with him to any work functions that require a date. Sometimes I leave with him in the morning, and he has his driver take me shopping all day; then he picks me up in the afternoon and we walk back into the hotel together. He has me on one arm and all of my shopping bags on the other. Perfect portrait of a mistress. When he's not working, he's free to spend time with his partner in a big city where no one knows them and no one cares about their personal business."

"So, it's okay with his company if he has a mistress, but having a same-sex partner would get him fired?"

"Yes. How's that for a double standard?" She rolls her eyes at the injustice. "Are you happy now?"

"No. Why can't you tell me who it is?"

"Ace, I swear I can't right now. I promise the time will come when I'm able to tell you, and you'll understand then why I can't tell you now."

"How long you think that'll be?" I ask, smiling.

"I'm going to choke you if you don't put this car in reverse!"

"So are you having sex with Zac Tanner or not?"

"Hell, no!" Lilly yells. "And it pisses me off that you would think for one minute that I would do something like that! He was at my house telling me that his parents were hiring an attorney and suing Catherine Hilliard for slander. He ran over from his grandma's pool—you know she lives three houses down from me—because his daddy told him not to call because they would probably be checking everybody's phone records."

"Well, his daddy should've been the one to come over there, not him."

"Oh, good word, Ace." She flips down the visor and starts fiddling with her sleek blond hair. "Can we get a move on? Please?"

"He could've dropped you a letter in the mail."

"You could just shut up and drive."

I pop in a Pink CD and do just that. My gut tells me that she's telling the truth, and by the time we get to the school parking lot, I feel like being friends again.

"Pull up behind the cafeteria and let's go in that side door next to the gym," she says, pointing. "You got your keys?"

"No, Lilly, I used a screwdriver to crank my car and left my keys at home."

"You are such a smart-ass." She whips out her school-issued photo

ID card, which has a picture of her looking like an advertisement for Crest White Strips and Pantene.

I whip out my school-issued ID card, which looks more like a mug shot of a startled primate. I swear, the woman taking the picture said "one," paused for thirty seconds, then said "two." I popped my lips and the bitch screamed "three!" and snapped the flash, and now I have this jewel of a photograph that I am supposed to wear around my neck every day.

I begged to have another photo made, but that vagina wart Catherine Hilliard refused. I waited a few weeks and claimed I lost it thinking that would do the trick, but Mrs. Hilliard was kind enough to fish up the same old photo to put on my new ID. Then docked my check $35 for her trouble.

"C'mon," Lilly says impatiently, "let's do this."

"Do what exactly?" I ask. "What are we going to do when we get into the school? You know the lobby might be locked and then Catherine Hilliard probably has dead bolts on her dungeon door."

Lilly points to a crisscross of bobby pins in her hair.

"Are you kidding me?"

"I can do it, trust me," she says, but I'm not feeling reassured. "Ace, I have to get in there, all right? I have to."

"What is it that you so desperately need?" I ask, stalling because I really don't want to get arrested again this week. "All Cruella de Vil had in her hand was pictures and postcards."

"I had one picture frame on my desk that day. It was black and white polka-dot with a little pink bow and had a picture of me in front of the Eiffel Tower."

"Maybe we should check your classroom first."

"You got everything out of my classroom, remember?" She gives me a mean look. "Did she have a picture frame in her hand or not?"

"It wasn't in the stuff I left at your house?"

"No, Ace, it wasn't in the stuff you *threw* across my front yard. I would've surely seen it as I picked each individual thing off the ground and put it back in the box."

"Oh," I mumble and look the other way. "I'm pretty sure she had it in her hand. I didn't see the front, but if you only had one then she's got it." I look back at Lilly. "Why is it so important to get this one little picture frame?"

"There's a memory card in it that I need to have back."

"Okay, I don't think it was a digital frame. I don't recall seeing a cord."

"It's not digital," she says. "There is a memory card taped to the back of the picture inside the frame." She looks around nervously. "Can we go now?"

I look at her. "What's on the memory card?"

"Pictures. Of everything."

"Oh. Okay. Well, pardon me for asking the obvious question here, but why in the hell would that be at school taped inside a damn picture frame and not at your house locked up somewhere safe?"

"It's not even mine! Here's what happened. I forgot to take my camera to Paris because I was in a rush when I packed, so the Gentleman let me borrow his. I spent a whole day on top of a double-decker bus taking these amazing pictures of the city to show my students, okay? His camera is very expensive and hi-tech, a lot like the one Chloe let us borrow today, and I couldn't wait to see how the pictures turned out. Are you with me so far?"

"Somewhat."

"I just used his camera that one day and the rest of the time he was taking pictures with it."

"Of him and his, uh, friend?"

"Yes. And he knew I was excited about the pictures I'd taken on his camera, so on the flight home, he gave me the memory card and told me to print off my pictures."

"So," I say, finally catching on, "the idea was for you to get your pictures off of the memory card, and then give it back to him because he had pictures on it as well."

"Jeez, Ace, I thought I was going to have to get out the crayons!"

"Right, because this isn't confusing at all." I look at her. "Please, continue."

"When he gave it to me I put it in my wallet, and by the time I got home it had fallen out and I had to empty my purse on the table and go through all of my junk. I was scared to death because I thought I'd lost it. So when I finally found the stupid little thing, I didn't want to risk losing it again. I taped it inside that picture frame for safekeeping. I'd brought it to school that Monday because, as you know, I don't have a printer at home and I wasn't about to risk taking that memory card to Walmart, so I was just going to save *my* pictures to the desktop at school where I *do* have a printer, then return the memory card to the Gentleman with just *his* pictures on it."

"Okay, that makes a little better sense."

"Well, as soon as I got the frame out of my purse at school, Mrs. Hilliard called me to the office and I just set the frame down on my desk, got up, and went to her office. I didn't know I was going to get fired and escorted out of the school! How could I have known that?"

"Good word, Lilly." I look at her. "You're too double-oh-seven for your own good, yet not double-oh-seven enough at the same time."

"Ace, for the love of God, can we please just get this done?"

"One last question," I say and she heaves a sigh and rolls her eyes. "Why are you so concerned about Catherine Hilliard finding this memory card? What difference would it make to her?"

Lilly opens her mouth, but doesn't say anything. She looks at me, then out the window. "Because," she says and pauses. "Because it would be such a scandal if those pictures got out and she is such a mean, hateful person that I'm sure she would love nothing more than showing those around and watching everyone's jaw drop."

"Well, okay, then, I guess I'm ready," I say and don't move.

"Great. Let's go." She unbuckles her seat belt and nods for me to get out.

"Wait." I put my hand on her arm. "What about the security cameras?"

"On the weekends, they only activate if there is an intrusion at the school."

"Like breaking into the main office?"

"No, like a broken window or a kicked-down door or something like that."

"How do you know this?"

"Sheriff Jackson told me."

"You asked him that?"

"Yes, Ace! I did. What of it?"

"Wow!"

"Ace, get out of the car!"

16

◇◇

We waltz up to the school trying not to look like the criminals we are about to become. I unlock the door and we walk through the commons area to the office lobby.

It's unlocked.

"It's a trap!" I whisper. "Let's get the hell outta here!"

"They don't always lock it, you idiot, and I think you know that," she whispers, then walks into the lobby like she owns the place. I skulk behind her looking around like a bleeding man in a shark tank.

We get to Chloe's office where she pauses, reads the "Out of the Office" note, and shakes her head. "I knew this would happen," she says quietly. "I knew he would cross that line eventually."

"So did I," I reply. "At least she's finally ready to get away from him."

"Yeah."

My stomach knots up when we get to Catherine Hilliard's office because I can't stop thinking about all the ways this could go wrong. I'm so damn nervous and it's so unbearably hot that I think I might pass out right there in the hallway. Lilly is on her knees working the lock with her bobby pins and I start to wonder where she picked up this proclivity for small-time criminal activity.

Then I hear it.

Click.

Lilly gets up and walks into Principal Catherine Hilliard's office, and I trail behind like Shy Ronnie in a *Saturday Night Live* skit.

"C'mon and help me look!" she says and starts rifling through the piles on Mrs. Hilliard's desk.

I walk around and pull open the top drawer on the left side. In there, I find a mixed mess of office supplies and a Cover Girl compact that looks like it was purchased around 1986. The second drawer is full of hanging file folders so I thumb through them, not looking for anything in particular when, at the very back, I see an unusually wide file with "L.L." written on the tab in thick black letters.

I pull it out, and when I place it on the desk a few pictures slide onto Mrs. Hilliard's desk calendar. I lean down to get a closer look and can't believe what I see. I gasp and can't stop staring. Smiling up from the photos are two very handsome gentlemen and I recognize them both.

There's a shot of them standing in front of the Eiffel Tower, one on the steps of the Paris Opera House, and one at a sidewalk café where it's quite clear they are more than just friends.

"Got it!" Lilly yelps, waving her polka-dot picture frame in the air. "Memory card's still taped to the back! Let's get out of here!"

She turns around, sees the pictures, and gets this look on her face like she had rotten eggs for lunch and they're on their way back up.

"Is this?" I take a gulp of air. "Are they—"

"Oh, holy shit!" she screams. "Where did those come from? Where the hell did those come from?"

"Back there." I point to the drawer. "Lilly, what the hell? Isn't that your uncle Rye?"

"Oh, my God! This is so much worse than I thought. Oh, my God! Oh, my God! Oh, my God! What am I going to do?"

"Well, to quote George Clooney in *Michael Clayton*," I say, shaking my head, "you are so fucked."

I scoop up the file, grab her by the arm, and hustle her out of the office.

"Lock it back up!" I order and then we haul ass down the hallway.

When we get back outside, Lilly trips as she steps off the sidewalk and falls down in the parking lot. I scramble over, help her up, and turn around just in time to see a patrol car turning into the drive.

"Oh, God! Please let that be the sheriff," she whispers as we pile into my car. I cram the file folder under my seat and turn the air conditioner on full blast.

The patrol car parks sideways behind me, effectively blocking any exit I might have planned. In my rearview mirror, I see Deputy Dumbass get out of the car and unsnap his billy club.

"Give me your school ID," I whisper. "Now!"

"Okay, we can handle this," she says, and starts digging in her pockets. "I just need to take a deep breath and get my head back on."

She comes up with the ID card just as Deputy Dumbass starts knocking on my window with his stupid billy club. I roll down the window and decide that now is *not* the time to be bitchy.

"Good evening, Deputy," I say and try to smile.

"What're you ladies doin' parked around here?"

"We were just working out in the gym," I say, hoping that will stave off any questions about why I'm sweating like a whore in church.

"We both teach here and sometimes we come in after hours to get our exercise on, but not very often because it's so *unbearably* hot in there." I mop my forehead with one hand and offer him our school IDs with the other. He looks at Lilly's, raises his eyebrows, and smiles like men do when they feast their eyes upon her image. He flips mine over, jumps a little, and hands them both back to me.

"I ain't never seen y'all back here before, and I patrol this parking lot every night 'cept Sundays."

"Who patrols it on Sundays?" I ask and Lilly punches me in the arm.

"Officer," Lilly says sweetly, and leans over so her tank top falls at just the right angle to expose her pink polka-dot bra. "It seems like we run into you every time we turn around, and you know what? I don't even know your name."

She throws open the passenger-side door and struts around to where the deputy is standing, and it's clear to me that she has his full attention.

"Lilly Lane," she says sweetly and holds out a delicate hand, "and you are?"

"Dax, ma'am," he says with a goofy-looking smile. He takes her hand and I think for a second that he might drop to one knee and kiss it. "Dax Dorsett. I'm from the coast and don't know many folks around here or where they work and whatnot, but I'm getting it all together." Dax taps himself on the head and is unsuccessful in keeping his eyes off her boobs.

"Well, Dax Dorsett from the coast, have you had supper?" Lilly asks, and I shoot her a hard look that she doesn't see because she is all about Deputy Dax Dorsett right now.

"Why, no, ma'am, I haven't," Dax says, and relaxes his stance. "I always ride by the school here, and then take a break for supper."

How convenient.

"Well, why don't you come join us over at Pier Six? You like pizza?"

Lilly says, and I'm shaking my head no, but I've apparently ceased to exist.

"Yeah, I love pizza. 'Specially theirs." He's grinning and looking at her tits again.

"We'll follow you there," she says and pauses, "unless you were going to arrest me for being a bad girl." She bats her eyelashes like a fourteen-year-old girl feeling the first sting of Cupid's arrow.

"Oh, no, ma'am," he says and his cheeks turn red. "No, ma'am, I wouldn't do that."

"Oh, you big sweetie!" Lilly says. "See you at the pizza place."

She blows him an air kiss, and Deputy Dax Dorsett hustles back to his patrol car like he's been called to the scene of a triple homicide.

"Lilly," I say when she gets in, "what the hell was that about?"

"Making friends, Ace." She smiles at me. "You should try it sometime."

"What?" I say, sounding more like a duck than I meant to.

She just laughs and says, "Drive to Pier Six, my friend, where we shall dine with that handsome deputy."

I shake my head and do as I'm told.

◇◇

17

Deputy Dax is waiting on us in the lobby of the Pier Six pizza parlor.

"Deputy Dax, would these be the ladies you were waiting for?" the hostess says, obviously smitten with him.

"Yes, ma'am, they are," he says politely. "Table for three, please."

"Inside or out?"

"Inside!" I say quickly before Lilly's romanticism gets the best of her and she wants to sit outside under the starlight. They both look at me and I smile and say, "I prefer a temperature-controlled environment if that's okay with y'all."

"Fine with me," Dax says and holds out his arm for us to walk past.

"It's not that hot outside, Ace," Lilly mumbles, and I'm glad I called that one first.

The hostess seats us at a table overlooking the lake and Dax doesn't sit until we do. We order a round of sweet tea and start talking about what kind of pizza we like.

"I really like anchovies, black olives, and pineapple," Dax begins, "and I like a lot of marina sauce, like a *whole* lot of extra marina sauce."

"Marina sauce?" Lilly asks and I cover my face with my menu. "Do you mean marinara?"

"No, I mean marina," he replies and points to the boat dock. "Just like right out there. And I don't like much cheese, either. Just a little sprinkle of cheese. Cheddar if that's okay."

"Oh," Lilly says. I put my menu back on the table and try to keep a straight face.

"And jalapenos!" Deputy Dax exclaims. "I love jalapenos! So you guys want to order an extra-large?"

I look at Lilly and she looks down at her menu and Dax Dorsett starts laughing.

"Man, I got y'all, didn't I?"

"What?" Lilly crows. "What was that?"

"Yes," I say, laughing with relief. "You totally got me."

"Guilty," Lilly chimes. "Got me, too. I was just going to agree with you and order a salad."

The good-looking young cop smiles and it is a dazzling smile indeed.

I glance at Lilly and she's leaning over, showing him her bra again.

"So how old are you, Dax," I ask, "if you don't mind my asking."

"I don't mind at all," he says warmly. "I'm twenty-three, just got out of the army. Did five years."

"Did you deploy?" Lilly asks.

"Twice," he says. "I tell you what, you don't appreciate how good we've got it over here until you spend some time in a place like that. Little things like Cheetos and gummy worms." He smiles at Lilly. "You like gummy worms?"

"Only the sour ones," she says and smiles.

"How old are you ladies, if you don't mind me asking."

"I do," says Lilly, shamelessly getting her flirt on. "A lady never tells her age."

I roll my eyes and say, "I'm thirty and, if it helps any, I graduated from high school with the lady here who never tells her age."

"Ace Jones!" Lilly exclaims, while Dax and I share a good laugh.

"Okay, ladies," he says, smiling. "What do you really want on your pizza? I eat any combination of everything so order whatever you like."

After a remarkably pleasant dinner at Pier Six Pizza with our new pal Dax Dorsett, Lilly and I set out to stalk that rat bastard Richard Stacks.

"Ol' Deputy Dax is a real sweetie," Lilly muses after we get in the car and buckle up.

"Yeah, and he's an army veteran," I say. "You know I have this image in my head of veterans being sweet little old men with mesh back caps or long-haired fellows on motorcycles, but there's this new wave of veterans now. It's all these hot young fellows who don't look old enough to drive, let alone walk around a war zone in a Kevlar vest with an M16."

"I knew you thought he was hot," Lilly teases as she reaches in the backseat for the camera. "I saw you checking him out."

"Me? You were the one shamelessly showing off your bra and looking at the poor guy like you wanted to tie him to your bedpost and make him your personal sex slave."

"I thought about it," she says and laughs.

"He really is pretty hot," I say, "and funny as hell."

"And *so* charismatic"—she looks at me—"and all this time you've been running around here calling him Deputy Dumbass. You should be ashamed of yourself."

"I am very ashamed of myself, and from here on out I'll be calling him Deputy *Hot*ass!" I exclaim and we both crack up.

"I really do like him and he seems so lonely up here without any friends or family—hey!" she exclaims. "I'm going to invite him to the next get-together we have at your place."

"Sounds good to me. Now let's get down to business," I say and start digging around in my console for the list of addresses we put together at Chloe's. "Fire up that GPS and let's get a plan together, because I wanna bust Richard Stacks's balls and make him eat 'em with a spoon."

"Whoa now, sister. Keep in mind that we promised to do this on Chloe's terms, not ours," Lilly says as she punches the addresses into the GPS.

"I just want to wrap my fingers around his throat," I say. "He is such a piece of human garbage."

"You got him pretty good already and you're lucky he didn't press charges," Lilly says, still looking down at the GPS.

"Guess he didn't want to go up to the police department and start whining about being hit by a girl."

Lilly looks up and points down the road. "All righty, the closest one is on Elmhurst Street, so take a left at the next light."

"Yes, ma'am."

The first address is a bust, along with the next three, but the fifth house turns out to be a peach. As soon as we turn into the subdivision, I see that glistening white Lexus shining like a polished diamond in the moonlight. I slow down as Lilly fiddles with the expensive camera, and I ask her if she knows what she's doing and she says she does, but I'm pretty sure she doesn't. At any rate, she leans over and snaps a picture, and the flash is so bright that it blinds us both and I almost run up into a landscaping ensemble that looks like it cost more than my car.

"Good word, Lilly!" I say. "We're gonna look like Tiger Woods out here running over fire hydrants and shrubbery! Turn that flash off!"

"I don't know how."

"Is that even his car?"

"Well, it has 'Stacks 1' on the tag so I think it's safe to say that it is."

"Who lives there?"

"I don't know," she replies. "Go check the mailbox."

"That's a federal crime!" I pause for a second. "You go check the mailbox."

"Pull the car back around there and I will."

"Seriously?" I ask.

"Hell, yeah!" she exclaims and gives me a serious look. "Think about Chloe. How pitiful she was today. She needs us to help her, Ace."

"Well, we need to remember that she was very specific with her 'no shenanigans' ultimatum," I say as I make a U-turn on the quiet street.

"Stop right here!"

I turn off my headlights and Lilly hops out, hijacks the contents of the mailbox, and is back in the car before I can say shit.

"Catalog, junk mail, graduation invitation, oh, yeah! Credit card statement!" She looks over at me. "Bingo!"

"Who still gets their credit card bills in the mail? Don't these folks know that there are small-time criminals like us out and about in their 'hoods? Raiding mailboxes," I say and crack up.

Lilly examines the billing statement and doesn't even give me a courtesy laugh, so I decide to follow the GPS directions to the last two houses just to see what they look like.

"So it's broken down into *his* and *hers* charges, and it appears that Mr. Tate Dannan does a lot of international travel and Mrs. Dana Dannan has an affinity for spas and liquor stores."

"Nice," I say. "So what now?"

"Well, it appears he was dropping loads of cash in Europe during the first two weeks of this billing cycle, and then the last two weeks he must've been around here because it looks like local charges." She flips the paper over. "Regular stuff like the Dodge Store and the Tobacco Shop," she says and pauses. "Oh, hold on a second! Here it is!" She waves the billing statement in the air. "Last purchase on this statement is a plane ticket!" She squints at the paper. "Twenty-eight hundred dollars. Damn!"

"So I'm gonna venture a guess and say that—"

"He could very well be back in Europe or some other faraway place," Lilly finishes my sentence.

"Or he could be in there playing poker with Richard Stacks."

"If Richard Stacks was going to play a card game, I guess you would be right in assuming it would be poker," Lilly retorts. "It's a long shot, Ace, but it's all we've got right now. Turn around."

"We're going back to the house?" I ask, getting excited.

"Hell, yeah, but let's park somewhere else."

"Oh, my goodness, this reminds me of when you thought that beaver-toothed boy was cheating on you, but the poor bastard was really just playing cards with his friends at that awful hunting cabin that we almost died trying to find."

"Why you gotta bring that up?"

"Well, it's the last time we did some down-and-dirty-out-in-the-bushes kind of stalking," I say, turning into an upscale apartment complex two blocks from our target.

"Hey, we should go get Buster Loo and pretend we're out walking the dog."

"If we had a dog," I say, "why would we *pretend* to be walking a dog?"

"You know what I mean!"

"Now, you wanna talk about getting our cover blown?" I say. "We'd get arrested for disturbing the peace! You know he barks his fool head off every time the wind blows."

"Right, okay. No Buster Loo. Let's go then." She crams the camera down in her bag.

"Wait! Let's get that flash turned off."

"I did that already."

"Are you sure?" I ask and she nods her head but doesn't look sure at all.

"C'mon, let's go!" she says and hops out of the car like a rabbit on Red Bull.

We maneuver through the landscaping at the edge of the parking lot, climb into and out of a deep gully, then walk along the short concrete fencing that outlines the more affluent neighborhoods on the west side of town.

Something moves in the darkness ahead of us and I don't know if it's a possum or the devil coming to get us. I yelp like a dog and scan the area for a varmint or a pitchfork. Lilly laughs so hard I'm afraid she's going to piss her pants. Then a bat swoops down, she screams like a banshee, and we both hit the grass and let the chiggers have their way with us for a few minutes.

"We are going to jail," Lilly whispers.

"It's not illegal to lay in the grass!" I whisper back. "What would we be charged with, Failure to Yield to Common Sense?"

"If that was a crime, you would've been sent to prison years ago!" Lilly giggles.

"Wow. That bat really stirred up your sense of humor."

"It's gone now."

"What, your sense of humor or the bat?" I ask.

"L-O-L," she says. "Both."

We get up, shake off like wet dogs, and make our way down to the house where Richard Stacks's Lexus is still parked in the drive. The backyard of the four-story estate is completely dark. I hop the short stone fence and land in some prickly holly bushes and Lilly cackles as I whisper-cuss like a sailor.

She hops the fence a few feet down, and we tiptoe across the pristine lawn onto a sprawling concrete patio. I ease up to the French doors while she creeps up to a large window.

"There's a man and a woman on the sofa, but all I can see is the backs of their heads," I whisper.

"I can see the woman's profile," she whispers back, "but I just barely see the dude."

"You think it's him?" I ask.

"Don't know," she answers, shaking her head, "but it'd just about have to be, wouldn't it?"

I decide to change positions and step back into a large wrought iron pottery shelf with about six hundred flowerpots on it. I turn around to grab it and think I've got it steadied when I see one little pot teetering on the top shelf. I watch in terrified silence as the pot falls, flowers first, straight down onto Lilly's head. She squeals and stumbles back into a patio chair and I watch in horror as the pot bounces off her head, onto the table, then down to the concrete patio, where it shatters into sixty million pieces. Lilly jumps up, looks inside the house, and, in a rush of movement, pulls out the camera, steps up to the window, and flash!

Yet again, I am blind, but that doesn't stop me from trying to get the hell out of there. In my sightless haste, I stumble over a yard gnome and fall face-first into a bed of monkey grass.

"Get your ass up and let's go!" Lilly calls as she rushes past me. "Here they come!"

I jump up and run through the yard like a rat on acid, hurl myself over the fence, and roll like Rambo down into the ditch.

I look around and Lilly is nowhere to be seen.

I hear a woman screaming for someone to call the police because there are burglars everywhere. In fifteen seconds flat, every backyard on the block is saturated with light and people are buzzing around like bees trying to figure out what all the fuss is about.

A spotlight sweeps the air a few feet above my head and I hear sirens and dogs barking, and I know I have to get back to my car. Fast. I strain my eyes against the darkness in the ditch and don't see Lilly anywhere, so I hunker down and scurry away.

I stay low to the ground as I crawl out of the gully and make my way back to the apartment complex where I'd left the car. The thought occurs to me that I would look a lot less suspicious riding around looking for Lilly rather than walking or being slumped down in a parked car literally twenty-five yards from where the manhunt is about to begin.

I'm peeking around the Dumpster box trying to make sure the coast is clear when my cell phone buzzes in the back pocket of my shorts. I scream like a toddler at the dentist and take off in a dead sprint toward the car. I drop my keys three times and my cell phone once before I finally get in, and when I do, I spin out of there like Ricky Bobby in *Talladega Nights* when he had that cougar in his car.

18

◇◇◇

I don't recognize the number of the missed call, so I dial it back and, lo and behold, it's Sheriff J. J. Jackson.

"Ace," he barks, "where are you?"

"Uh, in my car," I answer in a small voice.

"Would you happen to be close to the west side Walmart?"

"Why, yes, as a matter of fact—"

"Get over here and get Lilly before I change my mind and take both of y'all to jail!" he yells.

"Lilly," I say, trying to be coy, "where'd you find her?"

"In the damned field between Walmart and Mrs. Dana Dannan's house, where some *burglars* made a mess of the porch. Since Tate is out of the country, Dana was quite alarmed by the intrusion. Now get over here right now!"

"On my way," I peep like a baby chicken.

"Behind Dollar General!" he yells and hangs up on me.

I'm nervous as a tick on a bald dog as I pull up behind Dollar General, but much to my relief the sheriff is gone. Lilly is sitting on the curb covered from head to toe in dirt. She gets up and walks around to the passenger side of the car and taps on the window. I roll it down.

"Can I get in or do you want me to walk home because I'm so ridiculously filthy?" she asks with a dejected look.

"Nah, that's what leather seats are for," I say and motion for her to get in.

"Shit," she says, closing the car door, "I haven't run that fast since . . . ever."

"How did you get so dirty?" I ask, trying not to laugh. "Did you fall down?"

"How did you get so dirty?" she says, mocking me. "Well, this," she says and points to the black streaks in her golden hair, "is potting soil, my friend, from where you hit me in the head with a damned flowerpot."

"Accident," I say quickly.

"And this," she says and waves her arm across her body, "is from where I fell down in an irrigation ditch trying to get away from the scene of the crime."

She looks at me and I look at the road. She reaches over and plucks a cluster of twigs out of my hair. I can feel her looking at me so I look back at her and have to hold my breath to keep from laughing. She raises her eyebrows and eyeballs my equally dirty clothes and we both bust out laughing.

"But all is not lost, my friend," she says triumphantly and pulls the camera out of her bag, "because this picture is worth more than a thousand words."

She pushes a button and the camera comes to life and I cannot believe what I see on the tiny little screen.

"Chloe is going to die when she sees this," I say.

"Indeed," Lilly agrees.

19

◇◇◇

Saturday I get up early and take Buster Loo to the park for a nice long walk. He does the chiweenie high-step all the way down the road and around the first half of the track. When we round the bend and start into the woods, he stops and looks back at me as if to say, "Here's the spot. Let me go." I tell him to keep walking, but he just stares at me.

"Buster Loo, c'mon, we're not taking any chances on you humping a dog five times your size today," I say and take a few steps, hoping he'll follow.

Buster Loo doesn't move. He starts to whimper and whine and paw at the leash. I shake it a little because that usually gets him going, but he just stands there looking at me like I just flushed his favorite toy down the toilet.

"Buster Loo, let's go," I say in my most serious tone.

He turns his snout in disdain, then walks into the woods as far as the leash will allow. He falls over on his side and proceeds to flop around like a fish, snorting and honking and moaning. I just stand there and watch because I don't know what else to do.

"Well, so much for not being embarrassed today, Buster Loo," I say. He stops flopping and looks at me. "C'mere and I'll let you go."

He jumps up and starts running toward me and I take that opportunity to start walking in the opposite direction of the woods, hoping he'll follow. I feel a tug on the leash and turn around to see Buster Loo, wild-eyed and distraught, lying on his back with all four paws in the air. He's somehow managed to wrap his leash around both of his front paws and his rump and he's chewing on the part closest to his collar.

"Oh, good word!" I say just as an older couple appears from around the bend.

"Good mornin'," the man calls as they approach. He looks down at Buster Loo, laughs, and says, "Well, now, that's the first time I've ever seen a hog-tied dog."

"Yeah," I mumble, "me too."

"Have a good day," his companion calls.

"Thanks, you too," I say.

I walk back to Buster Loo and untangle him, but he's still upset and won't walk. I have to carry him all the way home because every time I put him down, he freezes up like a stuffed squirrel. At least I was spared from seeing Reece Hilliard and Daisy.

I take Buster Loo into the backyard, where his will to walk suddenly returns and, after being released from his enemy the leash, he speeds off toward the garden. I walk inside just in time to hear my phone buzz. I tell myself it's not Mason and, of course, I'm right.

It's a text from Lilly that says, "Call me," so I do.

"Jeez," I say when she answers, "why don't you just call *me* instead of sending a stupid text telling me to call *you*? That drives me nuts."

"Well, I didn't know if you were up yet."

"In the history of the world, have I ever slept later than you?"

"Uh," she says and pauses, "probably not, but who cares! I've got an idea!"

"Let's hear it."

"Cookout! Your place! Tonight!" Lilly says. "And invite Dax Dorsett!"

"So you want to use my grill to get yourself some meat, is that it?"

"Whatever works, my friend," Lilly says and we both start laughing. "So what about it? Is that okay?"

"Sure, why not?" I say. "The usual time?"

"Yes! That will be just fine."

"How are you going to communicate to Deputy Dax that his presence is requested here tonight? Do you have his phone number?"

"No, I've got the sheriff on that."

"Oh, that is so seventh grade," I say. "Are you going to bring a handwritten note asking him to be your boyfriend with boxes drawn for him to check Yes, No, or Maybe?"

"LOL," she says flatly.

"You know we could type up something and print it. Or do a little PowerPoint detailing all the reasons he should have sex with you."

"Shut up, Ace!" she says, laughing. "I'll text everybody and let them know what's up and you just make that guacamole dip I love so much."

"Done," I say. "Hey, Lilly? Two things."

"Okay."

"First of all, have you heard from Chloe?"

"No, have you?"

"No," I say. "Do you think we should call her?"

"Well," she muses for a second, "I'd love to tell her about that picture, or better yet, show it to her. But we better wait for her to call us. She was pretty clear about everything being done on her terms."

"Yeah, she was," I agree. "She'll probably call us when he leaves for work on Monday. I don't think we should tell her anything over the phone. We should wait until we can sit down with her so we can, like, I don't know, be a shoulder to cry on or something."

"Yeah, you're probably right about that," she says. "Can you imagine trying to explain *that* particular photo over the phone?"

"Exactly," I say.

"What's the other thing?"

"Well," I begin, not really wanting to have this conversation. "Aren't you worried about folks getting nosy at the party tonight? I mean, it didn't go unnoticed that you missed an entire week of school, and it was like playing dodgeball with all the inquiring minds that wanted to know where you were." She doesn't say anything, so to remind her that I have problems, too, I say, "All of that, plus all the talk about the Richard Stacks incident made for an exhausting couple of days." She still doesn't say anything, so I just get back to the point. "You know someone is bound to ask why you were out all week."

"Maybe not," she mumbles. "Maybe no one'll mention it."

"Logan Hatter will mention it, I assure you," I say. "So you might want to have a little powwow with him before either one of y'all start drinking."

"Yeah, you're right. I should've called him already."

"He won't care about that, but you will need to tell him what's going on. He's been after me hard about it."

"Okay," she says and sighs.

"Well, I better get on the house cleaning," I say. "See you tonight, lover girl."

"Au revoir, mon ami," she says with a chuckle.

Lilly arrives later that afternoon looking like a springtime dream in a strapless pink dress and sparkly wedge sandals. She looks at my flip-flops and khaki Bermudas and rolls her eyes.

"You don't even want a man, do you?" she asks.

"Not if I have to wear shoes like that to a cookout," I say, pointing to her feet.

"Here," she says, handing me two grocery bags. "Ethan Allen is on his way with the burgers."

People start filtering in and, before long, my patio table is covered with chips, dips, and tasty-looking desserts. I plug in the Christmas lights and fire up the tiki torches and notice that Lilly can't carry on a conversation without craning her neck toward the driveway. I go get the fan from my bedroom and set it up next to the picnic table to keep the flies away, then spot-check the food spread, making sure everything that needs a serving utensil has one. I sneak a handful of chips out of a covered basket and toss one to Buster Loo.

Logan Hatter taps me on the shoulder and says, "Hey, I'm telling you that it's not good to feed that dog table food."

"Logan," I say, turning and smiling, "Buster Loo ate a lizard yesterday. A whole lizard. I don't think a little table food every now and then is going to hurt him." He makes a gagging sound and heads for the beer cooler.

Ethan Allen arrives with what looks like seventy-five pounds of hamburger meat and six feet of smoked sausage. He fires up my old rusty grill and, in a matter of minutes, has a mouthwatering aroma floating across the backyard. Buster Loo stands guard beside the grill, circling it periodically to make sure no scrap goes undetected.

I look around, pleased that everything is going smoothly and everyone appears to be having a good time. I'm about to run inside and mix up the homemade ice cream when I catch a glimpse of Lilly standing by the gate, looking positively miserable.

"Hey, Lilly," I call. "Why don't you come in here and help me for a second?"

"Okay," she says. Lilly follows me into the kitchen and watches with zero interest as I lay out the ingredients of my supersecret homemade ice cream recipe.

"What's up?" I ask. "Has someone been giving you a hard time? Do I need to go out there and drop some 'bows on somebody's head?"

"No," she says and laughs. Then she sighs and pooches out her lips. "No one's mentioned anything about that."

"Not even Logan?" I ask, surprised.

"I didn't wait for him to ask. I pulled him aside and volunteered the information."

"What'd he say?"

"Nothing, really," she says with a sigh. "I was telling him that Catherine Hilliard was trying to pin some bogus crap on me, and he was listening with what appeared to be great interest until some guys nearby started talking about the NFL draft—so he wrapped up our conversation and took off."

"What! After the way he hounded me wanting to know what was going on!" I say, stirring up the mixture. "He better not ask me a thing about it later!"

"Ace, Dax isn't coming."

"Did he have to work?"

"I don't know."

"Did you talk to him?"

"No."

"Did you talk to J.J.?"

"No."

"So how do you know he's not coming?" I ask, filling up the first of three ice cream churns.

"Because I want him to so bad."

"Oh," I say, filling up the second, "so this is serious?"

"I can't stop thinking about him!" Lilly gushes. "It's driving me crazy. And he's only twenty-three years old! What the hell is wrong with me?"

"Not a damn thing," I say, topping off the third churn. "He's hot. You're hot. What's not peachy about that?"

"He's just a baby!" she whines. "I can't be crushing on someone seven years younger than me."

"Bullshit!" I say. "Dax Dorsett is a young man in his prime and I'm willing to bet he's more mature than you are." I wink at her and she scowls at me. "Now quit being silly and stir these bananas into that churn," I tell her and hand her a long-handled paddle spoon.

"Ugh, I hate homemade ice cream with bananas in it," she mumbles.

"So do I. That's why I made us a batch with Yoohoo," I say, turning to show her the churn of chocolate goodness.

"Now that's what I'm talking about!"

"Finally!" I say. "A smile! Great! Now take that outside and stick it in a freezer and plug it up."

I pick up the other two churns and follow her out the door. We're busy packing salt around the top of the freezers and don't see Dax Dorsett step up onto the porch behind us. Lilly hops up, whirls around, and almost knocks him down.

"Oh," she says, much louder than usual. "Oh, my goodness! I'm so sorry! Are you okay?"

"Oh, no! I'm not!" Dax grunts and feigns severe pain as he drops onto a patio lounger. "Oh, God, I think I'm hurt."

He's wearing a white T-shirt with a logo I don't understand, a hat with an unusually flat bill, plaid shorts, and some kind of weird tennis shoes. I don't really get the ensemble, but I still think he looks pretty hot and it's obvious to me and anyone else with a functioning pair of eyeballs that this young man works out. I look over and see Logan, who sports a slight beer belly, stand up a little straighter and puff his chest out.

"Oh, Dax," Lilly starts, "I'm so sorry. I didn't think you—" She stops and her cheeks get red. "I didn't see you there."

Ethan Allen glances up from the grill with a questioning look on his face and I just nod and smile.

Dax takes off his cap and brushes a hand through his short light brown hair.

"I think I might live," he says, "but just in case I don't, do you have any cold beer?" Lilly runs to the cooler, digs one out of the very bottom, and presents it to him with a wide sweet smile.

"Thank you, Miss Lane," he says, smiling back. "Join me?" He pats the seat next to him, and it's a wonder Lilly doesn't land on his hand she sits down so fast.

I look back at Ethan Allen and he's shaking his head.

"What kind of ice cream you makin'?" Dax asks, nodding toward the freezers.

"Vanilla, chocolate, and banana," she says, batting her eyelashes.

"Really?" he says and looks like he just can't believe his luck. "I love homemade banana ice cream! It's my favorite."

"Mine, too!" Lilly chimes.

I have to walk away to keep from laughing, so I join Ethan Allen at the grill.

"Somebody better call the donkey doctor," he says, nodding toward Lilly, "'cause that girl's ass is on fire!"

I start laughing and slap Ethan Allen on the back.

"You have such a way with words, Ethan Allen!"

"Thanks," he says, then turns to the crowd. "Burgers are done!"

◇◇◇

20

I sleep late Sunday and miss church for the second week in a row.

"I better go next week, Buster Loo," I tell him on the way to the park, "or they'll be sending out a search party."

No one is on the walking trail for as far as I can see in either direction, so I let Buster Loo off of his leash the minute we get to the woods. We walk all the way around and back home without seeing so much as one other person, and I can't help but wish all of our walks could be so pleasant and uneventful.

I call Lilly and she doesn't answer, which is disappointing since I'm dying to know how it went with Dax after she left the party with him last night.

Buster Loo and I take a long nap on the sofa and it's cloudy and stormy when we get up. I head out to the backyard to finish picking up the party trash and get it all bagged and under the patio just before it starts to rain.

I call Lilly one more time, but she still doesn't answer. I don't feel like cooking and have no interest in going out in the monsoon, so the only logical thing to do is order a pizza.

I spend Monday through Thursday at school having lunch with Coach Hatter and Coach Wills, ducking meddlesome questions about Chloe and Lilly and getting my ass chewed out at least twice a day by Catherine Hilliard.

I call Lilly Thursday night to see if she wants to do some stalking, but she's not up for it. I try to get some details on what happened with Dax and she says, "Yes, I saw that movie and I loved it," which is code for "can't talk right now because whoever we're trying to discuss is sitting/standing/lying right beside me," so I let her go without further ado.

"That's going to be quite a story," I tell Buster Loo as I flop down on the couch. "Your aunt Lilly has got herself a *young* man!" He hops up in my lap and starts nudging my hand with his snout, which is his code for "pet me now before I go crazy!"

After loving on Buster Loo for a few minutes, I decide to have dinner delivered by Pier Six. Normally I restrict myself to one pizza per week, but since my nerves have been so shot by all the drama, I don't mind making an exception. Thirty minutes later, I pile a plate full of piping-hot pizza, grab a cold beer, and sit down to a good screaming match on Nancy Grace.

I hear a whimper and look down to see Buster Loo sitting up like a Coke bottle, begging like he's never seen food before. I toss him a piece of pizza crust and he disappears to his secret hiding place behind the love seat.

During a commercial for adult diapers, my mind wanders off and I start thinking about the fact that I could actually lose my job because Catherine Hilliard doesn't like me and Richard Stacks wants retribution for me punching him in the face. Things like that happen in Bugtussle, Mississippi.

I decide it would be in my best interest to take another personal day on Friday because, first of all, I need more of a break than a two-day weekend can provide, and second, if I do get fired, I'll lose all my days anyway—so why not? I'm exhausted with the entire situation and I'm no good at keeping up an act. Especially one as dishonest and foolish as walking around at school all day trying to pretend everything is normal when it so clearly isn't.

The rumor mill is doing double time with Lilly and Chloe both still absent from school. Coach Wills said at lunch on Wednesday that people are starting to speculate that Richard Stacks beat up Lilly because he thinks she's the one that called Brother Berkin and told him that Chloe was in the hospital. Logan said he heard something along the same lines, as did Olivia West.

I was quite relieved that nothing had been said about Catherine Hilliard accusing Lilly of sleeping with Zac Tanner because, even after something like that is proven to be a sham, the accusation hangs in people's minds forever.

I've grown weary of the incessant animosity with Catherine Hilliard. I'm fighting a battle in a war I can't win because I'm on the wrong side of the sociopolitical slope. If Catherine Hilliard wants to fire me, she can damn well do it. And if she wants to finish ruining that school, she can damn well do that, too. I've had enough.

I sleep late Friday morning and get up in a terrible mood. I drag myself to the kitchen and make a pot of super-stout coffee, feeling more antisocial by the second. I look at the calendar on the fridge door and sigh. Friday the thirteenth. Great.

I join Buster Loo in the backyard, thinking some speedy-dog fetch will lift my spirits, but Buster Loo is more interested in sniffing around the perimeter of the yard. I look out at my garden and wish I would've gotten up earlier so I could've plucked a few weeds before it got so hot.

I go inside, pour another cup of coffee, and sit down at the kitchen table. I stare out the window and try not to think about Mason Mc-Kenzie. In trying not to think about him, I end up thinking about those jeans he bought me that I haven't been able to zip since last summer, so I decide the thing for me to do is to spend the rest of the morning in fat girl isolation at the gym.

◇◇

21

I forgo the walk of shame past the Bratz pack on the Boeing 747 treadmills and head over to the left side of the gym, where I get on an elliptical machine. After answering fifty questions on the nosy-ass monitor, I see 30:00 minutes pop up on the timer and wonder which one of my answers indicated that I wanted to spend that much time on this thing.

I'm huffing and puffing like the big bad wolf when my right foot slips, the left pedal goes crazy, and next thing I know I'm sitting astride the big plastic wheel cover with a raging pain in my cooter.

The only time my cooter has ever hurt this bad was when I was seven years old and had a friend over who wanted to ride bikes. My neighbor loaned me his so my friend could ride mine and off we went. I started horsing around, ran off the sidewalk, and landed cooter-first on that metal bar that girl bikes *don't* have. I thought for sure I would die from the pain that day, but somehow I managed to pull through.

At least only a few people witnessed that incident. Everyone in the gym is staring at me now and I see that fellow with no hair on his arms heading my way. I'd like to move, maybe get down on my belly and crawl away like a snake, but I'm paralyzed by the pain in my nether region. I assure the muscle-bound slickster that I'm not injured and get the feeling that he's more concerned about a lawsuit than my well-being, but at least he's considerate enough to offer me an ice pack.

An ice pack for my aching cooter.

I politely decline.

After several minutes, I limp back to the locker room to get my bag so I can leave with what dignity I have left. Which is none. I stop by the Red Rooster Drive-In on the way home to get some breakfast and end up ordering fried pickles and a bacon cheeseburger because I think I've earned a little comfort food.

Two and a half hours later, I'm sitting on the couch watching a *Biggest Loser* rerun with a pack of lima beans between my legs, when my doorbell rings.

"It's unlocked!" I yell. "Come on in!"

I turn around expecting to see Lilly because she's supposed to be coming over to discuss our stalking plans for the weekend, but it's not her.

It's Mason McKenzie.

"Well, isn't this shaping up to be a hell of a day?" I ask Buster Loo when he appears from behind the love seat.

I have on an AC/DC shirt that's a decade old and cutoff sweatpants with holes in the butt. My hair looks like a pack of rats just moved out and I have a bag of frozen beans between my thighs. To make matters worse, Buster Loo is having an all-out, balls-to-the-wall little doggie meltdown.

I cram the lima beans in between the couch cushions and flip around so the holes in my shorts are looking the other way.

"Hey there, Buster Loo!" Mason McKenzie says, picking him up. "How you doin', little buddy?"

Buster Loo is speed-licking him all over his face and wagging his tail so fast I'm afraid he's going to sling it off his little chiweenie ass.

I blink a few times and rub my eyes, but apparently I'm not hallucinating. Mason McKenzie is standing in my kitchen wearing a sky blue polo shirt, khaki cargo shorts, and brown flip-flops. His skin is nicely tanned and it appears his trips to the gym are a bit more frequent and productive than mine.

He's looking at me now, smiling like we're old friends.

"Hey, Ace," he says, "how've you been?"

Well, my nerves are shot, my cooter's frozen, and I'm on the verge of cardiac arrest because I'm still crazy in love with you.

"Great." I put on a warm smile. "You?"

"I'm good," he says and walks to the fridge.

"You hungry?" I ask as he digs through my refrigerator like he buys the groceries.

"Little bit." He turns around with a soda and a Pier Six pizza box. "Oh, wow, this is great!"

If I were ten years younger, I'd tell him to get his damned hands off my leftovers and get the hell out of my house. I'm not sure if I've matured or just gotten lazy, but I just sit and stare.

"Can I join you?" he asks.

"Sure." I wave to the love seat. "Have a seat." Buster Loo follows him into the living room, gets in his Coke-bottle stance, and starts paddling the air with his front paws.

"Aw, he still remembers the paw trick I taught him!"

"Yeah," I say. "He's a smart little dog."

"So what have you been up to, Ace Jones?" He plucks the olives off the pizza and tosses them to Buster Loo, who catches every last one before they hit the floor.

"Not much, Mason McKenzie." I still can't believe he's sitting in my living room, drinking one of my sodas and eating my leftover pizza. "You come up to see your folks?"

"Nope," he says and takes a bite of pizza.

"So?"

"So I heard what happened to Chloe and Lilly. And I heard you've been arrested once"—he raises his eyebrows at me—"almost twice, so since I'm the best lawyer I know, I decided I'd better come up for a few days."

"And do what?" I say with a deliberate lack of enthusiasm.

"Get Lilly her job back, for one," he says decisively. "Two, help Chloe get a divorce if that's what she wants. And three," he says and looks me right in the eye, "talk you into marrying me."

"Well," I start, trying not to stutter. "Well, that's certainly an ambitious plan." I try to breathe. "How long are you up for?"

"As long as it takes, baby." He smiles at me and I almost faint. "As long as it takes."

"What about the Law Office of J. Mason McKenzie?" I focus hard on appearing nonchalant.

"Got a young fellow that's burning it up. Name's Connor McCall. He's the real deal," he says between bites, "so he's handling the footwork and I'm right here if he needs me." He holds up a cellular gadget that I haven't even seen in commercials yet.

"How long you been in town?" I ask and immediately feel like a dumbass.

"Was that a pickup line?" He laughs.

"No," I say and start laughing despite myself.

"Actually, I just got here, Ace, and was on my way to Ethan Allen's when I saw your car was here and just—I don't know . . . I just wanted to see you." He looks down at my crotch. "Have you peed in your pants? Are you that happy to see me?"

I bust out laughing and tell him about the incident at the gym and he laughs till he almost chokes and, for one brief second, I allow the happiness to wash over me because, like Calgon, Mason McKenzie takes me away.

The doorbell rings again and I don't have time to say "It's open" before Lilly comes running in screaming, "Mason! Oh, my goodness! Mason McKenzie, oh, my God!"

He grabs her and hugs her and they are just so happy to see each other; then Lilly has a lightbulb moment and gets quiet.

"What are you"—she points at Mason—"doing here?" She points at me.

"Just visiting," he says, smiling at me, and I'm dying for one of those big hugs he just lavished on her.

Lilly nods her head and narrows her eyes at me.

"He's been here five minutes, Lilly, calm down," I say, and she looks down at my shorts.

"Have you peed yourself?"

"No, just shut up and let's go outside on the porch." I wave toward the kitchen. "Lilly, grab whatever you want to drink and come on." I reach down to pick up Buster Loo, but he scampers straight to Mason, who promptly scoops him up, and I swear the dog is smiling from ear to floppy ear.

◇◇

22

Lust is the great thief of common sense, so I must keep that demon in restraints. That is, however, easier said than done when a charismatic, six-foot-tall, blond-haired, blue-eyed, suntanned, well-toned sex machine that I want to make babies with is literally within my reach.

"You got the camera?" Mason asks as we settle into the overstuffed loungers on my patio. "I can't wait to see that picture."

"How do you know about the picture?" I ask, eyeballing Lilly, who takes a sudden and intense interest in my herb garden.

"Baby," he says, smiling like we were already sleeping together again, "I know *everything*."

"I know you're corny as hell. I know that," I say, rolling my eyes. "Lilly, did you get a print made?"

"Oh, boy, did I?!" Lilly exclaims and pulls a large padded envelope out of her shiny ruffled purse that's twice the size of Texas. She plops it down on the table and slowly withdraws a glossy eight-by-ten that we all gawk at in silence.

The photograph offers a full frontal view of Mrs. Dana Dannan, who is sporting an ensemble made of black leather and red lace with gold chains framing her bare boobs. Much to our collective delight, the picture also offers a side view of Richard Stacks the Fourth, who is butt naked and appears to be looking at the ceiling. His well-groomed and short but freakishly fat penis is staring in the same direction.

"Oh, my God," I whisper. "I couldn't see on that little camera screen that he was wearing a studded dog collar."

"Look at his dick!" Mason practically shouts. "It looks like a sea creature out of its shell!"

"Oh, my goodness," Lilly says somberly, "poor Chloe. Can you imagine having that thing coming at you for *over five* years?"

"Oh, I am going to be sick!" Mason says. "Put it away, Lilly."

"This is your copy," Lilly says cheerfully and slides the picture across the table. "I printed several."

"You should've left one in the photo kiosk," I say. "That would've been hilarious."

"Or made two hundred copies and stuck 'em on the windshield of every car in the parking lot," Mason adds with a snort, then looks down at his watch. "Well, ladies," he says, getting up and stretching, "I hate to break up the party, but I gotta run. I'll see you both at Ethan Allen's tonight."

"Sure!" Lilly says quickly.

She stands up and he gives her another big hug and I want to jump up and pounce on him like a fat kid on some birthday cake.

But I don't.

I sit in my chair like a statue. "Ace," he says, looking me in the eye, "I meant what I said earlier."

"What'd you say earlier?" Lilly pipes up and looks at me. "What'd he say earlier?"

"Nothing important," I say. "Bye, Mason."

"See you ladies tonight," he calls over his shoulder. "Let's try not to get arrested between now and then."

"What did he say earlier?" Lilly asks again.

"Just drop it, Lilly." I look at her. "You called him, didn't you?"

"What?" Lilly says. "Did someone mention Chinese? Who wants to go to China Kitchen?" She looks around like a dumbass, then raises her hand. "Me! I want to go to China Kitchen!"

"I know you called him, you dork," I say, getting up.

She gives me a feeble smile. "I didn't tell him to stop and see you."

"Yeah, okay, whatever," I say, turning around. "Let me go change shorts and we'll go."

"Great!" she says. "Hey! I'll call and check on Chloe."

"Good idea," I say, opening the back door. I stop and look back at her. "When's the last time you heard from her?"

"I missed a call from her earlier in the week, and when I called her back she didn't answer," Lilly says, digging through her purse for her phone.

When I walk back out on the porch a few minutes later, Lilly is perched on the edge of the lounger with a gloomy look on her face.

"What?" I ask. "What is it?"

"Her number's been changed," she says and pauses, "to an unlisted number." She tilts her head sideways and gives me a hard look. "When's the last time you talked to her?"

"She called me on, let me think, what day was it?" I pick up my phone and go to my recent calls. "Wednesday. She called Wednesday and asked if we'd found out anything about Richard."

"What'd you tell her?"

"I told her no. Didn't we agree not to tell her anything until we could sit down and talk to her face-to-face?"

"Yeah." Lilly sighs and shakes her head. "She is staying with him. She's cutting us off and she's staying with that bastard."

"Are you sure you dialed the right number?" I ask.

"It's on my speed dial, Ace!" Lilly exclaims. "Try it from your phone if you don't believe me."

I scroll down to Chloe's name, punch the green button, and get the same result.

"Forget China Kitchen," I say. "Let's get on with the stalking. I want enough dirt on Richard Stacks to bury him ten times over. And I wanna put everything we get on him in a big fat binder and take it to Chloe so she can finally see for herself that Richard Stacks *really* is the piece-of-shit human being that we always told her he was."

"Let's do it!" Lilly says and reaches for the padded envelope containing the pictures. "But before we go, you need to check this out." She pulls a sheet of paper out and holds it up for me to see. "I took that e-mail she sent us Monday, you know, the one with the mistress list that she cross-referenced with Richard's little black book?" I nod and she continues, "There were seventeen women on the list. One, of course, was our lady-in-leather, Dana Dannan, so I crossed her off, then put the rest of them in a spreadsheet."

"You made a spreadsheet?" I ask, looking closer at the data. "When did you get a printer?"

"Check it out," she says, ignoring my questions. "I put 'name' in the first column, 'address' in the second, then 'phone number,' and 'misc' in the last. We made the miscellaneous column a little wider so we'd have room to add comments after the Google search."

"We?" I say, smiling. "Who is 'we'?"

"Moving on," she says with a sly look. "We have four strippers, three call girls, two certifiable prostitutes, and seven local women not counting Dana."

"That's disgusting." I lean in for a closer look and see the spreadsheet has been titled "The Sluts of Richard Stacks IV." "Very Shakespearean name you chose."

"Thank you," Lilly says and points to the top box. "First up on the local list, we have an old favorite."

"Who is that?"

"Remember that skank who told everyone in town that she was having an affair with Richard, then went on to dish about his weird penis?"

"Jennifer Kramer?" I yell, squinting at the small print. "Are you serious? After all the things she said about him, she's still—" I pause because I can't find the right word.

"Yes, she is," Lilly says, "and now we know she wasn't lying about that oddball goober."

"Oddball goober," I repeat. "Did you really just say that?"

"Also making the list are two former secretaries"—she looks at me—"and one current."

"Big surprise there," I snort. "How nice of him to keep in touch with the others, too."

"Here's a good one." She turns the paper around and holds it up in front of my face.

"Brooke Valspar?" I bark. "Are you kidding me? Bruce Valspar's wife!"

Bruce Valspar is a textbook good ol' boy whose family owns a logging company just outside of Bugtussle. He's well over six feet tall, built like the Rock, and twice as sexy.

"Bruce Valspar would beat the ever lovin' shit out of him."

"Wouldn't he?" Lilly shakes her head. "And Bruce is so incredibly hot. Why in the hell would she cheat on a man like Bruce Valspar with a wimp like Richard Stacks?"

"That is beyond me," I say. "She must be crazy, and we need to be careful what we do with that. Bruce Valspar doesn't deserve to have his name drug through a mess like this."

"No," Lilly agrees, "but he doesn't deserve to have a wife whoring around with Richard Stacks, either."

"Yeah, but let's think on that a minute." I look at the list. "Don't the Valspars go to church with Richard and Chloe?"

"Yep."

"Wow." I nod toward the list. "What else?"

"A hairdresser and a real estate lady."

"Is the hairdresser just for haircuts or—"

"Well, Chloe sent the log-in info for their cell phone bill, and according to that he called her over thirty times last month."

"Wonder if she trims his muff?" I muse.

"Somebody has to, might as well be her!" Lilly laughs. "I bet she has to have a special set of shears to cut around that—"

"Oddball goober," I say. "I believe the term you're searching for is 'oddball goober.'"

"OMG! I wonder if he pats it down with aftershave after a trim?"

"Eek!" I say. "I can't think about that anymore! What about texting? Did you check that out when you looked at the phone bill?"

"That is an insurmountable task," Lilly says. "It took fifteen minutes to download, and you would need a small army to go over those numbers. I don't know how he has time to do all this screwing around as much as he texts. It's ridiculous."

"What a shit nugget." I look at Lilly. "What else?"

"Last on the list, we have this real estate lady."

"What's the deal with that?" I ask. "You think he's doing legitimate business with her, or you think maybe he's sporting that dog collar around her open houses to impress potential clients?"

Lilly starts laughing and shaking her head. "Oh, Lord, probably." She takes a deep breath. "Jeez, Ace, we gotta laugh to keep from crying."

"Tell me about it," I say. "So what should our next move be?"

"Let's get out of here," she replies. "I've got a plan."

"All righty then," I say. "Let's take my car so we can stay incognito. Don't get me wrong here because I know your car is way nicer, but I think it'd be in our best interest to forgo the means of transportation that screams Hey-Look-at-Me-Here-I-Come-Down-the-Road-in-My-Pussy-Wagon."

"LOL, Ace, funny," she says flatly. "Now take me to the Red Rooster Drive-In."

23

◇◇

While awaiting the arrival of our brown bags of greasy goodness, I peruse the list of Richard Stacks the Fourth's side dishes, and I can't stop thinking about his weird-looking penis and wondering how all of his whores react to it when they see it for the first time. Or anytime.

"We've got to nail him, Lilly," I say. "We have got to get him good."

"Yeah, I know," Lilly says. "Our only hope is catching him red-handed like we did with Dana. We've got to have hard-core evidence."

"Do you think it's even gonna do any good?" I ask. "I mean, let's say we get seven or eight more pictures of Richard in the act"—I give her a sideways glance—"and, to be honest, I think we'd be really lucky to get that many, but that's beside the point. The point is this: What if Chloe won't even look at them? What if she never speaks to us again?"

"That won't happen," Lilly says. "That can't happen."

"But you realize it's a possibility, right?"

"Yeah," Lilly mumbles. "I can't believe she changed her phone number and didn't even call or e-mail or anything."

"She dropped us like some hot potatoes."

"Some hot potatoes?" Lilly giggles. "Is that the best you can do?"

We crack up as the food arrives and I tip the carhop two bucks. I sort out the food while Lilly sips her cherry limeade.

"C'mon," Lilly says, putting her drink down and picking up her burger. "Let's eat on the way to Stacks and Stacks."

"Stacks and Stacks? Why are we going there?" I mutter with a steaming tater tot between my teeth.

"Because I need to put this on Dick Richard's car." She holds up a small dark object about the size of a half dollar.

"Dick Richard? I like that." I eyeball the device. "What is that thing?"

"GPS tracking dot," she says proudly, "magnetized and designed especially for tracking automobiles in real time."

"Where the hell did you get that? And do you even know what 'real time' means?"

"Got it from Deputy Hotass. Same place I got my printer." She smiles and picks the lettuce off her burger. "And 'real time' means that the instant the car moves, we can track it on the computer. No delay."

"Well, aren't you in tight cahoots with the local law enforcement," I say sarcastically.

"I'm in tight cahoots with Dax Dorsett," she says with a sly smile.

"You know I've been dying to hear the story on that," I say, putting the car in reverse. "So why don't you take it from the top?"

"Well, when we left your house last Saturday night, nothing happened."

"Nothing happened?" I ask. "What's up with that?"

"Well, you know, I told him I'd drive him home so I did. He was drunk as a skunk when we got there and I had to take his keys out of his hand and unlock the front door for him."

"Too drunk to get his key in the hole, huh?" I snort. "I see how that could be a problem."

"No doubt," Lilly says drily.

"What'd his place look like?"

"Oh, it was super-neat and very well organized," she explains, "but it's Man Cave all the way. Huge television, three or four game consoles, fridge full of beer and Gatorade."

"So?"

"So we go in and he tells me that I should sleep with him, which was exactly what I was thinking, so we go back to his bedroom and he takes off all of his clothes—"

"All of 'em?" I say between bites.

"All of 'em." She smiles and nods her head. "Every stitch."

"How was that?"

"That was amazing. He has some tattoos." She smiles and looks out the window. "He's the most beautiful thing I've ever laid eyes on."

"And?"

"And he fell on the bed face-first and started snoring!"

"What?" I ask, laughing.

"I couldn't wake him up. Trust me, I tried."

"That is hilarious!"

"Yeah, for you maybe," Lilly says with a smirk. "It was embarrassing as hell for me!"

"What'd you do?"

"I left. What was I supposed to do? Snuggle up to him and rub his back?"

"How did he get his truck? It wasn't in my driveway when I woke up."

"He said J.J. took him to get it early that next morning."

"When did he say that?"

"Monday night when he came to my house."

"How'd you get him over to your house?" I ask. "Did you put some banana ice cream out in your front yard under a box with a stick and string?"

"He did mow *down* on that banana ice cream, didn't he?" she says, laughing.

"Yeah, and he offered you some and you had to eat it because you lied and told him you loved it! That was great to watch."

"Won't do that again," she says and laughs. "Okay, here's how it went down. I ran into him at Pier Six Monday night," she says, smiling like the cat that swallowed the canary. "He was getting takeout and I was getting takeout so I suggested he take his takeout to my house." She leans her head back and smiles.

"Okay, that's clear as mud," I say, but she ignores me.

"So he did." She looks out the window. "He was so embarrassed about falling asleep, and he apologized about a hundred times. I kept telling him it was no big deal and he finally shut up about it. By that time, we'd finished eating so we had some drinks, talked about stupid stuff, and then it was *on*. Oh, my goodness, was it ever on."

"Did you feel awkward because you'd already seen his goods?"

"Not even a little bit!" she exclaims. "And if he felt awkward about anything at all, I couldn't tell. Anyway, I told him our situation and he had a few ideas." She pauses. "Actually, he's the one who dug up that info on all those skanky hos." She nods toward the list on the dash. "He's real smart with computers and electronics and junk like that."

"Did you discuss our stalking plans with an officer of the law before or after you had sex with him?"

"Uh. In between." She starts sniggering. "Oh, God, Ace, I think I'm in love."

"That good, huh?" I ask, trying to conceal my astonishment at this revelation. "Made you fall in love? Just like that?"

"It wasn't just the sex, although I have to say it was *above* and *beyond* anything I have *ever* experienced in my whole entire life. And I *like* him and I like hanging out with him. He's funny and sweet and he's so smart." She turns to me. "He is such a dreamboat. In every sense of the word."

"A dreamboat, huh?" I say, giggling to myself. I look at her and she is staring out the window with her elbow on the console, and her cheeseburger is dripping ketchup onto the gear shift. "Hey, lover girl, get your damn cheeseburger under control!"

"Oh, my word!" She snaps out of her daze and starts wiping down the console. "I am so sorry."

"Let me get this straight," I say with no small trace of skepticism. "You've spent the week getting freak nasty with a law enforcement officer and today you are going to stick a GPS dot on Richard Stacks's car in his office parking lot in broad daylight?"

"Abso-freakin'-lootley," she says. "Just pull into that little strip mall with Merle Norman in it and I'm gonna waltz over there and stick it under his bumper."

"Whatever you say." I pause. "I guess your new association does significantly lower our chances of getting arrested for this."

"Uh, yeah! This whole GPS thing was his idea," she says as I turn in to the parking lot. "Pull into the last space in front of the cell phone store. I'm gonna go around behind this building," she says, pointing, "because his car is backed in over there by those trees, so all I have to do is sneak up into that thicket and pop! It's on there."

"Okay, that's not nearly as dangerous as you made it sound," I say, looking over at her strappy silver high-heeled sandals. "You wearing those?"

"Of course I am. You know I walk better in heels than I do in tennis shoes," she says, "and I cased the place earlier so I kinda knew it wouldn't be that hard to do."

"Small-time criminal," I say, nodding in approval. "Fah sho."

"Fah sho," she says and gets out of the car.

I watch as she trots past the end of the building, then dips into the thicket separating the rear parking lot of the accounting firm from the back side of the strip mall.

Two seconds after she disappears into the brush, Richard Stacks the Fourth walks out the back door of his office and makes a beeline for his car. I think for a second about jumping out and chasing Lilly into the shrubbery, but he would be able to see my every move. I pick up my cell phone to call her, but hesitate because she never puts her phone on vibrate and Richard would hear it and we'd be busted for sure then.

Just as he reaches the front of his car, Lilly pops back out of the bushes and gives me a big thumbs-up. I start waving frantically with one hand and pointing with the other. She whirls around, sees him, and jumps back into the trees just as he glances down to where she was standing. Only after the white Lexus is well out of sight does she creep out of the brush.

She smiles triumphantly and starts taking long confident strides back toward the car, then stops short, looks to her left, and freezes. I follow her line of vision and my eyes come to rest on a petite silver-haired lady holding a giant ladybug purse.

I know that little old lady. Everyone in Bugtussle knows that little old lady.

It's Gloria Peacock.

◇◇

24

Gloria Peacock is a spunky senior citizen rumored to be one of the richest women in the South. Word is she knows everything about everybody in town and has known everything about everybody in town for the past fifty years. Maybe longer.

I look at Lilly, then at Gloria Peacock and take a deep breath.

They both just stand there like pistol-totin' cowboys at a shoot-out.

Lilly looks at her, then back at me, and Gloria Peacock looks at me, then at her. I'm looking back and forth between them, wondering how long Mrs. Gloria Peacock has been standing there with her big ol' ladybug purse.

Nobody moves.

All of a sudden, Lilly gets this look on her face like she just remembered where she was and starts walking toward Gloria Peacock, who steps into the shade as she approaches.

They have a brief exchange that ends with Lilly and Gloria Peacock both tossing their heads back and laughing like they just heard the best joke ever. Then Mrs. Peacock waves one of her frail, diamond-laden hands at me and smiles the biggest, most genuine smile I have ever seen.

Lilly comes and gets in the car.

"What was that?" I ask. "What was so funny?"

"Well, Mrs. Gloria Peacock saw the whole thing." Lilly glances back at the elderly lady, who has just gone inside Merle Norman. "She was very candid and told me that she knows everything that's been going on for the past week and would really like to sit down and speak with us."

"Sit down and speak with us? So are we, like, in trouble with her?"

"Oh, no," Lilly says and laughs, "not by a long shot!" She looks at me. "She says she has just what we need to get what we want."

"How does she know what we need and what we want?"

"I asked her the same thing, and do you know what she said?"

"How would I know that?"

"She said, and I quote, 'Sweetheart, I'm Gloria Peacock, and when I tell you that I have what you need, you don't ask questions; you just show up and say thanks.' "

"Wow," I whisper. "This is shaping up to be the weirdest Friday the thirteenth of my life."

"No doubt. She's expecting us at her house tomorrow at two p.m."

"Oh! You are lying!" I say, getting really excited. "You are freakin' lying to me! We have a date with Gloria Peacock at the Waverly Estate? No shit?"

"No shit!" Lilly says with no small amount of excitement. "I can't wait!"

"Me either! What are we going to wear?"

"Sundresses," Lilly says definitively. "Sundresses and heels."

"I am not wearing heels," I retort, "but I will wear some nice sandals."

"Then you should wear a strapless dress," she says and swings her hair around like she's posing for a photo shoot. "I'll wear heels."

"That sounds good." I take a deep breath. "Maybe this is a good sign. Maybe this means that this whole damned mess is going to work out somehow and everything is going to be okay." I nod my head. "I think it's a good sign."

Lilly agrees. "Well, when the richest woman in six states joins your team, it's hard to imagine you're gonna lose!" She looks at me and smiles. "Now, let's go stalk some whores!"

"Hell, yeah!"

She grabs her little netbook out of her gigantic hobo bag and flips it open.

"Okay," she mumbles as she pecks at the keyboard, "it appears that Dick Richard is heading toward Tupelo."

"Well, let's go," I say and we're off.

We spend the afternoon following Richard Stacks all over Tupelo and, all in all, it was a pretty dull afternoon. After stopping by three different businesses and two banks, he went to the mall, where he emerged with bags from Ann Taylor Loft and Barnes & Noble.

"Books and clothes," I say flatly. "Wonder who those are for?"

"The new John Grisham book came out this week," Lilly says, clearly as bummed as me, "and you know Chloe has the entire collection in hardcover."

"Great," I say, and we follow him to a liquor store and then to a flower shop from which he emerges with an armload of yellow roses.

"Yellow roses," I say. "What does that remind you of, Lilly?"

"Gee, let me think." Lilly pretends to mull it over. "Oh, wait, I know! It seems like we might have toted three apiece down a wedding aisle one time."

"Yes, and if my memory serves me right, we later stood behind a dear friend of ours and watched as she tossed a bouquet of those things over her shoulder and straight into a chocolate fountain." I look at Lilly. "If that wasn't a sign, I've never seen one."

"Do you think he could possibly be going to meet some whore tonight?" Lilly asks, but I can tell by her tone she knows that's not the case.

"Anne Taylor clothes, books, yellow roses, and a liquor store bag that most certainly contains a bottle of that really expensive wine she likes," I say and shake my head. "You know he's going home."

We watch in total disappointment as the black dot inches across Highway 78, veers off to the left, and then stops. The address pops up as 309 Parker Drive. Home of Richard and Chloe Stacks.

"Shit," Lilly says as she closes the computer. "What do you wanna do now?"

"Let's go see a movie," I say. "What time is it?"

"Three o'clock," Lilly answers, "just in time to catch an early show."

◇◇

25

When we leave the movie theater, the black dot hasn't moved.

"What the hell is she doing?" I ask Lilly. "Why does she stay with him? I mean, what's it gonna take? What is it going to take to get her away from that creep?"

"She's gonna have to make up her own mind about this, Ace," Lilly says, "simple as that."

"That's why we've got to have more than one picture," I say and tap on the steering wheel to emphasize my point, "to help her make up her mind."

"Honestly, Ace," Lilly says quietly, "I don't know if a hundred pictures just like that would make any difference to her because, in her mind, she's doing the right thing by staying true to her vows."

"She's been telling us that for the past five years, has she not?" I ask. "I mean, surely there is a clause somewhere in the Bible that allows a woman to protect herself from a lying, low-down, sack-of-monkey-shit, cheating, emotional-turned-physical abuser!"

"You know," Lilly says, "I ask myself over and over how someone as classy and beautiful and smart as Chloe got herself into such a fucked-up situation. Pardon my French, Ace, but this is so fucked up."

"That's exactly what it is!" I can feel my face getting red. "Why is she staying with him? A thousand pictures proving infidelity can't be as hurtful as getting slapped around like a rag doll! I'm sorry, but how is that not reason enough?" I look at Lilly and she's looking out the window, shaking her head. "Why is she not at my house or at your house right now? Why did we spend the afternoon following that bastard when we should've been at her house making her pack her shit and leave?"

"We can't do that," Lilly says quietly, "and you know it."

"This is so fucking frustrating!" I yell. "And what was up with all those pills she took? Was she trying to kill herself, or did Richard force them down her throat so she wouldn't be able to tell anyone what really happened? What about that?"

"I'm willing to bet she didn't do that to herself."

"Yeah, but when we were in college, would you have been willing to bet *then* that we'd be having this conversation *now*?"

"Not in a million years."

"Exactly." I pause. "I wanted to ask her about that the day we were at her house, but I couldn't do it. I told myself I didn't ask because I didn't want to upset her, but I think I was just scared of what she might say."

"I couldn't do it, either, Ace. I thought about it, too, and I couldn't," Lilly says, wiping her eyes.

"Maybe it was just an accident," I say. "I mean, Chloe wouldn't know an antidepressant from an aspirin and she had to be really upset that night."

"Yeah, you're right," Lilly agrees. "It had to be an accident."

"Had to be," I say and pause. "Lilly, this is all my fault."

"Don't start with that crap again, Ace!"

"Tell me how she would've met Richard Stacks if I hadn't called and told her about that counseling job that opened up right before school started." I pause and Lilly doesn't say anything. "Well, let me tell you then. She wouldn't have met him because she wouldn't have been here. She would've stayed in Jackson with her family and found a great job at one of those Catholic schools like she went to and she would've met and married a nice man."

"You can't think like that."

"Yeah, why can't I? Everyone always says, 'Oh, you can't think like that,' but do you know what I think? I think not thinking like that is just a cop-out for people who don't want to take responsibility for the hurt and pain they cause others!"

"You couldn't have known this would happen," Lilly says. "We didn't like him. We didn't think he was a good choice for her. We sat her down and told her that and she married him anyway. There is nothing else we could've done so stop talking that crazy shit."

"It's not crazy! I caused her to come up here, and it's my fault she's where she is right now because if I hadn't called her, she would've never met him. End of story! Whether I meant for it to happen or not is irrelevant."

"Fine, Ace," Lilly says harshly. "Take all the blame if it makes you feel better, but don't expect me to run around blaming myself for other people's personal choices. We have no control over that, and the only thing that matters right now is what we *do* have control over. That's my only concern."

"Okay, so what are we going to do now?"

"I don't fucking know."

We ride in silence for a few miles.

"Are you going to Ethan Allen's tonight?" Lilly asks.

"No," I say, "I'm just not in the mood for that scene. I don't know how I feel about being around Mason again."

"What?" Lilly wails. "You can sit over there and *say* whatever you want, but it's painfully obvious that you're still attracted to him. I was there today, remember? I saw the way you looked at him."

"What do you want me to say, Lilly?" I look at her. "Do you want me to just lay it all out for you so you can finally understand?"

"Yes, please do. I'm so tired of walking on eggshells around you every time this comes up. I would love nothing more than to finally understand why you refuse to give the man of your dreams a chance to love you."

"I gave him a chance last summer!"

"No, you didn't! You didn't even quit your job, and then you broke up with him because some stupid girl showed up at his house and you were always complaining that he was a—" She shakes her head and shrugs her shoulders. "What did you call it?"

"A gawker," I reply.

"Yes, a gawker! What a great descriptive adjective that is. It was starting to bug you because he noticed that there were other women on the planet besides you so you took the opportunity to bail on him when that girl showed up and he didn't get rid of her as fast as you thought he should have." She looks at me. "You would never have to worry about a *thing* if you married Mason and you should know that! Why can't you get it through that thick skull of yours that if he was interested in all those chicken-headed bitches, he wouldn't be trying so hard to be with you!"

"Chicken-headed bitches?" I say, chuckling.

"Yeah, sure, why not?" She looks at me and smiles. "Ace, I swear I'm not trying to be harsh or mean or judgmental here, but I just don't understand why you did that. Now he's back and you have the chance to—"

"No, you don't understand, Lilly!" I cut her off. "You have no idea how it feels to be a chubby girl on the beach with a man that looks like Mason! You don't understand that at all. And you don't understand how it feels to be at a bar and have every hot skinny chick in there staring him down like they want to *eat* his ass up with a fork and a spoon. And you don't know how it feels to stand by and watch these girls shake their fake tits and bat their false eyelashes, then look at me like, 'How *dare* you be with him!'"

"So what? He can't help it women act that way around him!"

"Yes, but when he takes the time to check them out from head to toe, then smile back, it makes me look like the biggest fool on earth. Like all I have to do is turn my head and—"

"You can't say you weren't happy when you were with him." She looks at me. "I've never seen you so happy."

"Of course I was happy!" I say. "I had the time of my life those first few weeks, but then we started going out more and it just got—"

"He's a nice, normal guy with a good personality," Lilly cuts in. "It doesn't mean he's going to cheat on you just because he smiles at someone with two legs and a cooch! That's ridiculous!"

"It's ridiculous to you because, like I said, you don't know what it's like. I just stand there beside him while he surveys the crowd, smiling and nodding, and watch people think, 'What is *he* doing with *her*?' Tell me one time you've ever felt that way and I'll shut up and go to Ethan Allen's tonight." I look at her. "Just one time. Tell me about it."

"Okay, never! But how in holy hell do you *watch* someone think?"

"Don't give me that shit!" I shoot back. "You know what I'm talking about!"

"Ace, you act like you look like a damn beached whale," Lilly says.

"Why do you do this to yourself? You have those sexy amazing legs that you used to show off with short skirts and shiny high heels. You have those big juicy boobs that show themselves off no matter what kind of top you wear. And all of this"—she reaches over and tousles my hair—"this dark, naturally curly *silk* on your head. You are *such* an attractive woman, but you couldn't allow yourself that because you wouldn't peel your focus off a pack of hussies you caught staring at your boyfriend. And who cares what the girl who came to the door looked like? Can't you see that you dumped *him* for how *she* made you feel! And now you walk around in flip-flops all the time feeling sorry for yourself. I don't get it."

"Lilly," I say, shaking my head, "you can't help it God blessed you with the body of a Greek goddess, and you will never know how it feels to be short and chubby, okay?" She starts to speak, but I hold up my hand. "Let me clarify one thing before you say whatever it is you're about to say." She nods and I continue, "I do not feel sorry for myself because I'm chunky. I love to eat pizza and drink beer and that means I'm always gonna have a muffin top spilling over the top of my britches, and that's okay with me. That's who I am. I know I don't look *that* bad, but I don't look good enough to stare down women who eat nothing but tofu, beets, and Bermuda grass and spend ten hours a day at the gym." I take a deep breath. "And even if I did, the gawking would still bother me and I'm sorry you don't understand how or why I can't get past that."

"So there's no way I could talk you into going to Ethan Allen's with me tonight?" she asks. "It's always so much fun when Mason comes home and you've been avoiding him for months. If you don't want to give y'all a chance, fine, but you should at least let him be your friend again."

"Lilly," I say and sigh, "I might sometime, but not tonight."

"Why did you let him in your house today?"

"He knocked and I thought it was you, so I just hollered and told him to come in."

"So he snuck up on you?"

"I guess," I say, laughing.

"Didn't have time to jump up and lock the doors and go hide in the bedroom?"

"No, I didn't. I just turned around and there he was."

"Seeing him made your day, didn't it?"

"No," I lied.

"Yes, it did, and that's why you stay away from him because you know you can't resist him when you're looking at him face-to-face."

"Lilly, you're getting a little carried away."

"Come to Ethan Allen's tonight."

"No."

"Please."

"Sorry, but the answer is no."

"Okay, whatever. I'm not staying out long anyway."

"Really?" I say, raising my eyebrows. "Do you have a *date* tonight?"

"He gets off at eleven," she says and smiles.

"So has he put the handcuffs on you yet?"

"I was wondering how long it would take for you to ask me that!"

"Well," I say. "Has he?"

"Uh, I can't comment on that because he told me anything I said could be used against me in a court of law."

"Oh, holy crab balls!" I say, laughing. I turn into my driveway and she starts stuffing all of her junk, Red Rooster trash and all, into her luggage-sized purse.

"Well, I guess I'll see you tomorrow," I say. "Hey, let's go in your car. They might not let us in the gate in this dirty ol' thing."

She laughs and says, "No problem. Pussy Wagon it is! I'll be here around one thirty and, in case you didn't know, I'm excited!"

"Me too!" I say and wonder what Gloria Peacock could possibly have that we need.

Maybe it's a million dollars.

◇◇

26

I put my cutoff sweatpants and AC/DC shirt back on, plop down onto the sofa, and feel a damp lump under my ass.

Lima beans.

Great.

"Buster Loo!" I call, taking the bag of beans to the garbage. "Wanna go outside?" He runs through the kitchen and torpedoes out the doggie door. We play speedy-dog fetch until he gets distracted by a squirrel and takes off doing a million chiweenie miles per hour. I go back inside, fill up his food and water bowls, and head for the shower.

When I get out, I walk in my closet and take the gold high heels off the top shelf. I go to the dresser and dig out a black lace bra and matching panties, then go back to the closet and flip hangers until I find what I'm looking for.

My super-frilly hot pink miniskirt. It was one of Mason's favorites.

I drop my towel, put on my undies, and take the skirt off the hanger. The wide elastic band stretches to the max under the strain, but I finally manage to get it over my hips. I pull on a black tee, slip on the gold shoes, and step out of the closet.

Standing in front of the mirror, I curse the cheeseburger I had for lunch.

I peel off the skirt, kick off the shoes, and put the ratty clothes back on. I mope into the living room, where I sprawl on the sofa and try not to think about how happy every female at Ethan Allen's will be to see Mason McKenzie walk into the bar.

After ordering an extra-large pizza with extra cheese, I flip through the DVR in search of something funny to watch because, yet again, I desperately need to be cheered up.

As I scan the seemingly endless selection of all the crap I've been recording, my mind spins off a million what-if fantasies, and after ten minutes I snap back to reality and remind myself that I am too old to be so pathetic.

The doorbell rings and I jump up and run to the kitchen door, but no one is there, so I run to the front door, only to be greeted by the smiling face of a nice young fellow in my third-period art class who is, of course, wearing a Pier Six Pizza T-shirt and matching visor.

"Hello, Ms. Jones," he says politely, and I get the feeling he is trying very hard not to stare at my shorts. "How you doin' tonight?"

"Oh, I'm great, Davis," I say. "Hold on a second." I run to the kitchen, grab a twenty, run back to the door, and give him the money. He starts digging in his pocket for change and I tell him to keep it for a tip.

"But, Ms. Jones," he protests, "the pizza was only twelve ninety-five."

"Yeah, Davis," I say, smiling, "that's for not telling everyone at school about these atrocious cutoff sweatpants."

"Can I tell 'em about your AC/DC shirt?" he asks. "'Cause that rocks!"

"Sure," I tell him, taking the pizza box and stepping back into the house. "Just make me sound way cooler than I am."

He pockets the money and smiles. "No problem, Ms. Jones. Thank you and have a good night."

As he walks off the porch, I suffer a wave of disappointment that my evening caller was not Mason McKenzie. Then I suffer a wave of being pissed off at myself for being disappointed and remind myself, yet again, that I am not and cannot be so pathetic.

So what if he said he wants to marry me?

Who cares?

I'm not falling for that one again.

I eat half the pizza, drink three beers, and fall asleep on the couch with Buster Loo in the bend of my knees. I get up at three a.m., put the leftovers in the fridge, and stumble back to my bedroom. My cell phone is lying facedown on my nightstand and I tell myself not to pick it up, but I reach right over and pick it up. When I do, I see that I have seven missed calls from J. Mason McKenzie. All received after midnight.

"I am too old for two a.m. booty calls, Buster Loo," I say to my little dog as he nestles into the covers. "Too freakin' old."

27

On Saturday I change dresses and shoes and hairdos and earrings and bracelets and necklaces and scarves about forty times each. It's a rare occasion when I worry about what someone might think of how I look, but this is Gloria Peacock we're going to see today.

The most stressful part of getting ready is finding something to wear that doesn't piss me off because it makes me look like a balloon-butt old biddy getting dressed to go to Mardi Gras or an overdone reject from a *Men in Black* casting call.

After I pile enough clothes on the floor to put a Lane Bryant store out of business, I go to the closet and dig out a dress that I snagged off a sale rack last year and haven't even tried on yet. It's a high-waisted white sundress that has a turquoise sash with a big fluffy flower sewn onto the left side. I put it on and, much to my surprise, it looks pretty decent. After checking all the angles, I decide to call it my magic dress because it covers everything that needs to be covered in the area of jelly rolls, cleavage, and thighs, and has the added bonus of matching a pair of fabulous sandals I bought on clearance last year. Problem solved.

Having beaten my hair to death with a hundred different styling attempts, I have no choice but to roll it up in a bun, but at least I have a nice white ribbon to tie around it. I twirl around like a schoolgirl in front of the mirror and smile at myself because I like what I see. And that almost never happens.

The doorbell rings and I strut down the hallway and into the living room, only to find Mason McKenzie standing in my kitchen looking like a hot mess on a humid day.

"You look great, Ace," he says, giving me a shy smile.

"Where'd you get the weed eater?" I ask snidely.

"What?" he asks, squinting at me like I'm talking way too loud. "Weed eater?"

"Yeah," I say, "the one you fixed your hair with."

"Oh, that's really funny," he says without laughing. "Where you headed?"

"To *the* Waverly Estate," I answer, thinking that will really impress him.

It doesn't.

"Oh," he says, "Mrs. Peacock and my grandmother are really good friends. Nice place." He pauses. "Why are you going out there, if you don't mind my asking?"

"Because Gloria Peacock invited me," I say with no small amount of pride, "and Lilly."

"Well, how nice," he says flatly. "Where were you last night?"

"What are you," I ask sarcastically, "my parole officer?"

"Why do you have to be so mean?"

"Why do you think you can keep showing up at my house unannounced and uninvited?"

"You are impossible," he says as he turns to leave. "You said you would be there. That's why I asked."

"Lilly said she would be there if I remember correctly."

"So we're back to this already?" he says as he pushes open the door.

"Back to what?" I fire back.

"Not speaking." He slams the door shut and Buster Loo rocket launches himself out the doggie door. I can hear him outside barking his fool head off.

I run back to the bathroom and start fanning myself so the tears won't run down my face and ruin my makeup. I look out the window and see Mason petting Buster Loo and scold myself out of the mood to cry.

I watch in complete agony as he puts down the little dog and disappears around the corner of the house. Buster Loo starts running speedy-dog crazy eights, stopping at every turn to throw his little chiweenie body against the fence, and my heart breaks for my poor daddyless dog.

Time slows to a snail's pace and I sit on the edge of the tub fanning myself like Scarlett O'Hara. After what seems like hours I hear a horn blow, so I do a quick mirror check and run out the front door, where Lilly is smiling and waving. I stuff my heartache back in that place I've kept it for the past nine months and I'm all smiles as I climb into her red BMW.

"Damn," she says, "we look good!"

"I concur," I say smartly. "Love that dress!" I lean over to get a look at her shoes. "Oh, good word, those are beyond fabulous." And probably cost more than that set of tires I put on my car last week.

"Thanks!" She beams at me. "Ready?"

"Am I?!" I exclaim. "Am I?! You bet your sparkly little purse I am!"

I ask her how it went with Dax and she talks about him all the way to the gates of the Waverly Estate, and that's fine with me because I am *more* than in the mood to sit with my mouth shut and listen to her ramble about her handsome young lover.

◇◇◇

28

The iron gates of the Waverly Estate look like they were hand-crafted by Michelangelo himself. We sit in the shade of this gigantic work of art and wait for the gate guard, sleek and sporty in starched white shorts and a blue polo, to make his way from the guardhouse to the car. He asks to see our identification, scribbles something on his clipboard, pushes a button on a device attached to his belt, and the glorious gates begin to move.

"Welcome to Waverly, my pretty ladies," he says with a deep Southern drawl. "Miss Lane, you can park right over there in any of those spots and a gentleman will pick y'all up and take you around to the pool where Mrs. Peacock is waitin'."

"Thank you so much, sir," Lilly says. "Have a nice day, sir." She rolls up her window and looks at me in a panic. "Are we supposed to tip these people?"

"Oh, my word, Lilly, you are such a dope! We are at a private residence, not the freakin' Peabody Hotel!"

"Well, you're supposed to tip anyone who provides you with a service." For all her many travels as a lingerie model, she obviously carried only her passport. I guess beautiful women don't get much experience tipping because they're always on the arm of a benevolent man.

"Well, give him twenty bucks if it'll make you feel better."

"Twenty dollars," she yells. "Are you crazy?"

"No," I say quietly, "but you could stop acting like you are." I look at her and smile. "Now shut up and let's at least *pretend* like we have sense enough to be here."

We get out of the car just in time to see a shiny blue golf cart pull up to the curb. Instead of straps to secure clubs, it has a seat on the back emblazoned with a majestic blue peacock in all its feathered glory. The driver appears to be a clone of the gate man, and I start having visions of Mr. Deeds in that mansion with that sneaky butler fellow.

"Ladies," the gentleman says with a friendly smile, "it would please me greatly to give y'all a ride."

"We'd love that," I say and try to smile big enough for the two of us because Lilly has lapsed into some kind of idiotic stupor and is looking around at all the trees and flowers with her mouth half open, and I worry for a second that she might start to slobber.

I elbow her and nod to the cart and she walks over and gets in, the whole time looking like a stupid-ass robot with long tan legs and expensive heels. When the gate-clone-staff man hits the gas, I lean over and whisper, "Hey, globe-trotter, what the hell is wrong with you? You're acting like you've never seen an azalea in bloom."

"There's just something about this place," she says dreamily. "I can't explain it." She looks at me, wide-eyed. "Don't you feel it? It's like an aura or something."

"Have you been smokin' weed?" I ask, and I'm not joking.

"No." She looks at me like I'm the moron. "This place is absolutely magical!"

"You are a freakin' fruit loop," I whisper, but she isn't listening.

"Look, there's a peacock!" she squeals. "A real live peacock!"

I roll my eyes and she continues to babble about the peacocks and the magic.

After a winding tour through what could easily pass for a privatized Garden of Eden, we roll to a stop next to a clover-shaped pool fit for a Hawaiian beach resort. Lilly is still thoroughly intoxicated with the loveliness of the Waverly Estate and has counted seven real live peacocks roaming the grounds. I bite my lip and tell myself now is not the time to call her a dipshit. Besides, she could just be giddy because she's falling in love for the first time in a long time.

Lilly slides off the backseat of the shiny blue golf cart, then walks over and hugs Gloria Peacock like the petite little lady just saved her from being eaten by piranhas. Gloria Peacock hugs her back and smiles that thousand-watt smile, and I wonder for a brief second if her teeth are real or if they're dentures. Very expensive dentures.

"We haven't officially met," she says, offering a hand laden with jewels more valuable than my house. And probably my life. "Gloria Peacock."

"Graciela Jones," I say, shaking her hand and trying not to stare at her rings, "but everyone calls me Ace."

"And why is that?" she asks quickly, and I'm caught off guard by her question so I stand there like a moron.

"Because she used to be so great at sports," Lilly gushes. "Ever since she was a little girl, she could play any sport she wanted and never even needed to be coached. She was what you might call a natural athlete. We went to basketball camp together when we were twelve and I just couldn't believe how good she was. I wasn't that good, because—"

"It's a nickname my dad gave me," I say in an effort to cut her off, but she doesn't even slow down. My face is burning from embarrassment, and it only gets worse when she rambles from my "has-been" prodigy status straight into how the Waverly Estate is more magical than Disneyland. We are standing directly in the hot afternoon sun, and I think I might pass out from the painful combination of heat and humiliation.

Gloria Peacock is kind enough to notice that I'm having a near death experience, so when Lilly stops to catch her breath, she invites us both to sit down. She waves her bejeweled hand toward a shaded little hut adorned with four oscillating fans.

Thank you, Jesus.

A female version of the gate-keeping-golf-cart-driving-staff-fellow glides into the hut and places a glass pitcher of sweet tea in the center table. She disappears, but returns in a flash with a bowl of lemon wedges and some tiny silver tongs. Another staff person appears and presents large clear glasses filled with square chunks of ice and some kind of weird plates that look like they're made out of bamboo. Yet another presents us with a platter loaded with tea cakes, candied pecans, cheese straws, chocolate-dipped strawberries, and four more sets of those adorable little tongs.

I look at Gloria Peacock and smile.

I am starting to see the magic.

And I want a pair of those little tongs.

"Help yourself," she says, smiling that big smile of hers, and I realize that I don't give a rat's ass if she's smiling at me with real teeth or elephant tusk dentures. I load my plate up like the black sheep cousin at a white-trash family reunion. Lilly, however, gracefully places just enough food on her plate to feed a small bird. A very small bird.

When we finish the sweet tea, snacks, and polite chitchat, Gloria

Peacock stands up and says, "Okay, girls, it's time to get down to business. Follow me, please."

We follow her around the pool and through a set of French doors flanked on both sides by what looks like fifty more French doors. Or windows. I can't tell. We step into a sunroom that looks like a Pottery Barn ad and from there into a marble-floored hallway capped with domed ceilings painted up like a cathedral. We follow her around a table topped with a flower arrangement the size of Rhode Island, down another glitzy hallway, and into a room that looks like a scene from *Mission Impossible*.

◇◇◇

29

"**W**elcome to my media room," Gloria Peacock says proudly. "Make yourselves comfortable." She motions toward a gigantic sectional facing an electronic arrangement as impressive as it is intimidating. The brown leather sofa is soft and smooth, and it makes me feel like I'm floating on a cowhide cloud. Lilly perches on the edge of a cushion and has this look on her face like she's not sure where she is or how she got here. I can't believe she's been acting like such a fool all day and apparently has no immediate plans to stop.

Meanwhile, Gloria Peacock is standing in the center of the room facing her electronic empire and appears to be conducting an invisible orchestra. She's waving and pointing, and I'm starting to wonder if she might be a little off her rocker, when all of a sudden the wall comes to life and I'm looking at a picture of me and Lilly talking to Deputy Dax Dorsett outside the gym the night we broke into Catherine Hilliard's office.

"Where did that come from?" I ask, stunned and secretly embarrassed for thinking she might be senile. Lilly's mouth is hanging open again, and I'm not sure if she's shocked to see our sweaty faces splayed across Gloria Peacock's larger-than-life magic computer monitor or if she's lusting after Deputy Dax, whose biceps look damn sexy on that big screen.

"Omega Security Systems," Gloria Peacock says, "my late husband's brainchild and my oldest son's life work."

She smiles and Lilly and I stare at the screen like a pair of teenage boys seeing boobs for the first time.

"My Will, General William Peacock, who I lost six years ago this September, spent twenty-two years in the army before he retired and went to work for the FBI." She pauses and seems to be lost in thought, but only for second. "Surveillance was his specialty, and this"—she waves a hand around the room—"is today's version of the work he began back in the fifties."

"They had video surveillance in the fifties?" I ask, trying to shake off the stupor and, at the very least, appear to have a grain of sense.

"Indeed they did, and my William designed the specs that became the foundation of COINTELPRO." She looks at me and my expression must convey my ignorance because she continues, "COINTELPRO is a surveillance system that the government put into action in 1956, but had to quit using in '71 because a bunch of idiots broke into a field office in Pennsylvania and"—she shakes her head and sighs—"what followed was nothing short of mayhem. Blown completely out of proportion."

"Coin . . . tell . . . pro?" I ask, and now I'm wondering if Gloria Peacock might be a Russian spy or something. "What is that?"

"COINTELPRO is an acronym for Counter Intelligence Program." She points at the screen and another image pops up, and I'm looking at myself standing outside the emergency entrance to the hospital wearing only one flip-flop. Sheriff Jackson has his back to the camera and is looking at the concrete, as are Lilly and Ethan Allen, and Deputy Dorsett is in the process of getting out of his patrol car.

"Oh, my God," Lilly whispers. "What was that movie? With Will Smith and Gene Hackman—"

"So how do you . . ." I trail off as she brings up a shot of me and Logan Hatter in the parking lot of Ethan Allen's. My mouth is wide open and Logan has his arm around me and his eyes are closed. "That is amazing detail!" I exclaim. "This is unbelievable." I pause, shaking my head. "But how?"

"*Enemy of the State*," Lilly whispers, and I look at her and she has this weird look on her face, and I start thinking that maybe she and Deputy Dax have been getting freak nasty on top of his patrol car and that'll be the next picture we see up on the big screen.

"Mrs. Peacock," I say and muster up all my courage, "is this legal?"

"Perhaps not," she says like it's no big deal. "My son had the cameras installed at various locations around town as a gift to the city to help cut down on crime. It was one of his father's last wishes. I think it was Will's way of trying to maintain the role of protector even beyond the grave, and I'm proud to say that more than a few criminals have been convicted using video evidence from our system here. Will Jr. went on to give that gift to several little towns in the tristate area, but ours is the only one to which I pay attention."

"So who all has access to this information?" Lilly asks, with obvious apprehension.

"Me," she says smartly, "and each town's local authorities and the feds, but they have to be granted permission and issued log-in information before they can use it. They can't just hack into the system any time they'd like. Will was very specific about the setup of the controls."

"Do the police know you have access to the system?" I ask, using my best *of course I don't think you're a criminal* voice.

"Why should they?" she asks, smiling. "Does it hurt to have an old lady like me surfing the databases from time to time? I think not," she says decisively, "especially since all of their equipment was a gift from the Peacock family."

"So you just sit in here and play God?" I ask and immediately wish I hadn't because I'm heavy on the *I was wrong and you* are *a criminal* voice.

"God," Gloria Peacock says coolly, "is not a woman, and I have too much reverence for Him to assert myself in that way."

"So what do you call what you do here?" I ask, and Lilly scowls at me but keeps her mouth shut.

"I call it my goodwill ambassadorship to people less fortunate than I," she says and levels a look at me that makes me look at the floor.

"Well, I guess that would cover everybody in the southeastern United States," I mumble, "at least."

"Mrs. Peacock," Lilly begins with an apologetic tone, "please let me apolo—"

Gloria Peacock cuts her off midword. "Lilly, it's perfectly all right," she says quietly. "I appreciate an honest skeptic. Now, Ace"—she turns her eagle eyes and ivory smile back to me—"let me answer your question about what I do here."

She brings up a photo of Richard Stacks and a redheaded woman fondling each other next to a Dumpster.

"Jennifer Kramer," Lilly whispers and shakes her head. "She makes me sick!"

"Like most people," Gloria Peacock continues, "I know what goes on in and around this little town, and when I hear something skewed I do my research, then make a legitimate effort to help the people who deserve it. Some are aware of my intervention, others aren't. In all honesty, most people have no idea I play any role in the resolution of their issues. A certain degree of secrecy makes it easy to continue getting things done."

She pauses, points, and the magic screen produces another picture of Richard Stacks. In this one, he's parked next to what appears to be the same Dumpster and there is a blond head in his lap.

"That has got to be Brooke Valspar!" I whisper and Lilly nods. "Why does she bleach her hair out like that?"

"I don't know but it looks awful!" Lilly agrees.

"These are just a few examples of the research I've done on Chloe's husband, but we'll get to that later."

"Okay," I say, not sure how to proceed.

Lilly just sits there and shakes her head.

◇◇◇

30

"First of all," Gloria Peacock announces like she's speaking from a pulpit, "I know that Lilly was fired and I know the *real* reason why."

"What?" Lilly exclaims and jumps off the couch like her ass is on fire. She opens her mouth to speak but Gloria Peacock holds up her hand, and I notice a diamond tennis bracelet slide down her arm.

"Mr. Reece Hilliard and Dr. Ryland Lane are both dear friends of mine."

"How do you know?" Lilly hisses like a cat, and I try to figure out how Lilly's psychotic mood swing factors into this odd turn of conversation.

"I know all about Reece and your uncle Ryland, my sweet girl," Gloria says, and Lilly looks like she's about to pass out. "I've worked closely with those two fine gentlemen over the years and I have known all along what you and only a few others know now."

I cover my mouth and gasp.

"Holy shit, Lilly," I croak like a frog.

Lilly's face is beet red and her eyes are wild. "Why are you doing this?" she demands. "Do you just sit in here waving your arms around, collecting pictures of them as well? Do you know what would happen if people found out?"

I try to wrap my mind around the fact that Lilly's uncle, an accomplished and well-respected professor at the University of Mississippi, and Reece Hilliard, a prominent banker who has the misfortune of being married to one Catherine Hilliard, really are going stinger to stinger in the story of the bees and the bees. They *were* the two gentlemen in the pictures I found in Catherine Hilliard's desk. I wonder if perhaps I've been hearing Lilly wrong for the past five months and she's been saying "the Gentle*men*" all along instead of "the Gentle*man*," and I just didn't pick up on it. She's usually not that shrewd so I make a mental note to ask her about it later.

She looks like she's about to lose her mind so I dismount the cowhide cloud couch and put my hand on her arm, but she shrugs me off and continues to stare at Gloria Peacock like she might kill her.

"Lilly," I say, "you need to calm down."

"Calm down!" she screams. "I lost my job because of this, and Catherine Hilliard accused me of having sex with an eighteen-year-old kid to justify it! Do you know how humiliating that is?" She turns that crazy nutcase glare on me. "Even *you* doubted me, and you're my best friend! I ditched our trip to Panama City Beach, and I thought you'd never speak to me again. When Zac ran over from his grandma's pool so we could discuss why Catherine Hilliard was trying to frame us, here you come with some damned Chinese food and then you throw all of my shit out in the yard!" She has tears in her eyes. "I went through all of that to protect them because what they have is so special and so sweet and I thought nobody knew, but people know." She looks at Gloria Peacock and the tears start rolling, taking heaps of mascara down with them. "*You* know. So what was the damn point? Why did I have to wreck my whole life being part of a cover-up if people already know?"

"People don't know, Lilly," Gloria Peacock says softly. "Reece, Ryland, and I are part of an elite and *very* private circle of friends. We don't have to be told things."

"I know I'm about to call Uncle Rye right now and tell him he's full of shit!"

"Lilly, please sit down." Gloria Peacock takes a seat on the sectional and pats the cushion next to her. "Ace, could you please get her some water out of the cooler?"

"Uh, sure." I look around for a cooler and see nothing that resembles an Igloo or a fridge so I wander toward the wall and stand there like I'm expecting water to fall from the sky.

"Third cabinet door from the left," Gloria says, nodding. "Would you bring me one also?"

"Sure," I say and step over to a line of cabinets that look like they cost more than my car and count down to the third door. Sure enough, it's some kind of little refrigerator stocked with imported beer, bottled water, and plastic bags stuffed with cut vegetables and fruit. I lust after the beer for a second, then grab three bottles of water and return to the sofa because I can't wait to hear the rest of this story.

Lilly's face is in her hands and she is sobbing uncontrollably. Gloria Peacock is rubbing her back and telling her everything is going to be just fine because we are going to make things right, and I don't know about Lilly, but I believe her. I wouldn't be any more convinced of victory if I were eavesdropping on Pat Summit in the Tennessee locker room.

Gloria Peacock looks up at me, holds up two fingers, then points back at the cabinets. I place my water on the marble-top coffee table and go back to see what's behind door number two.

Behind that door I find all shapes and sizes of blue and white tow-els. I grab a small one, wet it in the sink, and take it to Lilly. She wraps it around her face and calms down to heaves and sniffles. I pick up my bottle of water and sit back down on the sofa.

"Okay, girls," Gloria Peacock begins, "back to the facts."

"Okay," Lilly and I say in unison, and I can't wait to hear the facts.

"My use of this surveillance equipment could be construed as un-ethical or even illegal, yes." She looks from me to Lilly, then back at me, and continues, "But so is speeding and I've never run over anyone with my little plastic mouse over there"—she pauses, smiling—"not literally anyway. And as far as ethics go, I can't see a single thing on that screen that anyone standing on any street corner in the city couldn't see at any given time."

No! I don't want to talk about surveillance ethics and legality! I want to hear about Reece Hilliard and Ryland Lane getting it on! Damn it! I take a sip of water and try to hide my disappointment.

"So you have constant access to what anyone walking down the street can see with their own two eyes?" Lilly asks, and she sounds like she has marshmallows stuffed up her nose.

"Basically," Gloria Peacock says. "I'm kind of like a high-tech Robin Hood, if you will, watching out for people." She pauses and does the Ping-Pong glance again. "And when I saw Lilly put that tracking mech-anism on Richard Stacks's lovely white Lexus, I knew that you were the kind of girls that I could help. So I came home and did some research."

Oh. Forgot she witnessed that little foray in small-time criminal activity.

"So how does this thing work?" I ask, nodding toward the super-computer system. "How did you get those pictures?"

"You've heard of auto-face recognition?" She looks at both of us and we nod yes, but I've never heard of it and I'm sure Lilly hasn't, either. I mean, if they don't print it in *Cosmo*, she doesn't know about it, and if it's not on basic cable, then I don't. Gloria Peacock obviously senses that we have no idea what she's talking about because she goes into a brief explanation.

"Well, the concept has been around for a while and, as you can imagine, it started getting more mainstream attention after 9/11. In 2009, the FBI used facial recognition software to track down a double-homicide fugitive from California who was living in North Carolina. They accessed the driver's license databases of both states, did some cross-referencing, then found and arrested the guy. Think about it. You can't even open a checking account anymore without a valid driver's license. Ever wonder why?"

"I've never thought about that, but now that you mention it . . ." Lilly muses and the light of understanding begins to shine in her eyes. "So this is kind of like auto-tagging on Facebook when some kind of program or something scans your pictures looking for your friends?"

"Exactly," Gloria Peacock says.

"So," I say, "you can just say a name and your system, which was set up by your son as a crime-fighting tool for the city, can bring up images of any person who has a Mississippi driver's license because it's linked up with the state's driver's license database?"

"Actually it's linked up to databases in several states," Gloria Peacock says. "Would you like to see a demonstration?"

"I would love that!" I say with a bit too much enthusiasm because my mind is spinning out of control with names I'd like to yell at that computer.

Gloria Peacock returns to the center of the room and starts conducting her invisible orchestra again. When she stops, she says, "Search Catherine Hilliard."

Lilly and I look at each other, then back at the screen, where about six million thumbnail shots pop up.

"Let's narrow it down," Gloria Peacock says with a smile, then clearly articulates, "Search file for Ardie Griffith."

"Why is she searching for the school superintendent in Mrs. Hilliard's file?" Lilly whispers, and before I can think up a response, a photo flashes up on the screen and we both gasp and start laughing like two idiots fresh from the nuthouse.

"Ladies," Gloria Peacock asks with a triumphant smile, "do you both understand that I have what it takes to set things right in this little town?" Gloria Peacock looks up at the image and indulges in a very dignified little giggle.

"Just remember," Gloria Peacock says and smiles her big ivory-toothed smile, "complete confidentiality."

31

When Lilly drops me off, I feel like Oscar the Grouch, and not because I'm grumpy or have a pet worm, but because compared to the majesty of the Waverly Estate, my humble abode looks like a garbage can.

I had suggested on the ride home that she track Richard Stacks from the comfort of her home and we would stalk him only if he left town, because if he did anything local Gloria Peacock had it covered.

I can't help but wonder how rich she really is. She said her husband was a general in the army, then retired to the FBI, so between his salary there, his army retirement, and that high-tech spy machine he invented, he must've made some serious dough. I bet she couldn't use my two-dollar calculator to balance her bank account because it probably doesn't have enough room for all the zeros.

Maybe I should start looking for an army man to marry. Lilly's brother is a master sergeant stationed at Fort Carson, Colorado, so I could call him up and ask if he wanted to marry me.

Who am I kidding?

I know for a fact that he's in a committed relationship with a snow board and collects ski bunnies like some folks collect unicorns. He wouldn't have any use for my chubby ass. He's an asshole anyway. A very beautiful asshole, but aren't they all?

I throw my lovely dress onto the mountain of clothes I left on the floor, then go dig through the dryer for a clean pair of cutoff sweat-pants and a tank top. I unpin my bun and slick my hair into a ponytail and throw myself onto my fluffy bed. I wiggle around and get really comfy, then realize that something is missing. I haven't seen Buster Loo since I got home and that's about two clicks past not normal at all.

I call him a few times, and when that doesn't work I go with my old reliable tricks, "Buster Loo wanna treat? Buster Loo wanna go for a walk?"

Silence.

"Buster Loo wanna go outside?"

No Buster Loo.

Feeling a mild sense of panic, I jump up and check the doggie door to make sure it's working right, then search the backyard, but Señor Buster Loo Bluefeather is nowhere to be seen. I open the fridge and rattle some stuff around, then go to the pantry and crinkle a potato chip bag and shake a can of peanuts. No luck. I grab his leash and sling it around for a minute, but still no Buster Loo.

In a full state of panic, I run out the front door holding my breath as I scan the street, then jog up and down the road checking the ditches. I'm relieved that I don't see a little brown carcass. I run back to the house and check my car, my gardening shed, and search the full perimeter of my property. Having exhausted all of my immediate re-sources and my nerves, I slump down in a patio chair and start to cry.

As luck would have it, just when I'm getting super snotty, I hear a vehicle pull up in the driveway. I run inside to blow my nose and throw water on my face, and just as I'm patting my eyes dry, Buster Loo bursts through the doggie door and starts running around like he's being chased by an invisible vacuum cleaner. I pick him up and hug him like crazy and start crying again, all the while telling him how much I love him and how scared I was that he was gone forever. I wipe my face again and, still clutching Buster Loo, go outside to thank whoever was kind enough to bring my little chiweenie back home.

When I step out the door, I see Mason McKenzie standing in my yard. I decide to wait and get the facts before sailor cussing him for abducting my dog.

He's all smiles as he walks toward the patio, but when he gets close enough to see my puffy eyes and red nose, he starts looking like he just ate some bad eggs.

"Ace," he begins, holding out one of his big beautiful hands, "I'm sorry. I just miss him so bad I borrowed him for a little while. I didn't mean to upset you."

"Have you ever heard of a note?" I demand. "Or a phone call? Maybe a text message or any form of communication that might let someone know their little dog is not gone forever?"

"Look, I'm sorry," he says earnestly. "I meant to have him back before you got home. I miss him. I miss you. I miss us. Ace, please."

"Go get your own dog!" I yell.

"He is my dog!" Mason yells back.

"Get the hell away from me," I say a little quieter. "Get the hell out of here. Get away from me and don't you ever, *ever* steal my dog again."

"He's our dog," he says quietly. "I bought him for us."

"Oh, my God! Are you serious?" I yell.

"Ace, I want you back. I never wanted you to leave. Please, can you just calm down and talk to me?"

"What the hell is wrong with you, Mason?" I ask in my super-smart-assed sarcastic voice. "It's over between us. It's been nearly a year now if you haven't noticed. I wasn't good enough for you, remember?"

"Could you try to calm down, please?"

"You stole my dog! You stole my fucking dog! I don't need this! Your sense of self-entitlement makes me sick!"

"What?" He looks at me like I'm speaking Hebrew. "Why can't you just settle down?" He looks at me and I stare back, saying nothing. "Just so you know, Ace, I don't buy into your little loudmouth badass routine! It doesn't scare me." He looks at me. "You're the one who's afraid."

"Of what? What in the hell are you talking about?"

"You're afraid to give being happy a chance. You're afraid to let yourself go. You're afraid to drop your world-famous Miss Don't-Take-No-Shit persona and trust someone! You're afraid to trust me. You're afraid of being hurt and left alone like you were when your parents died."

"I cannot believe you are standing there talking about my parents," I say, feeling the sting of tears. I bite my lip and will them away.

"Do you think this is what Jake and Isabella would've wanted for you?" he asks quietly. "Do you think your mom and dad would've wanted you to spend the rest of your life pushing people away because you're so scared someone will hurt you as bad as their leaving you did?" I look down and he continues, "I don't. I remember them as two people who would do anything to see their little girl smile. Remember that birthday party you had at the end of sixth grade? Your dad rented one of those gigantic water-slide things and took it to the lake? That was one of the most fun days of my life, and I remember you having a pretty good time, too. Didn't you?"

"Of course I did," I say. "Everybody did."

"Exactly," he says. "They wanted you to be happy then and they would've wanted you to be happy now. They would've wanted you to be in love, to have a family."

"My parents have nothing to do with this," I say and then start lying for real. "For your information, I'm very happy with my life right now."

"Right, right," he says quietly and nods his head, "of course. Well, I'm sorry for coming here and trying to wreck your happy home. I won't bother you anymore."

And with that he turns and walks out the gate. I want to run after him and tell him how much I've missed him and how much I love him and that I want to have little Mason babies with him. Instead, I just stand there and watch him go.

I hear my cell phone and know by the ring tone that it's Lilly. I'm as thankful for the distraction as I am that she didn't send me a stupid text instructing me to call her because that would've pushed me over the edge.

"Hey," I say, trying to sound normal. "You actually called me. This must be some kind of emergency. What's up?"

"Richard Stacks left home thirty minutes ago and he's on Highway 78 headed west."

"He's going to Memphis, isn't he?"

"Yep. And so are we."

"All right then. I'll be right there."

"Ready and waiting!" Lilly exclaims.

"Hey," I ask before she hangs up, "would you mind if Buster Loo comes along?"

◇◇◇

32

Before I back out of her driveway, I make it clear to Lilly that we will not be discussing Mason McKenzie unless she wants to start dishing details about her uncle Rye and Reece Hilliard. So we hate on Principal Catherine Hilliard for the better part of the hourlong ride to Memphis.

"I can't believe she called me a slut!" Lilly exclaims.

"Well, I started to disagree with her," I say, "but I thought about it for a minute and decided she might be right."

"You are such an idiot." She shakes her head.

"Seriously, Lilly, I'm gonna beat the brakes off that heifer before all this is over."

"We should follow her home one night and jump her in her driveway."

"Oh, that's a great idea!" I say. "Let's turn around and do it tonight!"

"We'll definitely put that on our to-do list," Lilly says, "but tonight we've got bigger fish to fry."

"I'd like to fry his ass for real," I say and glance over at Lilly. "You don't think we're wasting our time following him all the way to Memphis, do you?"

"Not if we hit up the Rum Boogie Café afterward," Lilly says.

"What a fantastic idea," I reply. "Do some stalking, then cut a little rug to some blues."

"Hell, yeah," Lilly says and we slap high five like first-class dorks.

"Where's that dot?"

"Appears to be stopped at the Ladies4Gentlemen Club," she says, studying her netbook. "You need to take the next exit and then it's about three blocks west."

"What a surprise," I mumble. "A titty bar."

"Well, at least you don't have to worry about this being a wasted trip."

When I pull into the parking lot of Ladies4Gentlemen, it only takes a second to spot Richard Stacks's shiny white Lexus because it's parked right next to the main entrance. I survey the area to make sure he's not standing in the shadows somewhere getting his fat little weenie waxed by some random lady-for-hire. I take control of the camera because I don't believe Lilly when she swears the flash is turned off this time for real. I get out and squat down behind his car so I can capture his personalized tag along with the neon sign above the entrance. I snap a few shots, then see a gaggle of men walking toward the door so I run back to the car.

Buster Loo, bristled up and growling, is manning his chiweenie lookout post in the back window.

"Buster Loo," I say when I get in the car, "do you smell a bad man?" He barks and snarls and I take that as an affirmative.

"Buster Loo, you have always been an excellent judge of character!" Lilly says, and then looks at me. "You wanna go in?"

"Hell, no! Are you crazy?" I say and turn to snap a picture of Buster Loo standing in the back window with his snout and his ass both facing forward. "Buster Loo, you look like an elbow noodle back there."

"You've never been in a strip club before, have you?" Lilly asks, like I'm some kind of sissy.

"No, and I don't plan on going anytime soon," I answer in my most puritanical tone.

"We could dress up," she says, "like in a disguise."

"With what?" I ask sarcastically. "We brought overnight clothes and a dog."

She taps the small screen of her net book and says, "There's a place that rents costumes just around the block."

"You want to go rent a costume in downtown Memphis at nine o'clock on a Saturday night?"

"Why not?" she says. "Then we could go inside and get some *real* pictures." I look straight ahead and can feel her staring at me. "Ace, think about it. What are we going to accomplish sitting out here in the parking lot snapping pictures of his car?"

"What if he leaves?"

"Well, we'll follow him," she says sarcastically. "Just like we followed him up here. Now, c'mon, let's go. According to this, the store is only a quarter mile from here."

"I don't know, Lilly."

"Ace, would you consider for one second how Chloe's mind works? Is a nice glossy picture of his car gonna do it? Hell, no! He can deny that all day long, but if we get a picture of him getting a lap dance, well, now that's a little harder to explain, don't you think?"

"We've got this picture of the car plus that picture of him wearing a dog collar."

"You know that's not enough!" she says.

"Is it worth risking our lives to try and rent a costume in this part of town?" I ask. "And what would we be? Ren and Stimpy? Maybe some Smurfs? You could be Smurfette and I could be Hefty—"

"What? Smurfs? Hell, no!" Lilly sighs with exasperation. "We could get wigs and stuff."

"Oh, my God, is there a drugstore close by where I can pick up some lice shampoo?" I quip as I pull out into the traffic.

"Oh, good word!" Lilly hollers. "You can sit in the car and I'll do this myself!"

"Nah," I say, like a fickle child picking out a toy, "I don't wanna sit in the car. I think I'll try to find a Batman costume."

"Oh, good word," Lilly says again. "I am going to choke you. Turn in right here."

"If you choke me, you don't get to be Robin," I say with a smirk as I pull into the parking lot of Downtown Diggs and Costume Rental. "Is this place even open?"

"Their Web site says they're open till ten p.m." She looks at me. "Now move your ass, please!"

"This place has a Web site?"

"Shut up and get out of the car!"

I get out of the car and do my best to ignore the whistles and caws wafting through the dark humid air. Lilly struts to the door like she's on a fashion runway and I scurry behind her like I'm on a runway, too. The runway of Memphis International Airport, that is, about to get run down by a FedEx plane.

"Act cool," Lilly whispers. "They can smell fear."

"They can smell this," I say and pat my satchel.

"Oh, my God, don't tell me you brought your damn gun," she whispers and pushes the door open.

"Hell, yeah. Got her right here," I whisper back, keeping my hand on the bulge in my bag. "Never go to Memphis without the Pink Lady."

"Have you ever fired that at anything besides a watermelon?"

"Sure, I hit that fake deer in Ethan Allen's backyard once. Why?"

"Let's just find a good disguise and get out of here before you get in a shoot-out with a mannequin."

The large lady behind the sales desk eyeballs us as we start to look around.

"Evenin', ladies," she drawls. "Can I help y'all find somethin'?"

"Just looking," Lilly chimes. "Thanks."

The lady raises her eyebrows as we start browsing through a rack of black dresses. Several look like they might fit me, but even the smallest one looks twice the size of Lilly's skinny ass.

Something is not right.

"Are y'all sure I can't help you?" the saleslady asks, making her way over to us. "My name is Mrs. Ella Mae," she says and smiles a big warm smile, "and I really think you girls could use a little assistance." Her voice is smooth and beautiful and I start imagining her crooning old Southern hymns on Beale Street.

"Are these all plus-sizes?" I ask, holding up a dress that looks like it might fit me.

"Sweetheart, those are *men's* sizes," she says and gives me a look of genuine sympathy. "What exactly are you looking for?"

I stand there like a statue staring at the dress dangling from the hanger and all I can think about is that blue dress that belonged to Monica Lewinsky.

"Well," Lilly says, unaffected by the fact that she was just sifting through garments worn by drag queens, "we need to get in that titty bar down the road and get some pictures of our friend's husband. We don't want to be recognized but we don't want to draw a lot of attention to ourselves, either," she explains. "Do you have anything we could do that in?"

"Oh, absolutely," Mrs. Ella Mae says, still smiling. She turns Lilly around in a circle, sizing her up. "Must be a good friend of yours to go to this kind of trouble."

"She is, and he's a piece of dog shit," I offer.

Mrs. Ella Mae laughs out loud and takes me by the hand. "Now, let me see what you're working with, sweetheart." I turn for her and she nods her head and says, "Looks like I need a two long and a sixteen short." She looks back and forth between us. "That sound about right?"

"Sadly, yes," I say and she laughs out loud again.

"I like you all right, sweetie," she says, "and I'm gonna fix you two gals up. Just take me a minute."

I give Lilly a smug look. "She likes me," I say with a snort.

"She wouldn't if she knew you were packin' heat in her store."

"She might like me even better," I reply smartly.

"You girls try and find some shoes that fit you on that back wall over there and I'm going to roll out the wigs for you in just a minute," Mrs. Ella Mae calls from behind a blue paneled wall.

"Shoes and wigs," Lilly says. "This is fun!"

"Do you think catching cooties is fun, too?" I ask.

"Shut up and come on," she snarls at me. "Ace, I swear, you're not nearly as much fun as you used to be. Loosen up a little."

"Okay," I say, stung by the insult.

We try on all shapes, styles, and colors of stiletto heels because stiletto heels are the only shoes they have on the shelf at Downtown Diggs. I pick out a black pointy-toe pair embellished with rhinestones and Lilly chooses a leopard-print peep toe with red trim and black bead cat-eyes sewn onto the top. I remind her that we're aiming for low-key, and she reminds me that we're going to a strip club.

Lilly tries on every wig on Mrs. Ella Mae's wig cart and, after several minutes of self-admiration, decides on a long, sleek black one with blunt-cut bangs. I don't try on a single one and instruct Lilly to get me the short blond bob with tapered bangs. I don't intend to put it on my head until I run into a drugstore and get a shower cap. And lice shampoo.

"Put it on," Lilly says, handing me the wig. "Let's see how you look as a blonde."

"Lilly, I'm not putting this on my head until—"

She yanks the wig out of my hand and flips it over so I can see the "sanitized" tag stuck on the inside.

"It's like bowling shoes!" she whispers. "They get sprayed down or something after each use. Unlike the seats at the movie theater, where you don't hesitate to plop down and lean your head back on a seat that God knows who just had their head on!"

"Ugh. I never thought about that," I say and make a mental note to start taking a shower cap to the movies.

"Look around." Lilly waves her arm around. "This place is cleaner than both of our houses!"

I have to admit she's right. "Fine! Hand it here!" I say and take back my blond wig.

"All right, ladies," Mrs. Ella Mae says as she emerges from the back of the store holding a dress in each hand. "Here we go."

One dress is a slim tube of red silk and the other is a strapless black number shaped like a keg barrel and both garments look like they could stand straight up on the floor like fabric garbage cans.

"I think these will work just fine," she says in her melodic tone. "I just had to make a few adjustments to the bust size on yours, honey," she says, looking at me.

"Well, thank you so much," I say and tell myself to take that as a compliment. "Why is it so thick and stiff?"

"Coverage, sweetheart. The men who wear these dresses don't want their secrets given away by loose fabric."

"Oh, perfect!" Lilly squeals. "It matches my shoes!"

I roll my eyes as we walk back to the curtained stalls to try on our man dresses.

"Let's just keep them on," Lilly hollers from behind her curtain, "so we can hurry up and get back over there."

Reluctantly I slip my big black dress over my head and, much to my surprise, it looks fabulous. The stiff fabric does wonders covering flabby rolls of flesh.

A minute later, Lilly steps out of her stall looking like a Hollywood A-lister, and I wobble out of mine with my wig on crooked and stray waves of dark hair flying everywhere. Mrs. Ella Mae takes the wig off my head and uses her fingers to comb my hair back.

"Lord, child," she says, and I start to wish she was my grandmother. "You ain't cut out for this business, are you?"

"No, ma'am," I say as she strokes my hair and twists it up into a tight bun. "Not cut out for it at all."

She secures the ensemble with bobby pins, then steps back and says, "Look at you. You look good as a blonde."

"Thanks," I say and have no trouble accepting that as a compliment.

Lilly foots the bill for the rental and Mrs. Ella Mae gives us some garment bags and a key to the drop box outside.

"Just leave the key in the box with the clothes and stuff, girls, and, if you can, you need to let me know how this little adventure turns out for you." She hugs us both before sending us on our way. "Good luck! Y'all be careful now."

"Yes, ma'am," Lilly says and pushes open the door. "Thank you so much!"

The whistles and caws erupt double time when we get out on the sidewalk, and Mrs. Ella Mae walks out behind us and scolds the men for being so rude. Lilly smiles, waves, and winks at the pack of bellowers.

. I stick my hand in my purse and wrap my fingers around the Pink Lady.

◇◇

33

Buster Loo is snoozing in the backseat, so when I open the door it startles him out of his slumber. He jumps straight up on all fours and growls at me as I get in.

"Buster Loo," I say, "it's okay. It's just Mommy dressed up like a prostitute." I hit the button to lock the doors as soon as Lilly closes hers. "Hey, I need to take Buster Loo for a little walk and let him relieve himself before we start slumming."

"Okay." She looks around, then points back at the road. "There's a sidewalk."

"Uh, no, thanks," I say. "We'll just drive somewhere safe and do it."

"We don't have time!" she wails. "It's already ten o'clock!"

"We have to have time, okay?" I say, pulling into traffic. "I can see downtown from here. Find a hotel or something on your know-it-all computer."

"A hotel!" she says and heaves a sigh.

"Yes, one with a dog walk!"

"Oh, good word!" She opens her computer and studies it for a second. "Okay, turn right in two blocks and that'll take us to a cluster of hotels and restaurants and stuff."

I follow her directions, then drive through three hotel parking lots before I find one with a dog walk.

"You staying in the car?" I ask.

"Yeah," she says, texting with one hand and holding the computer with the other. "I'm gonna watch that dot and make sure he doesn't leave."

"We'll just be a few minutes," I say, hooking Buster Loo's leash to his collar. He jumps out of the car and pulls his leash tight, clearly excited by the new aromas. We make our way around the well-lit dog track with him sniffing and peeing and scratching, then sniffing and peeing some more. When we get back to the car, I open the door and he hops right in. I walk around, pop the trunk, and grab the on-the-go doggie refreshment care package that I keep back there at all times.

I'm about to pour some bottled water into Buster Loo's pop-up bowl when a car pulls up behind me.

"Excuse me, ma'am?" I hear a man say. "Are you a guest at this hotel?"

I turn around to see a cop getting out of his patrol car. He points a flashlight in my face and I squint and stumble backward.

"Uh, no, sir. I was just walking my dog."

"Walking your dog, huh?" He laughs. "Haven't heard that one before." He takes a step closer to me. "Have you been drinking?"

"Uh, no, sir, I haven't." Lilly gets out of the car and Buster Loo jumps into the back window and starts barking up a storm. "As you can see, there's my dog."

"What's going on?" Lilly asks.

The officer points his flashlight at her. "I watched you two circle a few hotel parking lots." He looks back at me. "Looking for customers?"

"Oh, my God," I mumble and look at Lilly. "This was your idea. Why don't you start explaining?"

"Actually, it's pretty clear what's going on," the officer says with an air of arrogance that makes my stomach turn.

"Officer, please," Lilly says and takes off her wig. "We're just trying to help a friend of ours. We're schoolteachers."

"Schoolteachers!" he scoffs. "Really? Do you have any proof of that?"

"I do," I say, turning to my trunk. "Right here."

I set the water bottle and the pop-up dish in the trunk and reach for my school bag. The officer pulls his gun and shouts, "Don't move! Do not move! Hands in the air!"

"Holy shit!" I yell. "Are you serious? I was going to show you my planning book for school! I teach art and have my weekly planner right here in my bag!"

"I can arrest you for using profanity while addressing an officer of the law, so I suggest you watch your mouth!"

I look at Lilly as if to say, "Start working your magic."

"Officer, please," Lilly begins. "Just give us a chance and we can show you that we are schoolteachers, not prostitutes. I can tell you for a fact that is her school bag and we both have ID cards issued by Bugtussle School District in Bugtussle, Mississippi."

"Bugtussle, Mississippi? Did you just make that up?" he asks, giving Lilly a hard look.

"No, sir," she says and sighs. "I did not."

"You expect me to believe there is a place called Bugtussle, Mississippi?" he asks sarcastically. "And where would that be located?"

"It's a little town about seventy-five miles southeast of here," she says. "Would you like to see my ID?"

"You," he says while looking at me, "don't move!"

"Yeah, got it," I say and roll my eyes. I'd like to take that gun and pistol-whip his brains out.

"You," he says to Lilly, "remove your purse from the vehicle and lay it on the hood for me." She does and he gets her wallet out, flips it open, and studies her driver's license. "So, there really is a town called Bugtussle," he says. "Where's your school ID?"

"Third slot up from the license," Lilly says calmly, and I stand there with my arms in the air, fuming.

"Sir," I say, "my dress is slipping down. Request permission to pull it up so I don't get in more trouble for indecent exposure."

"Pull it up!" he barks at me. "And where's your ID? I need to see your license, registration, and proof of insurance as well."

"Every bit of that is in the car," I reply, jerking my dress up. "And there is a gun in my purse." Lilly gives me an alarmed look and I continue, "For which I have a permit, of course."

"Why are you carrying a gun?" he asks, boring a hole in me with his beady eyes.

"Same reason you do, sir, for protection," I say, staring right back.

At this point, another patrol car pulls into the parking lot. The driver of that car gets out, takes a minute to look Lilly and me over from head to toe, then smiles.

"Rutherford!" he shouts at the cop holding Lilly's wallet. "What do we have here? Working ladies?"

"They claim to be schoolteachers, Parker," Rutherford replies, all business. "This one has a school-issued ID," he says and nods to Lilly. "And that one," he says and nods to me, "is carrying a concealed weapon. And they are not guests of the hotel."

"Well, well, well," Officer Parker says, still smiling. "A teacher dressed up like a hooker carrying a gun, huh? That's interesting. Where's your permit?"

"In the glove box, sir," I say, relieved that Officer Parker doesn't seem hell-bent on taking us to jail. "I was just walking my dog before we went, uh, to a club."

"Would you get that permit for me? And your license, registration, and insurance." He looks at me. "You're not dumb enough to pull that gun out, are you?"

"No, sir," I say. "I'm not even close to being that dumb."

"Okay," he says and nods to the car.

I dig out my license, school ID, insurance card, registration, and gun permit. I hand it all over to him, and he leans toward the car to get a closer look at Buster Loo, who I'm certain will pass out soon if he doesn't stop barking.

"That's a cute little dog," Parker says. "What is that? A wiener dog?"

"He's a chiweenie, sir," I answer. "Half weenie. Half Chihuahua."

"A chiweenie?" he says and laughs a little. "Is that bells on his collar?"

"Yes, sir," I say. "He likes the bells."

Officer Parker stops smiling. "Seems cruel to leave him in the car all night while you're out partying, doesn't it?" He looks down at my license. "Graciela Jones?"

"Okay, we're not doing that, like, stay-out-all-night kind of partying," I say in a rush. "We just let him ride with us because he likes to go, and I had to walk him before we went to the strip club down the road."

"Strip club?" Parker asks, obviously amused. "This just gets better and better." He looks at Rutherford, who is not amused. "Please continue."

"It's a long story," I say, looking down. "We have a friend—" I stop and Lilly picks up the conversation from there.

"We have a friend in a horrible marriage," she says. "Her husband recently went from being emotionally abusive to physically abusive. She was going to leave him, and then she didn't, and now she's not talking to us so here we are trying to gather evidence that we hope will convince her to leave him once and for all."

"Hey, Parker," Rutherford says. "Come check this out." He points to Lilly's computer. "That's a fairly sophisticated GPS tracking program." Rutherford turns to Lilly. "Is that your computer?"

"Yes, sir," she says.

"How did you come to be in possession of FF140X GPS software, Miss Lane?"

"We're high-tech hookers," I say and Rutherford glares at me.

"Wow," Parker says and looks at Lilly. He is more appreciative of her appearance than Officer Rutherford. "Where *did* you get that, Miss Lane?" Lilly looks at the pavement and says nothing. "I'm no expert, but I'm pretty sure that didn't come standard on your little laptop."

"Her boyfriend is a cop," I say and they turn to me. "He just got out of the army and moved to our area and they just started dating. He's got a lot of—" I pause and try to find the right word.

"Gadgets," Lilly says. "He was in communications and he has a lot of electronic gadgets." She nods to the computer sitting open in the passenger seat of the car. "It's kind of a hobby of his."

"Where was he stationed?" Rutherford the asshole asks.

"Fort Bragg," Lilly replies. "Hundred and first Airborne."

"Retired?" Rutherford asks.

"Five years," Lilly says.

"He's only twenty-three," I say and Parker raises his eyebrows and looks at Lilly.

"Thanks, Ace," Lilly mutters.

"Well," Parker says, handing me my handful of junk. "It appears you ladies are somewhat legit albeit suspicious."

"Oh, thanks," I say, and Rutherford shakes his head and snarls at me.

"Listen," Officer Parker says. "What y'all are doing here is noble and all, but it's also very dangerous. I'd like to advise you two to get in your car and drive back to—"

"Bugtussle, Mississippi," Officer Rutherford offers with a smirk.

"Bugtussle, Mississippi. I've been through there before. That's a nice little town so why not take your gun and your dog and his bells, and you girls head back down there and try to come up with a different, perhaps safer way to get dirt on your friend's husband, okay?"

"Yes, sir," I say.

They turn and start walking toward their respective patrol cars. I grab Buster Loo's dog bowl and the water.

"Miss Lane," Parker says over his shoulder. "Tell your boyfriend we appreciate his service."

"Will do, Officer Parker. Thank you!" Lilly calls. She turns to me as they drive away. "OMG, let's get out of here!"

"Where do you want to change clothes," I ask, placing Buster Loo's water and treats on the floorboard behind her seat.

"What are you talking about?" she asks as Buster Loo noisily laps up the water.

"Well, we need to take these clothes back before we head home." Buster Loo is munching hard on his grub.

"We're not going home, Ace," Lilly says, putting her wig back on. "I spent over two hundred dollars on these getups and it's not going to waste! We're going to that club and we're going to get those pictures."

"Officer Parker instructed us to go home."

"Officer Parker *advised* us to go home," she says and smiles. "There's a difference." She looks at me. "Now let's get back to the club before

Richard Stacks leaves with some skanky whore and we have to kick down a seedy hotel room door to get our pictures!"

"Oh, I've got a bad feeling about this," I mumble.

"Don't worry," she says and pats me on the back. "Everything is going to work out just fine."

"Whatever you say, Lilly." I look back and Buster Loo is balled up in the backseat with his eyes closed. "That poor dog wore himself out with all that barking."

"He did bark his little ass off, didn't he?" Lilly says. She reaches back and pats him on the head. "He's our little guard dog."

34

◇◇

The doorman at Ladies4Gentlemen looks at my driver's license, then looks up at me and says, "Dye your hair?"

"It's a wig," I whisper and he glares at me like I'm not worthy of his presence. I notice a button on his denim jacket that says "No Fat Chicks!" I want to tell him that a three-hundred-pound bulldog like himself should be happy with any chick, fat or otherwise, but decide it's in the best interest of the mission to keep my mouth shut.

"Cover's twenty dollars," he grunts and I fork over the money while giving him my best *Go F yourself in the A* look. I push through the turnstile and quickly surmise that this could possibly be the worst mistake I have ever made in my entire life.

And I've made some bad ones.

The bumping bass music rattles my skull, and the smoke haze is so thick that I can literally feel cancer cells forming in my lungs. I stare at the back of Lilly's head until she stops and I bump into her from behind.

"Jeez, Ace," she hisses, "ease up!"

We sit down in padded chairs next to a table that looks about as big as a Frisbee and twice as flimsy. I tell myself to be calm as I cast my eyes upon the T-shaped stage, where there are five topless Barbie doll–looking women twisted into various positions of peccadillo. Two are bumping and grinding on the stage extension directly in front of us, two are doing the same at the opposite end, and the one in the middle appears to be waxing that fire pole with her twat.

A gorgeous young lady with the biggest fake tits I've ever seen in real life saunters over to our table and asks in a sultry voice what she can do for us. Lilly smiles and bats her eyelashes, and the girl takes a seat on Lilly's lap and starts writhing around like she's possessed. Which she probably is.

"That's free for you, beautiful," she coos to Lilly, who smiles and blows her an air kiss. Then she comes over to my side of the rinky-dink little table, straddles my lap, and starts shaking those gigantic melons in my face. I'm afraid one of those rubbery-looking nipples is going to touch my nose so I squeeze my eyes shut, turn my head to the side, and curse the day I was born.

She gets off my lap and asks if I'd like a drink to help me loosen up. I want to scream at the top of my lungs that there isn't enough alcohol in the world to make me want her big fake boobs crammed into my eye sockets, but Lilly is giving me that I'm-gonna-kill-you-graveyard-dead look so I smile and order a draft beer. Lilly orders a shot of tequila, and that makes me cringe for real because nothing good *ever* happens when Lilly shoots tequila.

The waitress and her boobs bobble away and return what seems like ten hours later with the smallest mug of beer I have ever seen, a shot of tequila, a lime wedge, and a bottle of salt.

"That'll be fifteen dollars, ladies," she says with a smile, and Lilly slides a twenty into her thong.

I pick up my tiny mug of beer, take a big swig, and it's all I can do not to spew it across the room. I've never tasted horse piss mixed with peroxide, but it can't be too far from whatever frothy crap was poured into this glass. While I'm choking down the so-called draft beer, our waitress is shaking salt in between her watermelon tits, and just when I think I've got my gag reflex under control, Lilly drags her tongue across that salt patch, tosses back the shot of tequila, and starts sucking on that lime wedge like a runt pup on a fresh teat.

Now I'm really about to hurl.

A group of male patrons stare at Lilly like a pack of starving dogs slobbering over a choice cut sirloin, and I ask myself how much lesbian action these perverts need. I mean, there's a full-blown orgy taking place up on the stage.

I'm about to pass out from this excessive exposure to unadulterated debauchery when our waitress finally leaves, but not before promising to bring Lilly another shot.

"What the hell are you doing?" I yell. "That was the nastiest thing I've ever seen."

"Oh, calm down," she says, with her eyes on the stage. "It's just a body shot, you ignoramus."

"How many *other* people do you think have been licking that part of her body tonight?" I ask and shiver with disgust. "And who knows where else?"

"Ace," she says and turns to face me, "you have gotten so uptight! Why don't you let off the brakes every now and then! She's at the bar right now swabbing that area with an alcohol wipe."

"Oh, that makes it so much less gross," I say. "So sanitary."

I've never been more desperate to escape a situation in my life. I'm considering bolting when my eyes fall upon the face of Richard Stacks the Fourth, who is sitting in what must be some kind of VIP section because the furnishings are much more accommodating. He has one topless girl on his lap and another behind him rubbing her tits on his neck while he's caressing the nipples of the lap dancer. Multitasking at its finest. Oprah would be so proud.

"Lilly," I say, nodding my head in his direction, "look!"

She discreetly scans the crowd, and when she sees him her expression turns to stone.

"Give me the camera," she says, not moving her eyes.

"Lilly, you know your history with this camera and Richard Stacks. Why don't you let me do it?"

"Give me the damn camera." Her eyes do not move. I reach in my bag, grab Chloe's camera, and hand it to her under the table. She throws the strap over her shoulder, tucks the camera under her arm, and makes her way to the other side of the club, where she sinks into a crowd of people at the bar.

She pulls the camera up to her face, then jerks it back down by her side. The entire motion is literally as quick as a flash and no one appears to notice. She moves around and repeats the motion a few more times, completely unnoticed.

She makes her way out of the crowd, but instead of coming toward me, she starts walking toward Richard Stacks. She's out in the open now, walking full stride, when she pulls the camera up to her face again, only this time people notice. A clamor for security makes its way through the stinking, smoky air, and I watch in shock as she continues to walk toward Richard Stacks, holding the camera up to her face the whole time. Big bulging men that look like WWF rejects are hustling toward her, when Richard Stacks notices her.

He looks a little confused at first, then starts smiling like some kind of celebrity pervert, like it's all part of the game for him. When he finally recognizes Lilly, he jumps straight up out of his padded red chair, throwing his lap dancer to the floor, and the nipple masseuse wastes no time disappearing into the crowd.

Lilly slings the strap around her neck so the camera dangles down her back, and continues walking toward Richard Stacks, who looks like a hunter about to destroy his prey. The bouncers are a few steps from Lilly when she draws back and punches Richard Stacks in the jaw with her right fist, then hurls her left straight into his gut. When he bows over, she slams her bony knee into his face and sends his head flying back in the opposite direction. As the bouncers wrap their meaty fingers around her skinny arms, she raises her left foot and plants that leopard-print stiletto into his right thigh. His scream pierces the air above and beyond the deafening music, and everyone turns to observe the spectacle.

I don't know whether to laugh or cry, but I know I've got to get Lilly and get the hell out of there. Fast. I jump up and run after the bouncers, who are roughly escorting her toward an exit door. I make it just in time to see them shove Lilly out into the parking lot, where she stumbles and falls onto the pavement. I elbow my way out the door and help her back on her feet. The bouncers scowl at us and shake their heads in disgust. Like *we're* the white trash.

"Stupid cunts," the uglier of the two yells. "Get the fuck out of here."

I hear thunder and look up at the sky but don't see any clouds; then the thunder rolls behind me and I turn to see a flock of leather-clad men on Harleys roll into the parking lot.

"Holy shit!" I yell over the rumble.

"What?" she yells.

"Let's get out of here!" I wave toward the parking lot.

On the way to the car, we receive more than a few appreciative looks, head nods, and winks from the Men of the Motorcycle Mob. I bet they wouldn't be so impressed if they knew we were wearing men's dresses.

I press the unlock button on my keyless remote just as the door of Ladies4Gentlemen flies open and Richard Stacks comes running out into the parking lot, cussing like a madman. Which clearly he is.

"Oh, no!" Lilly moans. "It's the hospital scene all over again, only we don't have the sheriff here to protect us!"

"Get in the car," I say and unlock and relock and unlock the doors but they refuse to open. We are standing next to a white Maxima, but it's not my white Maxima because I don't have a clothes rack and a briefcase in the backseat.

"Wrong car!" I scream and start looking around for mine. I don't see it so I press the panic button and the alarm goes off and I realize it's coming from the other side of the parking lot. "Shit, you got thrown out a different door! C'mon!"

I kick off my heels and start running like my ass is on fire. Richard Stacks catches me just as I reach my car, and he spins me around and slaps me in the face so hard I see stars. Lilly runs to my rescue, only to be met with a swift backhand that knocks her to the ground. Richard steps over her and tries in vain to jerk his wife's camera off of the strap while Lilly flops like a fish and screams at the top of her lungs. I'm about to jump on his back and lodge the heel of my shoe in the base of his skull when a large, tattooed arm reaches out and grabs Richard Stacks by the hair.

The Biker Man pulls him off of Lilly, who, while getting back on her feet, screams a string of obscenities that would make a sailor blush. She falls silent when she sees the Motorcycle Men circle around us with their muscled arms crossed, looking mean as hell.

"You like to slap women around, you fat little freak?" the Biker Man roars at Richard, and the sound of knuckles cracking reminds me of microwave popcorn.

"Put me down right now, you scumbag!" Richard Stacks yells at the Biker Man, and I silently marvel at his stupidity.

"Scumbag? I'm the scumbag?" the Biker Man yells and his comrades roar with laughter. "Scumbags don't do this to women," he says, and backhands Richard Stacks across the face. I start to fall in love with him because he is one badass dude, plus he looks like the lead singer of Metallica. "So I think you qualify as the scumbag."

"You leave him alone this instant!" a small shaky voice cries from outside the circle of the Motorcycle Mob. "You do not lay another hand on him or I will sue you for all you're worth, which probably isn't much."

"And who are you, little boy?" Biker Man asks when he sees Lester Finks, Richard Stacks's longtime friend and lawyer, glaring up at him with beady, red-rimmed eyes.

"I'm his lawyer, you filthy sack of shit," Finks spouts, puffing out his chest, "and you're going to jail."

"What is this?" Biker Man asks. "A citizen's arrest?" The Mob roars with laughter once again. The biker closest to Lester picks him up, raises him over his head, and passes him off to his buddy. I watch in silent awe as the Biker Men toss Lester Finks around like a beach ball while the reluctant crowd surfer screams like a little girl.

"Lawyer man," Biker Man says, "you got a wife?"

"I—I'm not married," Finks yells as he's rolled over in the air again.

"Oh, yes, he is married," Lilly offers. "He's got a sweet little wife and three little kids at home."

"And a dog," I say and, realizing my opportunity, add, "And that piece of shit over there"—I point to where Richard Stacks is huddled behind my rear bumper—"has treated his wife like shit the whole time they've been married and just last week decided he'd start slapping her around." The Motorcycle Mob gets quiet and, for a second, the only sound in the air is the music thrumming its way out of the club.

The biker holding Lester drops him and turns his attention to Richard Stacks, who is attempting to crawl underneath my car.

"So you wanna be a wife beater, do ya?" Biker Man reaches down, grabs him by the foot, and pulls him out from under the car.

"She doesn't know what the hell she's talking about," Lester Finks crows, then flinches and takes a few steps back as the Biker Men turn their attention to him. "She's a lying bitch!"

"Let's review the situation, lawyer man. I just watched your fat buddy there," Biker Man says and nods toward Richard Stacks, who promptly steps behind Lester Finks, "slapping these two girls around." He glares at Lester. "Do you think I'm stupid? Do I look stupid to you?" He takes a step toward Lester and Lester takes a step back, stepping on Richard's toes.

"Uh, no, sir," Lester Finks mumbles, apparently having lost all of his balls during his crowd surfing. "Come to think of it, the facts do point in that direction."

"I thought so," Biker Man says. Sirens pierce the air and Biker Man looks at Richard Stacks, then at Lester Finks, and they cower together like scared puppies.

"Saved by the sirens," he growls, "but rest assured that if we catch you two around here again"—he smiles and Richard takes a step closer to Lester Finks—"we're gonna take you someplace the police won't ever find you."

Biker Man looks at me. "Hey, doll, are you okay?" I nod my head. "What's your name?"

"Ace," I say, shaking with fear, excitement, and admiration. "Ace Jones."

"Ace." He smiles. "I like that." He reaches into the pocket of his leather vest and pulls out, of all things, a business card. "Give me a call sometime, sweetheart."

"Okay," I say, taking the card and smiling from ear to ear. Turns out he owns a construction company. "Thank you, Mr. . . ." I look down at the card. "Thomas Compton."

"Call me Tommy," he says with a smile and a wink and I get weak in the knees. "And you better call me."

"Oh, you can bet I will," I say.

"Let's go, guys," he says, and our saviors hustle into the strip club.

Lilly stares after them with an agitated look on her face, no doubt wondering why no one gave her a business card.

"C'mon, let's get out of here, Lilly."

I get in the car and hear Buster Loo growling like a bear in the backseat. I look in my rearview mirror and see Finks and Stacks engaged in what appears to be a heated argument. I'm fantasizing about mowing them down when Richard Stacks steps around, jerks the passenger door open, and starts pulling at the camera again.

"I've had enough!" I scream. "I have had enough of this shit!"

I take the Pink Lady out of the console and get out of the car. When Lester sees the gun in my hand, he takes off running in a dead sprint toward the street. I know the police will be here any minute, but I stay the course. I walk up to Richard and press the barrel of the Pink Lady against his skull.

"Get your hands off of her." He continues to wrestle with Lilly so I pull back the hammer and finger the trigger. I glance down and see that Buster Loo has joined the fray by snarling and snapping at Richard's arm. When he slaps Buster Loo into the backseat, I spin the gun around and smash the butt of it against his temple three times. Pop. Pop. Pop. I slam Lilly's door shut and turn around to see an officer approaching me with his weapon drawn and I imagine a red dot floating between my eyes.

"Hold it right there, Bugtussle," Officer Rutherford yells. "Drop your weapon."

I drop the Pink Lady in the parking lot of Ladies4Gentlemen.

◇◇

35

"Jones and Lane," the jailer booms and his deep voice bounces back and forth between the cinder-block walls, creating an ominous echo.

"Right here, sir," Lilly calls, waving through the cell bars.

I look up and see Mason McKenzie and Ethan Allen Harwood staring at us, eyes as wide as saucers. Mason looks like he's about to crack up and Ethan Allen just looks shocked. Really shocked.

"What the hell?" Ethan Allen says as he takes in the wigs, the dresses, the stilettos.

"Been tryin' to hustle up a little extra cash?" Mason asks and starts giggling.

"Oh, thank *God* y'all are here," Lilly gushes and rushes out of the cell as soon as the jailer opens the door. "I was starting to feel like Paris Hilton, and I think they were about to make us strip and put on some of those nasty orange scrubs!"

Mason and Ethan Allen look me up and down as I exit the cell.

"Just don't," I mumble. "Don't say a word, and please tell me I can get my gun and the camera back tonight."

"The gun and the camera," Mason says with exaggerated bravado. "Yes, those items are waiting to be picked up, Miss Double-Oh-Seven." He motions us into a room. "Right this way, ladies."

"We have to get back to the car immediately," I tell Lilly as we approach the counter. "Poor Buster Loo has been all alone in that car in the parking lot of a strip club." I shake my head.

"It's not even been two hours, Ace," Lilly says, nodding toward the old-fashioned clock on the wall, the face of which is covered by what appears to be tiny iron bars. "Like I've told you a thousand times," she continues, "the doors are locked, he has water and treats, and he's fine."

"Yeah, I know," I say. "It's just been one hell of a stressful day." I glance up at the clock. "What's up with that? Do they think those numbers are going to make a break for it?"

"Security precaution," the man behind the desk says in a flat tone. "Names, please?"

We give him our names and he gives us our stuff, and we walk back out to where Mason and Ethan Allen are waiting in the hallway.

"Ready to go, hos?" Mason asks, laughing, and Lilly punches him in the arm and the four of us walk out the front door of the Shelby County Jail.

"Y'all wanna stop at a truck stop and take a shower?" Mason asks after we climb into his Escalade. "Maybe turn a few tricks, make a few bucks."

"Lot lizards," Ethan Allen drawls and shakes his head. "That's exactly what y'all look like. Y'all look like two lot lizards."

"Very high-end lot lizards," Mason adds.

"Take us to a hotel," Lilly orders. "Did y'all come prepared to spend the night?"

"We came prepared to spend this night and the next one, too, 'cause we are men," Ethan Allen says with much pomp and circumstance, "and men are always prepared to spend the night." He turns around and eyeballs Lilly and me. "'Specially after we pick us up a couple of hookers at the jailhouse."

"Which club did y'all say you were stripping—I mean stalking tonight?" Mason asks.

"Ladies4Gentlemen," Lilly says and laughs at Mason's stupid joke. "Just off Airways on Winchester."

"What in holy hell were y'all doing off in that part of town lookin' like y'all do?" Ethan Allen demands.

"Stalking Richard Stacks," I say.

"Well, was it worth it?" Mason asks.

"I guess we won't know until we see how Chloe reacts to this," I say and hand the camera to Ethan Allen.

"Good word," Ethan Allen says, "that ain't no way for a married man to act right there."

"No," I say, "and that's the least of his transgressions."

Ladies4Gentlemen is still rocking at one a.m. and Buster Loo is curled up and napping in the backseat. Both guys hop out of the Escalade and Ethan Allen walks around to the driver's side.

"What are y'all doing?" I ask.

"I'm driving you," Mason says, matter-of-factly. "Lilly is riding with Ethan Allen, and we are going to the Peabody."

"What, Mason, are you serious?" Lilly asks excitedly, turns on her stiletto heel, and hops in the front seat of the Escalade.

"Yes, you girls have been through a lot and I know you're tired. I think you're both very brave for what you did tonight, even if it was a *tad* bit stupid, so I got a room at the Peabody. Reserved it on the way up here."

"How did you know we were planning to spend the night?"

"Common sense, Ace," he replies simply. "That's it. Just good ol'-fashioned common sense."

I get in the passenger side of my car and immediately start sulking because I feel like a teenager who just got chastised by her parents in front of her friends. I silently pray for the ability to start keeping my smart mouth shut. Buster Loo rouses from his slumber and crawls into Mason's lap.

"Ace," he says after ten minutes of riding in silence, "can we just be friends? Can you just give me that at least?"

"Of course," I say, looking out the window.

"Thank you," he says, "and can I tell you that you look smokin' hot in that outfit?"

"Can I tell you that it's a man's dress?"

"Well," he looks at me, wide-eyed and mischievous, then in his Forrest Gump voice says, "well, I just don't know what to say about tha-at."

While Mason checks into the Peabody Hotel, I walk around admiring the grandiose lobby, wondering if the ducks ever parade around during the wee hours of the morning. Just as a security officer starts to give me the evil eye, Mason appears, takes my arm, and leads me to the elevator.

"She's with me, sir," he says with a wink. "Half price after midnight." This gets a nod and a chuckle from the guard, who turns and goes on his way.

"You understand that I need a shower?" I say as soon as we walk into the room.

"Oh, please," he says with a smile. "Please do, you nasty girl."

Two seconds after I get out of the shower, there is a knock on the door and Mason peeps through the hole and, in a very loud voice, says he didn't order any prostitutes and if he did he would've asked for two women, not a hot chick and a tall, ugly dude.

When Lilly and Ethan Allen are finally permitted to enter the room, I'm pleased to see that they have picked up cold beer and hot pizza.

"I can't believe Domino's was still open!" I say, grabbing a slice.

"Well," Mason says, "you're in Memphis, not Bugtussle, sweetheart."

"Oh, thanks for pointing that out," I say, and make a show of looking around the room. "And here I was thinking they'd built a Peabody in Bugtussle."

"You've been a bad enough girl tonight," Mason says with a sparkle in his eye. "You better check yo-self!"

"Jeez," Lilly moans, "there's the bed! Why don't y'all just get to it already!"

"Shut up!" I yell at her.

"What's all the commotion out here?" Ethan Allen asks, stepping out of the bathroom looking rather odd but very comfortable in basketball shorts and a T-shirt.

"Whoa!" I exclaim. "I feel weird looking at you wearing that!"

"Yeah," Lilly says. "It's like you look naked when you're not wearing your Wranglers and cowboy boots!"

"You wish you were looking at me naked, Miss Lane," Ethan Allen says as he stretches out on the bed.

"I've seen you naked, remember?" Lilly says. "When we all went skinny-dipping in the lake down by your house and your dad showed up with a spotlight?"

"Yeah and you liked it, too, didn't you?"

"Can't say I didn't!" Lilly laughs and helps herself to some pizza.

"Well, I didn't like it worth a damn!" Mason offers.

"It was a great show, Ethan Allen," I say. "I don't think your dad would've made you get out of the lake if he'd known you were butt-ass naked."

"Hey!" Lilly says, tossing her half-eaten piece of pizza in the trash. "Y'all want to run down to the Rum Boogie? Doesn't close till daylight!"

I finish off my third piece of pizza, toss Buster Loo the crust, then grab another beer and crawl into bed beside Mason.

"Can't do it, Lilly," I say.

"Me either," Mason says.

She looks at Ethan Allen.

"Girl, I'm already in my sleepin' duds."

"Speaking of duds, that's what all of y'all are!" she says, pointing. "Fine, I'm going to take a shower."

"Thank goodness, because you weren't gettin' in this bed with me till you cleaned up!" Ethan Allen says and even Lilly has to laugh.

"Do not touch me," I tell Mason as I wiggle in between the covers.

"C'mon, baby, put that blond wig and that man dress back on and let me spoon you," he says, and Ethan Allen starts laughing. Buster Loo jumps up into the bed and burrows into the covers between us.

"Oh, this is so nice," Mason says and pulls Buster Loo up close to him.

"Turn on ESPN," Ethan Allen says, and I start to doze while they watch *SportsCenter*.

Lilly comes out of the bathroom and hops in the bed beside Ethan Allen, who smiles and pulls the covers over them both.

"Hey, you two, don't be getting frisky over there," Mason says.

"Well, why the hell not?" Ethan Allen replies, turning off the lamp. "This is the first time I've ever slept with a hooker."

36

⬦⬦⬦⬦⬦⬦⬦⬦⬦⬦⬦⬦⬦⬦⬦⬦⬦⬦⬦⬦⬦⬦⬦⬦⬦⬦⬦⬦⬦⬦

I wake up the next morning and Buster Loo is snoring on my shoulder and Mason McKenzie is spread over me like a human blanket. I slide out of bed, look across the room, and see that Lilly and Ethan Allen are gone.

I get up and start the coffeemaker, then decide to take another shower because I still feel dirty from wearing that drag queen dress and going into that filthy club. When I emerge from the bathroom, Mason is leaning back on the pillows, watching ESPN.

He looks at me and smiles, then pats the bed and raises his eyebrows a few times.

"Thank you," I say, ignoring the invitation. "Thank you for everything."

"Thank you for not being so mean," he says.

"Where's Buster Loo?"

"Under there." He points to the foot of the bed.

"You want some coffee?" I ask.

"Love some," he says. I pour him a cup and join him on the bed. He drapes his arm around me, and we sit there drinking coffee and watching *SportsCenter*, and I hope he can't feel the pounding of my heart, which is about to beat its way out of my chest.

He leans over, puts his empty cup on the nightstand, then turns and looks me right in the eye. I sit there, petrified, hoping. He takes my head in his hand and pulls my face next to his and I'm sure that I am going to faint. Instead of kissing me, he buries his face in my wet hair, and I swallow a sigh of disappointment.

"Oh, I love the way you smell," he whispers, then looks me in the eye again. I think I'm going to pass out this time for sure. He takes my face in his hand, then sniffs my hair on the other side, brushing my neck with his lips as he pulls back.

I start fantasizing about crawling on top of him, when the door flies open and Buster Loo goes nuts. Lilly and Ethan Allen come in with coffee and doughnuts.

"Uh, did we interrupt something?" Lilly asks, smiling.

"Uh, yes, you did! We were about to have hot, lovely relations!" Mason says, and I wish my cheeks would stop burning. Mason, Ethan Allen, and Lilly just laugh so I force out a few giggles and try to act normal. Buster Loo is running around in circles, barking and honking and jumping at the doughnut bag.

"Buster Loo! Settle down, you crazy little devil!" I say as he jumps back on the bed and proceeds to speed-lick my cheeks, then hops in Mason's lap to do the same.

"Hey," Ethan Allen says, "we got y'all a snack and some good coffee. I can't drink the crap they have in the room."

"Here, have a doughnut," Lilly says.

An hour later, the four of us stroll down Beale Street, taking in the sights and the heavy aroma of stale beer. Buster Loo puffs his chest out like a big dog, and then tries to pee on a statue of Elvis.

We walk down by the river, then back to the hotel to get our bags and check out. Mason decides we should have a proper breakfast so we drive down to a place called Aunt Betty's Hungry Man Breakfast Buffet. Mason cracks the window and I pour water in Buster Loo's travel bowl and promise him we won't be long.

I'm chowing down on gravy and biscuits when I get a text message from Gloria Peacock inviting Lilly and me to the Waverly Estate. I accept and she immediately sends a message extending the invitation to Mason and Ethan Allen. I accept for them as well and can't help but wonder if she already knows about our little fiasco. Regardless, I can't wait to tell her the whole story.

"Heard from Chloe?" Ethan Allen asks over a mound of eggs, bacon, biscuits, and hash browns.

"No," I say with a sigh. "She changed her number and won't respond to my e-mails."

"What?" Mason says and looks disgusted.

"She did it before, a few years back," I say, "and when she finally gave us her new number, she apologized for her stupidity and said it wouldn't happen again."

"But it's happened again," Mason snaps, shaking his head. "That's pretty sad."

"I want to go to her house and talk to her face-to-face," Lilly says, "then help her pack her bags and get away from that shit bag."

"Don't know if that's gonna work out for you, Lil," Ethan Allen says, looking at his phone. "Gramma just texted and said she saw them going into the Baptist church across the street this morning."

"Gramma Allen knows how to text?" I ask in genuine shock.

"Gramma Allen has an iPhone," Ethan Allen says proudly, "and she's all eyes at church on Sundays."

"Hi-tech spy granny," Lilly says and we all laugh.

I snooze all the way home and when our two-vehicle convoy rolls back into Bugtussle just before lunch, I wake up and realize I've slobbered all over my shirt sleeve. Mason has invited himself to my place for a nap, so Ethan Allen turns off on Lilly's street and we continue driving down to mine.

Before I unlock the door, I make him swear there will be no funny business and, while showing him to the guest room, I find myself hoping he doesn't honor that promise.

I close the door to my bedroom and scold myself for being so ridiculous. I swear to myself that I will *not* have sex with him *and* I will *not* be mean to him, although I must admit that it's easier *not* to have sex with him when I *am* being mean to him. The sad truth is that I'm *dying* to do it, consequences be damned, but I'm too old to act like that. Yet I can't stop thinking about it. Sleeping in the same bed with him was nearly more than I could stand, even if he did fart all night long and into the morning.

I put on shorts and a T-shirt, crawl into the bed, and try to take a nap. I can't sleep because my mind is reeling, so I get up and tiptoe to the door of the guest room, where I hear Mason in there snoring away. Buster Loo runs to the front door and starts jumping at his leash, so I slip on my shoes, hook him up, and set out for a walk at the park. Lots of people are out and about in the wooded area, and I worry for a second that Buster Loo will pitch another hissy fit, but he just keeps walking on the leash like a perfect little chiweenie should. I'm exhausted when we get back home, so I fill up his doggie bowls, head to my room, and have no trouble dozing off.

After sleeping in separate beds all afternoon, we get dressed in separate rooms, and I am proud of myself for not busting down the guest room door and jumping on his ass like a cheetah on an antelope. Of course, it had more to do with my being tired than any semblance of self-control, but who cares? I stayed out of his bedroom.

◇◇

37

Ethan Allen and Lilly pick us up in the Escalade and we arrive at the majestic gates of the Waverly Estate at a quarter till four. The gate guard nods and opens the gate, and instead of the peacock blue golf cart with a single seat, the golf cart chauffeur appears in a peacock blue six-seater.

"How many of these does she have?" I wonder aloud.

"Probably a whole fleet," Lilly whispers.

The golf cart chauffeur drops us off at a thatched-roof patio that has a tile floor and a large teak wood table framed by six very comfortable-looking chairs.

Gloria Peacock hugs everyone and squeezes Mason's cheeks and asks about his grandmother and his parents and blah blah blah. After a round of sweet tea and peacock-shaped sugar cookies that look *and* taste like they came straight from Paula Dean's kitchen, Gloria Peacock takes us on a different route through her majestic estate to the *Mission Impossible* room.

"Before we tackle the Stacks issue, I have something for you girls," Gloria Peacock says matter-of-factly. "I have prepared a slide show that I think you will find both informative and entertaining." She smiles. "Are you ready?"

"Yes, ma'am!" I exclaim and can't wait to see what she's put together with her super spy computer. What follows is a series of photographs of Catherine Hilliard engaged in various positions of sexual endeavor with the Bugtussle School District superintendent, Ardie Griffith. In most of the shots, they are in the back of Catherine Hilliard's Cadillac station wagon on top of what appears to be a piece of memory foam with a blue polka-dotted sheet haphazardly spread over it.

"Where are they parked?" I ask. "And why wouldn't they pull that door closed?"

"I guess it might get too hot in there," Mason says, and he and Ethan Allen snort and laugh.

"Just hold on and I'll pan out so you can see." She pans out and my jaw drops as I recognize the vocational building that's right next to the high school. I quickly realize that it's the perfect place to hide because the U-shaped building provides the ultimate privacy shield, plus the whole area is fenced and locked. And since Ardie is the superintendent, he would certainly have a key.

Where they went wrong was not knowing that their meeting spot was clearly visible from the rooftop of the People's Bank, where Omega Systems just happens to have an eye in the sky. That and not pulling that back door closed.

For the record, Ardie Griffith is a very short man and Catherine Hilliard is a very tall woman, and together they make me think of a weasel humping a giraffe. The disgusting slide show ends with a shot of them reclining in the back of the vehicle, smoking.

"Wow," I exclaim, "that explains those yellow teeth."

"I have copies for you, Ace, in case things get hairy at school tomorrow," she says and hands me a padded envelope. I get excited thinking about the damage I could do with just one of these pictures. "Now, I understand you have pictures from your wild night last night so let's take a look at those."

I give Mrs. Peacock the memory card from Chloe's camera and, after some arm waving, the magic computer monitor comes to life.

The first picture is a shot of Buster Loo with his eyeballs and his asshole both facing the lens.

"Oh, look at that," Ethan Allen says and laughs. "Buster Loo posing for the camera."

"Don't make fun of my wiener, Ethan Allen," Mason whispers and punches him. "Dog, that is."

"Uh, I thought it was a *chi*weener dog," Ethan Allen replies.

"Either way," Mason says emphatically.

The next shot is of Richard Stacks with a stripper behind him and a stripper on his lap. "Oh, this is embarrassing," Ethan Allen whispers and nods to Gloria Peacock. "Couldn't y'all look at these some other time?"

"Shut up, Ethan Allen," Lilly whispers back.

He looks at the floor for the remainder of the slide show, which includes several incriminating shots of Richard Stacks the Fourth and his topless lady friends. Following those are some pictures of that red carpet, a few palm-of-the hand shots, and three close-ups of the parking lot.

Gloria Peacock turns to us and says, "Looks like you got him, girls."

"Looks like we did," Lilly says quietly, "but this is going to kill Chloe's soul."

"She killed her soul when she married Richard Stacks," I say. "This will be the beginning of the end of that."

"How are y'all gonna get 'em to her if she's not speaking to either one of you?" Ethan Allen asks.

"Don't know," Lilly says and I shrug.

"What if she doesn't care?" Mason asks. "What if, after all of this, she just looks at these pictures and is like, 'People make mistakes and I forgive him'?"

"That's what I'm afraid of," I say quietly.

"The Chloe we know and love is buried in there somewhere," Lilly says, frowning. "I just hope it's not too late to tap into the part of her conscious that would find this kind of behavior unacceptable."

"I've made every effort to have her here as a guest," Gloria Peacock says. "I sent a few e-mails, then a card, and of course I called several times, but was never able to speak with her personally. The only response I received was a blunt e-mail that basically said 'thanks but no thanks.'"

"She probably didn't even get the card, and the e-mail was probably from Richard," I say, feeling anger well up in my guts.

"So what's the plan?" Mason asks, clearly wanting to move things along.

"This situation must be handled with utmost care." She looks from me to Lilly and we nod our heads in agreement. "Go see her," she says. "Go to her house and break it to her gently."

"We can handle that," I say and Lilly nods.

Gloria Peacock waves and points, and her magic computer starts printing pictures, which she puts in another padded envelope and hands to me without a word. I look up at her and smile. She is officially my new idol.

When Mason and I get back to my house, he asks to come inside. We have a few beers on the patio and he asks if he can spend the night. I want to take him to my bedroom, tie him to the bedpost, and do unspeakable things to him, but I don't. I tell him he's welcome to sleep in the guest room.

"Again," he whines.

"Again," I say and smile.

◇◇

38

M onday morning I hop out of bed feeling like a million dollars earning twenty percent interest. I don't know if it's because Mason McKenzie is snoring away in my guest room or because I somehow managed *not* to go in there and jump his bones or because I have an envelope full of glossy pictures of that hussy Catherine Hilliard getting boned by that twerp Ardie Griffith.

I get to school twenty minutes early and set out to find Coach Hatter. I walk through the gym and into the athletic office without even knocking.

"What are you doing in here, Jones?" Coach Wills asks with a disapproving look on his broad, oily face. "Did somebody make you the coach of something and you forgot to tell me?" He belts out a hearty laugh followed by a burp.

"Well, I'm gonna start a flag-football team this summer and I thought I'd be the coach," I say, smiling. "Does that qualify me to step foot in here?"

"You can't be serious?" Wills says.

"Of course I'm serious!" I say. "I'm calling my team the Numbnuts and you're my number-one recruit!" I get a good laugh from the other coaches and Wills looks at the floor and, annoying as he is, I feel sorry for him because he's just a big dumb jock all grown up, trying to pass for an adult. "Just kidding, Wills." I give him a smile and a wink and pat him on the back.

"You're so mean to me," he mumbles, sounding a lot like Sponge-Bob's pal Patrick.

"Tell you what, if you sit by me at lunch again today, I'll rub your leg to make up for it," I say with a coy smile. This elicits whooping and hawing from the other coaches and Wills looks at me and smiles.

I look at Coach Lawson, the head football coach, and ask him where I might find Logan Hatter. I'm dying to pull out those pictures and pass them around the room, but I know now's not the time.

"He's not here yet, Ace. Anything I can help you with?"

"No, sir, I'll catch him later."

"Jones, are y'all sleepin' together again?" Wills says, unable to leave well enough alone.

"Maybe," I say and wink at him. "Maybe I've got my eye on you now." His big greasy face turns bright red.

"Oh, my goodness," Coach Lawson says, laughing and looking at Coach Wills. "Lay off of him, Jones. He's about to blow a gasket!"

"Y'all have a good day," I say, waving, then look back at Wills just before I walk out the door. "See you at lunch."

"Yeah," he says, waving a husky hand in the air. "See ya."

As I'm walking out of the gym I meet Logan walking in, and he can tell by the look on my face that something is up. We go to his office, he closes the door behind us, and I whip out the goods.

"Oh, holy shit," he whispers and looks at me. "How about *that*?"

"How *about* that?" I say, grinning from ear to ear because I love perpetrating mischief.

"Ugh. I'm gonna lose my breakfast if I keep looking at these." He looks up at me and then back down at the pictures. "You have to admit, though, Ace, some of that's pretty funny." I nod in agreement. "Can I have one? Or two? I'd like one for the wall in here and maybe one to hang on the bulletin board in the main lounge." He starts that idiotic sniggering and I start laughing.

"Maybe later and you can blame it on me. How about that?"

"Sounds good," he says, and then gets serious. "Where did you get those, Ace?"

"Can't say just yet," I say. He nods in understanding because he's a man and men don't freak out if they don't have all the details all the time.

I go to my classroom, check my e-mail, and surprise of all surprises, I have been summoned to Catherine Hilliard's office during my lunch break for yet another ass chewing. While this would normally ruin my day, today I can't wait to strut my stuff in Cruella de Vil's office.

The morning creeps by and I fantasize about letting the pictures fall out onto the floor where my students could see them and I could pretend it was an accident. The rumor mill would burn itself to the *ground* with news like that. But my students have done nothing to deserve that kind of punishment, so I forget about it and try not to stare at the clock.

When lunchtime arrives, I slide the envelope into my purse and strike out to see the principal. Her door is closed, of course, so I take a seat in one of the red plastic chairs in the narrow hallway.

My pulse is beating like a jungle drum and my stomach is churning like I just overindulged on lunchroom leftovers. I strive to look unaffected as I lean back and take a long, deep breath. I am determined to remain calm. I am determined to keep my cool. I cross and uncross and recross my legs and wonder what she would think if I walked in there and punched her right in the nose.

I try to think about something else, but the only thing that comes to mind is Mason hanging out at my house, and I am suddenly overcome with fear that he might find my vibrator. That makes me more nervous than I already am and I start laughing this crazy, ridiculous laugh and can't stop, so I start thinking about those peacock-shaped sugar cookies and wishing I had about six dozen to eat right now to calm my nerves.

Catherine Hilliard opens her office door and stands there looking like a beast of the Amazon in a two-piece mauve suit.

"Something funny?" she asks.

"Nope," I say. I stand up, look her square in the eye, and let a small giggle slip.

"I can see you now," she says with a smirk.

"Why, thank you so much, Mrs. Hilliard," I say with a broad smile and force myself to stop thinking about vibrators and peacock cookies. "I've been looking forward to this meeting all morning."

"Humph," she mumbles and I get the feeling she thinks I'm being sarcastic.

But I'm not.

She thinks she's about to get me good.

But she's not.

Not today.

Today the ass chewing will not go as planned.

39

I take a seat and watch her do the same, careful to maintain eye contact.

"So, Miss Jones," she says quietly, "you've been to jail again, I hear."

"I don't know what you're talking about," I lie in an effort to amuse myself.

"I understand that you had a gun in your possession and used it to assault a fine, upstanding member of our community."

"I don't recall seeing a fine, upstanding member of our community, but I did see that dirtbag Richard Stacks and his maggot lawyer at a strip club."

"At a strip club," she says with palpable disgust.

"Yes. Your fine, upstanding citizen was inside a strip club in downtown Memphis with two topless girls rubbing all over him and each other when we showed up with a camera." Her expression tells me that she was not privy to this information.

"That has nothing to do with the fact that an employee of this school district was sent to jail on a weapons charge"—she curls her upper lip—"at a *strip* club."

"It has everything to do with it."

"Didn't I tell you to mind your own business?"

"Didn't I tell you that you are a scab on the ass of humanity?"

"So you want to do this the hard way?"

"I most certainly do."

She places a yellow sheet of paper on her dusty desk and pushes it over to me.

"I verified with Shelby County that you were indeed incarcerated and that alone is grounds for suspension based on disorderly conduct. Even though you haven't been officially charged yet," she says and glares at me, "what you've done already will result in termination of employment with the Bugtussle School District regardless of what happens in court."

"Of course," I say, "I would expect nothing less from the principal of a school district infested with biased, unfair, and most likely illegal in-house politics."

"And your point is what?" Mrs. Hilliard says with a shrug.

"My point is," I say, reaching for my bag, "that everyone you try to screw is not going to bend over for you." She rolls her eyes as I pull the photos out of the manila envelope. Smiling, I flip to the one I like best, which is a shot of her with her legs spread eagle and Ardie's lumpy little skull pressed into the gap. I turn it around so she can see, and the look on her face makes my heart flutter with joy and triumph.

"Miss Jones," she says, reaching for the yellow slip, "perhaps termination can be avoided."

I snatch up the yellow piece of paper and stuff it deep inside my school bag.

"I don't think so, Mrs. Hilliard," I say and flip over a few more pictures for her to see, "because you are going to *fucking* fry for this."

She sits in horrified silence and I put the pictures back in the envelope and get up to leave.

"Ace," she says, lurching out of her chair and banging against the filing cabinet behind her desk. "Graciela, uh, Miss Jones, please sit down and let's talk about this. I need to know where those came from. Please," she pleads. "I'm sure we can work something out. We can come to some kind of agreement."

"Really, Mrs. Hilliard," I say, like I'm actually considering it.

"Yes," she says, "yes, of course, please sit down. There is something I need to show you." She starts poking around in the back of her desk drawer, no doubt looking for the "L.L." folder that Lilly and I stole last week, but she comes up empty-handed and visibly frustrated. "I know it's in here somewhere, and it's very important that I find it because it might clarify a few things for you." She starts to look panicked, and I stand in the doorway and bite my tongue because, unless she's planning to look in Lilly's panty drawer, she won't find that folder.

"Mrs. Hilliard, I really must get going. I need to clean out my room before the kids come back from lunch and start asking questions."

"No! No, please sit down, Graciela. Have you had coffee this morning? Can I get you some coffee?"

I smile because I *own* her now. "I don't drink coffee," I lie and turn to go.

"Please, Ace, please just have a seat. Please!"

"Oh, okay," I say and step back toward the chair. She looks so relieved I almost laugh out loud. I turn on my heel and say, "Did you think I was going to sit back down? Because I wasn't."

"Graciela, please, I beg you. Let's talk about this woman to woman. I'm sure we can work out some kind of a deal."

"The only deal you could interest me in is *your* lips on *my* ass," I say as I walk out the door.

"What do you plan to do with those, Ace Jones?" she yells, flipping back to bitch mode. "I will call the law and have you arrested for stalking."

"Do it," I say and keep walking, "and they can mark these pictures Exhibit A."

I hustle out of there because I know I've only got a few minutes before the bell rings. I run into Coach Hatter's room and tell him what happened. He follows me into my classroom and helps me pack up a few things.

"What about your students?" he asks.

"They're all working on independent projects for the art fair," I reply, "and Mrs. Jennings, you know her? She retired from my job several years ago and that's who they'll get to replace me until the end of the year, so they'll be in good hands." I look around my classroom and feel a pang of sadness. "Man, I'm gonna miss my kids, Hatt."

"You have to come back for the art fair."

"Hey, that's my favorite part of the year, and I wouldn't miss it for the world," I say. "If any of these guys need me, they know where to find me."

"They're going to be really upset when they find out you're gone," Hatter says, looking at his feet. "I'm gonna miss you, too, Ace," he says as he kicks a pencil around on the floor. "With you and Lilly and Chloe all gone, I'm gonna get lonely here."

"Aw, Hatt, you're so sweet," I say and look around my classroom, wondering if this is the last time I'll ever be in here. I realize that I've been set free from the very thing I've always used to justify not pursuing my dream of being a serious artist. I get scared for a second as I think about the consequences of walking out that door. I hesitate, wondering if I'm ready to walk away from my comfort zone.

All I have to do is go back to Catherine Hilliard's office and give her back this damned sheet of yellow paper. With the power I have over her now, I could run this school from the comfort and security of my classroom. But that's not what I want. "I better run," I say, giving him a quick hug. "Don't worry. Chloe and Lilly will be back soon. It's only a matter of time."

"But not you?"

"Not if I can help it, Hatter," I say, turning to go. "I think I'm gonna take this opportunity and do what I've always wanted."

"Paint?"

"Yeah," I say and feel a tremor of excitement just thinking about starting my own studio.

"Okay," he says. "Sounds good to me."

I walk down the hallway, out the door, and across the parking lot to my car. As I drive away from the school, I start thinking about my purpose in life. I've always known what it was. It's been in the back of my mind, just been sitting there, patiently waiting for me to act on it.

40

<><><><><><><><><><><><><><><><><><><><><><><><><><><><><><><><><><>

I go home, put on some comfortable clothes, and call Lilly to see what she's doing. Turns out it's not Deputy Dax. Maybe he wasn't all that impressed with us going to jail after getting into a tussle in the parking lot of a strip club. At any rate, we agree that today is the day to confront Chloe, so I pick up Lilly at her house and we head to the Stacks's residence.

I park at the community playground and we scamper across the street to 309 Parker Drive. I peek in the garage and see Chloe's shiny white Lexus SUV parked in one bay. The other two are empty. I give Lilly a thumbs-up and we walk up the steps to the front door.

After seventeen rings and a full nine minutes, I finally hear the lock move. When Chloe opens the door, Lilly steps back and nearly stumbles off the porch. I gasp and cover my mouth.

Chloe's hair looks like she cut it herself with meat shears in a dimly lit room. There is no trace of makeup on her face and her skin is pallid and pale as a ghost. She looks like she's lost about twenty-five pounds, which would put her at around eighty-five, and she's wearing some kind of gray silk wrap that looks like a cross between a kimono and a sarong.

"What are you doing here?" she demands and looks at us like we're trying to sell her a set of encyclopedias, and that pisses me off because we have been through hell and high water for her.

"Why did you change your phone number again?" I fire back. "And why haven't you called either of us?"

"Because you are both a bad influence on my marriage."

"What the hell are you talking about?" I snap, and Lilly steps forward to take control of the conversation.

"Chloe, we need to talk to you. It's very important."

"No, you need to leave right now."

"Chloe, we're your friends," Lilly pleads.

"Not anymore," she says like a zombie and tries to close the door. Lilly steps back but I wedge my foot into the doorway.

"Hold on just a minute, Chloe!" I yell. "I don't know what kind of drugs you're on right now, but you are going to let us in and you are going to listen to us."

"I'll do no such thing," she squeals like a child and starts banging the door against my foot, and that turns into a pretty painful experience because I'm wearing flip-flops. I drop a shoulder against the door and push it open. Chloe falls back onto the parquet floor of her foyer, screaming and waving her arms like a madwoman. I grab Lilly by the arm, jerk her into the house, and slam the door shut behind us.

"Uh, Ace," Lilly mumbles as I rub my throbbing foot, "I don't think this is what Gloria Peacock had in mind when she said to handle this gently."

"Shut up, Lilly," I say, standing on one leg like a chubby seagull. "Just shut up!"

Chloe jumps up like a cat and runs for the phone, screaming how she's going to call the police and have us arrested.

"Oh, hell, no! I'm not going back to jail," I yell at her, then grab her by the arms and shake her for a second. "Snap out of it, Chloe! What the hell is wrong with you? Who the hell *are* you?"

"Who the hell are *you*," she screams, "to break into my house and assault me? I have started over. I have started a new life and you are not a part of my new life."

"She has lost her damned mind," Lilly whispers.

"I heard that!" she screams, even louder. "Get out of my house and never come back again! Ever!"

"That's it," I say. "This is more than I can stand. I'm done."

"No, wait," Lilly says. "Chloe, could we please sit down in the living room?"

"No!" she screams. "Get out! Get out now! I know you've been following my husband and I hate you both for it."

"You told us to, you nutcase!" I yell at her. "You fucking told us to follow that piece of shit!"

"Ace, stop!" Lilly says. "Stop it right now." Lilly reaches into my bag and pulls out the envelope.

"You told us to follow him and we did, Chloe," Lilly says quietly as she slips the photos from the envelope. "We did just what you asked us to do"—she flips one of the pictures up so Chloe can see it—"and this is what we found." She flips another one and another one and keeps saying, "This is what we found."

"No, no, no!" she screams. "It's not true! You lie!"

"Jesus, Chloe, listen to yourself," I say sternly but with more empathy now. "You do not have to live like this. We are here to help you. We are here to save you. We are here to get you out of here."

"You are here to ruin my new life! And you have done it! You have ruined my new life and I will hate you forever for it!" she screams and falls on the floor and starts banging her head on the wall and screaming and crying, and it scares the holy hell out of me because I've never seen anyone act like that. Especially not my beautiful, perfect friend Chloe.

Lilly looks at me and I look at her and we carefully position ourselves on either side of her. I put my arms around Chloe, and Lilly puts her arms around both of us, and I whisper, "It's gonna be okay, Chloe. Everything is going to be just fine. We love you and we are here to take care of you."

"What took you so long?" she whispers and I look at Lilly, who, of course, starts sobbing her eyes out.

"I'm sorry. I'm so sorry we didn't come sooner," I whisper and stroke her hacked-up hair.

"I remember you coming into my room at the hospital and hugging me and telling me I was going to be okay, but then you never came back. You never came back, Ace. And I started to think I'd dreamed it. But then when I heard you just now, I remembered. I remembered that you were there."

"And we were here that Friday after you got home, remember?" I say softly.

"Don't you remember us coming to see you, Chloe," Lilly asks. "You made Ace hug me and she didn't want to."

"I will always be here, and so will Lilly," I whisper, not believing what an emotional wreck she has become. "We will always be here because we love you."

"What am I going to do?" she wails. "What am I going to do? I don't know what to do, and I haven't had y'all to help me and I don't know what to do." She looks down at the pictures scattered on the floor. "Are those real? When did you take those? Where did they come from?"

"Most of them Saturday night," I say quietly, "in Memphis."

"This past Saturday night?"

"Yes."

"Are you sure?"

"Of course I'm sure. Why?"

"He said he had an important meeting with a client in Memphis on Saturday night," she says slowly. "Let me see those. I want to see those pictures."

"Chloe," Lilly says, "I'm so sorry. Please understand that we don't want to hurt you any worse than you've already been hurt, but we wanted you to know the truth."

"Oh, Lilly," she says, "I think it would be impossible for me to hurt any worse."

She flips through the pictures two times, then lays them on the floor and gets up.

"Let's go in the kitchen and get some water." She looks at us through puffy red eyes. "I'm so ashamed of myself for how I've acted."

"Hey, you don't worry about a thing, girl," I say and breathe a sigh of relief that she appears to be somewhat back to normal.

Just as we get on our feet, the front door flies open and Richard Stacks charges into the foyer like a bull on steroids.

"What are you whores doing here?" he booms and nobody moves.

"You!" he says, pointing at me. "You stupid bitch! I have had enough of you!"

I take a few steps back into the living room and he comes at me hard and fast and I mentally prepare myself to get knocked out. Lilly makes a run for it, and I glance over at Chloe and see that she has pulled a long, narrow wrought iron candle holder off the wall. Just as Richard Stacks draws back a meaty arm to punch me in the face, Chloe swings that thing at his head like she's trying to knock a baseball out of the park.

"Enough!" she screams and, as I squeeze my eyes shut, I hear the candle holder crush against the meaty flesh of his head. "I have had enough, you lying bastard!"

Lilly is back from wherever she ran off to and is ransacking my purse, screaming, "Ace, why didn't you bring your goddamned gun? Where is the Pink Lady?"

Richard staggers but doesn't fall. He turns toward Chloe and roars like a lion. When he pauses to finger the trickle of blood next to his ear, Chloe swings again and hits his left shoulder. He takes the hit but stays on his feet. She stares him down as he totters toward her and the anger in her eyes is unnerving.

Her fear is gone.

When he's within arm's reach, he raises his right hand and I'm afraid for a minute that she's going to let him slap her, but she swings that candle holder around and hits him with a nut shot that puts him on the floor.

"Chloe," he says, barely audible, "Chloe, baby, I'm hurt. See what you've done?"

"You expect me to care?" she yells. "Do you *really* expect me to care?"

"Oh, my God," Lilly says and I can see that she is shaking all over. "Oh, my God!"

Chloe looks at him, drops the candle holder on the floor, and leaves the room.

"Where are you going, Chloe?" I ask and try to sound like I'm not scared shitless but, damn it, I am.

"To pack," she says calmly.

"What are we going to do now?" Lilly asks.

Richard rolls onto his side and moans in pain.

"How about get the hell out of here?" I say and we take off after Chloe.

Lilly rummages through the dresser drawers and I go through the closet and we're throwing shit in suitcases like the house is on fire. Chloe, on the other hand, is standing in the bathroom picking through her jewelry.

"Hey, Chloe," I say. "Can we get a move on?"

"Sure," she says, closing the drawer. "I just had to separate the jewelry that means something to me"—she takes off her wedding ring and drops it on the granite countertop—"from the jewelry that doesn't."

"Great!" I say and grab three bags and a suitcase. "Let's get out of here."

The three of us hustle down the hallway and past Richard Stacks, who is still clutching his balls. Chloe walks up to him and says, "Goodbye, Richard."

"Chloe," he grunts, "you can't leave."

Chloe turns and walks out the door, and Lilly hustles out behind her without so much as glancing his way. I pause long enough to holler, "Later, asshole!" right before I close the door behind me. We haul Chloe's luggage across the street, and I'm cramming it in the truck when I notice Chloe's next-door neighbor standing at her mailbox, staring.

"Shit," I say when she starts walking our way.

"What's going on here?" she asks, giving me the evil eye. I'm about to launch into an explanation when Chloe turns around and says, "Mrs. Franks, with all due respect, could you please mind your own business for once?"

Lilly and I look at each other in mutual shock.

"Why, Mrs. Stacks, there is no reason to be rude. I would simply like to know what's going on. Are you going somewhere?" She walks around to where Chloe is standing. "And, sweetheart, whatever has happened to your hair?"

"I'm sorry. I don't mean to be rude, Mrs. Franks," Chloe says patiently and swipes the lady's hand away from her hair. "But none of this is any of your business, so why don't you run along now?"

"Chloe Stacks, why, what's gotten into you?" Mrs. Franks says, looking at her like she's the Creature from the Black Lagoon.

"Well, Mrs. Franks," Chloe says, taking her arm and escorting her back across the street. "I guess you could say that I've finally seen the light about my relationship with my husband." Mrs. Franks gives Chloe a confused look and Chloe gently pats her on the shoulder. "Goodbye." Chloe hustles back to the car and gets in. "Ready?" she says.

"Indeed we are, my lady," I say, cranking the car.

"Let's get out of here."

"Where are we going?" Lilly asks from the backseat.

"Anywhere," Chloe says, looking at her house as we drive by. "Anywhere but here."

"I think I know a place," I say, picking up my phone.

41

◇◇

We are taken to the indoor patio of the Waverly Estate, and when we walk in drinks are set up and it's not sweet tea. Chloe doesn't seem to notice the grandeur of the place. I guess always having money numbs you to things like that. Or maybe she's distracted by everything that transpired today. I can't really say.

"Boy, when I picked y'all to hang out with, I really picked some doozies, didn't I? You girls remind me so much of my best friends, and I can't wait for y'all to meet. But that'll come later," Gloria Peacock says when we walk in. "Right now, could I interest anyone in a mai tai?" She waves a hand toward the bar, where I see several blue glasses filled to the brim and garnished with little umbrellas.

We each take a glass and a seat and she continues, "If you would allow me, I'd like to share with you a hot-off-the-press update on a topic of particular interest." She smiles. "Catherine Hilliard has been forced to resign her position as principal of Bugtussle High School."

"Well, that's the best news I've heard all day," I say.

"What?" Chloe says. "Why?"

"Somehow the State Board of Education in Jackson has been made aware of her recent misconduct—namely, placing a well-respected teacher on leave based on a ruse of false allegations." She smiles that big, pearly smile. "A little birdie must've told them."

"Or a little peacock," I say, twirling my drink umbrella.

"Oh, now, who's to say I have friends on the state board? And if I did, who knew they'd come through for me so quickly?"

"Who, indeed?" Lilly says, smiling.

"A related item of interest is that Superintendent Ardie Griffith voluntarily resigned his position this morning for reasons as yet undisclosed. Rumor has it the two of them plan to leave town tonight. Together."

"Ugh," I say, "that's good to hear, but gross to think about."

"Good for them," Lilly says with palpable disgust.

"Good for Reece and Rye," I say, and Chloe gives me a funny look. "Later," I whisper.

"How do you know all of this?" Chloe asks Gloria Peacock.

"We'll get you up to speed soon enough, dear," Gloria Peacock says to Chloe. "As you might guess, very few are privy to the details on this turn of events. Of course, the legal issues already in play have to be dealt with, but Mr. Mason McKenzie is on that project as we speak," she says and smiles. "Correct me if I'm wrong, but I do believe that things have been set right pertaining to the matter of Catherine Hilliard."

"Just like you said," I say and Lilly nods in agreement.

"Just like I said," she says with a smile and helps herself to a drink. "All wrapped up nicely without even having to go public with those horrid photographs."

"The public doesn't deserve to have to look at those," Lilly says. "Nobody does."

"Well, at least I got to show a few to Catherine Hilliard," I say. "So what do I do with the ones I have? Maybe make a collage, try to sell it online?"

"Ace, something is terribly wrong with you," Lilly says, laughing.

"Those will need to be shredded," Mrs. Peacock says. "Bring them in, if you don't mind, and we'll take care of that in the media room."

"Shit," I mutter to myself and have another sip of my drink. "Hate to see those go."

"Could I see them before they're destroyed?" Chloe asks.

"Trust me, sister," I tell her. "You don't want to see those."

"No?" she says.

"No," Lilly says. "Not your kind of material at all."

"So I'm assuming from what y'all have said that Mr. Griffith was having an affair with Mrs. Hilliard?"

"You assume correctly," I tell her. "The pictures tell that story in sordid detail."

"You're right," she says. "I don't think I want to see them." She raises her glass to her lips, then stops. "But what about Mr. Reece Hilliard? Isn't he the president of some big bank in Tupelo? I remember Richard telling me something like that."

"Yes, he is, but he's retiring soon and moving to New Orleans," Lilly answers. "And, Mrs. Peacock, I'm sure you're already aware that Uncle Rye is retiring as well?"

"Oh, holy bees' knees, this is getting good," I say.

"Of course," Gloria says, waving a hand in the air. "We're planning a grand celebration for the two of them to which y'all will be invited."

"What does Reece Hilliard's retirement have to do with Ryland Lane's?" Chloe asks pointedly.

"Chloe," Lilly says, "you've met my uncle Rye. Think about it."

"Oh," she says, then gasps and covers her mouth. *"Oh!"*

"Right," I say. "Oh!"

42

◇◇

To no one's surprise, the news about Chloe packing her bags and leaving Richard spread around town at the speed of light. Turns out Mrs. Franks had marched straight over to the Stacks's residence after we'd left. The door was unlocked so, naturally, she went right on in and saw Richard lying on the floor, bleeding.

Ethan Allen got wind of the story first and texted Lilly to see where we were. He called Mason, and they arrived in the patio room just about the time Gloria Peacock had finished filling Chloe in on the goings-on of the past week.

As soon as Mason catches a glimpse of Chloe's hair, he looks at me and mouths, "What the hell?" Ethan Allen doesn't notice it at first, and I watch him as he takes a seat. He looks over at her and is clearly startled by the shock of unkempt hair on her head. He immediately looks at the floor, then at Mason, who shrugs and shakes his head.

They both make a fuss over her to the point she gets annoyed and politely asks them to stop treating her like a burn victim. She tells us that Richard gave her a cocktail of pills every night, and she didn't know what they were and didn't care; she just took them because they made her numb. No one mentions the pills she took the night she was admitted to the hospital.

"I picked this up before I left," she says and pulls a really expensive-looking laptop out of her bag. "It's Richard's."

"That will be most useful, I'm sure," Gloria Peacock says, "but let's save that for later. The sheriff just arrived and you need to get that dealt with."

"The sheriff?" Chloe says, alarmed.

"Yes, the sheriff," Mason says. "Richard called his mother and when she got there, she took him downtown to file a report."

"What kind of report?" Chloe asks, baffled by this turn of events.

"Don't worry," Ethan Allen tells her. "J.J. will explain everything."

The sheriff comes in and looks uncomfortable at first, but when he sees the whole gang sitting around, he appears to relax a little. Deputy Dax isn't with him. I glance at Lilly and she's staring out the window, looking deeply disappointed.

"Chloe," the sheriff says, kneeling down in front of her. "Richard has filed assault charges against you and he's on his way to the hospital to see Dr. Rain, who will, no doubt, provide him with extensive documentation of his injuries."

"Somebody better call the hospital and warn them about his—" I stop short of giving a graphic description of his strange little penis.

"About his what?" Sheriff Jackson looks at me.

"Nothing," I say. "Please carry on." And he does.

"He had his mamma with him, and she started hollering about concussions and brain injuries, so I wouldn't be surprised if he spent a night or two in the hospital in an effort to make things looks worse for you."

"What a pussy!" I mutter and Lilly elbows me.

"J.J.," Chloe says, "are you here to arrest me?"

J. J. Jackson reaches for her hand and she lets him hold it. "No, of course not, Chloe," he says gently. "I was at the hospital the night you were admitted." He looks at me. "After I got your crazy friend over there under control, I went back to do some investigating. I got there just as Adrianna was leaving and she gave me an earful."

"But how did she know what really happened?" Chloe asks.

"She was walking past your room when she heard Richard talking to Dr. Rain, emphasizing how crucial it was that your being there was kept 'under wraps,'" Lilly says, making invisible quotation marks in the air with her fingers. "So, needless to say, she stood there and listened to the entire conversation, then went straight to the desk and called Brother Berkin. Then she called me."

"Then she got fired," I offer and everyone except Chloe gives me a shut-the-hell-up look.

J. J. Jackson nods to Mason. "Mason can take care of this easy as pie, okay? It's just a matter of filling out all the right paperwork."

Chloe looks at Mason. "What can you do? You're a real estate lawyer in Pelican Cove," she says, making it sound more like an accusation than a question.

"Well," he says, trying to act like that didn't sting, "I'm licensed to practice in Mississippi, Alabama, Florida, and Louisiana, and I know more about the law than just how to close a loan on a condo."

"Okay," she says. "What do I need to do first?"

"First of all," Mason says, "I'm going to draw up divorce papers citing infidelity and spousal abuse and add a clause stating that both parties agree to drop all charges pending dissolution of the marriage."

"What do you mean 'both parties agree to drop all charges'?" Chloe asks. "I'm the only one with charges against me."

"Right now," Sheriff Jackson says.

"Exactly," Mason says and continues. "You simply go downtown and file assault charges based on what happened two weeks ago and, while you're down there, you need to go ahead and take out a restraining order against him so he can't come near you as all of this unfolds."

"Oh, good word," I say and Lilly sighs.

"I'm telling you that he won't sign divorce papers," Chloe says. "Especially if I take out papers on him!"

"You see, that's the trick," Mason says and smiles. "Get the divorce papers signed first, *and then* file the charges."

"Is that legal?" Chloe asks.

"The paperwork is, yes," Mason says. "The process? Eh, not so much."

"All we're really concerned about is the paperwork," Sheriff Jackson says with a smile.

"So how is she supposed to get those divorce papers signed?" Lilly asks.

"Oh, I've got that all worked out," Gloria Peacock says from across the room. "All he needs to do is check himself into the hospital."

"And if he doesn't?" Chloe asks.

"Then we'll come up with another plan," Gloria says, undaunted.

"Okay, I've got to run," the sheriff says, letting go of Chloe's hand as he stands. "I don't need to know all of the details of this." He looks down at her in a way that it's obvious to anyone with eyeballs that his concern for her goes above and beyond what his profession requires. "Don't you worry about a thing, Chloe. Nothing is going to happen to you, I promise."

"Thank you, J.J.," Chloe says, blushing.

Upon his exit, Gloria Peacock turns to Mason.

"Sweetheart, how long will it take you to draw up those papers?"

"Couple of hours. I just need to get to my parents' house and get started." He pauses. "The only thing bugging me is how we're going to get this notarized."

"Well, Counsel," Gloria Peacock says with a smile, "I just happen to be a notary public."

"Mrs. Peacock," he says, shaking his head, "you are truly amazing."

"Thank you, Mason," she says in a chipper voice.

He gets up to leave, then turns around. "Oh, I almost forgot," he says. "I spoke with Tina Lucas, the attorney for the school district, on the way over here and she informed me that Lilly's hearing for Thursday has been canceled."

"Yippee!" Lilly exclaims, clapping her hands.

He looks at me. "You're gonna love this, Ace. When I asked about your situation, she didn't know what I was talking about. She put me on hold, then came back and said she couldn't find any documentation on you at all. Then she said it didn't make any difference since Catherine had resigned."

"Wonder where my paperwork got off to?" I ask sarcastically.

"Catherine Hilliard made off like a bandit with it!" Lilly laughs. "She was going to make damn sure you didn't get called before the board."

"Speaking of the board," Mason continues, smiling. "No more than five minutes after I hung up with her, the chairman of the board called and said he and Ms. Lucas would like to meet with the three of us next Monday morning at the county office."

"For what?" I ask.

"He said he was anxious to get the two of you back in the classroom, but would like to speak to us about, and I quote, 'finding a way to handle all of this privately without making it a public spectacle.'"

"Imagine that," I say with disgust.

"I'll tell you what he wants—he wants to sweep it all under the rug," Chloe says, "just like everyone does everything around here. He wants to make sure no one says a word about any wrongdoing and he needs you and Tina Lucas there to make sure this entire incident doesn't blow up in his face."

"You're exactly right, Chloe," Gloria says, then turns to Lilly and me. "Do y'all plan to attend the meeting?"

"I will!" Lilly says. "I can't wait to get back to work."

"I don't know," I say. "I'd like to make this thing so public that Anderson Cooper shows up to cover it."

"I don't know about all that," Lilly mumbles.

"It would be in everyone's best interest to let that opportunity pass, Ace," Gloria says. "I know how satisfying it would be for you to expose everything that's happened, but you have to remember that your first responsibility as an educator is to your students. Catherine Hilliard is gone. She lost. You won. It's over and it's time to move on. A smear campaign will do nothing but harm to the school's image worse than Catherine Hilliard already has, and that's not what you want, is it?"

"Of course not," I say. "She's made those kids so miserable for the past two years. Plus Olivia West and the rest of the seniors should be able to enjoy the remainder of the year in peace, without any"—I look at Mason—"public spectacle."

"Exactly!" Lilly says, beaming. "And we need to get back to work."

"Yeah," I say, unable to muster up much enthusiasm. "We need to get back to work."

"Good girl," Ethan Allen says, patting me on the back. "I'm proud of you, Ace! I know how hard it is for you to buckle down and keep your mouth shut."

"Thanks for that, Ethan Allen," I say and roll my eyes while everyone has a good laugh at my expense.

"What about you, Chloe," Lilly asks. "When do you think you'll come back?"

"I'm ready to get back to work, too. There is so much to be done this time of year and poor Mrs. Marshall is in there having to go it alone." Chloe runs a hand through her hair. "I just have a few things to take care of first, so it'll be later next week before I go back."

Her reference to her hair makes me uncomfortable, so I start messing with the plant next to my chair because I don't know what to say.

"Fantastic," Gloria says, pressing her elegant hands together as if to pray. "We're pulling this ship back up before it sinks!" I don't know what to say to that, either, so I keep fiddling with the greenery. "Oh, and Lilly," Gloria continues without missing a beat, "your uncle Rye wishes to speak with you, and I would consider it a personal favor if you would give him a call."

"Yes, ma'am," she says flatly and stares at her feet in shame.

"Goodness, we've had a lot on our plates today," Gloria Peacock says, getting up and stretching.

"Well, I better get moving," Mason says. "Got a lot to do this afternoon, so I'll see y'all tomorrow."

"I should be gettin' along, too," Ethan Allen says, getting up.

"Ethan Allen," Gloria Peacock calls.

"Yes, ma'am."

"Would you be so kind as to keep your ears open at the bar tonight and let me know what the word around town is on all of this business."

"Will do, Mrs. Peacock."

"And give your grandparents my regards, lovely people, Tillman and Quay."

"Will do, ma'am, thank you," Ethan Allen replies. "Chloe," he says, as he walks toward the door, "I'm glad you're all right and if you need anything, don't hesitate to call."

"Thanks, Ethan Allen."

"Ace, Lilly, Mrs. Peacock," he says and nods his head at each of us individually. "Have a good afternoon and take care."

We all chime in with good-byes and he puts his cowboy hat on and walks out into the sun.

"Nice boy," Gloria says, smiling after him. "Not many like him anymore." She looks at us. "That man would make an excellent husband and father." We all nod our heads in agreement. "I guess he just hasn't found the right woman yet."

"I think he's had so many bad ones that he's given up hope on finding a good one," I offer, trying to relieve a little bit of pressure she just put on the three of us.

"Hmmm," she says, "interesting. Well, ladies, I guess you understand that we have reached that point where stalking Richard Stacks would do more harm than good?"

"Yes, ma'am," I say and Lilly just nods.

"I think the three of you could use some serious downtime before we get those papers signed."

"How are we gonna do that again?" Lilly asks.

"Easy," Gloria Peacock says, waving her hand like it's no big deal. I've got it all planned out. Why don't the three of you stay here this afternoon?" she asks and my eyes light up. "We could all use a few hours in the spa." She looks at Chloe, then Lilly, then me. "Anyone for a little rest and relaxation?"

"Sounds good to me," I chirp.

◇◇◇

43

We follow Gloria Peacock through the majestic hallway, down a marble staircase, and into the most luxurious locker room I've ever seen in my life.

"There are some robes in there," she says, pointing, "towels, swimsuits, sandals, lots of other stuff. Please help yourself to whatever you need and I'll meet y'all out by the hot tub in thirty minutes. It's out that door and around to the left."

I grab a swimsuit that looks like it might fit me, then head to the robe closet and grab a big fuzzy one. I slide on a pair of fluffy slippers and prepare myself to be pampered.

Lilly, Chloe, and I slip into the hot tub and wait for Gloria Peacock to reappear. We sip water out of glasses and talk about how crazy the past few weeks have been. When Gloria shows up, she is wearing a blue one-piece swimsuit and her body looks like that of a twenty-five-year-old yoga instructor. She eases into the tub and tells us that two women have just arrived and are setting up to do pedicures, manicures, and facials, and the masseuse and his partner will be arriving shortly.

A staff lady appears several minutes later and informs Mrs. Peacock that the nail technicians are set up. Gloria asks Chloe to join her, and they get out of the hot tub and make their way to the cushy white pedicure chairs that are situated about a hundred feet away.

"Can you believe this place?" I ask Lilly, once they're out of earshot.

"No, I can't," she says, laying her head back. "Can you believe our luck that we're sitting here?"

"No, I can't."

"So what about that Chloe?" she asks, raising her head back up. "Clubbing Richard's nuts with that wall ornament."

"Man," I say, laughing despite myself, "what a day."

"What a day, indeed," she says. "This is just what I need right now."

"Yeah," I say. "So, uh, what's up with you and Dax? You haven't mentioned him in a day or two."

She takes a deep breath and sighs heavily before answering, "Old girlfriend just got a divorce and she's been staying with him for the past week."

"Aw, Lil, I'm sorry to hear that," I say. "At least he told you."

"He didn't," she says, leaning her head back and closing her eyes. "She answered his phone when I called last week and told me, in so many words, not to ever call him again."

"Jeez, that's got to be so embarrassing for him," I say. "I guess he was just too nice of a guy to make her leave."

"Whatever," Lilly says and looks like she's about to cry.

"Lilly, have you told him how you feel or have you led him to believe that he's just another notch on your lipstick case?"

"I haven't told him anything or led him anywhere," she says. "Honestly, I was hoping he might say something. I mean"—she bites her lip and looks away—"I know he's in love with me. I can tell."

"It's pretty obvious you feel the same way."

"Yes, I do," she wails. "Look at me! I'm miserable!"

"Yep, that's love all right!" I say and we share a giggle.

"What am I going to do?" she says. "He's only twenty-three and she's probably around the same age." She gets a pained look on her face. "Or younger. I can't compete with that!"

"Oh, bullshit, Lilly," I say. "Young chicks don't have a thing on us." I look at her and smile. "You're gonna have to tell him."

"You know I don't do stuff like that. There are rules—"

"Fuck the rules, Lilly," I say quietly. "I haven't seen you this much in love since, uh, let me think . . . since Freddie Pullen started school with us in the eighth grade."

"LOL, Ace. Freddie Pullen was and probably still is the biggest nerd on planet Earth." She tries not to but starts laughing. "I think you were the one with the hots for him."

"Oh, yeah, for sure. He was what you might call a techno-hottie."

"Maybe I should track him down on Facebook," Lilly says, rolling over in the water. "He's probably a zillionaire by now."

"Probably so. Remember him reading the *Wall Street Journal* during lunch?"

"Oh, Lord," she says and laughs. "How could anyone forget that? We were throwing French fries at each other and he was studying variations in the stock market. I don't think I'll look him up after all. I'm probably way too dumb for him."

"So does Dax have a list?" I ask.

"He does now," she says and sniggers.

The staff lady reappears with two flutes of champagne, which we graciously accept.

"Mrs. Peacock has asked me to inform both of you that the massage tables will be ready in ten minutes."

"Okay," I say, taking a sip of champagne.

"I'll come and show you to the parlors."

"Thank you so much," Lilly says.

"Parlors?" I whisper after the blue-clad lady disappears.

"To parlors," Lilly says, and raises her glass.

"To parlors," I say, clinking my glass against hers.

◇◇

44

After the single most relaxing afternoon of my life, Lilly and I leave the Waverly Estate with specific instructions from Gloria Peacock to lay low. Chloe graciously accepts Gloria's offer to be a guest of honor at the Waverly Estate, and the golf cart chauffeur takes her bags out of my car and loads them into the six-seater before we leave.

"That sure was nice of Mrs. Peacock to invite Chloe to stay," Lilly says as we drive away.

"No doubt," I agree. "There is no better place on Earth for her to be right now."

"Gloria Peacock certainly has taken a keen interest in us," Lilly says. "I wonder if Uncle Rye asked her to intervene."

"I thought about that," I say. "But it seemed like such a coincidence when we saw her, or rather when she saw us, that day."

"Gloria Peacock strikes me as the type of woman who can create coincidences as she sees fit," Lilly says, staring out the window.

"Good point," I agree. "Hey, you could ask Rye about it when you call him later."

"Yeah," Lilly says with a sigh. "I'll do that. When I call him later."

"On the other hand, maybe we shouldn't question the appearance of our fairy godmother."

"Whatever you say, Cinderella," she says quietly.

I drop her off at her pink dollhouse and head home. When I get there, Mason McKenzie's Escalade is sitting in my driveway. I walk through the gate and find him asleep in one of my backyard loungers with Buster Loo tucked under his arm. I smile despite myself and my heart starts to flip and flutter and I wish I could make it stop, but I can't. Buster Loo opens one eye, sees me, and goes ape-shit crazy.

"Hey," Mason says, rubbing his eyes.

"Hey," I say, smiling so hard my face hurts.

"Y'all have a good afternoon at the Waverly Resort and Spa?"

"Oh, absolutely," I say. "Massage, manicure, pedicure, cucumber facial, the whole nine yards."

"I'll give you a cucumber—"

"Don't say it!"

"Massage," he says with a devilish grin. "I'll give you a cucumber massage or a massage with a cucumber. Whatever you like."

"You should probably just stop right there," I say, laughing. "You could've gone inside, you know." I tell him.

"Well, I didn't want to piss you off, so I thought I'd hang around out here on the back porch like a stranger."

"Or a stalker," I offer.

"Or that," he says, getting up, and I see he has a boner the size of Nebraska. I can't help myself. I just stare.

"Oops," he says, grinning and adjusting himself. "My bad."

"Why don't you come on in the house?" I say.

"Are we gonna have sex?"

"Let me think a minute," I say. "Uh, no."

"Good, because I wasn't going to come in if you said yes."

He volunteers to take Buster Loo to the park and I use that time to straighten up the house a little bit. After wiping down the kitchen counters, I kick all of my clothes into the closet, then sweep and vacuum faster than I ever have. I wash and dry Buster Loo's doggie dishes and put down fresh water and two scoops of dog food. When Mason gets back, he wants to go to Ethan Allen's, but I tell him that we were instructed to lay low and I don't think that would qualify. We talk it over while Buster Loo chomps on his dog food in the kitchen.

We eventually decide on Chinese takeout and Red Box movies.

"Buster Loo wanna go for a ride?" Mason says, walking toward the front door. Buster Loo hauls chiweenie ass from the kitchen to where Mason is standing. Mason scoops him up, looks at me, and says, "Now we're ready." Buster Loo gives him a few quick licks on the cheek and Mason walks out the door telling him what a good boy he is.

"Did you get the divorce papers finished?" I ask after I get in his truck.

"Oh, yeah," he says. "That file is sitting in Mrs. Peacock's in-box right now."

"That was fast."

"Had to be." He looks at me. "Let's not talk about all that. I hate drawing up divorce papers. That's why I went the real estate route. Not as much angst." Buster Loo is perched on his left leg with his paws on the door and is rubbing his snout all over the bottom of Mason's window.

"Okay, but can you tell me how she's supposed to get them signed?"

"Mrs. Peacock said she had that all under control."

"Yeah," I say, "she mentioned that Richard Stacks had checked into the hospital. She's really connected, isn't she?"

"To say the least." Mason shakes his head. "There ain't a damn reason in the world he should be in the hospital. That is so ridiculous." He scratches his head. "Hell, his mother probably made him do it."

"Probably so," I say, laughing.

"How was Chloe when you left?"

"Doing good. Gloria Peacock had a stylist come in and cut her hair."

"Oh, God, when I saw that hair, Ace, I almost died!" Mason says, laughing. "I hate to laugh, I mean, it's not funny, but damn! It was like some kind of wild animal perched up on the top of her head. It was scary!" He looks at me. "You know, I've never seen her with a single hair out of place and that just shocked the hell out of me."

"Yeah, it was hard to look at."

"You know, that was really kind of you and Lilly going over there and getting her out of that house."

"We should've done it a long time ago."

"Can't force people to do something if they're not ready." He glances over at me. "Know what I mean?"

"I do," I reply and wonder if we're still talking about Chloe.

"So," he says, switching conversational gears, "Ethan Allen tells me you and Lilly really had it out about that Panama City trip."

"Yeah, I was pretty pissed," I say, "especially when I thought she was doing it with ol' Zac Tanner."

"Is that Dean Tanner's kid?" he asks.

"Yep," I reply. "Heck of a football player."

"Just like his daddy and his granddaddy," Mason says. "Football runs deep in that family. Has he signed anywhere yet?"

"He's going to the University of Alabama," I say. "It's a tragedy."

"Oh, God," Mason wails. "You're kidding me, right?"

"Wish I was," I say. "I'd rather see him go to Ole Miss than to Alabama."

"Was that a compliment or an insult? I couldn't tell," he says, pulling up to a Red Box. "What are you in the mood for?" He puts a hand in the air. "Wait! Let me guess . . . comedy?"

"Always!" I say. "Get us something funny."

"Done." He hops out and rents a few movies, then walks next door to China Kitchen and picks up our dinner.

After stuffing himself to the gills with General Tso's chicken, Mason goes into the living room and sprawls out on the sofa.

"What do you want to watch first?" he calls.

"I don't care," I say, "as long as it's funny."

"Come in here and sit down and tell me," he whines. "They're all funny."

I go over, pick up the movies, and sit by him on the couch. He drapes his arm around my shoulder and says, "You know, we don't have to watch a movie."

"Oh, yeah," I say, looking him in the eye. "But what would we do if we didn't?"

"Oh, I don't know." He pulls my face up close to his. "Anything come to mind?"

"Um-hmm," I mumble as he kisses me for the first time in almost ten months.

I drop the movies on the floor and we head for the bedroom.

45

◇◇

When the sun breaks through the curtains, I am wide awake and my heart is churning with feelings I can't get under control. Most prevalent by far is the crazy, nervous feeling of being madly in love with the man stretched across my bed.

I reach over and stroke his short blond hair and my mind spins off in a million different directions.

What have I done? Why did I do this? How long has it been since I've had sex? Who was the last person I had sex with? Was it him or Logan Hatter? What if I'm pregnant? What was that weird move he made just before he finished? Do I want to marry him? Should I make him leave or should I cook him breakfast? How many hot young things has he bedded since I left last summer? Why can't I remember the last time I had sex? What is he doing here? Would he be mad if I woke him up to do it again?

I decide to make some coffee and try to sort things out in my head before he wakes up. Buster Loo is standing in the hallway when I open the door and he runs past me without so much as a glance and rocket launches himself onto the bed, where he curls up next to Mason. Then he squints his eyes at me as if to convey his dismay at spending the night in the hallway.

I go to the kitchen and put on some coffee, and I'm staring out the window trying to tame my crazed thoughts when I feel Mason's arms slip around my waist. He pulls my hair back and kisses me gently on the neck. I turn around and he hugs me tight, cradling the back of my head in his hand.

He pours two cups of coffee and hands one to me. Smiling, he nods toward the patio, and we go outside and sit down. Buster Loo bursts through the doggie door and makes a real scene of running around and doing his speedy-dog crazy eights twice as fast as he usually does.

Mason looks at me and I look at my day lilies and everything in my mind falls away. All I'm left with is a pressing need to spend the rest of my life as Mrs. Mason McKenzie.

"So," he says quietly. When I look at him, my insides start to quiver. He cocks his head sideways and says, "What did you say your name was again?"

I bust out laughing and so does he. Then we sit and talk like old friends, laughing through two pots of coffee. He helps me make breakfast and insists on doing the dishes while I take a bubble bath. I soak in the tub and try not to daydream about happily ever after.

I hear him start the shower in the guest room, and five minutes later he steps into the doorway of my bathroom, wearing only a towel.

"Are you gonna flash me?" I ask.

"No," he says flatly, "I'm not the kind of man that flaunts my baby carrot."

I laugh out loud and say, "Baby carrot, indeed."

He raises his eyebrows and smiles, nodding toward the bed. I tell him to close the door so I can get out. He politely complies and I hop out of the tub, wrap a towel around me, brush my teeth, and shake out my hair. I grab my bottle of Sweet Cotton and spray my body down like I'm putting out a fire. When I open the door, Mason is lying in my bed with the sheet pulled up to his waist. His towel is on the floor and his baby carrot has transformed into a cucumber. I saunter around to my side of the bed and he starts sneezing like he just snorted a line of black pepper.

"What is that smell?" he says, rubbing his nose.

"Sweet Cotton," I say, cringing.

"Oh, God," he says. "It smells great"—he sneezes again—"but I think it's got my allergies stirred up." He sneezes sixteen more times.

I go back into the bathroom, dejected, and shower off half a bottle of Sweet Cotton. When I go back into the bedroom, he's on my side of the bed, reading *Cosmo*.

"What are you doing?" I ask.

"Researching the enemy," he says and smiles. "Come here, baby, and let me smell that hair."

"Better not," I caution as I slip into bed beside him. "You might have another attack."

He rolls onto his side, drapes his arm around me, and leans down close to my face.

"I might attack *you*," he says and pulls me up next to his cucumber.

An hour later, we're sitting in the kitchen talking about Chloe's situation, when his phone starts to buzz on the counter.

"Hand that to me, would you?"

"Sure," I say and tell myself not to look at the caller ID. But I just can't help myself. I look at the caller ID.

Allison.

That gets me good and pissed off.

Allison was the young lady who paid Mason a visit and caused me to pack up and leave him last summer..

I hold my breath and smile when I hand him the phone, praying my countenance doesn't betray me. He looks at the caller ID, gets up, and walks out the back door.

That pisses me off even more, and I think for a second about going out the front door and sneaking around back so I can hear what he's saying, but I remind myself, yet again, not to be so pathetic. Seven minutes and thirty-two seconds pass and he walks back in, says nothing, and sits back down at the table.

"What?" he asks. "What's wrong?"

I just stare at him, shaking.

"What is it?" he asks, and I think he honestly has no idea why I'm so upset.

"Who was that?"

"Nobody," he says, looking out the window into the backyard. "Why?"

My inner bitch and outer grown-up tangle in a vicious brawl, and I just sit there and stare at him like I might rip his head off and feed it to some wild hogs.

"Oh, my God," he says, getting up. "Don't tell me you're pissed off because I took a phone call outside."

"I'm pissed off because the caller ID said Allison, and, if my memory serves me right, I remember an Allison."

"Ace, really?" he says, walking into the living room. "I'm not having this fight with you again."

"Again?" I explode. "What the hell do you mean, again? We never had it to start with! Allison showed up and instead of asking her to leave, you took her by the arm and went outside and talked it over with her for almost an hour! What was I supposed to do? Just sit there while your number-one ex–booty call commandeered your attention in the driveway all night long."

"What's the point of being rude?" he says. "There was never anything serious between us."

"Please don't remind me that it was just a sex thing, okay?"

"But that's all it was! I can't help it she was upset! I can't help it she wanted more from the relationship than I did. I was just trying to let her down easy."

"Mason, I had been living at your house for over a month. I think we were a little past the point where you were supposed to let her down easy. Sorry, but that's something you should've dealt with long before I got there."

"I tried, trust me, I did. She's kind of a troublemaker and I'm sorry."

"See, if you knew she was a troublemaker, then why didn't you just ask her to leave when she showed up at the door?"

"I don't know, maybe because I made the mistake of thinking that you trusted me." He looks at me. "Rest assured, had I known the trouble it was going to cause, I would've slammed the door in her face and slid a note under it telling her to stay the hell away from me. I swear I would have."

"How could you *not* have known the trouble it would cause?" I say. "And how would you feel if I'd done something like that to you?"

"Don't give me that shit, Ace, because you dated Logan Hatter for how long? And how do I act around him? Hell, I like the guy!"

"That's different!" I shoot back. "He's friends with everybody you're friends with up here, and he has zero interest in us getting back together, and he is not the kind of person who would just show up at my house and spend an hour in the driveway talking to me if he knew you were here because he's not a home wrecker!"

"Oh, of course, that's different. How convenient for you. You know, you're the one who should be a lawyer, not me."

"What do you mean by that?"

"When's the last time you lost an argument?"

"I don't know, why?"

He shakes his head. "Why are you so hard to get along with?"

"How can you expect me not to be hard to get along with when you come to my house, weasel your way back into my life, tell me you are staying here until I marry you, then you take *her* call in my house, or rather *outside* my house! What the hell do you expect?"

"I meant it when I said I wanted to marry you," he says. "Don't throw that up in my face. And for your information, psycho, that was not the same Allison. The Allison who just called is Connor's wife— remember the new guy?—and she's helping him out around the office while I'm gone. He's working late and needed to know something, so she called me. But, please, let me thank you for thinking the worst of me!" He storms back to the guest room, and Buster Loo starts running up and down the hallway looking like he's about to have a nervous breakdown.

"I'm not doing this," he says, coming back with his bags. "I tried for months to call you after you left. I sent you roses. I sent you cards. I knocked on your door and you didn't answer. You have avoided me like the plague for over nine months. Nine months that I wanted to spend with you. Nine months that I wanted us to be together. But I see now. I see that, for whatever reason you've made up in your head, I'm a douche bag who can't be trusted." He pauses. "And if you loved me, if you really cared about me, you would not be treating me like this right now. So I'm leaving."

"Mason, wait, I'm sorry."

"No, Ace, I'm sorry," he says. "I'm sorry for coming back up here and trying to make this work."

"Well, I'm sorry that it hurt my feelings, okay? I'm sorry I wanted to stay away from you because you have so much power over me because I've always been so in love with you. It scared me when you walked out there to talk to her, okay? Because I was so afraid of losing you. It made me mad, hurt my feelings, and scared me because she was so beautiful. I couldn't understand how you could pick me over her. And everyone down there looks just like her. Everywhere we went, I felt like I was being judged and coming up short. I felt insufficient, okay? And it was more than I could stand, so I left and told myself to get over it, but I never did. I've missed you every day since I left. Every time my phone rings or buzzes, I want it to be you. I'm sorry. I'm crazy as hell and I know that and I'm sorry." I look at him with tears rolling down my face. "Why didn't you just tell me who she was and why she was there? You came back in, sat down on the couch, and started watching ESPN like nothing had happened."

"Because it didn't matter who she was or why she was there," he said. "That wasn't the important part." He looks me right in the eye. "The important part was that you didn't trust me"—he picks up his bags—"and you still don't."

"Mason," I say, "I'm sorry!"

"It's over, Ace. If you can't trust me, and you've made it clear that you can't, then there is nothing left for us to discuss." He walks out the door.

Buster Loo whimpers, and then disappears to his secret hiding place.

I stand there for a second with my mind reeling. I start feeling sorry for myself, and then start feeling sorry for my dog. For a second I feel sorry for Mason, because what if I really am a crazy, psycho bitch? What if I'm our only problem? This makes me mad at myself, but then I get mad at him when I start thinking about all the ways he could've handled the situation with Allison back then and the way he just handled that phone call.

I spend the rest of the day cleaning my house and being pissed off. I take Buster Loo for an evening stroll and calm down a little bit, but when I get home and see the movies on the coffee table, I get mad all over again.

"I'm not taking those back," I tell Buster Loo, who turns his head sideways as if to ask, "Why not?"

I walk over to the counter, dig through my purse, and pull out the business card that Biker Man gave me in the parking lot of the strip club.

"Compton Commercial Construction," I read, running my finger over the interlocking Cs. "Thomas Compton, owner." I pick up my cell phone and dial the number on the card. After three rings it goes to voice mail.

"Hello, Mr. Compton, uh, Tommy. This is Ace Jones. I met you in the, uh, in a parking lot last Saturday night." I pause. "And I was just giving you a call." Another pause. I press three to erase the message, and learn then that he has a different cell phone service because a voice comes on the line and says, "If you need more time, press two." I don't know what to do, so I just press the damn two button and keep talking. "Okay, so if you're ever down around Bugtussle, then be sure to give me a call!" I leave my number, then say, "Thanks." I add quickly, "And thanks for showing up when you did Saturday night. My friend and I really appreciated that." Pause. "Okay, so good-bye." I press the button to end the call.

"Shit!" I say and put the phone down. It rings immediately and scares the hell out of me. I panic for a brief second, then recognize the ring tone. It's Lilly.

"Gloria Peacock just called," she says. "Time to get those papers signed."

◇◇

46

"Here's the plan," Gloria Peacock says when we arrive in her dining room. "Lilly is going to create a distraction, and you," she says, looking at me, "and Chloe are going to slip into Richard Stacks's room and get him to sign these papers."

"Is he going to do that?" I ask, trying to hide my skepticism. "Sign the papers, just because we ask him to?"

"I'm not asking him," Chloe says. "I'm telling him."

Lilly and I stare at Chloe, and I see a smile creep across Gloria Peacock's face. I notice that Chloe's hair has been pixie trimmed and looks much better.

"Okay," I say to Chloe, "you, uh, seem really confident this will work."

"I'm taking all the wonderful pictures that y'all took with my camera," Chloe says. "I'm going to show those to him, give him the pen, and tell him that if he doesn't sign on the dotted line his fat-ass mother will have a stack of eight-by-tens on her front doorstep first thing in the morning."

I barrel laugh at that feisty little comment. "Oh, Chloe, I'm so happy for you and so sad for you all at the same time," I say. "This is crazy!"

"Why can't Chloe just walk in and act like she's there to see Richard?" Lilly asks.

"First of all," Gloria Peacock says, "visiting hours are over. Second, Dr. Rain is on duty tonight and I don't think he'd welcome you all with open arms."

"Nah, probably not," I say.

"Chloe, remember that Richard has to sign the bottom of all three pages, so you whip his emotions into a frenzy as quick as possible so he'll sign it just to get you out of there."

"Chloe, are you sure you want to go in?" I ask. "I mean, Lilly and I could get this done—"

"Absolutely not!" Chloe says, tapping the table for emphasis. "I am going to handle this myself!"

"Okay, then," I peep.

"Ladies," Gloria Peacock says, "there's no time like the present." She hands Chloe and me a pair of scrubs, hospital name tags, and clipboards. Then she gives Lilly a hospital gown, white leggings, and some really nice-looking house shoes. She tells us to change quickly and meet her in the garage, so we do. When we get to the garage, we find the golf cart driver standing next to a jet black Mercedes-Benz with jet black tinted windows.

"Is that our ride?" I ask, way more excited than the other two because they drive luxury cars every day.

"Yes, ma'am, it is," the chauffeur says, "and I'm your driver."

All I can do is grin like an idiot. Gloria Peacock comes into the garage with a handful of electronics and gives each of us a walkie-talkie the size of a pager and a wireless earbud.

"I feel like James Bond, for real," I say as I slip the communication device into my ear. "Is this some more magic from Omega Systems?" I ask Gloria Peacock.

"Good guess, young lady," she says with a wink. "Girls, I wish you the best of luck. Remember, stick to the plan. Get in, get out, and alert George if you hit a snag.

"Oh, wait, I almost forgot." She steps back into the house and returns a moment later with a large adjustable strap. "This is for Richard," she says. "Chloe, you need to get it out of the bag before you go in the room, and as soon as you get close enough, throw one end over his chest and one end under the bed." She turns to me. "Ace, you have to live up to your nickname here and grab both ends as fast as you can. Snap it together like this and pull."

"Just like a dog collar," I say.

"Something like that, yes. Y'all need to get this done quickly while you still have the element of surprise going for you, okay?"

"There are so many ways this could go wrong," I say.

"And there are so many ways it could go right," Mrs. Peacock says. "Worst-case scenario, it's a total failure and we have to kidnap him later to get it done." She smiles, and I can't help but wonder if she's serious. "We'll do whatever it takes."

"Whatever it takes," Lilly says with a smile.

"Whatever y'all say," I say, trying to sound confident.

We go over the plan one more time before we leave, then ride to the hospital in silence. George drops us off at a side door that Gloria Peacock arranged to have unlocked. Apparently when you donate millions of dollars to a hospital, multiple favors are only a phone call away.

We take the stairs up to the third floor and Lilly steps into the hallway first. She gives us an "all clear" and we creep into the hallway and stay a few feet behind her. I watch Lilly duck into an unoccupied room as Chloe and I keep walking. The challenge is getting past the nurses' station, and with each step, I get more and more nervous.

"Lilly," I whisper into the mic, "all set?"

"Ready," she whispers back.

I look at Chloe and she gives me a nod and pulls the strap out of the messenger bag.

"Do you have a pen?" I ask her.

"What?" Lilly says.

"Not you, dumbass," I whisper, a bit too loud. "I was talking to Chloe!"

"Of course I have a pen!" Chloe says and looks at me like I'm an imbecile.

"Well, excuse me for double-checking," I whisper, then into the walkie-talkie say, "Do it, Lilly. We're almost to the nurses' station."

I hear a table hit the floor and then Lilly yells, "What am I doing in here? Where am I? How did I get here? I've missed the school bus again!"

Everyone within sight jumps into motion and Chloe and I turn our backs as the crowd whirs by. When I look up, I see bed linens and towels flying out the door and into the hallway. Lilly slams the door shut and, as specified in the plan, rams the bed up against it. Calls go out for security as Chloe and I hustle past the nurses' station and slip unnoticed into Richard Stacks's room.

"What the hell is that noise?" he asks in a rough, scratchy voice. "Tell whoever that is to hold it down, if you can handle that, which you probably can't because I asked for a glass of water an hour ago, and apparently no one here is competent enough to put ice in a cup because I still do not have any water."

"Shut your mouth, Richard," Chloe says and stalks over to the bed. She tosses one end of the strap across his belly and the other end under the bed just like Gloria Peacock said. Richard makes a move to push the call button on the bed, but she slaps his hand away and says, "Now, you listen to me." I fumble around trying to grab the end of the strap that she threw under the bed and finally get hold of it and get the stupid thing snapped. "I have divorce papers and you are going to sign them."

"Yeah," he says, "and what if I don't?"

"I was hoping you'd ask that," Chloe says. She looks at me and I give her a quick nod and she grabs his right hand and I grab his left and I say, "Surprise!" as we zip tie each of his wrists to the bed rails. He starts jerking around and cussing and shaking the bed, so I grab the adjustable end of that strap and give it a good tug. I pull it so hard, it slides from his belly down to his hips and he gets really still and says, "Oh, my God, are y'all going to cut off my penis?"

"What?" I say.

"Richard, I don't plan on touching your penis again for as long as I live, okay? Besides, it's too short to get a good grip on when it's soft."

"Oh, my goodness." I try and fail to keep a straight face. "Pork Chop Penis," I tell him, getting hysterical. "You've got a pork chop penis!"

"How would you know?" he growls.

"She saw it when she took this picture," Chloe says and holds out the shot of him in Mrs. Dana Dannan's living room.

"I'll have you arrested for stalking and harassment," he tells me.

"I don't give a shit," I reply.

"Okay, Richard," Chloe says, getting in a rush. "We don't have much time so let me give it to you straight." She starts flipping through pictures, tilting them sideways so he can see. "Either sign the papers or these pictures will be on your mother's front doorstep first thing in the morning!"

"Nurse!" he yells. I pick up the plastic soda bottle on his nightstand and pop him on the forehead with it. The melee is still going full force out in the hallway, so I'm confident no one can hear him.

"Shut up!" I say. "Don't make this any harder than it has to be. Just sign the papers and we'll be on our way."

"This is blackmail, Chloe, and you will not get away with it," he shouts. "Nurse!" I pop him on the head again, a little closer to his eyeball.

"I'm gonna get that eye next," I tell him, hitting the bottle on my hand. Chloe reaches into her bag and I think she's about to pull out the divorce papers, but she doesn't. She pulls out a red cardboard cylinder about the size of a Lysol can.

"Yell for a nurse again and I'll give you a mouthful," she says, twisting the top on the container.

"Is that ant killer?" I ask. "Where did you get ant killer?"

"It's Sevin dust. I picked it up in Gloria's garage just before we left."

"That's poisonous!" Richard yells. "You two will not get away with this," Richard says, tugging at the zip ties.

"Yeah, I heard you the first time," I say.

Chloe puts the ant killer down and takes the divorce papers out and attaches them to her clipboard.

"Do you have a pen or would you like to borrow mine?"

"I'm not signing a damn thing, Chloe!" he growls. "You will go to jail for this."

"Hit him with that Sevin dust one time and see how he feels about it then."

"You crazy bitch!" he screams at me.

Chloe picks up the Sevin dust and sprinkles a little on Richard's forehead. "I'm warning you, Richard."

"Hey, Chloe, do you want me to call Mrs. Stacks and tell her to be expecting a package in the morning?"

"Would you, please?" Chloe says, like an angel. "Look, there is his cell phone. Why don't you just use that?"

"Excellent idea," I say, picking up Richard's cell phone. "Well, she's right here at the top of the recent call list. What a surprise!"

"No!" he yells. "Don't you dare!"

"You should really consider speaking quieter." She smiles at him and taps the ant killer. "Don't make me dust you!"

I turn the phone around so he can see. I hold my finger over the button.

"What's it gonna be, Richard?" Chloe asks. "We're running out of time."

"Give me the papers!" he says gruffly. I run around the hospital bed and take the clipboard while she stands guard with the bug powder. "Hold the clipboard down where he can sign it," Chloe tells me, and I get on my knees on the floor so I can hold it steady.

"You won't get away with this, Chloe," he mutters.

"Sure, I will," she says, picking up the pictures with her other hand. "Because I will always have these ready to box up and send to your mamma."

"Does Mamma not like her boy to go to the strip club?" I say in my best baby-talking voice.

"That old heifer would *die*," Chloe says and laughs. "Right after she murdered him."

"Give me the pen!" he wails. "Give me the pen, you heartless bitches!"

"Man," I say, putting the pen in his hand, "you are so damn pathetic." I hold the clipboard with one hand and flip the pages with the other while he scribbles his name across the highlighted lines. He stops before he signs the last page.

"This won't be a legal document," he says. "I'm calling Lester and telling him what you did and this will never stand up in court."

"Why don't you do that?" I say. "And I'll call Bruce Valspar and tell him that his wife gives you blow jobs out in the alley beside your office."

"What?" they say at the same time.

"We've got pictures of that, too," I tell Chloe.

"Brooke Valspar is my friend!" Chloe exclaims. "We're in the same Sunday school class! How could she!"

"She doesn't know what she's talking about, Chloe," Richard says, with his usual air of arrogance.

I look at him and say, "Bruce Valspar would beat you within an inch of your life if he knew about you and Brooke. Sit there and act like you don't know what I'm talking about and I'll call him as soon as we get out of here and tell him what happened and exactly where you are, and when he gets done with you, you really will need medical attention. Then I'll take those pictures Chloe showed you plus the ones I haven't shown her yet and tack those suckers all over the door of your church like Martin Luther did his Thesis. Got it?" He looks at me. "It's over, Richard. You don't have a leg to stand on and you know it. Now put your name on this fucking line, or I will not rest until I have completely ruined your life."

He signs the last line without another word. The fire alarm sounds and Chloe stuffs the pictures and ant killer back into her bag.

"That's our cue to get out of here!" I say, handing her the papers. I scramble around the bed, unsnap the strap, and roll it up as fast as I can. "What about the zip ties? I don't have anything to cut them with!"

"Then leave them!" Chloe says quickly. "We've got to go!"

We're hustling to the door when Chloe stops and looks back at her soon-to-be ex-husband.

"Don't you ever"—she points at him—"come near me again and don't you ever say one bad word about me. Understand?"

"Yes, Chloe," he moans miserably. "I understand."

"Let's go," she says.

We meet a nurse in the doorway and Chloe keeps moving past her, but I duck my head and say, "Nurse, we're from the sixth floor and this man has been placed on suicide watch. We've secured his wrists, but were unable to identify the powdery substance on his forehead. He's showing signs of lunacy. Please get the doctor!"

"Nurse," Richard yells, "help me! Stop those criminals!"

We bolt out of his room and I grab a gurney in the hallway. Security guards and nurses are running everywhere and a few firemen have just arrived on the scene.

"Madness!" I say, delighted by the chaos we created. Chloe and I pull our medical masks over our faces and push the gurney through the crowd.

"Sixth floor!" I yell. "Sixth floor, mental health coming through!"

I hear Dr. Sebastian Rain in a heated conversation with Deputy Dax Dorsett, who is accusing the good doctor of all manner of wrongdoing. When we get to the door of the room that Lilly has commandeered, I knock three times, then tell everyone to stay back.

"Sixth floor!" I yell. "Mental health! Give us some room, please!"

Lilly opens the door and Chloe pushes the gurney into the room.

Lilly jumps on the bed and lays down.

"Dax is in the hallway," I tell her.

"Oh, shit! He can't see me!" she says, looking around. "Hand me that pillow!" I give it to her and she pulls the pillow out, tosses it on the floor, and puts the pillowcase over her head. "Okay, let's roll!"

Chloe grabs one end of the gurney and I get the other and we push her out of the room and into the ruckus in the hallway. She starts singing "Row, Row, Row Your Boat" and making the motions with her hands. I keep my head down as we hustle our "patient" down the hallway and to the elevator.

"Excuse me," Dr. Sebastian Rain yells. "Could you please stop a minute and let me see that patient?"

"No, sir," I say. "Doctor's orders to get the patient confined and subdued as quickly as possible." We push Lilly into the elevator.

"*I* am a doctor," Sebastian Rain thunders and puts his hand out to stop the doors from closing, "and I demand to see that patient!"

"*I* don't give a rat's ass who you are," I say and shove him back away from the elevator doors just before they close.

"Ace, shit!" Lilly yells, hopping off the gurney. "Why did you do that? Now he's going to call security on us! Why in holy hell can't you just keep your damn mouth shut sometimes?"

"He was going to call security anyway," I yell back.

Chloe has her walkie-talkie to her face. "Pick us up at the loading dock, George. We are on our way."

"On our way where?" I ask Chloe.

"To the basement, and then we have to run like hell to the other side of the hospital, raise the dock door, and jump."

"How do you know that?" Lilly asks.

"Field trip last month," she answers. "Lilly, you better lose the floppy house shoes."

When the elevator doors open, we haul ass across the basement of the hospital, and I start thinking about every horror movie I've ever seen and get really freaked out. Then all of the alarms start going off and I hear people coming after us.

"Pull that red string!" Chloe yells as she slides to a stop next to the dock door. I pull the red string and she pushes the lock button; then the door flies open and I look down at a five-foot drop.

"Shit!" I say.

"Jump!" Chloe yells and over the edge she goes, followed immediately by Lilly.

I look back and see the guards rushing toward us, then close my eyes and leap into the air. When I hit the pavement, I'm sure I've broken both of my ankles and one of my legs, but I get up and run to the Mercedes like a *Biggest Loser* contestant toward a ten-pound advantage prize. We pile in and George hits the gas. We clear the area just as the police cars round the corner.

George doesn't let off the gas all the way back to the Waverly Estate. I finally exhale once we are inside the gates. I'm pretty sure Sheriff Jackson would have dragged our asses off to jail without so much as a smile after seeing the caper we just pulled off. He's our friend and all, but everyone has their limit.

"Holy shit," is all I can think of to say.

"Holy shit, indeed," George says, and smiles at me.

It's almost midnight by the time I leave the Waverly Estate. I check my cell phone, but I haven't missed any calls.

◇◇

47

I sleep late Wednesday morning and Buster Loo is sitting by the front door when I finally get up.

"Let me get some coffee, little buddy," I say. "Then we'll go for a walk." I start the coffeemaker, then rummage through the fridge, wishing I had some leftover pizza. I go to the pantry and pick through there until I find some animal crackers. When the coffee stops brewing, I pour myself a cup and go sit down at the kitchen table. Buster Loo is still sitting by the door.

"Are you in a hurry, Buster Loo?" I ask, sipping my coffee. He just stares at me until I pick up the cookie package, then his ears perk up and he torpedo runs to the kitchen and slides to a stop beside my chair. He sits up on his butt and starts waving his front paws up and down like he's trying to fan a flame.

"You'd think I never feed you the way you beg!" I toss him what could be a giraffe and he catches it midair and munches with great enthusiasm.

"I'm gonna have to sweep the floor again, Buster Loo," I say, but he's on his way to his water dish.

I finish my coffee, throw on some clothes, and Buster Loo and I set out for the park. I'm soaking up the perfect spring day, when I catch a glimpse of Reece Hilliard and Daisy coming around the other side of the track.

"Oh, shit, Buster Loo," I say. "They're coming our way!" I point at him. "You better behave yourself or you won't get a treat for the rest of the week!"

When we round the bend, I reel Buster Loo in to where he's only an arm's reach away. As we approach them, Buster Loo starts tugging and pulling. "Easy, boy," I caution, but he pays me no attention. By the time Daisy takes notice of Buster Loo, he's straining against his leash to the point that his eyeballs are about to pop out of his head.

"Good morning, Mr. Hilliard," I say when we're a few steps away. I hope he keeps walking because I'm a nervous wreck about my crazy, obviously horny dog, plus I don't know what I would say to him if he started a conversation.

All of a sudden, Daisy stops and starts backing away from Buster Loo. Reece Hilliard turns to check on her, and I start trying to come up with pleasant conversation that doesn't include me telling him how much I hate his wife and how lucky I think he is that she left town with Ardie Griffith.

Buster Loo stops walking as well because he has almost choked himself to death by pulling so hard against his leash. He leans back on his hind legs and starts honking like a goose. I stop walking and look down at him, wondering why getting him "fixed" didn't cut down on his enthusiasm for the lady dogs.

"Is he okay?" Mr. Hilliard asks, giving Buster Loo a funny look while scratching behind Daisy's ears. Buster Loo jerks like he's having a seizure and lets out a long honk, which prompts Daisy to stop whimpering and start growling.

"Oh, he's fine," I say, keeping an eye on Daisy, who is snarling and baring her teeth. I pick up Buster Loo and he stops honking and starts panting, and stares at Daisy like she's a gigantic piece of rawhide. "We better just keep moving," I say and do just that. "Have a great day, Mr. Hilliard," I call as I walk away. "Good to see you!"

"You as well," I hear him say, then, "C'mon, Daisy, what's gotten into you?"

When we get back home, I give Buster Loo a treat because he runs to the cabinet and acts like he might lose his little doggie mind if he doesn't get rewarded for his bad behavior. We go out in the backyard for some speedy-dog fetch, and I'm rolling around in the grass having a good ol' time when I hear my phone ringing. It's the "don't know 'em" ring tone, so I hustle onto the porch and pick it up.

"Hello," I say, breathing hard.

"Did I catch you at a bad time?" I hear a man say.

"Oh, no, not at all." I pause.

"Well, I got your message."

"Oh," I say, and it dawns on me that I'm speaking to none other than Tommy Compton, aka Biker Man, so I start trying to sound sexy. "Well, thank you for calling me back, Mr. Compton."

"Tommy," he says. "Please call me Tommy."

"Okay, Tommy," I say.

"How've you been?" he asks, his voice deep and sexy. "Haven't been brawling in any more parking lots, have you?"

That's pretty funny so I allow myself to indulge in my most ladylike giggle. "No, Tommy, I try not to make that a habit."

"Good to hear," he says. "Listen, I called you because I'm going to be in Tupelo for a meeting this afternoon and I was wondering if you'd like to meet me for dinner."

"Oh, really?" I say, surprised and excited all at the same time. "I'd love to."

"Do you like Japanese?"

"I love it."

"How about Ben Hibachi at seven?"

"Ben Hibachi it is."

"Great, see you then."

And, just like that, I have a date.

For the first time in a long time, I have a real live date with a real live man who is not Mason McKenzie. And I'm excited.

"I've got to get a move on, Buster Loo," I say when he joins me under the shade of the porch.

I think about calling Lilly, but decide not to because if I told her about the date, then I'd have to tell her about the big fallout with Mason and I'm just not in the mood. She's probably still in bed anyway. I decide to call Gloria Peacock, who assures me that everything is going according to plan. She tells me Chloe is downtown with Sheriff Jackson, who is helping her fill out all of the paperwork she and Mason had discussed.

I hang up the phone and go inside to take a shower. Then partake in a little beauty rest. Lilly sends me a text that wakes me up at 4:30.

"Whatcha doin'?" it says.

"Napping," I reply.

"Goin 2 c Dax 2nite," she sends back.

"Really?"

"Gonna run that b*tch off."

"Git-R-dun!"

"Hillbilly!"

"Good luck, call me if you need me," I text, praying she won't.

I roll my hair, put on my gold heels, and slip into the fat girl's version of the little black dress, which is a big black dress with lots of spandex. I stand in front of the mirror and adjust my bra so my boobs don't fall out of the deep V-neck in the front. I put on the biggest, most sparkly pair of earrings that I own, dab on some of my prized Vera Wang perfume, and grab my lip gloss.

I get to Ben Hibachi at 6:50 and decide to sit in the car for ten minutes so I won't look anxious and pathetic for being there early. I scan the area for a motorcycle but don't see one and start to panic, thinking I've been stood up. A neon green hatchback pulls up, but thank goodness, it's not him. That would just be weird to date a man with a Harley and a neon green hatchback.

A few minutes later, a gigantic white Chevrolet pickup truck pulls into the parking lot, and I watch Biker Man Tommy Compton get out and strut across the parking lot. I slump down a little so he doesn't see me and think I'm a freak for sitting in my car all alone. He's taller than I remember with a big beefcake body just like I like. He's wearing jeans that look like they were tailor made to fit his frame and a black button-down shirt with the sleeves rolled up. I watch him go inside the restaurant. I wait a minute, then get out and make my way to the door.

He's just sat down at the bar when I walk in, so I go over and slide onto the stool next to him. He glances at me and doesn't say anything. Then looks back and does a double take.

"Ace?" he says. "Sorry, I"—he pauses—"I didn't recognize you." He's giving me a weird look and I start wondering if I put eyeliner on both eyes or just one, then remember that I was wearing a wig when we met.

"You were looking for a blonde," I say, smiling.

"I was," he says cautiously.

"That was a wig," I say and bat my eyelashes like I've seen Lilly do so many times. "We were undercover that night."

"Undercover, huh?" He touches my hair and smiles. "You're beautiful."

I smile back. "Thank you, Tommy. You're looking rather handsome yourself." I silently curse myself for sounding so much like an idiot. Lilly was right! I am a hillbilly!

We order drinks, and I haven't taken two sips when the hostess calls out, "Compton!"

"That's us," he says with a smile, and I start to quiver inside. We take our drinks and get up to follow the hostess. He puts his hand on the small of my back and pulls out my chair when we get to our table.

"I hope it's okay that I asked for a table as opposed to a seat at the grill."

"Oh, absolutely," I say, glad for the privacy so I can keep him all to myself.

"I thought we'd have a lot to talk about," he says. "I'd love to hear all about that undercover operation."

I wonder for a second if he really wants to hear the story or if he's just trying to see if I'm a psycho.

The waiter shows up and we order another round of drinks. We discuss the menu, and I can't take my eyes off of him. He has to be at least seven, maybe ten years older than me and has more charm than a sack full of four-leaf clovers. I can hardly maintain our polite conversation because I can't stop thinking about how good he must be in bed. He's just sitting there making small talk about miso soup, but the way he's doing it is screaming out that he's a man with confidence, money, and a big pecker.

Three fine qualities if you ask me.

After we order, I lean over and say, "I've seen no hint of the person I met in the parking lot Saturday night."

He leans in and says, "I was just thinking the same thing."

"Has anyone ever told you that you look like James Hetfield?"

"All the time," he says and laughs. "I actually got mobbed at a Metallica concert a few years back and security had to bail me out."

"Oh, my God, are you kidding me?" I say, infatuation rolling over me like the midnight tide.

"No, I'm not," he says. "That's why I keep my goatee trimmed so short."

Our first course arrives and I regale him with tales of stalking Richard Stacks. He seems genuinely amused, intrigued even, and I stop worrying he'll think I'm a basket case.

"Sounds to me like your friend Chloe should start dating the sheriff, just to be on the safe side," Tommy says, cutting up his salad.

"Wow, it's funny you mentioned that because I think it could happen and that would be great," I say, pushing the carrots on my salad to the side. "So, I've told you all about me. Let's hear something crazy you've done."

"I bought a motorcycle," he says, shaking his head.

"That is pretty crazy," I agree.

"Yeah, well, all my friends got into it, so I rented one and rode with them one day and just loved it." He looks up from his salad. "I absolutely love that feeling. So I bought one."

I have a mouthful, so I just shake my head and hope he'll start talking again.

"And in case you're wondering," he says and gives me a coy look, "I don't frequent strip clubs. It was my friend Marko's birthday and he just got a divorce from a *terrible* woman and he wanted to go to a strip club, so we all went with him."

"I wasn't wondering that at all," I lie, and he looks at me like he's peering into my soul.

"Yeah, you were, don't lie." He smiles at me and I start to feel faint. I don't know if he's really that sexy or if I'm just giddy because it's been so long since I've been out on a date with someone I haven't known forever.

"I'm just glad you were there that night."

"Yeah, that dude is human garbage and that skinny little guy—"

"Ace," I hear someone say behind me. "Ace Jones?"

I turn around to see Molly Belle Harwood, Ethan Allen's younger sister.

"Oh, hello, Molly Belle," I say and know that I won't have to tell a single person about my date because everyone in town will know before the next chef fires up a stack of onions. "How are you?"

"I haven't seen you in church lately," she says. "You been doin' okay?" She lowers her voice, "I know a lot's been goin' on. Ethan Allen said—" Molly Belle Harwood's eyes drift over to Tommy Compton and she stops. "Why, who is this?" she says, smiling and holding out her right hand. "Hi, I'm Molly Belle Harwood. My brother is a good friend of Ace's."

"This is Tommy Compton," I say. "He's from Memphis."

"Nice to meet you, Molly," he says, mistakenly thinking her middle name was to be dropped in conversation.

"Well, it is so nice to meet you, too, Mr. Compton," Molly Belle coos. Her friends are at the door motioning for her to come on. She looks at me and winks. "I gotta run. Good to see you, Ace! And it was a pleasure to meet you, Mr. Compton." She walks past him, turns around and mouths "Sexy" and gives me two thumbs-up.

I start laughing and turn my attention back to Tommy. "I think she was impressed with you." He just laughs and waves it off.

"She has a really Southern accent," he says. "I mean, when you sound Southern to someone from the South, then you've got a heavy drawl."

"She comes from country folks," I explain. "Good-hearted, ol'-fashioned country folks."

He smiles at me as our dinner arrives, and I don't care if Molly Belle takes a picture of us and posts it as her profile pic on Facebook. I'm having the time of my life and don't care who knows it.

After dinner, we go to a bar with a small wooden dance floor and boogie till well after midnight. My feet are killing me by the time we walk out, but I grin and bear the pain.

"So, Miss Jones," Tommy says, walking with me to my car. "I don't know about you, but I had a fabulous time tonight."

"Me, too!" I say, tucking a wayward piece of hair behind my ear.

"You are a remarkable woman," he says, putting his hand around my waist. I stop walking and let him turn me around to face him. "So gorgeous"—he runs a hand through my hair, then glances down at my boobs—"and sexy." He looks back up at me. "I'm not going to lie to you. You've been driving me wild since the second you sat down next to me at the bar," he says, pulling me up close.

"Glad to know I'm not the only one who feels that way," I say, giving him a sweet smile.

"May I," he asks, looking at my lips.

"Please," I reply and close my eyes.

I feel his lips brush up against mine, and when he kisses me I know I'm in trouble. Deep and wonderful trouble.

"Come stay with me tonight," he whispers. "I'll bring you back to your car first thing in the morning."

"Okay." I smile and let him lead me to his big white truck.

48

The next morning, I wake to find Tommy fully dressed and hard at work on his laptop.

"Good morning, beautiful," he says when I roll over. "I got you some coffee." He points to a Starbucks cup on the nightstand. "Should still be warm."

"Thanks," I say, taking a sip. "Give me fifteen minutes and I'll be ready."

"Take your time, baby. They've got doughnuts downstairs," he says. "Would you like for me to run get you one?"

"I'd love one, thanks," I say, very much appreciating him giving me some time alone in the room. After he leaves, I jump up and start looking for my panties. When I finally locate those, I take three big gulps of coffee, then grab a pack of gum out of my purse and unwrap three sticks. I hop in the shower, and just as I get out I hear him come back in the room. I step out of the bathroom wearing only a towel.

"I'm sorry," I say, walking to the foot of the king-sized bed. "I just need to gather up my clothes."

"Sorry for what?" he says, smiling. "You just need to turn around and let me look at you."

"You're embarrassing me!" I say as he walks up and puts his arms around my waist.

"You don't really need this, do you?" he says, tugging at my towel.

"I don't know, do I?" I ask, unbuttoning his shirt.

"I don't think so."

When we leave the hotel an hour later, I feel like the biggest ho-bag this side of the Mississippi River. The morning sun shining on my gold high heels does nothing to alleviate that notion.

"I had a great time," he says, parking next to my car. "I'll call you."

"I had a great time, too," I say, opening the door. "Thanks for everything."

I get in my car, which is the only one in the parking lot of the bar, and feel more like a hooker than I did when I left the hotel.

And I don't mind at all.

I stop by Red Rooster and pick myself up a bacon cheeseburger and a butterscotch milkshake. The carhop, who appears to be in her early twenties, looks at my dress, my disheveled hair, and smiles. I start laughing despite myself and she giggles a little, but doesn't say a word. I take my burger and shake and tip her five dollars. The phone rings and it's Lilly, and I don't even get to say hello before she demands to know who I was with and where I was all night.

"You did what?" Lilly yells into the phone.

"I had sex with him!" I say. "Twice!"

"You had sex with Biker Man? Oh, my God, Ace! What were you thinking?"

"I was thinking that I'm a grown woman having a great time with a very attractive man. That's what I was thinking!"

"I cannot believe this," she says. "Molly Belle said he was sexy as hell."

"He is! He's sexy as hell."

"Does Mason know you had a date?" she asks.

"I'm sure he does by now," I say.

"Wow," Lilly says. "Okay. Back up and tell me what happened with you and him. I mean, he spends the night with you Monday night. Then you go on a date with Biker Man Wednesday night?"

"We got into it Tuesday morning and he left," I say, not wanting to go into all the details.

"Ah, so then you called Biker Man—what's his name again?"

"Tommy Compton."

"Sounds like a badass."

"Oh, he is."

"Ace," Lilly whines, "what are you going to do about Mason? He came all the way up here to help all of us and he's done so much and he wanted y'all to get back together and now y'all are broke up again—"

"We weren't exactly back together, Lilly."

"Well, he spent the night with you and didn't sleep in the guest room so pardon me for pointing out that strongly resembles a reconciliation."

"I know," I say, feeling the guilt monster gnawing in my gut.

"Are you sure you know what you're doing?"

"I don't know, Lilly," I say. "I've been pining over Mason McKenzie since the day I met him when I was eleven years old and I think it might be time to stop." I pause. "It never works with us. We tried in high school, we tried during college, and we tried last year and it just never works."

"You know you love him," she says, sounding like an old bitty who plays dominos in a retirement home. "You know you do."

"Of course I do and I always will," I say. "But that doesn't necessarily mean I should be with him, does it?"

"Ace, I don't know what to tell you, sister, but we've got that meeting Monday morning so you know he'll be in town until then." She pauses. "You're gonna have to talk to Mason about all this, you know that, right?"

"Yeah, I just don't know what I need to say." I sigh. "Lilly, I've really got the hots for Tommy Compton. I had the time of my life last night—"

"Hey, hang on, it's Chloe."

I munch on my cheeseburger while I hold the line.

"You are not gonna believe this!" Lilly exclaims when she clicks back over.

"What is it?"

"Chloe just called and invited us to visit her at 309 Parker Drive."

"What?" I say. "What the hell is she doing back there?"

"She said it was moving day."

"No shit," I say and sigh with relief.

"No shit," she says. "Come pick me up."

"I've got to run home and change and I'll be right there," I say and almost run over a carhop getting out of the Red Rooster parking lot.

I scarf the burger on the way home, run inside and change clothes. I check Buster Loo's doggie dishes and they're in good shape. I find him out in the backyard chewing on a bone.

"Buster Loo!" I say. "Come see Mamma!" He looks up at me, twists his head to the side, then goes back to chewing on his bone. "Okay, little buddy, see you in a few hours." I go back inside to get my keys.

"Okay," I say when Lilly gets in the car. "I've been thinking on the way over here."

"Oh, no," Lilly says, laughing. "You've been thinking again?"

"Shut up," I say, smiling. "You heard last night I was out on a date but you don't call me until eleven thirty the next morning. What were you doing, my friend?"

"Oh, Ace, you know how I always sleep late," she says with a smile.

"I know you mentioned running a bitch off from your boyfriend's house yesterday afternoon," I say, laughing.

"Hey, I straight ran that bitch off, too," Lilly says and we both squeal with laughter.

"High five," I say.

"High five," she says, slapping my hand.

"Tell me!" I say. "Tell me all about it!"

"Well, I cased the place before I went over there."

"Of course," I say, still laughing. "Because you're a professional."

"Right," she says with a smile. "The first time I drove by, her car and his truck were both in the driveway, so I ran to Red Rooster and got a milkshake. When I went back, his patrol car was there."

"So you knew she was there?"

"Oh, yeah, she was there. I pulled up in the driveway and walked right up to the front door and rang the bell." As she goes into the details of the brouhaha that transpired when Dax opened the door, I drift off and start thinking about the Allison that showed up at Mason's last summer. Maybe she was just as in love with Mason as Lilly is with Dax. "So anyway, she threatened to slash my tires. Can you believe that? Slash my tires? How white trash is that?"

"That's very white trash," I say. "Sounds like I'd like her."

"Ace!" She punches me in the shoulder. "So she's going nuts and the neighbors start coming outside, and Dax tells her she can either go back in the house or get in her car and leave and not come back." She looks at me. "She went in the house, but the neighbors did not."

"Oh, Lord," I say. "I don't have to worry about people gossiping about me because you'll be the talk of the town for weeks after all that."

"Well, he walked me to my car and asked if we could talk later." I felt a pang of jealousy wondering if Mason had told that damn Allison the same thing. "I told him that we most certainly could and apologized for causing such a scene." She takes a deep breath. "Then I grabbed his arm and told him that I was in love with him and he wasn't just a fling for me."

"Whoa, baby, how did he respond to that?"

"He looked shell-shocked for a second, then said, 'Can I come to your house in an hour?' and I said, 'Why, hell, fuck-a-billy yeah!'"

"You didn't say that."

"No, of course I didn't, but a 'yeah, sure' seemed like such a lame ending to my fantastic story."

"It is a fantastic story," I agree. "So he came over?"

"Yep. He packed her ass up and put her on the road and came and spent the night with me, yo!" She throws her hands up, making what she obviously thinks is a gang sign.

"What are you doing with your fingers there?" I ask, laughing.

"Oh, who knows," she says.

Lilly reaches over and turns up the radio. While she's car bopping, I start daydreaming about Tommy Compton.

49

◇◇◇

When I turn into Chloe's subdivision, the first thing I see is a fifty-three-foot moving van backed into her driveway. I park on the curb and we get out and walk to the garage, where Chloe is speaking to six men wearing moving T-shirts.

"They just got here," she says proudly, "and I'm taking everything."

"Really," I say. "That is awesome, Chloe."

"Not because I want it," she says with a smug grin, "but because I want the neighbors to see me taking it. I know that's not really a good reason, but—" She shakes her head and points to a jug of weed killer. "Would you care to take that and spray the grass?"

"Spray the grass?" I ask, looking at her like she's crazy.

"Yes, you know that green stuff out on the lawn," she says, pointing, "all of it. But don't get any on the shrubs," she says. "The landscapers will be here any minute to excavate those."

"You're taking the shrubs?" Lilly asks, joining us.

"I'd take the bricks if I could get them loose," she says and turns to crawl up the ladder, then stops. "I thought I'd get this done before Richard gets released from the hospital because I'm afraid if we have another confrontation—" She stops. "I might kill him." She looks at me, then Lilly. "I have so much anger, so much hate."

I think she's about to cry so I start trying to come up with something funny to say, but she pulls herself together and continues, "Lilly, would you help me throw some stuff down from the attic?"

"Sure," Lilly says, "absolutely, Chloe, anything you need."

"Do you think it's too much to spray the yard?" She looks down at me with those big brown eyes.

"Oh, hell no!" I exclaim and pick up the weed killer. "I think it's the best idea ever."

"Do you really?" she asks, smiling. "When I had the idea, I was thinking that you would be proud of me for coming up with that."

"Oh, I am, Chloe," I say. "When you told me, I was standing down here thinking that I couldn't have come up with a better idea if I'd thought about it for a week."

"He'll get lots of letters and fines from the homeowners' association and I just thought that would be pretty funny."

"It will be *so* funny!" Lilly says.

I'm in the backyard spraying weed killer on Chloe's perfectly manicured lawn, when I hear shouting coming from the front yard. I run around the side of the house and see that bridge troll, Bobbie Sue Stacks, shouting and wagging a fat stub of a finger in Chloe's face. I make it to the sidewalk just as three moving men step out onto the front porch and Lilly steps out of the garage.

"Everything okay, Mrs. Stacks?" one of the men shouts.

"You stop right now!" the elder Mrs. Stacks shouts back. "This stuff belongs to my son!"

"Everything is fine, gentlemen," says the younger Mrs. Stacks.

"Please continue moving *everything* from the house into the van. Thank you." She smiles that sweet smile of hers and the moving man tips his hat and says, "Back to work, guys."

"I said for you to cease and desist immediately," Mrs. Bobbie Sue Stacks screams.

"With all due respect, ma'am, I don't know who you are and I don't want to be rude, but if you would stop shouting at my crew and me right about now, that would be great."

"You gather up that crew and get out of here," Bobbie Sue yells, walking toward him. "And you"—she stops when she sees me and starts waving a fat finger my way—"this is all your fault, Ace Jones!"

"My fault?" I say and look at Chloe, who is motioning the moving men back to work.

"Yes," she crows. "If you would've just stayed away from Chloe, everything would've been just fine, but no, you had to come over here and put the idea in her head that she needed to get a divorce!"

"Hey, Bobbie Sue," Chloe says, and when Bobbie Sue Stacks turns around, Chloe pokes her in the chest and says, "some things I can figure out on my own!" Bobbie Sue staggers back and opens her mouth to say something, but Chloe grabs her by the collar and pulls her up close to her face. I get so excited that I almost pass out right there on the sidewalk.

"Bobbie Sue, I'm leaving Richard and there is not one damn thing you can do about it. Now, if you want to play dirty, I can play dirty, too, but you might want to run over to the hospital and speak with Richard before you start that fight, because when he signed the divorce papers, he gave me everything but the house."

"My Richard would *never* sign anything over to you," Bobbie Sue snarls.

"Oh, but *your* Richard did," Chloe says. "And I'm not taking all this crap because I need it; I'm taking it because I *can*! I'm just emptying this house to make a *statement*! Now get your ass out of here before I take it upon myself to make your son's dirty laundry public knowledge— and trust me, you old hag, there is plenty of it."

For some reason Bobbie Sue looks at me, so I give her the finger.

"You will pay dearly for this," she hisses to Chloe.

"I won't pay for a *damn* thing." Chloe takes a step toward her and Bobbie Sue takes a step back. "And don't you *dare* threaten me! You do *not* know what I'm capable of!" She looks at me. "Ace, do you still have those pictures of Rich from the strip club?"

"That and so much more," I chirp, delighted to be involved in the conversation.

"Would you like to see those?" Chloe asks, pushing Bobbie Sue backward. "Or would you like to leave?"

"I'll leave," Bobbie Sue Stacks stammers, "but you'll hear from my lawyers."

"Will I?" Chloe says, getting in her face. "Will I?"

"You could be bluffing about those pictures!"

"Would you like to call my bluff?" Chloe asks. "You push me and I'll rent a damn billboard and put up a life-size picture of your boy *and* his fat ugly penis for everybody in town to see!"

Bobbie Sue Stacks gasps in horror, then scurries to her Lexus and drives away.

I look around and see faces in almost every window of the surrounding houses. Peepers everywhere, but no one dares to venture outside. I guess they don't feel like tangling with a three-man team of crazy women.

"Now," Chloe says, turning to me, "let's all get back to work."

"What are you going to do with all this stuff?" Lilly asks, eyeballing the stacks of boxes in the carport as we walk back up the drive.

"Well, I'm keeping most of it for my new project."

"What's that?" I ask.

"I'm starting a shelter for battered women," she says, "with Richard's 401(k) money."

I can't help but laugh. The irony never ends.

"Well, I've got grass to kill," I say.

50

<><><><><><><><><><><><><><><><><><><><><><><><><><><><><><><><><><><><><>

"Hey, let's go to Ethan Allen's tonight," Lilly says on the way home. "We haven't hung out there in a while."

"Sounds good," I say. "We're a little behind on solving the world's problems from the comfort of a worn-out barstool."

"Right," she says and giggles. "Uh, is it going to be okay if Mason shows up?" she asks, and I wonder if she's been scheming behind my back again.

"Have you talked to him?"

"No, I haven't. I'm just saying—"

"It'll be fine if he does," I say. "I've been thinking about that and I've come up with a plan."

"Yeah, what's that?" she says, flipping through my CD case.

"I'm going to apologize."

"For going on a date with someone else?"

"No. For everything besides that," I say. "I've acted like a fool toward him so many times and I think it's time for me to stop." Lilly gives me a skeptical look. "I figured something out today."

"Oh, Lord." She rolls her eyes and smiles.

"No, really, I did," I say, turning into her driveway. "The only reason Mason and I can't be together and be happy is *me*. I don't trust him and I never have, and that's not his fault or that stupid Allison's fault. It's *my* fault. I do not trust him and I don't think I ever will because I'm just not a trusting person and I can't help it."

"So?"

"So I'm going to tell him all of that and then I'm going to tell him how sorry I am for all the times I acted like a loony tune and I'm going to tell him that I think he's the greatest guy ever and deserves to be with someone who can trust him."

"Oh, goodness," she says, opening the passenger door. "You better come inside and sit down. Sounds like you've had a real revelation."

"I have," I say, following her into the house.

"How much of this enlightenment can we attribute to having sex with Tommy Compton?" Lilly asks, handing me a bottle of water.

"I don't know," I say, following her into the living room.

"You know the new will wear off of him, too, and he's going to have his own special set of problems to deal with, right?" she says, sitting down.

"Yes, Lilly, I am aware of that, and let me thank you for raining all over my parade." I plop down on her fluffy sofa.

"Not trying to rain on any parade, I'm just saying—"

"Well, I'm just saying that I'd like to spend some time with someone whose new didn't wear off fifteen years ago and I think it might be refreshing to have a new set of man issues to deal with."

"That is not fair to Mason and you know it!"

"I can't help that."

"Ace Jones!" Lilly says, shaking her head. "Just keep in mind that we're all friends here and the rest of us still love Mason like a brother."

"I'm not trying to piss anyone off, Lilly! That's not the plan at all."

"Well, no offense, Ace, but I think it would've been a little bit better if you'd waited until Mason went back to Florida before you started gallivanting around town with another man."

"I was in Tupelo," I say. "It's not like I took the guy to Ethan Allen's—"

"I'm sorry. What you do is your business," she gives me one of her pitiful looks, "I just can't help but feel sorry for Mason because he came up here to help us and he's done so much, and he had his mind set on getting you back."

"How do you know that?"

"Ethan Allen told me."

"Of course."

"So you're gonna give him the old 'it's not you, it's me' line?"

"Lilly, it's *not* him and it *is* me."

"You can't trust Mason, but you think you can trust a man with a Harley that you met in the parking lot of a strip club?"

"Now, *that* is not fair!"

"What about Logan Hatter?" she asks.

"What about him?"

"Did you trust him?" It sounds more like an accusation than a question.

"Hell, no!" I say. "We partied, had fun, and had lots of sex. I never entertained the slightest notion of a serious relationship with him. It was just fun for a while, then it fizzled out, and now we're friends and that's it. I was never in love with him."

"So that's the problem?"

"What?"

"You're in love with Mason, but you can't find it in your heart to trust him, no matter how much he's done to show you that he loves and cares about you. You can't do that one little thing for someone you do love?"

"I could pretend to."

"Yeah, we both know how good you are at that." Lilly shakes her head. "Don't you think it would be better to have this conversation face-to-face in a private setting, like, say, your house, rather than at a bar surrounded by noisy drunk people?"

"Of course I do," I say. "I tried to call him this afternoon when I took a break from killing the grass, but he didn't answer and hasn't called me back."

"Great. So it won't be awkward at all to see him at Ethan Allen's?"

"No, it won't, because I'm going to ask him to walk down to the lake, and I'm going to tell him I'm sorry and everything else I just told you."

"Oh, Lord," Lilly says and sighs. "Why does it have to always be so damned complicated with you two?"

"See, that's exactly what I mean. It shouldn't have to be."

"Okay, then." She starts fiddling with the pillows on the love seat. "All I want is for you to be happy, so if this biker fellow makes you happy, then do what you have to do, I guess. I just feel sorry for Mason." She looks at me. "What was the fight about this time?"

"Well, his phone rang and I looked at the caller ID and it said 'Allison.'"

"Allison, as in Allison that came knocking on his door the night you packed up and left?"

"Well, the caller ID said 'Allison,' and he picked up the phone, walked outside for about ten minutes, then came back in and I completely lost my shit."

"I don't blame you for that. Why the hell would she be calling him?"

"That's the thing, you see, it wasn't *that* Allison," I say and Lilly groans. "You remember he told us about the guy he hired that does such a great job? Connor McCall?"

"Yes, I remember he mentioned that."

"Well, Connor's wife apparently helps out a lot at the office and guess what her name is?"

"Please don't tell me it's Allison."

"It is," I say, feeling even more ashamed of my behavior after telling the whole story out loud. "She was calling to ask Mason a question about a case that Connor's working on for him."

"OMG, Ace, no wonder he hasn't called you back."

"I know, Lilly. That's what I'm telling you. Everything I've done pertaining to him has been wrong. And it has to stop! He's a great guy who I will always love, but I can't seem to unfuck my mind when it comes to him and he doesn't deserve to be treated like that."

"I'm starting to see your point, but it's still sad."

"It's sad I'm such a crazy bitch!" She starts laughing. "Don't you say a word!" I say, pointing at her. "I just owe it to Mason and I owe it to myself to put this thing between us to rest."

"I wish you the best of luck."

"Thanks," I say, getting up.

"Hey, we've been going everywhere in your car lately, how about I pick you up tonight?"

"Would you be so kind?" I say.

"But of course," she replies. "Eight p.m.?"

"Which really means between eight thirty and eight forty-five?" I say, giving her a knowing look.

"Something like that, yeah."

*   *   *

When I get home, Buster Loo is sunning himself in the backyard. I flip the latch on the gate and he jumps up and starts running around in circles, barking like a maniac.

"It's just me, Buster Loo," I say, walking into the backyard. He speeds over to where I am, so I lean down and give him a good scratch behind the ears. "Buster Loo's a good boy," I say several times and he relishes the compliments despite their repetitive nature. "Buster Loo wanna go for a walk?" I ask when he's had all he can stand.

He takes off and jumps through the doggie door and is sitting at the front door when I walk inside. I hook him up and we head out.

On the walk to the park and all the way around the trail, I can't think about anything but Tommy Compton. The dinner, the dancing, the way he touched me, it was all so enticing. I try not to compare him to Mason, but I can't resist. Mason is so familiar, so wonderfully safe, whereas Tommy Compton is new, exciting, and a little bit dangerous. I wonder if and when he'll call me back, then get all panicky thinking about how devastated I'll be if he doesn't. I double-check my phone to make sure I haven't missed any calls, then shove it back into my pocket, embarrassed for being so juvenile.

When we get back home, Buster Loo makes a beeline for his water bowl and I make a beeline for the shower. Then we curl up on the sofa together and watch an old *Saturday Night Live* rerun. At seven o'clock, I get up and start stressing over what to wear to Ethan Allen's.

I never stress about what to wear to Ethan Allen's.

I stare into my closet and try to figure out what would be the most appropriate thing to have on when you tell someone that it's over for good and forever. It's too hot and sticky for jeans, but I know the mosquitoes will be out en masse if we end up down by the lake. I don't feel like trying to squeeze into anything and being uncomfortable all night, so that drastically reduces the list of possibilities. What I'm left with is a stack of cutoff sweatpants and the one pair of khaki shorts that actually fit me without pissing me off.

I stand there wondering why I even bother looking through my closet because I wear those damn shorts everywhere I go. I guess I just like the thought of having more clothes to choose from even though, in reality, I don't. Oh, well. At least I'll be comfortable. Mosquitoes be damned.

I pick out a shirt, slip on my sparkly flip-flops, and head to the bathroom to do my hair and makeup. I'm filling up Buster Loo's water bowl, when I hear Lilly honking her horn out in the drive.

"Hello, sister," she says as I get in. She's wearing a strapless peach top, a denim miniskirt, and sky-high heels.

"Don't you look oh so sexy?"

"Well, I'm expecting company later," she says with a coy smile. "A lot later."

"Got a midnight caller lined up, do ya?"

"He gets off at twelve thirty."

"So you're gonna get all sauced up, then go home and wait for him in that hooker outfit?"

"Yep. That's pretty much the plan."

"Well, lucky Deputy Dax Dorsett."

She starts laughing. "Have you heard from any of your men since you left my house?"

"Hell, no!" I say and try to ignore the pang of disappointment.

"I talked to Ethan Allen and he said Mason would be there tonight."

"I figured as much."

"Said he was there last night, too, and got *drunk*."

"Well, he's staying with Ethan Allen, so, of course, he's going—" I stop and start second-guessing myself.

"What?"

"I don't want to do this. I don't want to have this conversation with Mason. I really don't."

"You went on a date, Ace, and he had to hear about it from Molly Belle Harwood. The least you can do now is tell him the truth about how you feel."

"I'm gonna need to do some serious drinking before I do that."

"I don't know if that's a good idea." She eyeballs me. "You know how you get when your nerves are all out of whack."

"I start feeling sick."

"Exactly."

"I'm already there."

"Great."

◇◇◇

51

Mason isn't at Ethan Allen's when we get there, so I hustle to the bar and start downing Killian's Red. Ethan Allen doesn't say much to me and I know he's probably a little irritated by the fact that he had to hear about my date from his little sister instead of hearing about it from me.

The guilt monster returns and commences eating me alive so I try to drown it with beer.

Ethan Allen's is packed and Lilly goes to the end of the bar and helps run drinks like she did when the place first opened. I keep my seat and continue to get tanked-up. Since I skipped supper, it's not long until I feel that buzz.

I go to the bathroom and, when I come back, someone has taken my seat at the bar. I'm scouting out another place to sit when I see Mason walk in. My gut wrenches and my heart starts to pound and I realize I'm in desperate need of another beer. When he sees me, he goes in the opposite direction. I watch him walk to the end of the bar, where Ethan Allen hands him a glass of what I'm sure is Crown and Coke.

I stand there in the middle of the crowd wondering what I should do, and for some odd reason I start thinking about Gramma Jones. She kept a book of quotes and, of all the crazy things she made me memorize over the years, the thing standing out in my mind at the very present moment is a quote that said, "I was seldom able to see an opportunity until it had ceased to be one." She was a big fan of Mark Twain.

"Hey, Ace!" I hear someone say and turn around to see Logan Hatter. "Heard you and Lilly are coming back to school next week."

"Yeah, Hatt, we have a meeting at the county office Monday morning about that."

"That is great!" Logan says and gives me a bear hug. "Glad to hear it!"

Coach Wills walks up behind him, looks down at me and says, "Hey, Jones. How's it going?"

"Wills, how are you?" I look around. "You here with Hatter?"

"Yeah," he says and I look at Hatter, who shrugs and smiles.

"All my lunchtime pals left me," he says, grinning. "I had to find a replacement."

I laugh despite my dreadful mood and high level of intoxication. "Good for you, Hatter."

"Hey, Hatt," Coach Wills says, "check 'em out over there." Wills is staring at a group of college girls huddled around a corner table. "Looks like they could use some company."

"That appears to be the case, Wills," Logan Hatter says. He looks at Wills, then smiles at me. "My protégé."

"Lady killer in training," I say, watching Wills make his way toward the unsuspecting girls. "He should have a warning label."

"Ah, that'd ruin all the fun," Logan says and takes off after him. "See ya, Ace."

"Bye," I say, but he doesn't hear me.

I look around, but Mason isn't at the end of the bar. I signal for Lilly to bring me another beer.

"You better slow down after this one," she says, looking genuinely concerned.

"Where did Mason go?" I ask.

"Ace, if it's making you this miserable to tell him how you feel, then you might want to reconsider some things."

"No," I say. "I'm getting this done. I'm getting it over with."

"Well, he walked next door to pick up some pizza, so he'll be back in a minute."

"Let me know, will ya?"

"Yes," she says, patting me on the back. She shakes her head and disappears into the crowd. A few minutes later, she taps me on the shoulder. "He's in Ethan Allen's office."

"Did you tell him I wanted to talk to him?"

"Yes," she says and starts patting me on the back again.

"What'd he say?"

"Nothing."

I make my way back to Ethan Allen's office and knock on the door.

"He's at the bar," Mason says.

"I'm not looking for him." I push the door open and stand there, overcome with anxiety and the smell of Pier Six pizza. I realize that I'm starving.

"What can I do for you?"

"Can I have a piece of pizza?"

"Are you serious?"

"Yes, please. I'll pay you for it."

His countenance softens a little and he pats the chair next to him. "C'mere," he says. "Have as much as you want."

I sit down beside him and help myself to two pieces of heavenly perfection.

"Thanks, I was hungry," I mumble.

"Yeah, and you could be a little drunk, too."

"Maybe."

"Maybe, hell," he says, smiling. He reaches over and tousles my hair and I get a whiff of his cologne.

"You smell so good," I say, looking at him.

"Don't I always?" he asks, still smiling.

"Indeed you do, Mr. McKenzie."

"Let me take you home," he says, laughing. "You're drunk, you just ate half my pizza, and I know you're about to get sleepy."

"I don't think I ate *half* your pizza."

"Pretty close to it."

"Maybe like a *fourth* or something like that."

"I round up," he says.

"You round up? What are you, some kind of cowboy?"

"C'mon, let me drive you home before you fall asleep in that chair."

"I've only had five mugs of beer, but I *am* feeling rather drowsy."

"You always were a cheap drunk."

"Thank you."

"I'll let Lilly know I'm taking you home."

"You are too kind," I say, getting really sleepy.

On the way home, I struggle to stay conscious while he scans the radio stations. When we pull into my driveway, he hops out and opens the door for me. He takes my hand and walks me down the sidewalk to the steps leading up to my front porch.

"Why are we going to the front door?" I ask.

"So we don't upset Buster Loo," he whispers. "Now go inside and get in bed."

"Would you like to come in?"

"No," he says with a sigh. "I think it's best if I go."

"Mason," I say, "I'm so sorry for how I've acted toward you." I sit down on the bottom step and spew out a long, clumsy apology that doesn't remotely resemble the one I'd rehearsed when I was sober.

"Ace, baby," he says. "Just stop. I know what you're trying to say and it's okay. Okay? C'mon and get up now." He reaches down and helps me up. "I know what you're telling me."

"What am I telling you, Mason?"

"That it's finally over."

"But I want you to know that it's all my fault," I say and tap my chest. "I'm the one with a problem, not you!"

"No, it's not your fault," he says quietly. "You are who you are and you're just fine." He takes my face into his hands. "I just want you to know that I love you. Just like you are. I always have and I always will." He kisses me on the cheek and walks back to his truck.

52

<><><><><><><><><><><><><><><><><><><><><><><><><><><><><><><><><><><><><><>

I wake up the next morning with a pounding head and a dog snout in my face.

"Buster Loo," I moan, "Mommy's sick." He licks my forehead, and then rests his little snout on my shoulder. "You're such a good boy. What would I do without you?" I get a soft "Rrrmph" as a reply.

I lie in the bed for a long time, petting Buster Loo and thinking about Mason. I get up and look in the mirror then head straight for the shower. I can't stop thinking about what he said.

I take a double dose of ibuprofen, fix a Sprite, and curse myself for forgetting the cherries last time I went grocery shopping. I ease down onto the sofa and Buster Loo hops up beside me and snuggles up in the bend of my knees. We watch the news for about an hour and I'm feeling a little better, so I go to the kitchen and start rummaging through the cabinets for something to eat that doesn't have to be cooked.

My phone starts buzzing in the bedroom and Buster Loo starts barking and running around in circles, and I don't make it back there before the call goes to voice mail. I look at the missed call list.

Tommy Compton.

A few minutes later, the voice message alert starts beeping and I stare at the phone and try to sort out my feelings. I press the button to play the message.

"Hello, Ace Jones, this is Tommy Compton calling to check in. I was wondering if you'd like to come to Memphis tonight and let me take you out on the town. Give me a call back when you can. Thanks."

"Oh, Lord," I moan. I look at Buster Loo. "What the fudgecicle am I gonna do now, little dog?" He twists his head to the side, barks, and runs down the hallway. I hear him jump out the doggie door.

I decide it's in my best interest to put off returning that call because I'm so damned confused. I can't get Mason's words out of my head and feel like I'm walking out on my best friend, but at the same time, I'm dying to go to Memphis and go out with Tommy Compton.

My phone buzzes again and my heart jumps into my throat. I pick it up and look at the caller ID.

Gloria Peacock.

"Hello, dolly," she says in her chipper tone. "What might you be doing this fine day?"

"Not much," I say. "How are you?"

"Oh, I'm fantastic, thank you," she replies. "I'm calling to see if you would like to join me for lunch? I'm having some friends over and it's going to be a really good time. I'd love for you to be here."

"And I would love to be there, Mrs. Peacock," I say, relieved for the distraction. "What time?"

"Noon," she chirps. "I'm calling Lilly now."

"Great," I say. "How's Chloe?"

"Chloe, I'm happy to report, is doing quite well. Turns out her grand-mother was my dear William's second cousin. Small world, isn't it?"

"Indeed it is," I say.

"Oh, and Ace, I had a talk with Chloe about the pills and, as I sus-pected, she had no idea what an extra dose of what she now knows was Xanax would do to her."

"She was just trying to calm herself down."

"She was, so I don't think we have anything to worry about."

"Great."

"See you at noon," she says and clicks off the line.

Five minutes later, I get a text from Lilly.

"YFHS—I'll pick you up at eleven thirty!"

I send back, "YFHS????"

"Yeeeeeeeee freakin' haw, sister!" is her reply.

"And you call me hillbilly?"

"UR1."

53

◇◇◇

When we arrive at the Waverly Estate, we hop on a blue golf cart and take another ride across that extraordinary expanse of property.

"I don't know what state is known as the Land of Enchantment but that's what this place should be called," Lilly says. "Look at that peacock!"

"New Mexico," I say.

"What?"

"New Mexico is the Land of Enchantment."

The golf cart rolls to a stop next to the clover-shaped swimming pool.

"Have a wonderful afternoon, ladies," the golf cart chauffeur says. "You'll find Mrs. Peacock around on the patio."

"Thanks," we say at the same time.

"I'm gonna go swimming in there one day," I whisper to Lilly as we walk past the pool.

"I just want to get back in that hot tub," she says.

"Girls!" Gloria Peacock says as we round the corner and step under the shade of the Patio of a Thousand Fans. "So glad you could make it!"

"Wouldn't miss it for the world, Mrs. Peacock," I say, giving her a quick hug.

"And thank you so much for having us," Lilly chimes, hugging her like she hasn't see her in ages.

"New friends"—she waves a hand at us—"meet my old friends!" She motions toward three ladies sitting at the patio table who appear to be approximately the same age and social status as Gloria Peacock.

"This is Graciela Jones," she says and lays a diamond-encrusted hand on my shoulder. "Everybody calls her Ace."

"Ace," the smallest lady snaps. "What kind of a name is that?"

"That's Birdie," Gloria says and I want to ask the ol' biddy what the hell kind of name that is, but I don't. "Birdie Ross. We've been friends since kindergarten."

Birdie Ross is wearing a light blue T-shirt that makes her ice blue eyes glow. She's the only one of the four older ladies whose hair has not faded to gray. Well, I'm sure it's turned gray, but whoever does her coloring must do an excellent job because she looks like a natural blonde.

I wonder if people call her Birdie because her nose bears more than a passing resemblance to a parakeet's beak or if it's short for something awful like "Bernadine." She looks very familiar to me, but I can't re-member where I know her from. I decide not to ask about her nick-name. Mainly because it might not be a nickname and I'm not in the mood to humiliate myself in front of Gloria Peacock and her friends.

"Nice to meet you, Birdie," I say.

"Why do they call you Ace?" Birdie asks. "You play a lot of cards?"

The other two ladies start laughing and Gloria says, "Birdie, you're impossible!"

"Actually, I used to play a lot of *sports*," I say, smiling. "It's a nickname I picked up on the soccer field when I was a little girl."

"Wait a minute," Birdie says. "Your last name is Jones?"

"Yes, ma'am."

"Are you Essie Jones's granddaughter?"

"Yes," I say, feeling a little sting at the mention of her name. "I am."

"I thought you played basketball," Birdie says, peering at me with those ice blue eyes.

"I did," I say, wondering what in the world was going to come out of this old lady's mouth next. "In high school. I played soccer in Nashville when I was a kid."

"I thought so!" She claps her hands. "Essie Jones was one of my favorite ladies in the Garden Club. I remember she was always talking about her granddaughter and she only had one, and that's you?"

"Yes, ma'am," I say again. So *that's* where I know her from.

"She was always bragging about you playing basketball. She was so proud of you. And I always remember thinking what a strange name you had." She looks at me. "Your real name is Graciela, huh?"

"Yes, ma'am." I start to feel like a recording.

"What a beautiful name." She pauses and I pray she won't start talking about my parents. "I personally saw to it that her yard was kept up after she passed," Birdie says, shaking her head. "She had one of the most beautiful yards in Bugtussle."

"She still does," Lilly offers.

"We were so happy when you came home to live in that house," Birdie says. "So happy. And I know Essie was happy, too. I bet she was up in heaven just a-smilin'."

I laugh a little and try not to tear up, and Mrs. Peacock puts a hand on Lilly's shoulder.

"This is Lilly Lane. Ryland Lane's niece."

"Oh, I know that Ryland Lane!" Birdie crows. "He is *such* a good-looking young man."

"Well, he's not so young anymore," Lilly says.

"He is to me!" Birdie says and everyone laughs.

While Birdie regales Lilly with tales about her uncle Rye, Chloe joins us on the patio.

"Chloe!" I say, looking her up and down. "You look fabulous!"

Chloe has on short khaki shorts, a white V-neck tee, and she's barefoot. Her pixie-cut hairdo has been highlighted and she has a fantastic tan. The only makeup she's wearing is peach lip gloss. She comes over and hugs Lilly and me.

"You look amazing!" Lilly whispers to her.

"A week here would make anyone look amazing," Chloe says, smiling.

"Hello, Chloe!" Birdie calls out. "Did y'all know that Chloe's grandmother and William Peacock were second cousins?"

"Yes, Mrs. Peacock mentioned that to me," I say.

"I didn't know that," Lilly says and Birdie launches into an explanation of the Barksdale and Peacock family trees, and the other two women at the table roll their eyes. As she's talking, Gloria Peacock walks around and stands behind them.

When Birdie stops to take a breath, Mrs. Peacock says, "This is Daisy McClellan. She's from Bugtussle, but she sold out and moved to Seaside, Florida, in the early nineties."

"You live in Seaside?" I ask, genuinely impressed. "That place is unbelievable!"

"I do," she says. "I bought one of the first cottages built on the beach." She smiles. "Life is too short to be landlocked."

"Daisy," Birdie hollers, "Mississippi is *not* landlocked! We have forty-four miles of coastline!"

"And Bugtussle is a six-hour drive from that coastline, which is a bit too far for me."

"It'd only be five if you didn't drive like an old lady," Birdie says.

"But, Birdie, I *am* an old lady," Daisy says and smiles.

Daisy McClellan is the most beautiful grandma-aged woman I have ever seen in my life. She has dark brown eyes, high cheekbones, and a little button nose. She had to be drop-dead gorgeous in her heyday.

"And this is Temple Williams," Mrs. Peacock says, "a dear friend of mine from Tupelo."

Temple Williams has almond-shaped eyes, mocha skin, and her gray hair is pinned back in a loose bun. From the small diamond cross around her neck down to her expensive-looking turquoise sandals, she exudes class and elegance.

"Nice to meet you, Ace," she says and nods at me, then Lilly, "and you as well, Lilly."

"Temple is the only one of us who's managed to keep her husband alive," Birdie offers.

"Oh," I say, "congratulations." I pause. "Uh, on that."

"Fifty-five years in June," Birdie says. "Isn't that right, Temple?"

"It is, Birdie. Thank you for remembering."

Birdie looks at me. "I do crossword puzzles and Sudoku to keep my brain sharp."

"Oh, okay," I say. "I like crossword puzzles."

"Why are y'all still standing up?" Birdie asks.

"Oh, sorry," Lilly says and quickly takes a seat.

"Birdie Ross," Gloria says, laughing. "Whatever will we do with you?"

After we're all seated, we're served sweet iced tea with lemons and a large plate of hors d'oeuvres, and I start thinking again about how badly I need a pair of those little silver tongs. Birdie tells us all kinds of crazy stories and Daisy throws in colorful details here and there while Gloria Peacock and Temple Williams sip their drinks and laugh. I stop dreading getting old and start looking forward to it because it seems like these women have a big time all the time.

After refreshments, we move inside to the patio, where the drinks are kicked up a notch.

"Don't let me drink too much, Daisy. You know how I get," Birdie says, picking up a glass.

"Don't we all," Temple says.

"So," Gloria says and looks at me. "I heard you had a date."

Everyone stops what they're doing and looks at me.

"Well, let's hear about it!" Birdie says, sitting down next to me on the couch. "I'm a fan of details, by the way." She winks and pats me on the knee.

"With who?" Chloe asks.

"Tommy Compton," I say. "One of the guys we met that night at the—" I stop, not wanting to say "strip club."

"At the *club*," Lilly finishes my sentence.

"You went out with one of those men from the motorcycle gang?" Chloe asks with a look of horror on her face.

"They weren't a *gang*, Chloe," I say.

"Oh, this is going to be a good story!" Birdie says. "I dated a Hells Angel one time. Boy, was he exciting!" She gives me a knowing look. "And he was great in the sack!"

"Birdie Ross!" Temple says. "Too much information!"

I look at Birdie and smile.

"She really liked the guy and had a great time," Lilly says, commandeering the conversation. "But she's having a little trouble letting go of this other fellow."

"Mason?" Chloe asks.

"Yes," Lilly says. She looks at the older ladies. "Ace has quite a dilemma on her hands. She's met this new guy who she's really attracted to, but she can't let go of this old guy that she's been in love with since she was eleven years old."

"How old are you now, honey?" Daisy asks.

"I'll be thirty-one next month."

"That's a long time to be in love with someone," Temple says. "What's this new guy have that the old one doesn't?"

"A motorcycle?" Birdie asks.

"He's just new and different and we don't have this murky past full of failed attempts to be together." I look at Birdie. "And yes, he does have a motorcycle." Birdie smiles and gives me a thumbs-up.

"Ace, you and Mason were made for each other and everybody knows that but you," Chloe says. "I don't see why you won't just give in and marry him."

"Whoa, now," Birdie says. "That's a big step."

"You should know," Daisy says.

"Daisy," Birdie says, "you've made that step more times than me. Only difference is that my husbands all died and you left yours!"

"I'll leave a cheater before I outlive one!" Daisy says. "Every time."

"So you're trying to decide between Mason and this new guy?" Gloria says, thoughtfully.

"Well, I made my mind up to end it with Mason, but when it came time to do it—"

"You couldn't," Chloe says.

"Oh, no, she did," Lilly says. "She just had to get really drunk first."

"That's the best way to handle a difficult situation," Daisy says. "Doesn't mean you were doing the wrong thing, it just means it was a hard thing to do."

"Exactly," Birdie agrees.

"Well, I think there's a reason it's taken you so long to let go of this—what's his name?" Temple asks.

"Mason," Lilly says.

"Let's call him ol' reliable, can we?" Birdie says. "Mason makes me think of a bricklayer that pissed me off one time."

"Okay," Temple says. She smiles at Birdie, then looks back at me. "Why have you held on to Mr. Ol' Reliable for so long?"

"He's her dream man," Lilly says, and I just sit there.

"Dream man?" Birdie scoffs. "That's a quaint notion. Tell us about him, sweetheart."

I take a few minutes and fill them in on my past with Mason, careful to omit the more embarrassing details about the Allison fights. Then I tell them about my date with Tommy Compton and Lilly follows up with a detailed summary of how we met him.

"I'll say one thing about the new guy," Temple says, after taking it all in. "A man willing to hit another man, no matter how much he deserves it, will cause you trouble at some point."

"Temple, he'd just seen these two girls get slapped!" Birdie cries.

"Even so," Temple says with an air of finality.

"You have to watch a man when he's mad," Daisy says. "What a man says in anger will tell you a lot about his character."

"He was really nice to us," I say and Lilly agrees.

"That's good," Daisy says. "But Temple's right. A certain temperament can mean trouble down the road."

"She's the one with a temper," Chloe says. "I can't believe you went out on a date with him!"

"Well, what are you going to do now?" Daisy asks.

"I don't know."

"What are your options, again?" Birdie asks.

"Go back and apologize to Mason—" I begin.

"Who bought her an engagement ring last summer before she got mad and left him."

"Thank you, Chloe," I say. "Or go out with Tommy tonight, which I really want to do."

"Then go out with Tommy and see how it goes," Daisy says. "You got rid of your safety net, ol' reliable Mason, so you might feel differently about things now that you don't have him to fall back on." She smiles. "I say give it a whirl."

"I agree," Birdie says. "Give the Biker Man a fighting chance." She looks at Temple. "Not literally, of course."

I look at Gloria Peacock, who smiles at me. "Follow your heart. It won't lead you wrong."

"Mine did," Daisy says. "More than once."

"I think you were following something besides your heart, Daisy," Birdie says.

54

<><><><><><><><><><><><><><><><><><><><><><><><><><><><><><><><><>

I leave the Waverly Estate later that afternoon with no more clarity about my situation than I arrived there with despite all the wonderful wisdom and advice of Gloria Peacock and her friends.

After Lilly drops me off at home, I grab a chew toy and go out in the backyard. I play fetch with Buster Loo until he gets bored and disappears into the house.

I'm thinking about returning Tommy's call when my phone rings.

It's Tommy Compton.

"Hello," I say, trying to sound sexy.

"Hey, Ace," he says and the butterflies go crazy. "What are you doing?"

"Oh, just thinking about you."

"I called earlier and left a message," he says. I smile to myself and relish how cool and *not* desperate I've made myself look by not promptly returning his call.

"Yeah, I got it," I say. "I was about to call you."

"Were you really?" he says in the deep, sexy voice.

"I was," I say and my mind is made up about this situation.

"What were you going to say?"

"I was going to say that I would *love* for you to take me out on the town tonight."

"You like Rendezvous?"

"Love it."

"Great. Can you be here at seven?"

"Sure can," I say, thinking that I could be there in an hour if he wanted me to be.

"Okay, I'll text you my address."

"Fantastic," I say.

"See you later."

"Buster Loo!" I say, tossing the phone onto the table. "Mommy has a date tonight!" Buster Loo just glares at me and hops through his doggie door.

I stand in my closet and wish I didn't love pizza and cheeseburgers so much. Buster Loo joins me and scratches around at the shoe boxes in the bottom of the closet.

"See anything that looks good, Buster Loo?" He whines and snorts, then runs under the bed.

I finally decide to wear the same white dress I wore on my first trip to the Waverly Estate despite the fact I'll be eating ribs. I pluck it out of the closet, steam it, and hang it on the doorway of the laundry room. I dig out a pair of heels to wear to dinner and grab my sandals to wear dancing. Lilly would be so disappointed in me for taking sandals. She just doesn't understand that everyone doesn't have a gift for enduring foot mutilation like she does.

I leave my house at 5:30 p.m. so I'll have plenty of time for my GPS to lead me around all the wrong ways to get to the residence of Tommy

Compton. When I finally do arrive in his neighborhood, I'm afraid someone will call the police on me because it's obvious that dirty, not-so-new cars aren't commonplace in this part of town. I curse myself for not driving through the Jiffy Clean in Tupelo.

"What have I got myself into?" I mumble as I step out onto the pebbled drive. The house has a three-car garage that's attached and a two-car garage that isn't. I walk to the front door and ring the bell.

When Tommy Compton opens the door, the smell of cologne drifts my way and I allow myself to be intoxicated by his aroma. He's wearing another pair of those jeans that look like they were sewn to fit his frame, and judging from the size of his house, he could probably afford a closet full of tailored clothing. He's wearing a gray polo T-shirt that's snug in all the right places.

"Well, hello, Miss Jones," he says and takes my hand. "Won't you come in?"

I step inside the foyer and he steps back and looks me over.

"You look wonderful," he says, and gives me a kiss on the cheek, which almost causes me to pass out right there on the marble floor.

"As do you," I say, shamelessly eyeballing his biceps.

"We have reservations at eight, so let me throw on a shirt and we'll go." He motions toward the living room. "Have a seat." He starts to walk away, then stops and spins around. "I'm sorry, would you like something to drink?"

"Oh, no, thanks," I say, walking into his living room, which is framed by four colossal columns. He disappears somewhere inside his mansion and returns a moment later wearing a short-sleeve black polo.

"Very Grecian," I say, waving toward the columns. "I like it."

"They valued philosophy, arts, architecture, and sports and weren't afraid of hard work or battle," he says. "My kind of people." He looks at me. "Have you ever been to Greece?"

"No, but it's on my list of things to do." I follow him out to the garage, where I see the Harley, a ski boat, and what has to be a brand-new Camaro. It's black with charcoal racing stripes.

"Where's your truck?" I ask.

"In the other garage," he says. "Would you rather go in that?"

"Oh, no," I say, walking to the passenger side of the Camaro. "Of course not."

He smiles and we get in. He backs out of his garage a little faster than I expected, then speeds out of his subdivision like we're leaving the scene of a crime. When we get on the bypass, he passes everyone on the road and I wonder why I didn't notice his expeditious driving habits when I rode with him in Tupelo. Maybe because we were in town with a bunch of traffic lights.

He speeds across I-240 and I'm relieved when he gets off at Riverside Drive. The traffic slows us down and he turns right on Union, then left onto Second Street and pulls into a parking garage. I grab my purse, which is heavier than usual because of the sandals, and he takes my hand and walks me to the restaurant.

My feet are killing me by the time we get there and I wish I'd left the high heels in the closet. I hobble down the steps to the restaurant, clinging to the stair rail like a leach.

We have an amazing dinner, during which I'm extra careful not to drop any BBQ sauce on my white dress, and he asks me if I'd like to take my purse back to the car before we head over to Beale Street. I ditch the heels and slip my poor, aching feet into the sandals and toss my purse into the backseat. I don't worry about anyone seeing it back there because they would need a two-thousand-watt lightbulb to penetrate the tint on the glass, and since I've never even heard of a flash-light that bright I'm sure my purse will be safe.

"Did you bring your gun tonight?" Tommy asks as I close the passenger door of his beautiful black sports car.

"No, I knew I'd have you to protect me," I say and he smiles.

"Did you shrink?" he asks as we're walking out of the garage.

"No, I changed shoes."

He looks down at my sandals. "How very practical of you," he says, and I'm not sure it's a compliment.

We go dancing and drinking and have the best night ever, despite the sandals. I don't even mind when he speeds us back to his house because I can't wait to be alone with him again. He escorts me up the spiral staircase to his bedroom, where his appreciation for Greek culture is even more evident, and in the middle of the largest bedroom I've ever seen sits the biggest bed I've ever laid eyes on.

"California king?" I say, eyeballing the mountain of throw pillows.

"Yes, ma'am," he says, peeling off both his shirts. "Would you like to get in the hot tub?"

"I didn't bring a swimsuit," I say.

"Good," he says, smiling.

◇◇◇

55

On my way back to Bugtussle the next morning, I try to find something wrong with Tommy Compton, but as far as I can tell, he's perfect. I'm exhausted when I get home, but throw on some junky clothes and take Buster Loo for a walk.

After a shower, I crawl into my bed, which seems small compared to the luxurious California king on which I snoozed for a few short hours this morning.

I sleep until late afternoon, when Lilly wakes me up by pounding on the back door. After I unlock the door, I fix her a glass of tea and myself a glass of Sprite and we head for the living room. She tells me she's been out house hunting with Chloe, before launching into the date she went on with Dax the night before and I'm content to just sit and listen.

"Well," she says finally. "How was *your* date with Mr. Compton?"

"Amazing," I say. "He's amazing. His house is amazing."

"Where'd he take you to eat?"

"Rendezvous."

"Oh, I *knew* you were going to say that!" She gives me a wicked grin. "Well, how do you feel about everything, uh, else?" she says and I know she's talking about Mason.

"Tommy Compton is right for me on so many levels, Lilly. I really, really like him, and what I want is for Mason to find someone who makes him feel like Tommy makes me feel." I look at her. "I've got it bad for Biker Man."

"Would you marry him?"

"Don't get all carried away now," I say and smile at her.

"I guess you know Chloe and Ethan Allen are both a little pissed at you for ditching Mason and dating someone while he's still up here." She waves a hand in the air.

"Yeah, I'll give that some time and swoop in with a lengthy, heart-felt apology and everything will be fine in a week or two."

"Yeah," she says. "I'm just happy to see you so happy!"

"Same here, *mon ami.*"

"Oh, I can't wait to get back to work. *Je suis ravi!*" she says.

"Whatever that means."

"It means I'm delighted!" she says. "Well, I gotta run. I've got to meet Chloe at another house in about thirty minutes."

"Is she looking to buy?" I ask.

"No, she just wants to rent until she gets all her affairs sorted out."

"You think she'll go back to Jackson?"

"Really," Lilly says and gives a coy smile, "I think the only Jackson she's interested in is J.J."

"That would be so awesome if those two got together," I say. "He would be so good to her, she wouldn't know what to do."

"Well, I think the interest is mutual," Lilly says with a knowing look. "I give it a month and they'll be together."

"That just makes my day."

"Mine, too," she says. "Well, I've really got to go or I'm going to be late. You doin' anything tonight?"

"Watching *Saturday Night Live*," I say.

"Ace, you're such a party animal."

After she leaves, I watch the news for a while, then end up falling asleep during *SNL*. I wake up Sunday morning with a terrible crick in my neck.

56

◇◇◇

I get dressed for church and take a dose of ibuprofen, hoping that will restore my ability to use my neck. Sadly, it does not. I waddle into the church foyer like a penguin, eyeballing my surroundings, and have to turn my head, neck, and shoulders toward anyone who speaks to me.

"Well, hey there, Ace Jones," I hear and turn my entire upper body around to see Molly Belle Harwood smiling at me with a Bible in one hand and a Coach purse in the other.

"Hey, Molly," I say. "How are ya?"

"Great, thanks," she says as Ethan Allen steps up behind her.

"Got a crick?" he asks.

"Yes," I say. "Thanks for noticing."

"Sleepin' in strange places will do that," he says and Molly Belle slaps him on the arm.

"Ethan Allen!"

"Good morning to you, too, Ethan Allen," I say. He nods and walks away.

Molly Belle leans in. "So are you still seeing that man you were with the other night?"

"Yeah," I whisper. "I went to Memphis to see him Friday night."

"Fun!" she says quietly. "I don't care what Ethan Allen says, I'm happy for you. You can't live your whole life doing what other people think you should."

"Thanks, Molly Belle," I say and I really mean it.

"Besides, that dude was smokin' hot."

The church bells start to ring, so she says good-bye and hustles down to where her family sits every Sunday in the third pew on the left side of the sanctuary. I pick up a bulletin and make my way to the balcony. During opening prayer, I hear someone sit down beside me. I open my eyes and twist around to see Mason.

"Good morning," he whispers. "Care if I join you? Bottom floor is packed."

"Not at all," I say and smile. He winks at me and I wonder if there will ever come a time in my life when seeing him doesn't make my day. After the service, he invites me to eat lunch at his grandmother's house and I politely decline. I've never fit in with his family, plus I'm sure they've all heard I'm dating a member of a motorcycle gang.

I go to Red Rooster and order the chicken strip basket because it doesn't feel right to eat anything other than fried chicken for lunch on Sunday even if it is served in a red-checkered box.

On the way home, I notice the crick in my neck is gone. Gramma Jones was right. A trip to the Lord's house and a bite of fried chicken really can cure whatever ails you. Or maybe the ibuprofen finally started working. Who knows?

When I get home, I put on some more comfortable but not totally skanky clothes, which means my trusty bermudas and a shirt that didn't come from a concert. I'm walking out the front door with Buster

Loo when I see a motorcycle coming down my street. I freeze on the front porch and Buster Loo starts tugging at the leash. The motorcycle slows as it nears my drive and I see the signal light come on. Then Tommy Compton pulls into my driveway on his Harley.

"Hey, baby!" he says after he takes off his helmet. "Wanna go for a ride?"

Buster Loo starts to growl when he gets off his bike.

"Is that your guard dog?" he asks, laughing.

"Yeah, I was about to take him for a walk," I say, not at all sure what to do.

"Take him later," he says. "Come with me. The boys are riding the Trace today and I wanted to swing by and see if you'd like to go."

"The Natchez Trace?" I say, trying and failing to imagine a more boring ride.

"Yeah, we ride it every now and then."

"Okay," I say. "Would you like to come in a minute?"

"Sure," he says and moves his bike up next to my car so it's in the shade.

"Nice yard," he says, walking up the sidewalk. "You do all this your-self?"

"It was my grandmother's place," I say. "I just do upkeep."

"Well, you do a great job," he says, taking his boots off on the porch.

I take a reluctant Buster Loo back into the house and try to get him to go into the backyard, but all he wants to do is sit and growl at Tommy.

"I don't think your dog likes me," he says, walking around my living room.

"Oh, he's just mad because he thought we were going for a walk," I say. "Would you like a drink? Water? Coke? Diet Mountain Dew?"

"I'd love some water."

I take him some water and offer Buster Loo a treat, but he's not interested in a treat. Tommy reaches down to pet him and Buster Loo snaps at his hand.

"Buster Loo!" I say. "Bad boy!" I look at Tommy, who is trying not to look pissed off, but I can tell he is. "I'm so sorry. He never, and I mean *never*, does that."

"Mean little dog," Tommy mumbles, and Buster Loo starts barking and going crazy. Tommy starts to look really irritated and I pick up Buster Loo and try to calm him down, but he's completely lost his little doggie mind. He wiggles out of my arms, hits the ground running, and goes straight over and starts gnawing on Tommy's pant leg.

"Hey, now!" Tommy says. "These are two-hundred-dollar jeans!" My heart sinks as Buster Loo starts gnawing on his other pant leg. "Could you put him in another room or something?"

"Sure," I say, wanting to pull a Lilly and start squalling my eyeballs out. I walk over and try to pick up Buster Loo, but he runs to the door and starts barking and jumping and acting even crazier. I look out the door and see Mason's Escalade in the driveway. I look around, in a full state of panic, wondering where he is, and then he walks in the back door.

Everyone just stands there for a second, looking.

"Uh, Mason," I stammer. "This is Tommy Compton." The look on Mason's face makes me feel sicker than I already am.

He reaches out to shake Tommy's hand and says, "Hello, I'm Mason McKenzie."

"Hello," Tommy says, and gives me a funny look.

In the meantime, Buster Loo runs over to Mason and starts hopping around next to his feet. Mason picks him up and says, "Hey, little buddy."

"And he is?" Tommy looks at me.

"A friend," I say, looking at Mason, who is glaring at Tommy.

"Right," Tommy says, looking at his watch. "Well, it was nice to meet you, Mr. McKenzie, but I need to get going." He looks at me. "Maybe another time?"

"Sure," I say and he starts walking toward the door.

"How did you get here?" Mason asks. "Did you walk?"

Tommy turns around and the look on his face makes me shudder, and not in a good way.

"No, Mr. McKenzie, I rode my bike. Not my Schwinn, of course. I'm referring to my motorbike, which is a Harley-Davidson CVO."

"I didn't see a *motor*bike when I pulled up so I hope I didn't park on top of it."

"Let's hope you didn't, Mr. McKenzie."

"Well, Mr. Compton, if I need to move my Cadillac Escalade so you can leave on your *bike*, please let me know."

"That won't be necessary," Tommy says and walks out the door.

I look at Mason.

"Sorry," he says, "didn't know you had company. I'll be on my way."

"No, Mason, just wait a second, please." I run out onto the porch, where Tommy is putting on his boots.

"Tommy, I'm so sorry."

"No need to apologize, Ace. You could've just told me you had a boyfriend." He looks at me. "I really should've called first."

"I don't have a boyfriend!"

"You've got something," he says, nodding to Mason, who's walking past my car.

"Oh, there it is," Mason says and starts pointing. "I see your bike, there under the tree. Missed it on my way in."

Tommy just stares at him, and then turns to me. "Friends don't act like that."

"He's my ex-boyfriend," I say, not knowing what else to say.

Mason gets in his truck and leaves.

"Ace, you're a fun girl," Tommy says. "Smart, gorgeous"—he looks down at my boobs—"so very sexy." He takes my chin in his hand. "I've had a great time with you. I really have." He pauses and I know what's coming next. "But I'm a simple man and it's pretty clear you're in a complicated situation." He nods toward Buster Loo, who is in the window barking his head off. "Not to mention that rabid beast of a dog hates my guts."

I sigh and force a smile. "He's really a sweet dog," I say.

"Yeah," Tommy says, smiling. "That's what I was thinking just after he snapped at my hand and just before he started trying to gnaw off my leg." He smiles at me.

"I'm so sorry, Tommy," I say and realize that I'm getting sick of making apologies. Every time I turn around I'm apologizing to somebody for something.

"No worries," he says. "Hey, since your boyfriend left, do you think I might get a kiss before I go?"

I nod and he plants a soft kiss on my lips. It's sweet, but the fire is gone.

"Why don't you give me a call when you get things sorted out?"

"Yeah, I'll do that," I say, knowing I won't and knowing just as well that he won't be holding his breath waiting on me.

"See ya," he says, slipping on his helmet.

"Bye."

And just like that, I'm all alone again.

◇◇◇

57

I wake up Monday morning feeling more miserable than ever. I throw on some clothes, half-ass comb my hair, and skip the whole makeup routine.

When I pull up at the county office, Lilly is waiting in her car. She meets me at the front door and says, "What happened to you? You look like shit!"

"Thanks and I don't want to talk about it."

Mason pulls up a second later and walks into the building, completely ignoring us.

"Oh, boy," Lilly says and sighs. "C'mon and let's get this over with."

Mason is completely professional throughout the meeting and his coolness toward me makes me feel invisible. The chairman of the board, Cecil Ricks, wants both Lilly and me to stay on paid leave for the rest of the school year, which is only three weeks, and return in August.

"Let all the talk die down," he says, looking at Mason. "Somebody else will be on the cross by the time school starts back."

Tina Lucas, the school's attorney, places employment contracts in front of us, I guess to serve as motivation.

"I'm ready to go back to work now," Lilly says.

"Lilly," Mason says quietly, "I think it would be best if we went with what Mr. Ricks is suggesting. Everything came out when Catherine left and now the rumors are flying like crazy. If nothing else, I think it'd be best to let Zac Tanner graduate in peace."

"Why do you think Catherine Hilliard targeted Zac Tanner?" Tina Lucas asks, looking at Lilly.

"I have no idea," Lilly says and shrugs.

"I'll tell you why," I say. "Because at the beginning of the school year, Amanda Tanner came into a teachers' meeting and jumped all over Mrs. Hilliard in front of all of us. What better way for Mrs. Hilliard to punish Amanda for standing up to her than by doing some damage to her kid during his senior year of high school."

"I don't think Zac was actually that *damaged*," Mr. Ricks says.

"Well, his girlfriend dumped him when she heard the rumors so that had to hurt a little," Lilly says.

"Hurt the kid, hurt the parent," I say. "Great philosophy for a high school administrator, and what amazes me more than anything is how such a poor-quality person could get hired for that job in the first place." I stare at Cecil Ricks. "How *does* that happen?"

"Well, Ardie was insistent and now we all know why," Cecil says, adjusting his tie as he attempts to shift the blame.

"Ardie doesn't have a vote, only a recommendation, Mr. Ricks," I say. "You and the rest of the board members voted her in."

"Ace, drop it," Mason says. "She's gone. It's over."

"Well, Mr. Ricks, I just want you to know that I think you're a real shit bag for letting that woman torture all of us for the past two years."

"Ace!" Lilly and Mason yell at the same time.

"Miss Jones, may I remind you that you haven't signed your contract yet?"

I look at the contract on the table. "And?"

"And if you want your job back, I suggest you start minding what you say."

"You know what, Mr. Ricks? I don't think I want my job back because you and your little cronies make me sick."

"Ace," Lilly says and gives me her meanest evil eye.

"Miss Jones," Cecil Ricks says in a condescending tone, "may I remind you that this isn't a Harper Valley PTA meeting."

"Really," I say, getting up, "I don't see a lot of difference in this place and the one in the song." I push the contract across the table to Tina Lucas, who looks like a deer caught in headlights. "I don't want my job back. You can have it. Because your political bullshit didn't just hurt Lilly and me and Zac and Amanda, it hurt the whole school. You lost almost a dozen great teachers and you don't even care. Instead of having the best, most fun year of their lives, two graduating classes had their senior years terrorized by Catherine Hilliard. All because of your stupid small-town politics."

"Ace, you need to stop talking," Mason says, getting up. "Mr. Ricks is not the only person on the school board."

"Yeah, but he's the chairman," I say. "And before I leave, Mr. Ricks, I also want you to know that you are the biggest *pussy* I have ever seen in my life."

Lilly and Tina gasp, Mason comes over and takes my arm, and Cecil Ricks just stares at me like he cannot believe someone would say something like that to him.

"Miss Jones, Mr. McKenzie mentioned that you'd like to attend the art fair tomorrow night. Initially I'd agreed to let you go, but now I'm afraid I can't allow that. I don't need you up here making inflammatory comments about the board. Things are stirred up enough as it is."

"Right," I say. "Let's all just omit the part where you take any responsibility for this mess and paint me as the problem for noticing. That's brilliant. I think I'll run against you next year because your position here"—I tap the table for emphasis—"is going to be up for grabs and everyone knows it."

"That's enough, Ace," Mason says.

"Miss Lane, will you be signing your contract?" Tina Lucas asks in a nervous voice.

"Yes! I will be!" Lilly exclaims and grabs the pen out of Mason's hand. She signs it and slides it across the desk.

"This meeting appears to be over," Mason says quickly. "Tina, can you shoot me a copy of Lilly's contract for my file?"

"Of course, Mason," she says.

Mason motions toward the door. "After you," he says and Lilly and I walk past him out into the foyer. "Keep walking," he says and we go on out the door.

"I cannot believe you!" he says to me when we get outside. "Lilly, I'll send you a copy of your contract when I get it. Right now, we all just need to get out of here." He gives Lilly a quick hug, shoots me a scolding look, then takes off toward his truck. When he opens the door to put his briefcase in, I see his luggage stacked neatly in the back.

"Ace Jones, I swear I've never seen anything like that in my life," Lilly says, shaking her head. "And I've seen you do a lot of crazy shit."

"Fuck those assholes," I say.

"What are you going to do?" she says. "You just gave up your job in there."

"I get paid until the end of July," I mumble. "I'll think something up between now and then."

"You wanna come to my place and hang out?" Lilly asks.

"Nah, I'm just gonna head home."

"Hey, I'm sorry about the art fair."

"It's okay," I say, and get in my car and leave.

On the way home, I call Chloe.

"Hey, I know you're mad, but just listen to me for a second," I say when she answers.

"I'm not mad at you, Ace," she says sweetly. "I was, but I got over it. You're a grown woman and it's not my place to judge you."

"Thanks, Chloe," I say. "Listen, would you be interested in renting a nice little house that's fully furnished?"

"Sure," she says. "Where is it?"

"557 River Birch Drive."

"That's your address."

"I know," I say. "Chloe, I've got to take some time. I've got to get away for a while."

"You mean like you did in college when you went to Europe?"

"That's exactly what I mean."

"Okay, you've got a deal," she says.

◇◇◇

58

All of my bags are packed and I have no idea where I'm going.

I go through the house and make sure the toilets are flushed, then pull the trash can out to the curb. I take my extra set of keys and hide them under a lounge cushion on the back porch.

I hear the rumble of a truck and know that Ethan Allen is in my driveway. I sit down on the lounger and wait for him to walk around the corner. He appears at the gate and Lilly is right behind him.

"Ace," she says, running up and hugging me. "Chloe said you were leaving!"

"Yeah, I've got to, Lilly." She sits down beside me and I look at her. "I've got to get away from here."

"I'm worried about you," she whispers. "Where are you gonna go?"

"I don't know," I say. "I'll figure it out as I go along, I guess."

"Hey, Ace," Ethan Allen says, taking off his cowboy hat. "Listen, I'm sorry I wasn't as nice as I should've been at church yesterday. It was just killing Mason that you were going out with that motorcycle man and he's my best friend and all."

"Ethan Allen, you don't have to explain a thing to me," I say, looking at him. "I'm sorry for what I did to him. And I'm sorry you had to hear it from someone besides me."

"All right, then," he says, then looks at me and smiles. "Well, since you're all packed up and ready, I know somewhere you could go."

"You obviously haven't talked to him since our little meeting this morning."

"Of course I have," he says. "He told me about you getting all up in that Cecil Ricks's ass and said he almost had a stroke, but you said a lot of things that fella needed to hear."

"Are you serious?"

"He actually got to laughing as he was telling me about it."

"It was pretty funny," Lilly says with a nervous giggle. "I mean, now that it's over."

"Look, you already got your stuff packed," Ethan Allen says. "You quit your job and you found somebody to rent your place here. I know it looks to *you* like everything is falling apart, but it looks to *me* like everything's coming together like it's supposed to."

"Not that we want you to go, of course," Lilly says, looking down.

"But you need to go," Ethan Allen says, getting up and stretching.

"And you need to stop thinking you don't deserve to be happy," Lilly says. "Because you do."

"I never said that."

"You never had to."

"Why don't you make us all happy and hustle on down to Mason's house?" Ethan Allen asks, putting his cowboy hat back on.

"He doesn't hate me?" I say, getting off the couch.

"Are you nuts?" Ethan Allen says. "C'mere, girl, and give me a hug. You think that man from the motorcycle gang would've bothered him so bad if he hated you?"

I hug Ethan Allen, then hug Lilly, and reach under the lounger cushion and get my extra keys.

"Give these to Chloe, will you?" I say.

"Sure will," Lilly says and starts fanning herself with her hands.

"Don't do it, sister," I tell her. "Don't start."

"What?" she says, then wipes a tear. "I'm not crying!"

Ethan Allen puts his arm around her and says, "Don't worry, lover girl. You've that handsome pup to keep you company, remember?"

"Hey, you two," I say as they're walking down the steps. "I'm not doing this if y'all are about to call him and tell him I'm on the way." They look at each other, then look back at me.

"Okay," Ethan Allen says. "Whatever it takes to get you back down there."

"Promise?"

"Promise," Lilly says. "You just go on and surprise him."

"I'm going," I say.

I walk back inside and find Buster Loo standing with his nose to the front door.

"Are you ready to go?" I say, and he chiweenie sprints over to where I'm standing. We go out the back door and he takes off and starts running speedy-dog crazy eights all around the yard. "Empty that little tank, Buster Loo," I tell him. "We've got a long ride." He does his business, then runs up to the fence like he understands what's going on. He looks at me as if to say, "Let's get this show on the road."

"I can't believe I'm doing this," I tell Buster Loo as I pull out onto the highway. "But here we go. I'm going down there and I'm going to trust him." Buster Loo barks two times then hops in the backseat and I hear him scratching the blanket on the floorboard. "I trust him," I say to myself, surprised at how good it feels to say that out loud.

I pull up at Mason's house in Pelican Cove just after midnight. All the lights are out and I let Buster Loo run around and do his business. When he comes back, I pick him up and take him to the door. I ring the bell. Then I ring it again.

What seems like nine hours later, I hear footsteps and my heart starts to pound. I hear him turn the dead bolt and feel like I'm going to hurl. He flips on the porch light, opens the door, and stands there rubbing his eyes. Buster Loo starts pawing and twisting and flopping, and Mason reaches out and takes him from me. Buster Loo promptly lavishes his cheeks, nose, and ears with doggie kisses.

I stand there looking at him, not sure what to say. I'd rehearsed a thousand lines on the drive down, but none seem appropriate now that I'm actually standing here looking at him.

"Ace?" he says. "Is everything okay?"

"Yes."

"Did you drive down by yourself?"

"Yes, well, me and Buster Loo."

He steps back and opens the door. "Well, don't just stand out there on the porch. Come on in."

I walk in and he turns on the lamp in the foyer.

"You never took down our pictures," I say, looking at the walls.

"Why would I?"

He fixes us both a glass of ice water and we sit down across from each other in the living room.

"So," he says, smiling. "What can I do for you?"

"Well," I say, taking a deep breath, "I'm unemployed, I've rented my house to Chloe, and I'm looking for a place to stay."

"Well, I've got three guest rooms, but they're all full of junk."

"I don't believe that."

"No? Well, it's true. There's only one room in the house where I have any extra space."

"Yeah," I say, smiling as the nausea starts to fade. "Which room is that?"

"Mine."

"I'll take it."

"Are you serious?" He smiles. "You're back?"

"Yes," I say, "if that's okay with you."

"I can't think of a time when anything's ever been more okay with me." He looks at me. "Does anyone know you're here?"

"Chloe, Lilly, and Ethan Allen."

"Great, so everybody?"

"Yeah," I say, laughing.

"You wanna go to bed?"

"I'd love to."

The next morning I get up to the smell of gourmet coffee and salt water. I walk down to the kitchen and see Mason out on the porch, reading the paper. I pour myself a cup of coffee and join him outside. Buster Loo is curled up next to his feet.

"Good morning, sunshine," he says when I sit down across from him. "Nice hair."

"Thanks," I say, taking a sip of coffee.

"Do you think I should call an exterminator?"

"For what?"

"To try and find the rats that made that nest on your head."

"Funny." I smile.

"How's your coffee."

"Absolutely wonderful," I say. "As always."

After breakfast, we take a long fabulous walk on the beach. When we get back, I hop in the shower and then get dressed. Mason is sitting in the kitchen when I go back downstairs.

"Wanna go for a ride?" he says.

"Where to?"

"It's a surprise."

We get in his truck and he drives a few blocks, then pulls into the parking lot of a building that looks like it would fit right in on Bourbon Street.

"I know you know what this is."

I stare at the place with tears stinging my eyes. Actually being here and seeing it really puts things into perspective. It's one of the coolest buildings I've ever seen.

Then it hits me. He didn't just buy me a neat-looking building, he bought me a doorway to the biggest dream of my life. How could I withhold trust from someone so willing to invest in what he believes I could do? It occurs to me that Mason has more faith in me than I have in myself.

"It's a little dusty," he says, getting out, "because it hasn't been cleaned in a while, but I'll have that taken care of first thing tomorrow." He looks at me. "Well, are you coming?"

As I walk toward the front door, I'm overcome with feelings of shame for ever doubting him. He unlocks the door and I follow him inside.

"This is for you, you know," he says, looking around. "It's all for you."

"Mason, it's so perfect. I—" I stop because I get choked up.

"Shhh," he whispers, putting a finger on my lips. "There's only one word that I want to hear come out of your mouth right now."

"Thanks?" I say, with a feeble smile.

"Nope," he says, pulling a small black box out of his pocket. He flips it open and my jaw drops as I stare at the large round diamond.

"Will you make me the happiest man on earth?"

"Yes!" I say, hugging him. "Yes! Yes! Yes!"

"That's the one," he said, slipping the ring onto my finger. "That's the word I was looking for. Please feel free to say it as much as you like."

"Yes," I whisper, looking at the ring on my hand. "It's beautiful!"

"Yep," he says, pulling me into a hug. "Just like you."

ACKNOWLEDGMENTS

I would like to thank my sweet, funny, and infinitely patient husband, Brandon, without whose constant encouragement and continuous support I would've never finished this book. You were right.

To each and every person who bought the ninety-nine-cent copy, this would not be happening for me if it weren't for you. Not only did you purchase a self-published book by a first-time author—you took the time to tell your friends and family about it. To all of you, I am eternally grateful.

To Molly Reese, whose e-mails always make my day. Thank you for always being so nice about the attachments I forget to attach and for taking on the role of part-time therapist.

To Susanna Einstein, for turning a big dream into a marvelous reality.

To Larry Kirshbaum, for giving me the opportunity of a lifetime.

To Danielle Perez, my gracious and wonderful editor. There are no words to properly express how much I appreciate your involvement in this project.

To Heidi Richter, my publicist, for making it all so much more exciting.

Very special thanks to my parents, Barry and Wanda Raines, who, God bless their souls, have been with me through the best of times and the worst of times. And thanks to my brother, Brent, for reading the book and pointing out that I had the tequila-shooting sequence out of order.

Special thanks to Mandi Harris, Molly Crow Wren, Sandy Jackson, Melisa George DePew, and Jenny Miller Little. Where would I be without y'all? Thanks also to Tina Houston, Amy Gahagan Moore, Frances Yates, Mary Jo Smith, and Rhonda Lauderdale Goodwin. You guys were with me from the very beginning.

Thanks also to two of the best high school English teachers in the history of the world, Mrs. Carolyn Jackson and Mrs. Debbie Milton. It took a lot to make me pay attention.

Finally, I would like to thank Amazon for their Kindle Direct Publishing Web site, Barnes & Noble for PubIt!, and Mark Coker for Smashwords. These companies are giving writers unprecedented opportunities in the world of self-publishing.

Photo by Rachel Wade

Stephanie McAfee was born in Mississippi, and she now lives in Florida with her husband, young son, and chiweenie dog.